Behind the Door

Hidden Motives Series – Book One

ISBN 9781520386171

Cover Art by Kelly Martin— **kelly@kam.design**

Editor — Jill N. Noble-Shearer – jill.noelle.noble@gmail.com

Dedication

This is my first novel and I have much to be thankful for.

To my editor, Jill N. Noble-Shearer, thanks for believing in my work and for all the kind help. Without you, Behind the Door wouldn't be published.

To my husband Mauricio for his love, unwavering support and hilarious critiques.

To my parents Olmar and Nilse, the best one can have. My eternal love and thanks for everything.

To my brother and my sister, Jackson and Dani, for the sense of family you give me.

To Mike, my teacher, my friend and my translator, who has rendered this novel so faithfully into English because he understands exactly how I think, my eternal gratitude.

To Rachel, for friendship made in heaven.

To Alisson, my best male friend, for understanding me and being such an admirable guy.

To Andreza my BFF, for all the support with her constant phrase: Everything is going to be all right; we are going to be happy; we just have to wait!

To Mary and Rui, Sibblings life gave to me.

And to the wonderful friends who are part of my world, I love you all. Thank you for being in my life and inspiring me.

Chapter One

Present Day — Simone

Simone met Carl on a trip to New York.

At forty-two, she thought she knew her own mind and all there was to know about life. She was good at her job. She believed the choices she'd made over time had given her a life that, if not happy, was at least interesting. Carl changed all that.

A reasonably attractive and quite intelligent woman, owner of luminous brown eyes and medium-chestnut hair, Simone considered her best features were her generous smile and her full lips, always shiny with colorless lip gloss.

Simone was a psychiatrist, specializing in paraphilias — sexual behavior disorders. Dozens of men and women with sexual problems of all kinds came to see her.

Carl had appeared in the middle of a presentation she was giving for the Society Sex Therapy and Research Conference at the New York Academy of Sciences.

Simone was on the stage, facing the audience. Behind the comfortable red leather chairs, the frameless glass walls of the 40th floor allowed a perfect view of Manhattan´s sunset.

Simone was the ever-punctual type. She never failed to be first to a meeting. Perhaps this was an unresolved disorder of her own, a neurotic love for the clock. Carl caused a stir as he sought a seat.

"Loewenstein, in his psychoanalytical contribution to the theory of masochism, says the phenomenon is challenging since it contradicts the basic human characteristic, which is to avoid pain and displeasure, thus departing from standards of normality."

She couldn't finish her thought because, besides arriving late and still standing up, the guy decided to jump in. "But, Doctor, what is pleasure and what is displeasure? And what is normal? Who has established that?"

He'd interrupted her presentation. She had to respond. She couldn't avoid it. "Studies are carried out to learn what normal behavior is. This is what is practiced by the majority of the population in a given country, region or culture. Deviations from such behavior are considered abnormal. Generally, there is a group consensus as to what is good— pleasurable—and what is not. Based on these findings, pleasure and displeasure can be determined."

But the tardy disrupter proved unhappy with her explanation. "With due respect, Doctor, I still don't understand."

She sighed a bit impatiently. Seeing that the man would not desist without an answer, she decided to discourage him. "Your name, please?"

"Carl."

"Carl, my time is limited. Could you kindly leave your questions 'til I finish? There will be ample opportunity for them then. I won't be able to conclude my talk, otherwise."

"There is a seat in the last row." She pointed.

"Thank you and excuse the interruption."

He finally went to find a seat and left Simone to pick up her train of thought.

The lecture lasted fifteen minutes longer without further interruption. Afterward, during the coffee break, Carl approached her.

He was attractive and fair-skinned, though not handsome in the classical sense. Charming and magnetic, he had a square and angular face, far from what could be called pretty. His eyes were light brown, his dark hair flecked with gray. He was a tall man and at first sight, you couldn't tell if he was lean or muscled under his suit. But he was certainly well proportioned.

"Okay, Carl, what do you want to know?"

He seemed shy. She sensed it in his sweet smile, the one only shy people use when they want to be accepted. That was her mistake — she believed in the assurance the shy pass to others that they are gentle, calm, agreeable and pose no risks.

"The question I tried to ask before was what is normal sexuality and what is not?"

The way he spoke showed great interest. He looked her right in the eye while awaiting her response and reaction.

"I think I know where you want to go. Who defines normality? Who has the authority to do it? You don't have a medical background, do you? You're apparently unfamiliar with diagnostic standards. Is that correct?"

His little smile said "bingo." Then he said, "Your diagnosis is right on the money. I'm a lawyer. I really don't have the slightest idea about diagnostic standards."

This truly surprised her. A lawyer? At a sexology workshop, she would have expected a psychologist or a therapist or a gay person trying to understand himself. But a lawyer?

"And what brings a lawyer to a sexual disorder workshop?"

"I'm here because I need to build a defense in a case involving sex games that led to a woman's death. I need to understand the subject better so I can do my job."

Right, she thought. *A lawyer lost among shrinks. Wonderful. Any more surprises?* And "lost" was the correct word because the subject involved medical statistics...a bit out of a layman's depth.

"What *games* are we talking about?" Simone made quotes in the air with her fingers when she said "games." She wanted to show she didn't think any sexual activity that led to death was sportive material.

"Sadomasochist games," he replied, eyeing her intently.

"And you want to understand what's normal about that kind of game?"

"I need to understand. But your response a little while ago didn't help me. When you base something on studies where you ask people questions, you'll have to agree that most of them don't tell the truth. So how can you know if a given behavior is real or just a lie, and the majority not really a minority?"

"What do you mean by people lying in a study of that kind?" she asked, eager to get a lawyer's point of view.

"They just lie. Most people are too stupid and frightened and dishonest to answer a questionnaire truthfully. Even more so when it comes to a taboo subject like sex."

His body language said nothing. It didn't reveal what he thought about the subject. He seemed to be trained not to physically give away what he felt. Simone hadn't been able to read him yet.

"But we have to start from the premise that responses are true. If we don't, we'll never establish a standard." She rabbit-punched the palm of her right hand with her left in emphasis. "Regarding sexuality, it's very easy to identify sadism and masochism because we use a standard that shows only fourteen percent of the population has had an experience of that kind. I'll grant you that's not an exact figure but we have to work with the idea that about eighty-six percent of the population behaves differently."

"They behave differently or they're lying."

He was insistent. Clearly, he needed answers that fit the case he wanted to build, and the ones she offered didn't satisfy him.

"Maybe," she said. "What's normal for you?" Better for her to ask the question, she thought. That way she could understand what he really wanted to hear and then she'd be rid of him.

"Normal is to feel pleasure and do everything you can to get it. The rest is prejudice, nonsense or cowardice!"

His heated tone at last showed that behind his noncommittal lawyer's façade was someone with fire in his belly.

"People kill in pursuit of pleasure. You should know that better than anybody. You're defending such a person."

"Yes, the case I'm working on is basically that. Death for pleasure. Someone who puts pleasure above all else. Risking death. And that's not wrong or good or bad. It's the desire of someone to have that pleasure—someone who accepts the consequences." He stressed these words as if to show he truly believed what he was saying.

"True. But considering you're here, lost among shrinks, it seems your argument's not strong enough to convince the judge."

He smiled vaguely, as if agreeing. He ran his hand through his hair, showing impatience, apparently frustrated. "Not only the judge. I need to convince him and the whole jury. The charge is first-degree murder. They'll say it was premeditated. When my client goes to trial that will be taken for granted because sex frightens people. Unconventional sex terrifies them. Sex is easy to condemn."

"Can you sleep at night after you've defended a murderer? I've never been able to understand lawyers. You always defend one story and it's not necessarily the true story. My whole life has been dedicated to the search for truth."

"I hear you. But I understand the situation and I know he didn't intend to kill, only to give pleasure. It was an accident and…"

Apparently, he believed his own words.

"Lawyers always seem to say that. But you're right that unconventional sex terrifies the average person." She glanced at her watch and saw she was two minutes late for the resumption of her presentation. It disconcerted her. "Oh. We have to get back." She turned and took a step.

"Dr. Bennet, could you help me with my case?"

He placed a hand on her arm. Though partly absorbed by the sleeve of her jacket, the touch sent a frisson all through her.

"My name is Simone and I swear I don't see how I can help you."

"Simone, can we talk again after this gathering wraps up?"

"Yes, certainly." Out the window went her desire to go back to the hotel, take a bath, get something to eat and go to bed.

The other lectures were meat for a sexologist but probably not much help to a lawyer. Carl did, nevertheless, keep quiet and pay close attention. After the final presentation, he waited at the door with his hands in his pockets.

"Carl, you went the distance," she said, a tiny bit pleased to see him there.

"I toughed it out. How you people do complicate things. It's impossible to understand some of those terms you use!"

"Just like you lawyers when you write."

He nodded in agreement. "But our handwriting's more legible." He beamed and showed his perfect teeth.

"How can I help you? You've just met me. You don't even know what I do. You don't know if I'm capable or knowledgeable enough to be of any service to you. And from the little you've told me about your client's situation, it's complicated."

"I'm not a psychiatrist but I've been practicing law for twenty years. In my field, we also get to know people, to form speedy opinions about a person's character or worth. You can help me. I know you can. Sexuality is your area. I liked your book. Even though I didn't understand half of it, I could see that you approach problems with an open mind."

She couldn't conceal her pleasure when he mentioned her book. It had taken so much work, so many hours of research, to write. Recognition was always welcome.

"I can't have preconceived notions in my profession. I'm truly happy to meet someone from outside the academic world who's had the grit to read it."

"It was hard. It's pretty technical. You write with objectivity but it doesn't let a reader see much of your personality."

My personality? she thought. If she wanted somebody analyzing her personality, she'd write fiction, not a work of scholarship.

"It's a scientific undertaking, an extension of my doctoral thesis, not a novel. But getting back to your case. If you know something about my career, you also know I don't live in New York. I live in Woodbridge and I work in New Haven. I'll be here for just three days and I only have one free. I don't see how I can help."

"I'd like to hire your services. I want your help with this case. My office will pay you for your time. I really need help. I need an expert opinion. I'll go to Connecticut if necessary, or you can come here if possible. It's not that far, after all."

His eyes were timid and sweet and pleading with her. She never turned down a call for help. She nodded without having the vaguest idea what she could do for him.

"I can try. I'll need more details about your proposal."

"Can we discuss the case over dinner? I'll tell you what happened so you can think about whether you can help me and how."

Simone was prudent as a general rule and even more so because every day she treated people with serious behavioral disorders. Prudence had to be her name. But now she set prudence aside. Her curiosity about Carl took over, along with her attraction to this elegant, opinionated man.

* * * * *

When they got to his car—a black Mercedes sedan—she couldn't help analyzing it. The vehicle one chose to drive said a lot about the owner.

She pointed to the parked car.

"You drive a safe and quite traditional sedan for someone who defends the unconventional. Oh well, the world is full of 'do as I say' and so on."

"It's a good-looking and fast car. I like to take control of a powerful machine, and for clients, it shows gravitas. But I'm not the car. It's only a car."

Her remarks had clearly made him uncomfortable.

"Relax, I wasn't being critical. It was an observation."

"I am relaxed. I just get edgy when someone analyzes me. I feel like a lab rat."

He courteously opened the door for her and helped her into her seat. His warm hands on her made the attraction grow.

"Part of the job. Excuse me," she said.

"Don't worry about it. I'm starved. How about you?"

Amazing how lawyers can so slickly change the subject.

"Famished." But her hunger had passed. She was dying to take a glance in the rearview mirror to see how she looked, to make sure she was presentable and that her hair wasn't a mess.

"How does a tasty risotto sound?"

"Sounds good. It's on my list of comfort food."

He nodded in agreement and kept quiet for most of the fifteen minutes it took to reach a quaint restaurant with dim lighting in the Meatpacking District.

He greeted the waiter with a smile. He was apparently an *habitué*. They seated themselves at a pleasant table beside a glass wall with water trickling down it. Very soothing. Only then did he speak. "Do you know anything about wines, Simone?" He spoke without looking up from the menu, which he seemed to be studying as if it were a case.

"Yes, I know they're made from grapes." She laughed at her own weak joke.

"But do you like wine?"

"I do. But I don't understand everything that I like."

It was getting late. She decided to stop analyzing Carl's personality. The menu was downright seductive and her hunger had returned with a vengeance. It was hard to choose. She wanted to order everything. He chose right away and waited for her to make up her mind before picking a wine. He didn't ask her opinion. Maybe he was afraid of another lame attempt at humor.

"How long have you been a doctor?"

"Thirteen years next January." She felt as if her ballroom days were over when she said it. She was forty-two now, a difficult age for any woman. Confessing to the fact took an act of courage.

"And was there any particular reason for specializing in sexual matters?"

"I didn't have much interest during medical school. I wanted to be a psychiatrist but sexology didn't appeal to me. Then two years after I graduated, and with an appointment book full of patients, I began to understand that most problems involve sexuality." She paused to taste the wine. It pleased her uneducated palate. "So tell me about your case."

"A complicated situation. Two lovers who liked to play sex games of all kinds. One night, the woman died in the middle of one."

His description was so nonchalant, he could have said, "I went out for a loaf of bread."

"What was the game like?"

"She had a fantasy she lived out over and over. She liked him to squeeze her neck during intercourse. That day, he squeezed too hard."

"And why did he squeeze too hard? Do you know? Did he lose control or was it intentional?"

"She kept asking him to squeeze harder. The more he squeezed, the more she wanted. He squeezed and squeezed and squeezed until she died."

He seemed as if he was watching the scene, his gaze far away while he described what happened.

"And you're certain that's what took place? That it wasn't rape followed by murder?"

"I'm absolutely certain!" he snapped. "He didn't want to kill her. He only wanted to give her pleasure."

Good lawyer. Passionate about the case, she thought.

"But he did kill. Squeezing the neck during the sex act to give and feel pleasure is called hypoxyphilia. Many accidents and deaths occur that way."

"So it's not uncommon?" he asked, sounding half curious and half relieved.

"No. There are even famous people who've died that way. The main problem is that it's very hard to know if the one who caused the death wanted it to happen or not. At times, it's not an accidental crime; it's just disguised strangulation, an obscured rape. It's necessary to be sure."

"That's not the case." Apparently he was certain.

"You seem convinced of that. The killer's account is persuasive?"

"I don't like the word killer. It implies guilt. I've known him a long time. He would never intentionally kill anyone."

"I wouldn't say that. We're all capable of killing. It depends on the circumstances and the restraints we have — or lack of them. You have no idea of the number of people who come to me who have killed or were about to kill and who are absolutely peaceful people, people who are apparently normal and level-headed."

"No one is normal up close."

"Up close. Apart from the statistics on standard conduct, we don't know very well what normal is."

"Then I'd better not get too close to you, Doctor, or my abnormality will show." He laughed, as if it were a good joke.

"I need to find out how to help you so I can know if I need to get close." She really wanted to get closer to him. He intrigued her more and more.

"Simone, I need to clear a person. He is a close friend and partner. I need to know the death was not premeditated, that it was not intentional. To prove innocence, I need to be convinced, technically convinced, I mean. For that, I need a psychological study of hipoxophilia." He placed his hand on his throat as if to squeeze it.

What was this man doing to her? Just touching his own throat made her want him to touch hers.

"Hypoxyphilia," she corrected. "But just studying hypoxyphilia will help you clear someone?"

"It will. I need to know what makes someone feel pleasure from that, to know what's going on inside someone's head to make her demand such intensity. I want to understand what that behavioral deviation is and to understand what leads her partner to satisfy her desire. I want to know what motivates him."

He spoke these last words with an emphasis that left no doubt he needed an answer.

"I think we have to be more objective."

"*We* have to be? So you're agreeing to help." He seemed relieved.

"The case seems interesting. But we need to look at the event itself to be able to find out if it was hypoxyphilia or plain and simple death from asphyxia. I need details to help build your argument."

"Simone, you'll get all the information you need. He wrote a minute description of what happened with a wealth of detail."

"He what? He described it?"

"That's exactly what he did. And he didn't just describe the death. He wrote the history of their relationship as if it were a novel."

"Do they have names, or is it a professional secret?"

"Mark and Lara."

"But are those their real names?" She was already thinking about Googling deaths by hypoxyphilia to try to find something.

"There are no lies in the text but first, you'll read, then you'll be able to say what's real. At first, I'd like you to just stick to the text. Please don't go to other sources 'til you finish it. That will eliminate any bias."

As if he'd read Simone's thoughts, Carl had put a damper on surfing the web. But, she reflected, he was right. Better to read the text and afterward look for additional information. Besides, the book is almost always better than the film.

"How are we going to do this? Will you lend me what he wrote?"

"Let's do it this way; I'll let you take the first chapter. You read it and then tell me if you can help me. If you say you can, we'll draw up a contract covering fees and confidentiality and you'll have access to the rest of the story."

The lawyer had returned to life—contract, fees and confidentiality!

"Sounds good to me."

He opened the briefcase he'd put on a chair, took out a yellow envelope and handed it to Simone. It felt like it held about ten pages.

"Simone, I suggest you eat. You still haven't touched your food and risotto is good only when it's hot." He pointed at her untouched plate.

She tasted it and closed her eyes, signaling her approval. "It's wonderful. I love risotto."

"I do too. And I can make a great one."

Besides being interesting, the guy could cook. She wanted to take him home and keep him in captivity.

The dinner went well. Carl was cultured and a good conversationalist. She guessed he was more or less her age, based more on when he said he'd graduated from law school than on his appearance. She soon found out she wasn't far off. He was forty-three.

"I'm very curious to know what makes a pretty woman like you decide to spend her life delving into the human mind."

"Thank you for saying 'pretty.'"

Simone had never thought of herself as a pretty woman. She'd always looked at herself as being more "interesting" than pretty. Her hair and eyes were light brown; she exercised regularly and had a good shape. Nothing spectacular.

"The human mind is the most fascinating place that exists." *And your bed's probably number two,* she thought, a bit tipsy now from the wine.

"I prefer Paris."

He laughed. Wine can turn even the most severe lawyer into Mr. Cool.

"I agree. It's a more beautiful and less complicated place. But the trip into the human mind is much more intense and rich."

"Are you married, Simone?"

The wine speaking again, she thought.

"No husband in the world could put up with a life like mine. I'm a workaholic."

"But have you ever been married?"

Did he really care about her life or was he just being polite?

"Yes, a long time ago, and I have a daughter. I was sure that would be your next question."

"Indeed, it was. Classic, right?"

"To be expected. And you? Tie, black briefcase, wife and children waiting at home?" She was praying for him to say no.

"I left the tie in the car. As you've noticed, the briefcase is here. I'm a classic."

"And the wife and kids are at home?"

He dismissed that with a wave of his hand.

"No wife at home, no children. With all the time I spend on the job, they'd have to look for me in the classifieds whenever they wanted to talk to me. But I do have a plant."

So he really does have a sense of humor, she thought. *A bit on the harsh side but it's there. Just keep some alcohol in his blood.*

"That feat's beyond me. I can kill any plant. I always forget they need water." She paused. "Carl, the meal was wonderful. I don't mean to be inelegant but tomorrow the first presentation is at 9:00 a.m. and I still have to go over my notes."

"When will you have time to read the first chapter?" He was obviously in a hurry for answers.

"I promise I'll do it tomorrow night. Leave me your phone number and I'll call you on Saturday with my thoughts, okay?"

"I'm anxious to hear them but all right. Here's my card."

He gave her his business card, which seemed a pretty cold thing to do. Professional. *Wake up, Simone,* she admonished herself. *That's exactly what he wants with you, a professional relationship.*

"I'll need your cell phone. These are office numbers and the day after tomorrow is Saturday."

"I'll be at the office all day. Call me there."

"Talk about a workaholic. I just don't understand the live…what? Fern?"

"It's a cactus, Simone. It's just like me—tough, prickly, not very pretty and extremely resistant."

"Careful, Carl. The inside of a cactus is soft and watery."

"If you say so…" And he kept silent, looking deeply immersed in his thoughts or in another dimension throughout the journey to her hotel. Once there, he wished her goodnight and left.

Chapter Two

The man intrigued Simone more and more but clearly he only wanted her professional assistance. He hadn't come on to her. But he had said he thought she was pretty. She smiled, content.

Women considered brainy, like her, longed to be appreciated for other qualities. Without false modesty, she was sure she was smart. Nice to know someone thought her pretty as well.

She reached her room exhausted. She looked around. She simply adored hotels — their impersonality and what waited behind the locked door...the very image of immaculate orderliness. She threw herself on the bed and lay there completely dressed for a few minutes. She was tired but her mind was in turmoil. Thoughts swarmed inside her head. She breathed deeply and decided to take a bath. Then she wanted to sleep.

But she couldn't sleep after the bath. Feeling relaxed and refreshed, she got under the covers. The night outside was cool, about 50 degrees. The temperature inside her room, however, felt just right. The yellow envelope she'd tossed onto the table when she came in called to her. *I'll just take a peek,* she thought.

As she opened it and removed the printed pages, she said to herself she'd just read the first one. A simple glance changed her mind.

The text was written as if it were a book. And with a dedication:

To Lara.
My life, my world, my love.
Without you there is no color,
no joy, no laughter.
There is no poetry.
Miss you day and night.

Hard to sleep after a declaration like that. No one had ever written or said anything of the kind to her. She wanted to know who such a romantic soul was. Just a page...

* * * * *

Mark's Journal — Lara

Reaching the big four-oh is a crisis for anyone. Man or woman, it doesn't matter. You feel as if half your life has slipped away and you don't know where it has gone. I wasn't thinking much about midlife; I was just living. But life springs surprises that give us pause.

Over the last forty years, I'd had my share of joys, successes and loves, or rather, I thought I'd had loves. I'd also had doses of disillusionment that turned me skeptical about affairs of the heart. I was prepared to live alone.

I'd gone through two marriages. I was very young the first time. To this day, I can't explain why I ever got married. The second time, I was more mature but the marriage was a greater source of boredom than of good memories. No children from either. Paternity has never appealed to me and I refused to give in to my first ex-wife's whims in that regard. I was fortunate she was an intelligent woman who accepted my attitude. The first marriage failed because she began to insist on kids and I said no. We went our separate ways.

In the second marriage, neither of us wanted children. Our relationship ended day by day. It ground us down. I concluded that marriage is the graveyard of love. Tie the knot and it dies. I resigned myself to that.

I was convinced I'd never love again. I was absolutely certain that trap called love wouldn't get me again. Instead, I'd have a few flings, a bit of fun here and there.

I bought an apartment to reflect my decision. It was big and spacious but just for me. No women's closets and their thousands of shoes and handbags. No cozy nooks to lull me into dreams of cradles. Functionality, practicality, isolation. That was my house. I had a dog — all the company I needed.

My life was planned. I'm a lawyer and a good one. My career was increasingly successful. My clients liked my work.

With my PhD studies completed, one of my pleasures was teaching. I'd call it a hobby. Though it can wear you out and it pays peanuts, it's extremely enjoyable. Teaching is a stage for frustrated actors. I'm quite reserved. But when I'm acting, or rather, teaching, and when I'm practicing law, I'm someone else. My best traits come to the fore and I fulfill myself within the persona I take on in those roles.

When I reached the point where I said to myself that all I wanted was to go on this way, life showed me it had other ideas. We are not life's drivers but rather its passengers.

I met Lara at the home of my friend and ex-brother-in-law, Peter. A confirmed bachelor and gay man, he loved to throw lively parties for "interesting people" as he liked to put it. But they weren't always as interesting as he thought and I made a habit of making excuses whenever he extended me an invitation. But on that particular day I found myself at loose ends. The office was under control and classes were finished at the university, so I decided to take a chance and see what Friday night might have to offer.

I was sipping whisky when a woman started to walk toward me. A knockout, I thought. She was sensual, blonde and tall, almost as tall as I was and with eyes the color of the Caribbean. With her firm bra-less breasts and shapely legs, she was, pardon the expression, a luscious butterscotch sundae. To this day, I still remember our first conversation word-for-word.

"How ya doin'? I'm Lara."

"Mark."

"Are you here all by yourself because you haven't found anything to your liking or because you're just nasty?"

Impossible not to laugh at such a come-on.

"Both."

"You do seem nasty but you're too good-looking not to have something else to do."

"Has anyone ever called you brassy?"

"More than once. But it'll do you no good to call me on it. I say whatever I feel like saying. The advantage we'll have in our relationship is I'm honest. How many people can guarantee you that?"

"Our relationship? Hey, I know you're gorgeous and gorgeous women think they can do whatever they want and the world will smile. But you seem crazy to me, and crazy people scare me."

"I know. You like boring and normal people." She drew a square in the air with her index fingers.

"No, just normal is fine."

Luckily, Peter now came over to rescue me from this surreal insanity.

"Mark, I see you've met Lara. Lara, this is my lawyer Mark who gets me out of life's tax imbroglios. Mark, this is Lara, my marvelous architect who's responsible for my house. How nice. I wanted you two to meet. I don't know why it hasn't happened before because you two are my bosom friends. I think you have a lot in common."

He finally stopped to breathe and gave us both a bear hug the way he did with everyone, more to cause embarrassment than to show affection.

That's all I needed to hear. I'd spent my life building the image of a serious and dedicated lawyer and now someone was telling me I had something in common with a mad woman. I needed to think about the image I was projecting to the world. The same thing must have occurred to Lara because she laughed.

"Dear Peter, I think you're mistaken about the similarities. I've already introduced myself to your friend. I like him but he's frightened."

"Frightened and present. It's weird when people talk about me as if I were somewhere else," I reminded them.

"Mark, Peter chose you to be my blind date this time."

"This time?"

Peter seemed a little surprised about her statement but didn´t offer a denial. "That's right. I'm eternally trying to marry off Lara. She's been my friend for as long as I can remember. But I realize that the man who can put a wedding ring on her lovely finger has yet to be born."

I liked hearing that the goddess was single.

"Peter," she purred. "I've already told you. I'd marry you today."

"Sure you would. And you'd spend your life covering for a closet queen?"

"And how closeted you are! At least I'd be married to a great friend, which is more than some couples I know who've been together for thirty years can say."

The banter of those two was living proof that I'd drunk too much. I'd never heard such off-the-wall chatter. Damn whisky! Or had I wandered into a Woody Allen film?

"Getting back to the two of us, Mark..." Lara said.

"There is no 'two of us.'"

"Not yet. That's true. But there's going to be." She placed her hand on my arm and went on. "Peter, dear. We're going, okay? A million kisses. Lovely party." She kissed Peter on the mouth.

"What do you mean, 'we're going'?" A better look at the girl's breasts and I changed my mind. "Okay. We're going. But where?" If she'd wanted to go to North Korea, I was going. She was hot!

"Peter, has this whisky been doctored?"

"Mark, spur of the moment for once in your life. Let Lara take you away."

"Are you sure she's not a psychopath?"

"No, not at all. Take a chance and see. Tomorrow we'll find your body some place. And if you've gotten lucky, there'll be a smile on your face. Go, my friend. You've been a stick in the mud for too long now. Live a little."

So that's how Lara entered my life. And everything changed.

Present Day – Simone

Simone felt too worked up to sleep. But she was pleased to have perhaps resolved the first enigma. Carl was a criminal lawyer, Mark a tax lawyer. Mark was Carl's colleague and maybe a law school classmate. An emotional attachment clearly existed between them. So Carl's defense of Mark involved more than a professional relationship.

She tried watching TV but sleep didn't come. She got worried. In a little while she'd have to go to work. She'd be a mess.

At last, after tossing and turning for an hour, she nodded off until the alarm clock woke her. She rose and fixed herself up the best she could. She applied a touch of makeup and put on a black suit, sheer stockings and high heels — her serious professional uniform — and headed for the workshop, feeling tired but happy. She loved her profession and she loved to talk about her expertise.

* * * * *

Upon taking the microphone to start her presentation, Simone saw Carl seated among the participants. Quite a surprise, considering she hadn't thought she would see him until the following day.

"Good morning, everyone. I hope you're all well rested."

Their animated response helped to perk her up.

"Let's continue on the subject of sadomasochism," she went on. "Today, I'm going to return to one of the foremost authorities on this subject, Freud."

"Always Freud," someone burst out.

"Yes. Always Freud because he is the source. Everyone else has copied him, contradicted him, followed in his footsteps or been inspired by him. But no one has ever been able to be free of him for one simple reason. In many regards, he was right."

"Everything for Freud was sex. I think he was a pervert!" a girl in the front row interjected. She looked too young to be at a workshop with trained professionals, too young to really understand anything about sex in theory or practice. Her opinion was more than suspect.

"Considering that, from a psychiatric standpoint, perversion is any act not involving traditional sex — that is, penis-vagina — you may be right. But our point was not Freud's sex life but rather his contribution to the study of paraphilias and perversions. May I continue, or does anyone else wish to add something?"

The room fell silent and she reached the end of her presentation without further hiccups. When she looked for Carl he had disappeared. What had he been doing there? Testing the knowledge of the expert he wanted to hire? Trying to get information to buttress his case? Or just lured by curiosity? Well, her curiosity about the lawyer was increasing… She thought maybe she should accept his proposition…

The day drained her with its controversial subjects and endless discussions. When it was finally over, she went straight to the hotel and filled the bathtub to unwind. She took a bottle of whisky from the wet bar, put ice in a glass and couldn't resist picking up the manuscript.

Mark's Journal – Who is that Girl?

"Okay, Runaround Sue. Where are we going?" I'd given up fighting her.

"Dancing!" she replied with a winning smile.

Now I realize she understood what that smile did to others. Whenever she wanted something she'd turn it on and become a mischievous child just waiting for her wishes to be satisfied.

"I can't dance, Lara."

"No problem. I'll teach you and if you're really hopeless, you can stand around and watch me." She flashed that smile again.

"Lara, you don't seem quite right to me."

"And what's right to you?"

"We have codes of behavior and laws in this country that say what's right and wrong."

"Borrrring. I'm talking to you, not the lawyer you hide behind."

She jabbed me in the chest. Oh how I wanted to bite that pink finger with its red nail. I imagined her running her nails across my chest and got lost in the fantasy.

"Hey, Mark. Four, three, two, one... Ground control to Major Tom," she sang.

I wasn't sure if she meant me. "What? I don't understand..."

"You were in space. Are we going dancing or not?" An annoyed expression on her face showed she was impatient and she was tapping her right foot.

"Okay, lady. Let's go drag ourselves around some dance floor. But I've already warned you I'm no good at that. Do you know someplace?"

"Lots of them. I love to dance. And I know just the one that'll bring you back to planet Earth and get you out of that suit. It's called Behind the Door. Ever hear of it?"

"No. I don't know what's behind the door or in front of it. I don't go to nightclubs. I'm a day person. I get up early. But let's head there and see how the creatures of the night behave."

Such a sacrifice would surely get her into the sack with me — if I still had enough energy left after going through the aforementioned door.

"Did you drive here or do you want to go in my car?" she asked.

"No. I don't like to drink and drive."

"My God! You're right out of some bygone era! What's your sign? Let's get my car." She was already striding for a nearby parking lot.

"My what?"

"Sign of the zodiac."

"I think it's Capricorn. My birthday's January 5. Why?"

"I'm an amateur astrologer and your sign explains a lot, you poor thing. You're a typical Capricorn."

We got to her car and, contrary to what I'd expected, she had a monster SUV. Rolls of paper were strewn everywhere. She began dumping and tossing them all into the back seat along with countless plastic water bottles.

"Excuse the mess. It's my work car." Despite the apology she seemed unembarrassed.

"At least you hydrate yourself. Okay. Now explain, 'You poor thing. You're a typical Capricorn.'"

"You Capricorns are complicated. You're closed, loaded with traumas, reclusive, serious and traditional. Oh yes, and hard workers too."

While she drove, I watched her. A ten! She could call me whatever she wanted but she would be mine tonight!

"Hey, that seems pretty offensive!"

"No, no it's not. We are what we are, in thrall to astral energies. It's not your fault."

"In that case, I feel better. I'm a stick in the mud but it's not my doing."

"Darling, I'm not calling you a stick in the mud — yet. By the end of the night, maybe." She laughed.

"And you? Do you have a sign?"

Now she laughed with gusto. "Everybody has! I'm a Gemini."

"I know: Crazy, wild, with psychopathic tendencies and an excess of sincerity."

"Almost right. The excessive sincerity comes from the moon in Sagittarius."

"Oh, and now we have the moon..."

"Okay, boring subject. So tell me about yourself, little goat." She poked my ribs with a fingernail.

"Little goat?"

"Yes. Capricorn is represented by a goat."

She explained a bit more about astrology and went on to discuss a hodgepodge of subjects. The woman chaotically connected one thing to another. For years I hadn't spoken so much and about so many different topics. She wasn't just gorgeous, she was smart. But I grew increasingly certain that she had a grave psychological problem. This was confirmed a little while after we got to Behind the Door. The building appeared to be just a house. I detected no hint of it being a nightclub except for the people going inside and the number of cars parked out front.

Upon entering, we were registered, asked for our ID, charged a fee and handed cards that recorded what we might consume. They made us leave our belongings in a locker to which they gave us the key. They made it crystal clear we were to lock up everything, especially our cell phones. Aggravating my suspicion that I was falling into some kind of trap, a bouncer body-searched me.

"Hey! This is illegal."

"Relax, sir. This is normal procedure here. It's for your safety."

A woman wearing tight jeans and something like a bodice searched Lara, who then turned to me and smiled.

"C'mon, Mark, this song's great to dance to."

She began dancing as she headed inside, pulling me along. Well, she wasn't dancing, exactly, but more like gliding in a trance, eyes closed and her body moving sinuously to the music. It was like walking into a movie where there's a beautiful girl who knows all the moves. I felt like a spectator who wanted to touch the star, now boogying to the sound of fireworks. She was singing too.

"Do you want to drink something, Lara?"

"Yes. That would be wonderful, Mark. Whisky."

She winked. Does anyone still wink these days?

Her hair was starting to look windblown and she kept looking more and more beautiful as the night wore on. Or I was drunk, even though I'd had only a couple of drinks at Peter's place...

The mob at the bar made getting the drinks take a while. When I got back, Lara was doing an erotic dance with another man. I felt jealous and I'd only just met her. I wanted to tell him, "Hands off. She's mine!" What was this? I never got jealous.

"Maaark, come here and meet my friend. This is Leo. Leo, this is Mark, my new friend."

"Oi, Marko, such a pleasure."

Another gay guy. She knew a few...

"How's it going? Want a drink?"

"No, thank youuuuu. Lara, are you going behind the door tonight?"

"I don't know. What do you think? Would my friend have a heart attack?" She pointed to me.

"Better now than a month from now," Leo said.

"Right." She turned to me. "So what were we talking about, Mark?"

Present Day – Simone

The phone rang and Simone jumped out of the tub to answer it.

"Hello?"

"Hi, Simone. It's Carl."

"Hi, Carl. I'm reading the manuscript now."

"That's why I'm calling. How far into it are you?" His voice sounded eager.

"Not too far. Only a few pages. But it's very interesting. It holds your attention."

"Oh yes. It's detailed. I think the idea was to convey everything he felt."

"He's done that so far. I don't want to put it down. Too bad I've only just started. I had no time during the day."

"Have you eaten? Would you like to go out to dinner?"

"Thanks, Carl, but I'd like to read more since we're going to be meeting tomorrow. I'll get something from room service."

She was dying to go out with him but she had to make a decision by the following day and she needed to read more.

"What do you like to eat most?"

"I eat practically anything. But don't worry. We can lunch together tomorrow if you wish."

"Okay. It's a date. Excuse me for calling at this hour."

"It's not so late. Don't worry."

"Have a good night, Simone."

"You too, Carl. Sleep well."

She called room service and ordered a bowl of soup. Then she popped a bottle of wine but it tasted like diesel fuel. She returned to the tub and continued her reading. She wanted to have a response the following day based on professionalism, not just on the lawyer's brown eyes.

Mark's Journal – Behind the Door

"What's all this Behind the Door giving me a heart attack?" I had a feeling I wouldn't like the answer.

"Do you know what this place is, Mark?"

She half shouted to be heard over the music.

"Apparently it's a nightclub."

That's what it seemed to be: a dance floor, people dancing, a bar, drinks, dim lighting.

"This is a swing house."

"Really?"

I'd never been to one before. I had a preconceived notion that swing houses were for couples who lacked the resolve to end worn-out relationships and were just trying to disguise their desire for two-timing.

"Behind that door is the club." She pointed to a closed door. "Here's just for dancing. Want to go in and take a look?"

"What happens in there?"

"You've really never been in one of these places?"

She seemed nonplussed, as if she'd just discovered I'd never been to McDonald's.

"No, I haven't. I've always thought they were for ugly and old people."

"Nope. Not at all. All kinds of people come here. Here's how it works. You can touch somebody. But if you get no for an answer, stop right there. If somebody touches you, and you don't like it, just step away, unless you want to touch back. No one forces anything."

"And?"

"It all happens naturally. If you want to do something with someone, you can do it right there or in a private place or in a place for others to watch you."

"What are you saying?"

"Getting laid, Mark. Sex," she said without any emotion, as if it was a thing that happened every day in everybody's life.

"Interesting."

Oh man, how I wanted her and I didn't care even if it was right there in the swing house.

"Come with me. I'll show you."

She grabbed me by the hand and pulled me through the door. What she'd just said had me feeling like a three-peckered little goat. But I was worried about running into somebody I knew. What madness!

Inside was darker than the dance floor. The few lights lit up almost nothing. Amid sighs and moans and a sort of background music, people wandered about, looking around as if choosing a product, considering its advantages carefully, a real meat market. A woman rubbed her hand across my chest and kept moving.

"I'll show you the rooms," Lara said.

The first one we entered had a round bed where people sat feeling each other up. One man was fondling a woman's bare breasts while tongue-kissing another woman. There was no way a person couldn't get turned on by something like that.

"What's this?"

"The community couch. Everyone can use it. Want to sit with these people for a while?"

"No, not now. I want to see more."

We continued on.

"Here are the private cabins where you can close the door."

From the sounds I was hearing, some people were making use of the privacy.

"Here are the fish bowls."

She pointed to a few glass-sided rooms. I drew close to one and saw a couple screwing. I can't describe the adrenalin that was coursing through my veins. Between all I was seeing and my sexy tour guide, I'd never been so turned on in my life. My heart pounded. My dick throbbed. Just a little more and I'd have Lara on the floor.

"Hey! A woman just grabbed my ass." What a weird feeling, to have that done by a stranger.

"Take it easy. That's how it is here. Relax. It you don't like it, just keep moving. If you do, touch back. It's all spontaneous and knowing how to take no for an answer."

"I can touch anybody?"

I felt like a kid in a candy store with a C-note.

"Yes, indeed. It doesn't mean you'll get anywhere, though."

At this point, I did what I'd been aching to do all night. I put my hand on Lara's left breast and waited for her reaction. She closed her eyes and smiled. I'd hit the jackpot!

"Now it's my turn." She wrapped my neck in her arms and kissed me, her mouth and tongue soft, sweet and hot. I began to run my hands all over her body. I felt as if I were on drugs. I lost my sense of time and place, with people moaning all around and a couple screwing a few feet from us. I raised her skirt as we kissed and caressed each other. I wanted to come right there. I slipped my hand between her legs. She must have had a quarter inch of panties. She was moist and juicy.

"Mark…"

She placed her hand on my penis and began to massage it. I didn't want to pop my rocks right then. I thought about work, deadlines, anything to keep me from blasting off. I wanted to come inside her. She pushed me a little to one side and I didn't know what was going on.

"Lara, excuse me for getting carried away in the middle of a corridor. Is everything okay?"

"Of course, I only wanted to give you this."

She handed me a condom that seemed to have come from thin air. I slipped it on, lifted her buttocks and held her against the wall. Then I drove my dick into her pussy as far as it would go. She grew wetter. She squeezed. She ground her hips. Her legs tightened around my waist. She began to come. She moaned. I couldn't hold back any more and unloaded in the most satisfying, ecstatic climax I'd ever had.

A couple stood there watching us. I felt like an animal in a zoo.

"That was good, right?" She spoke languidly, breathing on my neck.

"Good? I've never come like that in my whole life."

"I know how you feel," She laughed. "It's like a drug cascading through your whole body. Come here."

She opened a door to a couch, a roll of paper towels, a red lightbulb and nothing else. We went in and she locked the door.

"Let's finish the right way what we started outside."

She started to strip and so did I. Before she was completely naked, she took a condom from her bra then threw the bra onto the floor. She was gorgeous! In seconds I was naked too. I drooled at the sight of her voluptuous body. She pushed me down on the couch, put her mouth around my penis and began to suck it. A true professional.

"You're nuts!" I exclaimed.

"You don't know the half of it," she said.

Then she mounted me and began to ride, slowly at first, then at a gallop, and then as fast as she could, obviously desperate to come. Though the couch was hard, cold and uncomfortable, I lost all notion of time and let my lust lead the way in that tiny room. We screwed and screwed. Sounds of sex, sighs and moans swelled all around us.

When we finished, we dressed in silence, drained and exhausted. I didn't know what to say.

"Shall we go?" she asked with a fatigued and somnolent expression.

At last! I'd thought the woman would never wear down.

I searched for something to say. "Okay. You want to eat something?"

"Absolutely. I'm starving."

"Me, too."

"Will you drive?" she asked.

I thought of the drinks I'd had, but who could be prudent after what had just happened? "Sure."

"There's a Coney Island hot dog joint near here that's great."

I thought a woman like her would want a good restaurant and red wine. And she suggested hot dogs. Were there any more surprises to come?

"That's what you really want?"

"That's what I want."

So we went to Coney Island and I saw that sophisticated lady turn into a little girl. She wolfed down two dogs smothered with sauerkraut, mustard, onions, chili and some other garbage that looked like grated cheese. We said nothing for a while. She really seemed to have needed the junk food and the silence, which she broke first.

"Did you like the experience?" She had mustard on her upper lip.

"Which one?"

"All of 'em," she said with her mouth full.

"I'm still dazed by it all. Behind the Door and all... It was the most intense experience

I've ever had the most adrenalin I've ever felt. But it's just ended. I'm still digesting it. Do you go there a lot?"

"There and some other places. I like adrenalin. My therapist says I'm hooked on it. So sometimes I go to those places. I do that."

"And the world accepts it?"

I couldn't begin to understand. Therapist? Addiction to adrenaline? I decided I'd think about that the next day.

"Your expression says you don't think so." She laughed humorlessly.

"I can tell you I'm overwhelmed right now. Our sex was crazy…was off the Richter scale. I haven't felt anything like that in a long time." In reality, I'd never felt such extreme pleasure but I couldn't admit such a thing without looking like a complete wuss.

"You finished? Did you like the hot dog?"

Funny. She asked me that in the same way she'd asked the other question. Nonchalantly.

"They were very good. I don't much like hot dogs but surprisingly, I liked those."

"I know. You're suit and tie, wine and table linen. Little goat. Respectable life, traditional sex, proper meals and prim women. I'm off the menu. I'm too nouvelle cuisine for you."

"Not at all. I was going to invite you out tomorrow, I mean, tonight. It's 3:00 a.m. now."

When was the last time I'd stayed up so late? Maybe when I was sixteen.

"Wow! Seriously? We have to see where your moon is because for the first time you've actually shocked me." The girl's face showed true surprise.

"Finally!"

"Okay. I'll give you my number. Call me this afternoon if you still want to, after the adrenalin wears off. I'll take you back to your car now. I have to sleep. Tonight, I'm going out with a hunky lawyer and I mustn't look a mess."

She went whistling off to the car, pulling me by the hand. And I was wondering about the depth of the quicksand I was slipping into.

We didn't say a word on the way. She turned up the radio and sang along. She had talent. She bounced around and had a good voice. But against the wall or on the couch she was Tony, Emmy and Oscar material.

"Here we are."

"Thanks for the ride."

She gave me a smack on the cheek, and I wanted more than that, but I didn't know what to do.

"See you later," she said.

"See you then."

And she left. I suddenly realized I'd forgotten to get her telephone number.

Chapter Three

Present Day — Simone

Simone no longer wanted to sleep. The story she was reading had her so aroused that she began to caress herself and ended up masturbating. She fantasized about a certain elegant, be-suited lawyer with brown eyes.

It didn't help much. She felt edgy. She was now beginning to understand what had led to Lara's death.

Addiction to adrenalin. The woman warned right at the start that she had a pathology. Her addiction could have been the result of any number of causes. Normally, some kind of disorder brings it on. The addict seeks intense thrills, sometimes danger. The worst part is that such people have little sense of real danger. They don't wish for death but they don't fear it either.

Maybe Carl was right. Lara hadn't been murdered; her death had been an accident. Accidents happen to people with that kind of problem. What could have been Lara's pathology? Then there was Mark, a man apparently with his feet on the ground who was drawn to the flame. Many men like him are attracted to psychopaths. But he was rash. And maybe Lara wasn't psychopathic. It was hard to diagnose with so few pages. But a shrink's mind can't read something without diagnosing it. Maybe the whole tale was made up.

For now, she would give the manuscript a rest. She was really tired and she could always continue reading it tomorrow. She thought about drinking some wine but alcohol would disturb her sleep and this time, she wasn't going to toss and turn all night. She grabbed a bottle of mineral water, opened it, poured a glass, then she took a potent pill guaranteed to knock her out. She drank the water and went to bed, falling asleep almost immediately. No dreams that night.

* * * * *

Simone was still asleep when the phone rang at eleven in the morning.

"Good morning, Simone."

Carl's crisp voice stunned her a bit.

"Good morning, Carl. How are you?" She sat up in bed to try to shake off the drowsiness and not make it obvious that he'd awakened her. She'd always felt a Catholic's guilt about sleeping late.

"I'm fine. Ready for lunch?"

"I am indeed."

What she really wanted was coffee and toast. But that was okay.

"What do you prefer? Japanese, Italian, a nice piece of meat?"

"Japanese is always a good choice." *And a latte to go with it.*

"I'll come get you, okay?"

"Okay. Thanks."

She jumped out of bed, took a quick shower and resolved that today she wasn't going to be Doctor Simone. No suit. She'd be sexy. As a good friend of hers used to say, "Don't let my brain dazzle you. Let my derriere make you drool!" She put on a touch of makeup, the "I was born beautiful" kind. Then she pulled on tight jeans, a white blouse with sleeves rolled up to the elbows, a brown belt and high heels. There. She felt confident and she still had half an hour to read a little more.

Mark's Journal – Te Revoir

What an infernal night. Dreams full of people moaning, red lights and loud music kept waking me up. I finally got out of bed at dawn, put on a pair of sneakers and went for a run to try to sweat the booze out of my blood and get my head on straight.

But one thought wouldn't go away. I needed to see that woman again! That thought grappled with another. *She's everything you don't like in a woman. She's unpredictable, too liberal, half crazy and a creature of the night. Among other "qualities".*

But her siren's song won the battle. I'd see her again. *Okay, Mark. Just one more time.*

I got home drenched but reinvigorated. I took a shower, picked up the phone and then I remembered. I hadn't taken her number. What now? Peter! Oh no. Anything but Peter. I'd have to explain to him why I wanted it. And he was a professional gossip. So, face Peter or not see Lara?

"Hello, Peter?"

"Hi," a sleepy voice answered. "Who has the audacity to call at this ungodly hour?"

"It's me, Mark, and it's 10:00 a.m. It's getting late."

"Getting late? Only if you're going to tell me to run for it because the police have an arrest warrant for me. It's early morning and Saturday!"

"Excuse me. Relax. No warrants. Your taxes are in order."

"I'm relieved. But if my taxes are in order, where's the fire? Wait a minute. I know where it is. It's inside your pants. Post-Lara Syndrome." He started to laugh.

"Post-Lara Syndrome?"

"Oh yes. I know the effect she has on people. When I'm a grown-up gay I want to be just like her. Irresistible!"

"You are a grown-up gay. It's nothing like that. We had a conversation yesterday and she told me she's an architect and I really need her phone number for some remodeling in the office."

Right away I knew that wasn't a credible excuse.

"Okay. I can go back to sleep. You're not going to call her on a Saturday to discuss work. I'll give you her number on Monday."

Despicable little fag!

"No. If you can give it to me today, I'll be grateful because then I can schedule an appointment with her for Monday. It's pretty urgent."

"Right! And the office caved in and there's an architectural emergency there. Be humble. Get down on your knees and say, 'Peter, you beautiful, sexy queen. Give me luscious Lara's number because I want to punch her skivvies today.'"

"Peter, you queer son of a bitch. Give me Lara's number because if not, that token bill I send you because you're my ex-brother-in-law will suddenly become a real one!"

"Ouch. That hurt. Bad boy. At least satisfy my curiosity. How was it last night?"

"We talked a lot. I liked her. We had dinner and I forgot to get her number."

"That's all? And you want me to believe you want to go out with her again because you talked... It must have been a very nice chat indeed. But that's not enough. Oh no. You can increase the bill. I'm not giving you the number. Uh uh."

"Peter, that's all that happened. I'm a gentleman and I wouldn't attack a woman on the first date."

"I know you wouldn't. As for Lara..."

I didn't like what he was saying. It sounded as if the whole world knew what she was like.

"What about Lara?"

"I thought she'd attack you. As soon as she saw you at the party, she went crazy for you. She wanted me to introduce her to you and when I hesitated she went over and introduced herself. I thought she was going to go down on you right there."

"Really? I thought you'd sicced her on me."

"No no no. I'd told her a little about you and she didn't even care. But when she actually saw you, she started salivating."

"Great. Now give me her number and you can go back to sleep."

"Don't I get a little kiss for that?"

"Good grief! Never! But today, if I'm lucky, Lara is going to get one."

"Mark, seriously. You and my sister didn't work out. I don't know why. I think you were too young, too much alike. But I think you should try to relax sometimes. All you do is work. Maybe Lara's craziness is what you need now. It'll be a good distraction. Don't think for once. Just do it."

"I'm sure she is not what I need. She's off the wall. But she's drool sexy, right?"

"She's not my style but sexy? Yes. She's also a good person. Don't judge her by appearances, okay? There's a super lady underneath all those curves. I don't believe she's someone to get serious about. Just go there and have fun, man!

"You know her well?"

"Yes. We became friends a long time ago and later on she became my architect. And she's very professional."

"You're an operator, Peter. Always making friends and getting discounts."

"It's my charm that does the trick."

"Right. Sure. But I'll take what you're saying to heart."

"I like you, ex-bro-in-law. And I like Lara. I wouldn't allow you two together if I thought you wouldn't hit it off. I'm not talking about marriage. I just think she can get you out of your rut and put some fun in your life. She's the right person for that."

"Okay, Peter. Let's see. The phone number?"

"Here it is. Write it down and don't call me until you have some titillating news."

I sat there for fifteen minutes just holding the phone and wondering if I really should call her. What did I have to gain by starting a relationship with someone like her? Sex! Amazing sex, and I didn't have to marry her. Just screw her. Courage, my friend!

"Hello," a child's voice answered.

"Hello. My name is Mark. I'd like to speak to Lara. Is this her cell phone?"

She'd said she was single but I'd forgotten to ask if she had any kids.

"Yes, it is. I'm Roberta."

That was nice. The little girl had introduced herself.

"Nice to hear you, Roberta. May I speak to Lara?"

"Yes. Auntieeeeee! A man on the phone wants to talk to you."

Wonderful! She was just her aunt. And the kid had a promising future as a soprano.

"What man? What phone? Roberta, have you been playing with my cell again? I'm going to talk to your mother because with you I'm talking to the wall."

"But Auntie, the phone was ringing and you were way over there. I don't remember his name. Here's the phone."

"Hello."

"Good morning, Lara. It's Mark."

What more could I say? We met last night at Peter's and screwed each other's brains out afterward?

Laughing, she said, "So that's your name."

At that moment, two kids began to shout in the background.

"Excuse me, Mark, but my nieces are impossible today. It's my Saturday to watch them."

What kind of person could leave kids in the hands of a wild woman like her? Well, without knowing the parents, he couldn't possibly judge their sanity. Interesting. The woman had a family. Nieces and a brother or sister somewhere.

"Are you going to babysit them all day?"

Say no, say no. I already had a hard-on just talking to the woman. I was back to being a teenager again when the mere voice of a woman gave me an erection.

"No. I'm going to have dinner with you. You asked me out last night and besides…Peter called me ten minutes ago." Laughter filled her voice.

So that swishy bastard had already started gossiping. I could have strangled him.

"And the kids?"

"Do you want them?"

She laughed again. How could someone who'd turned in so late and had screaming kids around her manage to be laughing so merrily?

"I can't handle kids. They don't like me."

"Kids like everybody. Just buy them off. They're the most venal creatures I know. Give them a piece of chocolate and they'll respect you. Give them a whole box and they'll pledge undying love. It's easy."

Whenever I thought the woman couldn't amaze me more, she did so.

"And you? What do I have to do for you to give me your undying love?"

That was a stupid thing to say. I was a prudent man who knew how to choose his words. What kind of idiocy was that?

"Take me to dinner and we'll see if you're really a bore or if you can prove otherwise. Maybe I will respect you."

Present Day – Simone

Carl arrived on time. Good. Point for him. Simone appreciated punctuality in anyone. But when it came with a handsome man in jeans, a pale blue shirt and stylish loafers, it was erotic.

"Dr. Simone."

He waited for her with the passenger door open. She considered adding politeness to the list of requirements for being erotic.

"Counselor." She returned the formality without knowing whether or not he was kidding.

"Gotten far with your reading?"

On second thought, she reflected, maybe politeness could be dropped from the list. Where was "Good morning?", "How are you?" "Sleep well?" She was disappointed. She'd gotten all dolled up and he only showed interest in her brain.

"Yes. I finished what you gave me and I'm anxious to read more."

"Is that a yes?"

Yes, you can take me to bed or to a chair. You can take me anywhere, she thought. But that was not the yes he wanted.

"Yes. We have to discuss the terms but I'll work for you. The story truly has my interest. It's intriguing, to say the least."

The restaurant Carl had chosen was modern and impersonal. A few Japanese motifs adorned the walls. He guided her to a normal table by a window. Simone would have preferred one of the low ones with cushions for seats. The well-illuminated ambience was definitely all business, not intended for romantic encounters.

"Okay. I have a draft contract for you here and I'd like you to take a look so we can establish our responsibilities."

He opened his briefcase and handed her another yellow envelope. Oh, lawyers and their contracts. Don't they ever use the word "agreement"?

"I'll do that."

Just then, a very good-looking, smiling man came over to their table. He had brown hair, green eyes and high-quality, salon-tanned skin, or it could have been the real thing. He was tall and smartly dressed.

"Carrrl, I've been missing you so, my friend. How nice to see you're in such lovely company.

He cordially extended his hand to Simone.

"I'm Peter, the hunkiest and most charming friend Carl has."

"Hi, Peter. This is Dr. Simone Bennet. Simone, Peter is my good friend."

"Good afternoon, Peter. It's a pleasure to meet you. Would you like to join us?"

At that moment, another man arrived. He was even better-looking than Peter. He had blond hair and shocking-blue eyes and kissed Peter lightly on the lips.

"The pleasure's all mine, Simone. But as you can see, my dashing companion is here. Almost as handsome as I am. You've already noticed the difference, right?"

"Really?" Peter's companion said. "The difference is that I'm well-mannered while my company is a little bit savage... Good afternoon, everyone. I'm Charles."

Peter's joking continued. Simone wasn't listening anymore. Her heart was racing. Here was one of the characters in the novel. He had to be Peter, the gay friend. If so, the story might be real. She'd had her doubts. She thought maybe the story was just an imaginary text the suspected murderer had written to defend himself. Now, with Peter standing in front of her, she didn't know what to think.

After the twosome bade Carl and Simone adieu, they ordered lunch and Chardonnay. Only then did they continue talking.

"That's...Peter? The Peter in the narrative?" Simone spoke more excitedly than she should have for someone who was expecting to receive a fat fee.

Carl appeared not to notice. "Yes. That's Peter himself." He ran his hand through his hair, which she'd already taken as a sign of impatience.

"The characters *are* real..."

"That's right. They all exist or existed."

"I can speak with everyone who has been or will be mentioned?" She felt her curiosity growing every minute.

"I think with one of them it won't be possible. The others, if necessary."

She felt a bit foolish. Such a stupid question. One of them was dead.

Carl maintained a professional attitude throughout the meal. They agreed on all the details of their collaboration—fee, travel expenses, all of it. But what most interested her was missing. She found out nothing more about the man himself.

After lunch, he gave her another envelope, a brown one this time, that probably contained twenty more pages. He wouldn't give her the whole thing until she'd signed the damn contract, and then, to her disappointment, he suggested he would drive her to her hotel so she could continue the analysis of the text. Definitively, his only interest was her mind.

When she arrived at her hotel, she found her room immaculate, just as she liked it, clean and organized. She turned on the air conditioning, took off her shoes, changed into a comfortable pair of sweats and a t-shirt then filled a glass with canned orange juice she found in the mini bar. She then sat on the couch to read the text, figuring she could take a bath later.

Mark's Journal – Chitchat and Chili

She suggested we meet at the restaurant. Afterward, I'd take her home. Something to do with practicality, she said.

She chose a Thai restaurant in an old house in SoHo. The atmosphere seduced me right away. Half-light, low tables, motifs from some Asian country I couldn't identify. The waiters were all Asian and they did their best to make the customers comfortable.

We were led to an almost floor-level table where we sat on cushions. As we selected items from the menu, Lara was a hurricane, fidgeting and making suggestions at the same time. She waved her hands as she spoke, those delicate but firm hands, and used her index finger a lot.

"Mark, what do you want out of life?"

From where did she pluck that question? Quite an out-of-the-blue way to break the ice on an almost first date.

"In how many words?"

"Short and sweet."

"Money, health, knowledge, peace, travel. I want to be happy."

I thought it was a nice reply. It showed ambition, concern with quality of life and culture. I thought she'd approve.

"Hmmm. Only that?"

I'd used my seduction manual repertoire and all I got was "hmmm"? Was that a good "hmmm"? A bad one? It definitely wasn't what I'd expected.

"What does 'hmmm' mean?" I finally asked.

"Hmmm is hmmm. I was expecting something like that from you. You really sell that idea. Very Capricorn. Except for the travel. You must have a moon in a more adventurous sign."

"And what do mean by 'very Capricorn'?

The lady had forgotten I was a complete ignoramus on the subject.

"Capricorns are ambitious, wise and long-lived. They're the sign of the zodiac that lives most intensely."

She spoke with the same seriousness that I did when I explained taxable events to my students.

"Capricorns are also hot, bouncy and good company?"

Suddenly, I was acting like a teenager who wanted her to think I was funny.

"That depends on the wisdom they've acquired…" The minx gave a vague response, leaving me up in the air. Then she went on. "Now, if you're asking if you're hot, I enjoyed screwing you last night. I think we can do even better. It was the first time and there's a lot more to come."

She pointed her finger at me and I gagged on my whisky.

"Thank you." I felt like a perfect idiot thanking her for the praise.

"That's not praise. I said it can get better. I don't believe in good sex the first time. There's no such thing because nobody really knows what the other wants."

"Then why Behind the Door?"

"That's just it. The first time nobody knows where to put their hands." She waved hers at me. "Adrenalin gushes there. Lust runs rampant. Screwing's easier. When did you ever get laid with someone the first time like that?"

I wanted to answer "every time." Something in her expression thwarted me.

"Okay. I understand. Almost never. But aren't you afraid of what people might think about you?"

She shrugged as if to say, *I don't give a damn what people think.* She sighed. "What are they going to think? That I like sex? Better they know immediately, right? I'm sick of people who play hard to get. Teasing and not delivering. It's better to know where you stand. If you can't swallow, don't chew!"

"That's quite an attitude. It's startling. I bet it sends a lot of guys racing for the exit."

"Yuh. Most do. Men think they're great lovers. But they can't handle a trial run. They're afraid. They're in a hurry. They don't know what they want. But some stay. Like you, for example. Dining with me just to be polite but berserk for more."

She laughed while I blushed with embarrassment. I couldn't even open my mouth to apologize.

"It's that obvious?" I finally managed.

"That you want more? Of course. It's plain to see. But take it easy. I do."

Just then dinner came to my rescue. I felt like a little kid nabbed stealing candy at the supermarket, ashamed, afraid the waiter might have overheard. But I reminded myself he hardly spoke any English.

"You certainly are direct," I told her.

"Yes indeed, my friend. I've seen a lot in my short life. I've bent over backward to please. I've been a puppet. That wasn't for me, so one day I decided to stop."

More than a hint of pain showed in her eyes…unsettling to find in such a young and beautiful woman. Who could have hurt her so much that she'd come to behave as she did?

"I know how it is," I said. "It's like apnea. What's pleasurable at the start of relationships doesn't last because it's not real. You've decided to be real, once and for all."

"Apnea?"

I'd finally said something that had surprised her.

"Yes. I like to go diving. Sometimes I dive without air tanks. I hold my breath. It's called apnea and you can do it for only so long. At the beginning of relationships, people hold their breath. When they can't do it anymore, they go back to being who they are and relationships end."

"I adore that description."

Now I wanted to shout and jump up and down. I'd hit the bull's-eye!

"Hey, do you dive?"

"I'm crazy to learn. Is it good?"

Suddenly, she was five years old, eager for something new and completely changing the subject.

"For me, diving is the greatest feeling of freedom that exists."

I remembered the sensation of being underwater. The silence. The blue vastness on all sides. The sense that the world had stopped. It made me happy. I think I smiled.

"It truly makes you happy."

"Yes, it does. It's something I really love to do."

"What's it like?"

What do you know! I was going to teach her something. I felt macho again.

"When you dive you always need a companion because it's not safe to do it by yourself. Despite that, as soon as you're down there, it seems you're alone. You're floating in an immense swimming pool where you can't see the sides. There are few sounds, only rising air bubbles when you use air tanks. Sometimes somebody bumps a tank against something but generally it's just silence. You don't feel walls. You feel free. Maybe it's like being an astronaut. You're in space but with the welcoming wet touch of water."

"There must be Pisces somewhere in your chart."

There she was again with the horoscope.

"Do you use the horoscope much to govern your life?"

"There's an enormous difference between the horoscope and astrology. I don't consult the horoscope ever. I study astrology. Astrology is a science. Did you know that it used to be taught in schools in France?"

"Really? I thought it was only a filler in a newspaper."

"Oh, that too." She laughed. "But when done seriously, it's pure science. It's mathematics."

She began to explain a few principles. I became interested in the subject. It seemed what she was saying could have some scientific basis...some...

"Let me throw a question back at you, Lara. What makes you happy?"

She raised her arms and opened them wide. "This makes me happy. A good wine, a good meal, good company, a good surprise, trying something new, good sex. I don't need much."

"What do you want for your life?" I pressed her.

"In the short term, peace."

"Peace? Like world peace?"

Was she a candidate for Miss America?

"Nooo. Like peace in my life."

"Define that for me, would you?"

"Running my life at my own speed. Not having to account for where I go and what I do. Taking care of my needs."

Easy to understand why she was single. That description was the antithesis of marriage, of the ones I'd had, at least. Pain seeped through her words. Suffering of some kind had led her to think that way.

"That's why you're single?"

She didn't answer my question directly. "I sincerely think marriage and living together are a trap. And you said something interesting today. I'd never thought that perhaps what kills a marriage is this apnea almost all of us experience."

I felt pleased she'd understood something about life because of my explanation.

"Then you've done apnea because of someone, right, Lara?"

"Sure. Of course. A few times. I started out in life doing apnea, being somebody's poodle. Then I saw the best thing would be to show right away who I was. I wouldn't have to go crazy, trying to meet the expectations of others.

But I soon discovered that people don't want who you are. They watch. They observe. Then they end up thinking 'I'm going to change her!'"

"That's it."

I remembered my ex-wives and their demands for changes for the sake of the relationship. "We have to talk" gave me a migraine the moment I heard the words.

"And I understood that nobody changes for anybody. We only change when it's important for ourselves. So don't buy bananas when you want to eat apples. A banana's a banana. Eat it or go find another fruit stand."

The dinner went well. She was very pleasant company. We discussed life in general, travel and our jobs. Her depth and maturity belied her appearance. I silently gave Peter credit for having advised me not to judge this book by its cover. When I realized three hours had passed, during which I'd truly enjoyed myself, I laughed and felt happier than I had for a long time.

We left the restaurant in a merry mood because of the drinks and each other's company. I was glad to be taking her home. Knowing where to find that woman was invaluable information. And I was going to drive, even after having a few drinks. That was a novelty!

I opened the car door for her and helped her to get comfortable. My habits usually weren't so direct but the effects of the alcohol made me fasten her seatbelt and kiss her. The woman was irresistible. Two legs were wobbly and the third one firm when the kiss ended and I took the wheel.

I started the car and left the parking lot. We stayed quiet for about three blocks. Then she began to tickle my neck with her long nails and slip her hand under my seatbelt toward my crotch.

"Lara, are we going somewhere?"

"We're already there. Relax." She unzipped me and took hold of my erection. "I want to do something with you."

She took off her seatbelt and took me in her hot mouth. I almost came then and there.

"I'm going to pull over." I began to slow down.

She raised her head and told me to reduce speed but not to stop. Jesus!

She went back to business. She paused and undid my belt. She produced a condom from nowhere and slipped it on. She must have been a magician who had pulled condoms out of her ear in some previous incarnation. She lifted up her skirt. No panties. She mounted me with her back to the wheel.

"Don't you dare stop this car, Mark. Relax. Feel the adrenalin. Just don't close your eyes."

Feel the adrenalin or relax? How could I relax with the adrenalin roaring through me? Not close my eyes? Not close my eyes! I was driving, for Christ's sake! May God's will be done. Or the devil's… She gyrated languidly as I tried to watch the road. I was going slowly. Feel it all and still keep my eyes open. She suddenly moved faster, squeezed harder and gushed. Good. Seconds later, I closed my eyes and braked — the car. No way could I brake anything else. I came 'til I was drained. Her smell filled my nostrils. The smell of sex filled the car.

"A little spice in life sometimes, right?" she remarked after we'd caught our breath. She kissed me, dismounted, removed the condom, knotted it, put it in the glove box and retook her seat. All in a New York heartbeat.

"Oh. You drive me wild, wild!" I felt incoherent. My lawyer's eloquence had gone to the moon on a one-way ticket. I was whipped. Out of it.

"You're sexy. You're so serious you always make me want to steer you off the straight and narrow, to shake you out of your tree."

"You're out of your tree! What if we'd had an accident?" I lowered my head onto the steering wheel.

"First, there's a lawyer here to get us out of trouble. Second, have you ever heard of fatal accidents at fifteen miles an hour?"

I wasn't insane but she aroused indescribable instincts in me. First, uncontrollable lust. Second, uncontrollable lust. But she also aroused apprehension, fear and the desire to wring her neck. All at the same time.

"Will you take me home now, handsome? We're going the wrong way."

I hadn't even thought to ask where she lived.

Chapter Four

Present Day — Simone

Simone analyzed Mark and Lara's relationship. It was certainly out of the ordinary. It looked as if he'd gone into it driven by desire. It wasn't yet possible, however, to know what she wanted. They appeared to be playing the same game — mutual attraction. Simone saw Mark's growing interest. As for Lara, a certain indifference seemed to temper her behavior. Mark was simply being swept along. And Lara seemed to be in control.

Impossible not to imagine what came next. Hot, spontaneous sex. The psychiatrist in Simone tried to focus on symptoms. Everything led her to believe it was a matter of a pathological relationship where one party was seductive, fearless and inventive. The other, the victim, was a sensible, correct person who nevertheless was susceptible to the excesses of the other. To what point was that the case? She'd have to go deeper into the text and the relationship.

Thoughts crowded her mind. Easy to see why Carl believed in Mark's innocence. She could also believe in it from reading the narrative. But how true was it? The text seemed very exact, very profound. *Some writers are like that,* she thought. They could reach the point of making a reader believe a story was true. But what if he'd made it up, created a story designed to obtain a "not guilty" verdict? Simone's conscience grew uneasy. She might hold the key the defense needed to acquit...an innocent man or a guilty one?

Enough of Lara! Simone decided to read the contract Carl had given her. It must have been fifteen pages long. She wondered if he'd ever thought of writing phone books. Why were lawyers so wordy? Was it to justify their fees? Or because they were frustrated novelists? She looked over the papers and saw the same old boilerplate. Endless clauses. Why did he want one covering confidentiality? She was a psychiatrist. It was her duty to maintain confidentiality in her work. It wasn't necessary to put it down on paper. If she violated his privacy, she'd lose her license to practice medicine. Okay. If Carl wanted it in the contract, he could have it.

The document tired her. She needed to talk to her partner, Edward, before she signed the contract.

Edward had been her med school classmate. They became friends early on and always worked side by side, including many shifts spent on night duty at various hospitals. They went on to open a practice together as both had become psychiatrists. Theirs was a successful partnership. They always helped and depended on each other, and they never did anything affecting the practice without clearing it with each other. She wouldn't sign a contract or engage in an activity that kept her outside the office for a while without at least listening to what he thought about it.

She got her cell phone and called Edward.

"Hello. Good afternoon, Edward."

"Hi, Simmie. How's it going? Where are you?"

"Still in New York. I'm fine. Excuse me for calling on Saturday afternoon but I've received an unusual proposal to assist a law office with defending one of their clients."

"You've changed your profession? Are you going to abandon me?"

"Ha ha. That's not funny. It's a complicated case of death by hypoxyphilia and they want my help with the psychological aspect. What do you think? Should I accept? I'll have to be out a bit but I think I can keep it to weekends when I'm needed."

"If you think it may be good for you, you know you can count on me for whatever. We're partners... What about the research? Have you given up?" He sounded worried.

"Oh no. Of course not. It's my priority. I'm thinking about it all the time. How are we doing?"

Simone was doing research for her new book, which would deal with couples' sexual fantasies. Edward had suggested they do some fieldwork on the Internet. They had opened a false account and signed up on a suitable site. They introduced themselves as a couple seeking to find a "boyfriend". Dozens of e-mails came in. They decided to choose a few and, as a couple, meet the responders to see why the men offered themselves for such activities or why they fantasized about them. Edward and Simone also wanted to separate those prospective participants who would really go the distance from those who merely wanted to fantasize.

"We have a number of *candidates* but I'm waiting for you before we respond. The propositions are irresistible." He chuckled.

"Any worth looking into?"

"Yes. There are one or two out of a couple of hundred with whom I think we should schedule a meeting. I'm having fun with this. The more I get to know about our fellow humans, the more I think there's no such thing as normality, common sense or levelheadedness. This research is doing me good, too."

"Thank you, Edward, for everything and always. You know I love you, don't you?"

They always said that and it was the honest truth. Perhaps the greatest love that exists is between friends. It is the least selfish. It asks for nothing and simply gives. The two of them would always be the best of friends. It was one of the few certainties Simone had in life.

"You're welcome, my lady. Have fun and relax a bit."

"I'll try. And you? Any romance on the agenda?"

"I wish. I'm going to pick up Noah and take him to the movies. Probably I'll have to face another torture session with Beth."

Noah was Edward's son, whom he'd had with his ex-wife Beth. Or rather, Beth had had with him. She'd gotten pregnant on purpose...the way many women do when faced with the imminent end of a failed relationship. To put off the inevitable. The divorce had been hell for Edward, full of blackmail and constant shouting. Now, a few years had passed since the height of the storm, and things were a bit better, a bit calmer. But Beth, from a station in life much lower than Edward's, had no compunctions about making quite unpleasant scenes in step with her frequent alterations of mood.

"Beth never changes... Aren't you tired of all her acting?"

"Tired? I could kill her with my bare hands if I wouldn't end my days in jail..."

"Resist, Bruce...resist..." Simone quoted the *Shark Tale* cartoon they had watched some years ago in the company of their respective children, Noah and Tamara, and Simone and Edward both laughed.

"I will, my friend. Come back. I miss you."

"Miss you too. I'll be back on Monday."

"A big kiss and I'll see you then."

"Kisses, my friend." Simone hung up the phone, still smiling.

Okay, Simone thought. *No snags with the contract.* She took a pen from her purse and signed it. The die was cast.

She didn't know yet whether Mark's story was true or false. Her curiosity kept growing. But it had not outstripped her desire to get to know Carl better. She couldn't make up her mind whether he had awoken her "woman attracted to handsome man" side or merely her psychiatrist side, which wanted to fathom his personality.

Who's kidding whom? she finally said to herself. She wanted to grab the guy and do with him what Lara had done with Mark. She stood deadlocked one-to-one with Lara in desires and fantasies. But as to making a move, Lara led, two-to-one.

Simone decided it was time to visit her own shrink. She'd begun to engage in mental competition with a dead woman. She even knew what the good Dr. Edgar would say: "Put your fantasies into practice or practice something without fantasizing. But practice. You're too involved in your work, too starved for affection." One-zip for Dr. Edgar but now Simone should get back to work...back to reading text.

She asked room service to send up a latte and a pastrami sandwich and after its arrival, she ate quickly, sat on the couch, put her feet on the coffee table, settled her reading glasses on her nose and began to read.

Mark's Journal – Doctor's Orders

I dropped Lara off at a modern and bright building made of glass and steel. She didn't ask me in. I don't think I wanted that. I was still shaken by everything that had happened in the previous days and needed to distance myself for a while. Something inside me was shouting, "Danger!"

"Thanks for the lift, Mark."

She pecked me on the cheek and left the car. What the...? She screws me blind, kisses me on the cheek and gets out of the car. I almost asked her to give me a call. The roles had reversed. Dammit, I was the man in the relationship, not some needy chick!

"You're welcome, Lara. Sleep well."

"You too."

She said nothing else, turned around and went inside. I headed home with a weird feeling. I needed to talk to someone. I started going over my friends in my mind. Should I talk to Augie? He'd tell me to keep punching her shorts and then he'd ask for her phone number. He'd say she was too much for one man to handle. Then it hit me. There was only one person capable of giving me a feminine opinion to help me understand what was going on.

I got my cell, synchronized it to the hands-free system in the car, found Peter's number and called him. Peter must keep his phone hung around his neck because he answered quickly.

"Hellooooo."

Peter sounded half asleep. Again? I was starting to think he was in constant hibernation or I was pathologically inconvenient.

"Hi, Peter. Did I wake you up...again?"

"No. I'm just lying here in bed watching *The Godfather* like a worthless rag without friends, without romance, without anything to do."

Pitiful poof, I thought. "Well, I wanted to talk to you about something."

"Do you know what time it is? It's two in the morning! The children should be asleep."

"Sorry, Peter. I thought you'd be out cruising 'til sunrise."

"I'm referring to you. You go to bed early. What are you doing up at this hour in need of friends? Have you finally discovered you're gay?"

"I lost track of time. I was taking care of a few things and didn't realize it was so late."

"Taking care of things with whom? I've got a feeling…for somebody who usually turns in at eleven… Let me see. Her name's spelled L-a-r-a." He giggled.

"Right. That's her. I wanted to talk to you but not over the phone—I'd prefer live and in color. Can we do something tomorrow?"

"Not tomorrow. Tomorrow's Sunday. I'm going to the stock cars. I'm already in Charlotte."

"Stock cars? You don't like that stuff."

"I detest it. That abominable noise. Those cars hurtling around. But the doctor recommended I find a beautiful and rich guy who loves sports. So I thought about where I could fill the prescription. The stock car track is packed with them. I'm going to follow my doctor's orders."

"Peter, stock car fans are men. What the doctor suggested wasn't exactly that."

"Oh. That's what you think. Gays who are really gay blend into the crowd and always have their eyes open. Look. Twenty percent of the world's population is gay. A hundred percent here are men, so... Twenty percent of stock car fans can be gay! I'm going to get lucky. Monday, I'll be available. How about lunch?"

"Where did you get that twenty percent?"

"It's empirical. Just look around."

"Okay. Right. Twenty percent? That's a lot. Let's have dinner. I can't go to lunch because I'm breaking in a new lawyer who just passed the bar and I have to keep an eye on him. He's smart enough but you know how it is."

"Is he good-looking?"

"He probably is, Peter. The women at the office began to use more perfume after he came on board."

"I'm coming down to your office. He might be just what the doctor ordered."

"You can't show up at the office. And besides, he's a penniless rookie lawyer. He doesn't meet your specs. We'll have dinner. You choose the place but please not one that's too intimate. You and I at a table eating by candlelight would ruin my image."

"Ruin your image? I'm gorgeous. All the men say so. And the women persist in trying to straighten me out. People would say you're a man of breeding and fine taste!"

"You truly are clueless. See you Monday, Peter."

"Wait a minute. I have to wait 'til Monday to find out what happened between you two? I'll call Lara—"

"Please, Peter."

"Please yes or please no?"

Goddamn homo from hell! "Please no!"

"I'll consider it if you tell me everything before I watch the rest of *The Godfather*. You've already made me miss a good part of the movie."

"I don't know why somebody who is as gay as you are is so hooked on *The Godfather*. It's too macho for your taste."

To my knowledge, he'd already seen the trilogy at least thirty times.

"I've got it bad for Corleone Junior. Whenever I watch the films I imagine a man like that in my life."

"Peter, sometimes I'm in total disbelief about how gay you are. You could be a little bit more masculine. And Corleone Junior's name is Michael."

"I love you too. Good night."

"Good night, my brother."

I thanked the Lord above Peter had gotten off the Lara kick. He could be irritating. But the truth was — although I loved harassing him for being gay — my ex-brother-in-law was the closest thing I had to a brother…or sister, for that matter.

Chapter Five

Present Day — Simone

On Sunday morning, Simone awoke from an excellent night's sleep. She lounged in the bed for a few minutes, allowing herself time to wake up, then she stood, took off her light-blue silk nightgown, went to the bathroom and took a shower. After completing her toilette, she ordered breakfast. She was famished and asked for almost everything on the menu. She loved to take her time and eat a large breakfast on Sundays. She ate slowly, savoring the fact it was a holiday — no pressure, no schedules — but then she remembered she had to call Carl and tell him about the contract.

"Good morning, Carl. I signed the contract. Do you want to come pick it up?" Suddenly, she felt rude. She hadn't even asked him how he was. Maybe his behavior was affecting hers.

"Good morning, Simone. I'm glad you've decided to help me. I want to give you some more of the story."

And to see me again before I leave, right? she thought.

"I intend to head for Woodbridge early, about six o'clock this evening. The traffic is beyond belief on Sunday. What time do you want to come over?"

"I'll be there at four. I'll take you for coffee if you like. We can talk a little more."

"Thanks, Carl. Sounds good." Simone smiled to herself, hung up the telephone and decided to get dressed. She chose jeans and a white shirt — her casual "uniform" — but she put off doing her makeup, deciding she had plenty of time to put on her face later.

With some time left, she decided to look at the e-mails that had come in for her research. She took her MacBook, put it on a small table near the window, sat, connected to the internet and opened the fake e-mail account she and Edward had created called clairepaul@himail.com.

They had signed up on a couple of sites, one called livelife.com and the other myidealcase.net. The message they addressed to men read:

Hi. We're a couple. Claire is thirty-five and I'm thirty-six — which wasn't true. She and Edward were both forty-two but they believed the younger ages would make them more marketable — *and we want a boyfriend. Claire loves to have sex with other men and I love to watch and sometimes join in. We can't identify ourselves.*

Discretion is fundamental. So is safety. We don't want any kind of financial relationship. Write to us and send a photo. From there we can arrange a meeting. Kisses. Claire and Paul.

Simone began to read the e-mails and respond to the most promising ones, with a hidden copy to Edward.

Lusciouslover wrote: *Hi! You guys done this before? Where do you live?*

Amazing. The guy was invited to have sex with a couple and all he wanted was the address. *Must be a mugger,* she thought. *Delete.*

Loverboy said: *Hi, princess. How you doin'? I'd love to get to know you better. I smell good, I'm handsome and I've got a big one. I love safe drool sex. I live alone. Let me know.*

This one made Simone laugh. In his eagerness for free sex, he had forgotten the husband. He just wanted the princess. And the language…

Paul wrote: *That's great. We got the same name. Photos attached.*

Simone got a shock when she looked at them. How grotesque. There were only pictures of the guy's penis in various stages of tumescence or lack thereof. No face. Nothing. Didn't he own a mirror? His cock was crooked and he was showing it online. Simone, the psychiatrist, diagnosed him as demented.

Marriedman said: *Hi. Well. I'm married. I'm thirty-two and I really would have to be very discreet. I don't have photos of my whole body. I'm sending just a regular photo. What are you both really looking for? Where do you live? What do you want out of this relationship? What's your line of work? I work for the government. Discretion is essential for me.*

In accordance with the standards Simone and Edward had established, this one would get an answer: *Hi, Hubby. Wonderful that discretion is important for you. For us too. We really want a boyfriend, someone for three-way sex with no holds barred. We go for everything inside four walls. We live... We'll discuss details later. We're in the legal field.*

Depending on how this one replied, they'd think about phase two of the research — Internet chats with no image. Phase three would consist of an actual meeting between Edward and the potential candidate and phase four — a second encounter, including Simone. Then they'd ditch him.

Alwaysdiscreet wrote: *Gud evning Paul I don like to identeefie my self neither. I nice an discreet I not lyke uther men I difrent, polyte like sex and frenship an had difrent kynds uv relationships all safe relax.*

The man had attached a naked photo of his whole body. Simone marveled at his nerve. Some people really were totally uninhibited.

She analyzed the text and concluded he was an exhibitionist who massacres language but was definitely courageous. She decided to respond in recognition of his merit.

Dear discreet. What's your name? What type of experiences have you had? How old are you? Can you explain to me why you're different from other men? What do you mean you've had different kinds of relationships? What did those relationships involve? Affection, just sex or...?

Popipopi said: *Hi Claire and Paul. I hope you like the photos but I'm not really that photogenic. Hee hee. As you can see, I'm six feet tall and I'm twenty-eight. I live alone. I like to go to the gym not to body build but to run. I do speed among other aerobic exercises because I like to maintain my* sexual vigor. *I imagine you've been looking for some time for a compatible person who can satisfy your needs. I'm not a person who likes to talk about himself. I prefer to use modesty to describe myself. I love to have flings but not often. I learned from a girlfriend of mine that I was addicted to sexual flings. At first, I confess it was strange but then I developed a taste and we did it whenever it was convenient. Like you, I value discretion. I have an important job where my image is a crucial factor. Don't get me wrong. I like flings I just don't feel comfortable with letting relatives and friends from the corporate environment know about them.*

With photo and spare punctuation. *Important job, my ass,* she thought. Quite an interesting case. Already had experiences with a girlfriend addicted to flings. Simone decided to respond.

Hi. What's your name? Could we set up a meeting in a public place? You, Paul and me? We like your profile. Your discretion and knowing you have experience is very good. Amateurs are horrible in any area. In this one, it's even worse. When you're available we can agree on a place for us to meet. Okay? What's your profession?

There was a correspondence from someone with whom she'd already exchanged a few e-mails. Time to move to phase two with this one. She'd chat with him on the Internet. allyoucaneat had written: *Hi there, my favorite couple. What do you think about scheduling some kind of meeting for us to get to know each other better? I think we've already exchanged all the information we need by e-mail. I'd like to go a little deeper into our relationship or we'll be old and bald before we satisfy our fantasies.*

Time passed quickly. She'd had a lot of fun by the time she finished. She enjoyed doing this kind of research. She scheduled a chat with allyoucaneat for the following Saturday afternoon. She'd be at home then and more at ease.

After answering the e-mails, Simone packed and prepared to leave. Carl arrived at 4:00 p.m. as scheduled, his dark hair wet, as if he had just taken a shower. He was wearing blue jeans and a black polo shirt, both tight enough to allow her to admire his muscled body...

They went to a small coffee shop near the hotel. Simone gave the signed contract to Carl and they discussed some practical points of her job and defined schedules, nothing personal, all about work.

Carl was obviously in a hurry — he gave some excuses and left half an hour after his arrival. Simone went back to her hotel, checked out and left for home.

Chapter Six

Present Day — Simone

After returning from New York, Simone had a crazy-busy week, patients coming and going, classes, research for her new book...she barely noticed the days pass and then suddenly it was Friday.

That damp, gray Friday afternoon was signaling the approach of summer's end. Simone wanted nothing so much as to go home, fill the bathtub and sip a glass of wine. But she was still at the office and had one more patient to see, a new one. He'd taken quite a bit of her time and was already in the waiting room.

Simone customarily took a ten-minute break between appointments. She leaned back in the chair behind her oak desk and watched the drizzle outside her office window.

Her office was cozy. The dark furniture suggested seriousness and solidity. A Persian carpet's reddish hues and paintings on the walls lent the room a European flavor. Shelves full of books were visible through the glass doors of varnished oak cases set against pastel walls. The ambience belonged to times past.

The computer and the intercom seemed out of place. Bonaparte had inspired it all. Simone had once visited his Malmaison office, Josephine's house, in France, during her exchange program, and had decided one day she would decorate her own office exactly like that. And so she had.

Every new patient offered her a different challenge. Delving into someone's soul was always complex. Patients often undermined their own therapy. They didn't reveal everything they should or related a fanciful version of facts. Only a few expressed problems clearly or knew exactly what they expected from treatment. Some patients were referred by friends, relatives or spouses who wanted to see them make changes, changes the patients themselves had not the least desire to undertake.

The intercom sounded. Mona, the secretary Simone shared with Edward, informed her it was time for the session. Simone sighed and went to her leather armchair. In her office, the patients settled onto a classic, dark-green velvet couch where they could put their feet up, lie down or just sit. Simone sat stationed in front of them, observing their reactions and taking notes.

The man who came in was quite ordinary and of serious demeanor. He stood about five foot nine, appeared to be in his late thirties, wore glasses and had sandy hair and light-brown eyes surrounded by small wrinkles. Dressed in designer jeans and shirt, he'd probably left his coat in the waiting room closet.

"Good afternoon, Dr. Bennet," he said, offering her his hand. His touch was warm when they shook hands, a sign he wasn't nervous about their first meeting.

"Good afternoon, Alvin. I see you've been recommended by a colleague, Dr. Schuster." She glanced at his appointment card as she replied.

"Yes. Very well recommended, in fact. Dr. Schuster holds you in high regard, Dr. Bennet."

"And what brings you to me, Alvin? Tell me a little about yourself."

"Dr. Schuster believes my case falls within your area and that my problems are sexual in nature."

Direct and to the point, she thought. "If you don't mind, first I'd like to know something about what you do, a little about your life in general."

"I run a successful IT firm. I like computers, have good clients and have no financial difficulties."

No question about that. The fees Simone charged were sky high, the best way yet she'd found to select patients. Even so, she had at least eight hours of appointments per day.

"I've been married for five years. I have one child, a son, and we get along very well. I also have a very good relationship with my wife."

"I see that you want to clearly delimit your therapy. You've no problems with children, work or your wife. So let's go back to where we started. What brings you here?"

"I think I'm addicted to sex. I think about sex all day long. I fantasize. I like to see my wife having sex with other men. I like to have sex with women I don't know. I like to take part in orgies. I like risky situations." The man spewed each statement without stopping to breathe. The strange thing was that he spoke about his fantasies and what he considered to be problems without any emotion. It was as if he weren't talking about himself but about someone else.

"This bothers you? These adventures and fantasies?"

"No. Not me, personally. It doesn't limit my life. But I'd like to understand them because sometimes my wife suffers on account of them and also because sometimes I end up in high-risk situations. Controlling them would help me to avoid or minimize the problem."

"Please define 'risky situations'."

"Sex with strangers, men and women. Sometimes with several people the same night. No protection at all."

He paused and looked at Simone, apparently waiting for her reaction. She never tipped her hand. She was a high-stakes poker player when it came to hiding what she was thinking.

"Of course, it's risky. There are many deadly diseases. You know that. And there are also people with serious psychological disturbances who may be very dangerous."

"It's just that it's stronger than I am. Sometimes I promise myself that I'll stop. I swear I won't do it again. But suddenly, it's as if something takes possession of my body, and I can't master my emotions."

Again he spoke of powerful emotions, of a complete lack of control over his libido. But neither his voice nor his gestures showed the least trace of feeling. He could have been reciting the phone book.

"Would you be able to give a name to what takes over your body?"

She thought it would be good to clarify whether he had some mystical or religious belief that led him to think spirits were possessing him and determining his actions, or whether he had a schizophrenic personality.

"Adrenalin. I'd call it that. It's strong. I start to shudder and it's impossible not to satisfy my desires. Your office is impeccable, Doctor. Excellent taste!"

At first, Simone didn't understand. The change of subject took her totally by surprise. From sex to interior decorating. What else was there besides sexual compulsion? A touch of attention deficit perhaps? The psychiatrist in her sought feverishly to fit the patient into a psychological category.

"Thank you," she responded without a hint of being thrown off balance. "Let's continue. I'd like you to tell me about one of those experiences so I can get an idea of what we're dealing with."

"Right. Last Saturday night, for example, I was at home. Earlier, the three of us — my wife, my son and I — had gone out to eat. When we got back my son went to bed and Stella, my wife, and I started to watch a movie. She soon felt sleepy and decided to turn in. After a while, scenes of having sex with strangers began to fill my head and an adrenalin rush hit me. I took the car and ended up at a swing house, the only one in town that lets men in stag. I headed straight to the restricted area. Right away, I found three men having sex with one woman at the same time."

"Did you join in?"

"I stood there for a while, just watching. You have no idea how much it turned me on to see that woman with those men all over her. She was moaning. It was intoxicating to see how aroused she was. The sweat glistened on her body while one man was kissing her, another was penetrating her and another was fondling her. She stopped kissing, looked at me and motioned to me to come over."

"You joined them?"

"Yes. In fact, I took my pants off so fast that afterwards, it was hard to find them. We were in an open area. They were on a kind of public bed. People could hang around and watch what was going on or even participate. The woman pushed herself away from the man who was penetrating her and motioned for me to lie down with her. She didn't say a word. I lay down with her and began kissing her. She mounted me and started to ride me. I was out of it. I only felt the adrenalin and her body against mine. A man began to suck one of her breasts. Another was kissing her neck. Then the other man got behind her, and she paused for an instant and then bent forward to let him take her from behind. We both screwed her at the same time and savagely. That nameless woman got even sweatier and the three of us came almost at the same time."

Simone, as always, kept her poker face but Alvin's account had been graphic and had aroused her. She imagined a certain lawyer in the place of the patient. Her body reacted strangely and she didn't like that one bit. She really needed to get laid, she thought.

"How did you feel afterward?" she asked.

"I was afraid because I'd had unprotected sex."

"Unprotected? You mean without a condom?"

"Yes. I got carried away. That had never happened. But the adrenalin took over and I couldn't think straight. Now I'm really afraid it will happen again."

"And you're afraid you may have contracted a disease. You'll have to take tests. But it can take up to six months for the most serious diseases to appear in the results. I suggest you talk to your wife in the meantime to prevent contagion."

"I think I'll have to do that."

The patient was making her uneasy. Something inside her warned there was much more to his story. Especially because he showed no emotion when he spoke. His last comment didn't convince her that he'd speak to his wife.

"It seems to me that you have your emotions well under control. You describe highly troubling events and yet I don't see that they affect you. You talk about strong urges, loss of control and fear of consequences. But your face and body language show no feelings at all."

He appeared surprised at her observation.

"Maybe it's my personality. I'm very reserved. I think Dr. Schuster was right when he said that having a domineering German mother didn't help me much, emotionally speaking. According to him, her constant insistence that I hide my feelings was very effective. But believe me, Doctor, they're there."

He now looked sad, as if remembering some past suffering. Perhaps. Could be a repressed personality. Too early for any diagnosis.

"I understand how far you've allowed yourself to be taken over by this adrenalin. As for the health and safety risks, they aren't my concern here but I have to alert you to them. That said, why have you come to me? You would like to take control over it, understand?"

"First of all, I want to understand. I need to understand if I'm normal, abnormal, if I need treatment. Then I want to have more control so I don't put myself in such dangerous situations, as I said at the beginning of our conversation. But the fundamental thing is to understand."

"And because the risk isn't yours alone but your partner's as well."

"Uh huh…that too."

At this point, Simone thought of Carl and his need to understand. She thought for a split second that maybe her mission was to make people understand the reasons for their behavior, not to change it. Only they could do that. She felt a pang of frustration.

"I'm going to try to help you, Alvin. I'd like to see you once a week for now. Later, we'll be able to space out your time. I think a weekly session will be more productive at the beginning."

"I'd like twice a week if possible, Doctor. I want to resolve this quickly."

"That depends more on you and your determination, Alvin, than it does on me and the number of sessions. We'll start with once a week. Besides, as you've probably noticed, your appointment is the last one on Friday. I'm booked up. My secretary's already gone home. We'll just have to adapt to the way things are."

"All right, Doctor. Whatever you think is best. Naturally, I count on your discretion. My case isn't something that can be published."

"Of course. I have a duty to keep everything here in confidence."

What's this? she thought. *In the last week, everybody's suddenly questioning my professional integrity.*

"I mean," he went on, "I wouldn't like my case to appear in one of your books."

Again, in less than a week, someone was referring to her book.

"You've read my book?"

"No, Doctor. It's not my area. But Dr. Schuster told me about it and thinks you're probably writing another one."

How strange, she thought. She'd never mentioned her plan for a new book to Samuel. Had Edward told him about it? She made a mental note to call Samuel or ask Edward.

"You have my word. Besides, I didn't mention names in my book. I just talked about cases and behavioral statistics. Your secret's safe with me."

"Excuse me if this request seems impertinent, Doctor. But it's the old saying. Secrets are kept only if everybody is dead."

He laughed when he said that. Strange. Strange behavior. She definitely did not like the man. She'd see him one or two more times to form an opinion about why she didn't like him and then, if necessary, she'd recommend another psychiatrist.

"I understand," she replied.

She accompanied the patient to the door, wished a nice weekend to Mona and walked to the parking area.

Simone and Edward's office occupied a beautiful old house, which they'd bought and refurbished years ago. It was a Tudor-style house, with an oak door. In front of the house Mona had planted a lovely garden that gave the place a very cozy appearance, and the lawn next to the small parking lot was very well manicured.

Simone climbed into her car and then went directly home.

Simone's house, on Elderslie Lane in Woodbridge, Connecticut, was spacious and comfortable. The red brick English Tudor with white window frames and fluttering lace curtains boasted a gloriously green lawn for this time of year.

The interior decoration was European, in keeping with Simone's taste. You might say her house was an extension of her office, or vice versa, due to its paintings, Persian carpets and dark, velvet-upholstered furniture. It all lent an air of comfort, security and excellent taste.

Table lamps were scattered about the house. When she switched off the overhead lighting and switched on the lamps, the atmosphere grew warm and intimate. Many picture frames sat on little tables and on the grand piano in the living room, which she played only when she was very happy or very sad, and never for others. All these things gave her a profound sense that her house was her home.

Simone entered through the front door and proceeded directly into her bedroom. A canopy oak bed occupied the center and two Louis Philippe chairs with flower upholstery sat in a corner, a soft white rug in front of them. The room's décor was the complete opposite to that of her professional and practical image, but it was a reflection of her deeply hidden romantic soul.

She took off her clothes and went to the bathroom—a very clean and immaculate white marble area, where an antique claw-foot and porcelain bathtub had a place of honor—and she filled said tub with hot water and a splash of bath oil.

After taking a long, hot soak, Simone dressed in a comfortable bathrobe and went to the kitchen, the only modern part of her house, all in white and steel with state-of-the-art home appliances. She poured a glass of Californian pinot noir then she looked in the refrigerator and felt truly grateful to her maid Lola for having made soup. It wasn't the ideal menu for a Friday but it was just what Simone needed.

She heated the soup in the microwave, put it in an elegant bowl—just because she was alone didn't mean she was going to eat from a plastic bowl—then she sat down to eat.

Afterward, Simone wandered around the house a bit. She straightened picture frames, paintings and cushions. The maid persisted in not returning them to their former positions whenever she cleaned. Simone believed Lola moved things only to show she'd done her work. The disorder irritated Simone.

She thought about exercising but decided to leave it until Saturday morning. Surely her muscles could endure a day off. She felt exhausted. Nevertheless, she had to do a little more of her work for Carl.

Simone headed for her favorite easy chair, burgundy velvet, soft and comfortable, and she sat down, putting her feet on the ottoman and simply sitting for a while, savoring the wine and listening to the growing patter of raindrops against the windows. Then she picked up the manuscript and began to read.

Mark's Journal — Tell Me Her Secrets

Peter and I couldn't get together on Monday. We both were too busy. But on Tuesday, we made it to a happy hour and I was anxious to talk to him.

"How's it going, Peter?"

He wrapped me in his customary bear hug and even gave me a smack on the cheek. I grew embarrassed and he got a kick out of my reaction.

"Fabulous! And you?"

"Okay. What are you drinking?"

I was already at the bar with a whisky. The place was packed and all eyes were upon us, after my dear friend's triumphant entrance. We were at Terroir Tribeca, a wine bar with a modest menu.

"I'll have wine. I hate whisky. Too macho for my taste. I'm beat. I spent the night dealing with suppliers. You'd think those Chinese could do a bit more to consider our time zone. Making a purchase at one in the morning is not my cup of tea."

"What are you importing this time?"

I'd have to know that because the import tax problem would be all mine. Peter behaved like a reckless child sometimes. He'd gone to China, bought a lot of merchandise, and only afterward asked me about taxes and legalities. Maybe his throw-caution-to-the-wind attitude was the secret to his business success. I could never act that way—maybe because I know the law and its consequences, or maybe because I'm more prudent by nature.

"Clothing for teens. I've already mailed you the documentation. I need your opinion yesterday."

Just now, it was possible to believe Peter was actually a businessman.

"You and all my clients are always in a hurry. But when I hand you off to one of my associates you all want to skin me alive."

"Well, I do understand. But I want you and only you taking care of me." He laughed. "So let's get to it, my friend. You called me here to talk about Lara. At least tell me what's going on to make you want more information so badly."

"You don't beat around the bush, Peter. Have you ever tried subtlety just once in your life?"

Peter put on the face of someone ransacking his memory for when that might have happened. "Yes. I remember one time I tried. It didn't work so I gave up. Now speak to me."

"We've gone out twice and I'm interested. But at times, she doesn't seem quite right to me so I've come to a specialist for his opinion."

"Really. Nobody in the world has had more flings than I have. I've begun to keep track of my conquests with roman numerals for aesthetic reasons and because I ran out of letters in the alphabet."

"Peter…"

"Okay. I don't exactly know what you want with Lara and I know her only as a friend, and she's a very good friend. But you know, being a good friend isn't the same thing necessarily as being a good girlfriend."

"You've known her for a long time?"

"I've known Lara for years."

"Tell me everything about her."

"I'm the wrong person for that. Talk to her therapist. I only know what she allows to be seen. She guards her emotions. I don't know even a tenth of it. I cry on her shoulder often, but she's never cried on mine."

"Tell me what you know."

"She's Sean's older sister. He was my first boyfriend. I met Lara just before she graduated from college. She came and went, and at the time we all ran into each other at her grandmother's house in the Hamptons. Those were very good summers. My romance with Sean lasted about three years. We stayed friends afterward and sometimes I'd go out to the house in the summer. I inherited Lara in the process. I still go there occasionally, but the house now belongs to Lara, and Sean's living on the other side of the world."

"China?"

"Oh no! Texas."

It was hard not to laugh. Peter was the type of New Yorker who viewed the rest of the country as the back of beyond.

"Lara was always the way she is now—beautiful, blonde, nice, restless, talkative, friendly and…mysterious. Impossible to know what is going on inside her. She's the best friend in the world. She listens to everybody and gives advice. What she does is never a secret. It's kind of strange how her life is an open book. The guy she's seeing. Where she's off to. But I've almost never heard her express her feelings. She won't confide whether she likes such and such a person or tell you if she's sad or depressed."

"Are you saying she's shallow to the point of not having deeper feelings?"

"No. On the contrary. I know she has deep feelings. I've seen them a few times. She just isn't capable of putting them into words. It seems she doesn't trust people. It's as if she's afraid of being betrayed at any time."

"Many boyfriends?" *Say no!*

"Lots of short relationships. As for a real boyfriend, holding hands and introducing him, I've never seen one. But I'm going to warn you, and I'm talking about the fifteen years more or less that I've known her. It seems nobody lasts."

I'd last, I thought. But then I asked myself why I would want to last in the life of someone I had just met.

"She's fickle?"

"Uncommitted. I think she doesn't want to get married, have kids, those things in the life cycle."

"Life cycle?"

"Yes. The same old story. You meet, fall in love, reproduce, decide to stay together in boredom 'til divorce or death do you part. Amen…ah, and get your ass fat in the process."

He was right. I couldn't contradict him because that's how relationships really were. And I thought the same about marriage because I'd been there, and Peter knew it.

"You've really never seen her with a boyfriend?"

"No. I always see her pulling somebody by the hand. But I've never seen it go on for long… Hey, my friend. Wait a minute. You've got that defiant look. You're thinking 'I'm going to be different'. Well here's my best gay advice of the day. Don't make plans. For once in your life, get out of your rut. Let life lead you wherever it may. Don't force it. Don't try to mold it. Go with the flow."

"Duly noted, Peter… So, how about the stock cars? Did you follow doctor's orders?"

"Are you kidding? The place was a Cro-Magnon convention of high school dropouts. It made the Addams Family look normal!"

"Don't exaggerate, Peter."

"It's the honest truth. I wasted my time. But I'm devising a new strategy. I think I'll become a patron of the New York City Ballet. There are definitely a few gays around there and I'll be benefiting the arts. Glamour and sex, and even selflessness. And the bodies…oh my God!"

We chatted for a couple more hours. At times, Peter shed his gaiety and behaved like a businessman. As always, he was fun to be with.

I went home wondering how to approach Lara again. I was too restless to sleep. I served myself a whisky and paced in my kitchen for a while, thinking… Should I call her directly? Invite her to dinner? What was the best way? I was on the verge of calling her several times—I grabbed my cell phone, searched for Lara's number, put my finger on the button—but then I'd stop. I'd had a few drinks already and alcohol is never a good adviser. I decided to leave it until the following day. I could almost hear Peter expressing his approval of my "prudent" decision—something like, "That took real courage, my friend".

To hell with Peter. I decided to go to my room and sleep, safely…

Chapter Seven

Present Day – Simone

Simone was sitting on the sofa in her house, manuscript on her lap, when a phone call pulled her from her reading. Her daughter, in an exchange program in France, the same Simone had been to some twenty years earlier, wanted a bit of attention. After their brief conversation, Simone was about to return to the manuscript when the phone rang again. Tammy again, she thought. But when she answered she heard only breathing at the other end of the line.

"Hello?"

Nothing. The breathing continued and she heard soft music in the background.

"Hello? Who do you wish to speak to?"

Just breathing and music. Someone with nothing better to do on a Friday night, she thought and hung up.

The same thing happened three more times. The phone would ring, she'd pick up and then…nothing. She finally lost patience and put the phone on mute. *Could I have a secret admirer?* she wondered.

She glanced at the eighteenth-century, mahogany clock that stood to one side of the broad living room. Ten fifteen. Friday was almost history. She sighed. Another week had gone by, during which she'd done nothing but work. Nothing else. She felt sad and lonely. It would be good to have an admirer—a real one. She should go out and try to meet some flesh and blood people.

Possibilities? Call a friend and go out to a bar, where she'd try to find "the one"? That wasn't her style, thank you. What should she do to get rid of this sudden blue feeling? Maybe read a little more? Watch a movie? Sit in a corner, feeling sorry for herself? That was definitely the worst option and light years away from the way she'd learned to behave. She would return to her reading. A head full of ideas was all she needed.

Mark's Journal – Where's the Party?

Two weeks had passed since I'd last seen Lara. Whenever I tried her cell, it was always out of the area. I even ridiculously staked out her apartment inside my parked car, hoping to see her arrive. My somewhat obsessive feelings for the woman began to worry me.

Peter had no information about her whereabouts. He told me she was like that.

Sometimes she'd disappear and hole up in the house in the Hamptons. Sometimes she'd hop a plane and go to Paris. He thought she had an apartment there because she went so often.

But late that Friday afternoon, she finally called me. I was all set to give my first class of the semester after summer vacation. It was good to be getting back into the classroom, to return to the world of youth and dreamers.

"Hello, Mark," she said melodiously.

"Hello, Lara."

"You recognized my voice."

"No, your number."

I wasn't about to give her the pleasure of knowing that her voice had become quite familiar to me already.

"What are you up to?"

"Getting ready to leave the office and then head to the university. I'm giving a class today."

"Oh, how depressing! A class? I want to take you to a party. Blow off the class."

Living up to responsibility was certainly not one of the lady's fortes. I admit I felt sorely tempted to do as she had proposed. But my sense of duty won out.

"What time's the party?"

"I think it starts at ten. But we can get there a little later. They haven't hired us to do the catering."

Funny girl…and great, I thought. Perfect for me. I'd demonstrated my professorial integrity. Now to agree when to meet.

"My class ends at about nine-thirty. I'm free after that."

"Okay, little goat. I'll pick you up wherever you want and you won't have to feel guilty about driving drunk. I will get us a driver."

"Little goat."

Again referring to my sign of the zodiac. It was her way of calling me a standard-issue square, according to what I'd understood of her characterization of it.

"Okay. Here's what I'll do. I'll leave school and go home. You can pick me up there."

"Fine. What's your address?"

"I live in Tribeca." I gave her the details.

"Hmm…a successful lawyer."

"I try my best…"

"See you in a while, my favorite lawyer."

"See you, Lara."

After I've finished my class, I went directly home, where I took a quick shower, put on some cologne, dressed in a gray suit, white shirt and dark-gray tie. Then I double checked my hair, my tie and my suit…and when I looked at myself in the mirror for the last time I thought, *all you need now is to check your lipstick… You are behaving like a nervous virgin going on her first date; stop it, man!* Then I went pacing into the living room, waiting for Lara.

Lara came by my place as agreed. She'd called beforehand to have me wait in the lobby. She arrived in a black Lincoln with a driver, as promised. The car's tinted windows were so dark, it crossed my lawyer´s mind the owner would be breaking the NYS Vehicle and Traffic Law, but maybe it was only the effect of the night and dim light in front of my building. Then she opened the door and invited me inside and I forgot all about the law. She was lovely and radiant and wearing a blue dress made of some soft, shiny fabric with a line of buttons down the front.

"Hi there, suit!" She kissed me in a way that said she wanted more from me than just a date for a party. One of the things that bothered me about Lara was she never let me take the initiative. I felt a bit castrated.

"Hi, pretty baby. You look stunning!"

I was sincere. She looked fantastic. She wore some kind of eye shadow that made her eyes appear even more beautiful and mysterious than usual. She could have stepped out of a Bollywood film, her eyes were so seductive.

"I missed you!"

"I missed you too. Where have you been? I tried to contact you." I attempted to sound casual because I didn't want to seem desperate.

"Around." She tossed her hands.

"Around here? Around there?"

"No. I went to France." She spoke as if going to Europe and back in just a few days was routine.

"Come here." For a change, I took the initiative and embraced her. I loved her scent and the feel of her body. But more than that, I was happy just to be near her again.

After the car pulled out, I hugged her once more and she stayed in my arms quietly for a few moments. A very warm sensation that pleased me a lot. Then the idyll was over… She pulled out of my arms, lifted up her dress, took my hand and put it between her legs. No panties.

"I missed you down here too," she whispered.

The touch of her warm, moist softness supercharged my existing eager erection.

"You're crazy," I said, glancing at the driver.

But he had his eyes on the road.

"I want you right here, right now," she responded.

There went my hopes of a comfortable bed with Lara lying naked on it.

"Right now?"

"Yes!"

She turned to me and unzipped my fly. She began to rub me. She lowered her head, took me into her mouth and began to suck. Her tongue went 'round and 'round. I just closed my eyes and told myself to let it be.

"You may be crazy but you're wonderful crazy," I mumbled, not wanting the driver to hear.

I took a peek and he still was watching the road.

Lara now opened a small silver purse and took out a condom. She slipped it on me, pulled up her dress and positioned herself facing me. Then she eased onto my rock-hard penis.

"The driver will kick us out of the car," I whispered in her ear.

"Don't worry. He's a true professional and I always use his services. He's just going to cruise around and watch us in the rearview mirror. Don't you like that? Don't you like somebody watching you?"

Her arms now tight around my neck, she began to move her hips. I forgot the driver. We were in the middle of the city and I forgot the passing cars. I simply gave in to the pleasure. I lost track of time and space... She had that power over me. As if she could sense I was going to come, every time I got close she'd slow down. She'd nibble my neck and kiss me. Then she'd speed up again. She did that several times until I was ready to go nuclear. We humped and bumped for all we were worth.

"I'm going to come so good, so good, Mark. Come, come with me."

At that point, I didn't need an invitation. I blasted off for so long I thought I'd gone into orbit. I finally opened my eyes and spotted the driver slyly peeking at us in the rearview mirror. It embarrassed me.

Lara began to tidy herself. She adjusted her wrinkle-proof dress. She touched up her makeup but I think only her red lipstick had smeared. To me, she'd never looked so perfect. What a start to a party!

"You know, Lara. Someday, I'd like to take you to a bed and do this in a more comfortable position."

She laughed lustily, as if I were joking.

"You old-fashioned little goat. Are you saying that doing it this unconventional way is no good?"

"I'm not saying that at all. I love it. I'm just saying that...for us...unconventional would be in bed. This is our third time together and each time we've done it unconventionally. I'd like to have more time, more privacy."

"Greedy little goat. Don't forget that old saying...be careful what you wish for."

By the time we got to the party, it finally dawned on me that the driver had been circling per Lara's instructions. The bash took place in an opulent penthouse almost opposite the Met. It flaunted striking decorations, black and white marble, crystal chandeliers everywhere and floor-to-ceiling windows, through which Central Park could be seen, to the museum's right.

Lara definitely knew some high rollers, I said to myself. Not that I'd come from poverty. Far from it. My father was a successful attorney who'd given me a privileged life. But after law school I set out on my own. I took a position with another law firm. I forged my own career. I had never wished to be seen as someone's son. It was a hard row to hoe. But every success tasted like a glass of ice-cold champagne on a hot night.

Right away, Lara found the host, a man of about my age, and introduced me to him.

"Freddy, this is Mark, a friend of mine. Mark, this is Freddy, also my friend, and this is his party."

I felt jealous. That was the word, exactly. Mark is my friend like Freddy is my friend for me meant: "I also screw him on a park bench, on white sofas in this apartment, on top of the table with twenty settings." My imagination ran amok.

"Hello, Freddy. Thank you for having me."

"Welcome, Mark. Any friend of Lara's is a friend of mine. Now please, enjoy yourselves! And once again, Lara, thank you for everything."

He excused himself and headed off to greet another arriving couple.

The gathering intrigued me. It seemed a menagerie of high society. I saw Wall Street bankers, New York Social Register types, well-heeled foreigners, politicians and theater people. Only a bishop in a miter was missing. As I circulated with Lara, she spoke to everyone. No question she had connections. Many of the guests seemed to be her clients. They all praised her work as an architect and offered congratulations for her remodeling of the penthouse. The party was its inauguration.

"You designed this place?" I asked.

"Yes. But it has nothing to do with my taste and everything to do with Freddy's. After his divorce, he told me he was fed up with female fussiness and wanted something really masculine, black on white. So that's what I did."

"It looks great."

"It looks like a hospital to me. But to do my work well, I have to satisfy the client's wishes and not my own."

He really hoped she was just satisfying the client's professional wishes.

Just then, a very attractive and well-dressed woman of about fifty came up to us.

"Lara?"

"What are you doing here?" Lara snapped. It was the first time I'd seen as much as a hint of rudeness in Lara.

"I came with the senator. He's a friend of Frederick's. I'd like to talk to you."

"What happened? The vultures have started to circle New York? The carrion in Washington's all gobbled up? I have zero to say to you."

"Lara, please. Give me a chance."

"Excuse me, Mark. I'm going to talk to Freddy."

Lara hurried toward the host. I had no idea what was going on.

"You'll have to excuse my daughter. Sometimes it seems she's never been taught any manners. I'm Sabine Stevenson Eberle, Lara's mother."

Lara's mother? And she treated her like that? My God. I'd always wanted to have a mother. What I'd just witnessed shocked me.

"It's a pleasure to meet you, Mrs. Eberle. I'm Mark, a friend of your daughter's."

"How nice to meet one of Lara's friends. What do you do, Mark?"

"I'm a lawyer."

"Is it a prominent firm?"

The woman had just been mistreated by her daughter, had just met me and was asking for my resume. What the...?

I was about to answer when Lara scampered back. She grabbed me by the arm and began dragging me toward the exit. What a horrible habit that was, pulling people this way and that whenever it suited her.

"We're out of here, Mark. I just said goodbye to Freddy."

She ignored her mother.

"What was that all about, Lara? That woman was your mother."

"Correct tense of the verb. She was my mother, once upon a time. For years, I haven't considered her as such. But I don't want to talk about it."

I didn't know Lara well enough to pursue the issue. But the party had definitely been the fastest one in my life. It lasted precisely one half glass of whisky.

At some point while saying goodbye to our host, she must have called the driver because he was right in front of the building waiting for us. Lara remained silent, so I gave my address and took her to my apartment.

I lived on Laight Street, near St. John's Park. I loved my apartment, one of the symbols of what I'd managed to accomplish through my own efforts. It was spacious, well decorated — according to my taste, anyway — masculine and certainly homier than the stark luxury we'd just left.

I'd purchased the place from another lawyer after his divorce. The décor was conservative, with lots of wood and navy blue. But I liked it.

My dog — a five-year-old golden retriever and my faithful friend — was waiting for me as he always did.

"Hi, Tommy."

He gave me his paw, just as I'd taught him to. I was proud of my boy. Good manners. Lara patted him and he leaned his head on her. She apparently liked dogs and he, attractive women.

"He's beautiful!"

"Yes. And good company too."

I led Lara over to the couch. I wanted to hug her and calm her down. She looked very upset.

"Want something to drink?"

"What have you got?"

"Well, I don't have caustic soda and absinthe. But there's whisky, wine, champagne…"

"I'll take a whisky. When I don't feel good it comforts me. It's sentimental."

"You serious?"

"Yes, I am. When I was a little girl my father used to drink whisky. It was his favorite tipple. I'd sit in his lap, marveling at the glass, at the golden drink. When the ice melted and there was only whisky-flavored water in the glass he'd give me a sip. Having a whisky takes me back to those days."

I poured some for her and was glad for the first real sentiment she'd shared with me.

"Ice? Soda? Water?"

"Just ice. Three cubes, please."

"Feel like talking?"

"No. I want you to hug me."

Ah. Finally, a bit of non-sexual intimacy. I hugged her and thought she was going to cry. But she didn't. She stayed in my arms for a long time, patting Tommy, who had stationed himself at her side. At last she sighed deeply, moved away, took a sip of her drink and sighed again.

"Is that bed of yours somewhere around here?"

"It certainly is. Want to lie down?"

I foresaw not the least prospect of sex in that scenario. I was not disappointed.

"Yes, I would and I'd like you to lie down with me. I don't want to be alone."

"Of course. I'll get the bathroom ready for you to use." So I left Lara sitting on my bed and went to the bathroom, where I tried my best to find a few things I considered feminine, like cotton, body lotion, some makeup remover I didn't know I had and a box of Kleenex, and I put them over on the sink cabinet.

I found Lara in the same position over on the bed, looking lost in thought.

"Hey, kid, the bathroom is ready for you."

"Thanks, Mark," she said, snapping out of her trance. She climbed from the bed and went to the bathroom.

When she came out, I saw she had removed her makeup. Her eyelids were no longer black. She seemed very young and vulnerable.

"I put an undershirt of mine on the bed if you want to use it."

"Thanks, but I sleep in the nude."

Lady, stop trying to spoil my good intentions, I thought. "Fair enough."

She got under the covers. I lay down naked beside her. Maybe there would be a chance to make love to her later... She'd be back to her old self after a while. She cuddled up to me and I thought it would be very hard just to sleep with her. But I soon did and slept deeply.

When I woke up, I gave thanks it was Saturday. I looked for Lara but she'd gone. For some reason, that didn't surprise me. She seemed to be a girl of comings and goings, arrivals and departures. Nevertheless, I was disappointed not to see her there. At least I'd partly reached my goal. She'd been in my bed. But no sex at all.

I found a note on the table. "Thanks for everything. Kisses. Lara."

And nothing more.

Chapter Eight

Present Day – Simone

Simone's Saturday started seamlessly. First, she did her morning exercises. Then she went to the supermarket to restock the fridge. After that, she headed for the beauty parlor to have her nails done with the clear varnish she considered suitably professional. She lunched at a mall before returning home.

The moment Simone walked in the door, she sensed something was wrong. She glanced through the kitchen toward the back door and gasped. The rear window stood wide open. The curtains were fluttering. Wind and rain were coming in. Everything had been closed when she'd gone out and it was the maid's day off. She told herself she'd probably left the window half shut and a gust had blown it open wide. Besides, her neighborhood was absolutely safe.

She went inside, put her purse on the kitchen island and closed the window. Things appeared to be in order. But she had the uneasy feeling that someone had been there. Nothing was out of place yet nothing was exactly as it should be. Simone was a perfectionist who knew every detail of her house and the precise position of every item in it.

Someone had been there! The photos on the piano had been moved. They faced a different direction from the way she liked them. She was certain of it. Only last night, she'd positioned them turned toward the living room. Now some looked out the window, while others watched the wall and still others the door.

She inspected the rest of the house but nothing else made her uncomfortable. She must be getting old. It probably hadn't even been last night when she'd arranged the photos. Anyway, who the heck would sneak into somebody's residence just to look at pictures?

Yet the feeling of an alien presence persisted. She decided to check all the doors and windows. If she'd been a bit more childish, maybe she'd have peeked under the bed. She contented herself with the visible, bearing in mind how unlikely it was for someone to have entered without taking something. But this wasn't the first time she'd had the impression someone else had been in her home. Twice recently, Simone had come home and thought someone had been there. Maybe Lola had moved things around on cleaning day. That was probably it, and Simone had been so busy she hadn't noticed. It was just like Lola to clean and leave things out of place. Things like that made her nervous.

To calm her nerves, Simone meditated for an hour. She liked to empty her mind and she used to do a session at least twice per week. She had even created a special place in her house — a meditation area, a calm room with indirect light, comfortable cushions and a bedroll on the floor. An hour spent meditating relaxed her mind and helped her keep control of her emotions.

After she finished her session, she tried to decide what to do next but the cool, rainy, lazy day provided a fine excuse to stay at home without remorse for not taking advantage of the weekend. Not that she liked going out in the sunshine. She much preferred to remain indoors to read, study or paint, despite those who told her she was wasting her life and should find a man.

Simone enjoyed her privacy and possessed the psychological strength to resist social pressures. That bothered people. They couldn't understand the idea that no company was better than bad company. Once in a while, she'd agree to go on a blind date set up by a friend just to please those who wanted her to meet "Mr. Right". Inevitably, it led to nothing. A long time ago, she had decided Mr. Right didn´t exist. All her illusions on the matter had vanished.

She had reached the conclusion that what she sought for her life with respect to romance wasn't available in the market. Perhaps she was too demanding. But she'd studied so much and had acquired so much cultural baggage, she couldn't settle for having someone just for the sake of it. None of this, "I'm unhappy but at least I'm married".

Immersed in her thoughts, Simone suddenly remembered she'd scheduled an online date with one of the candidates involved in her research.

Simone glanced at the clock and realized she was late for her online date and she hated to be late. Her date was with allyoucaneat@loftmail.com. He called himself Victor, surely a false name, as were hers and Edward's. She turned on the computer, went into the chat room and saw he was already waiting. She started to write.

Hi, Victor. Sorry about the delay! It's Claire.

Hi, Claire. I thought you'd stood me up. Thirty-five minutes is more than just a delay.

He seemed angry. But it was impossible to be sure when someone was writing.

I'd forgotten. Paul and I went out and got back just now.

Paul's with you?

Yes. Right next to me.

Tell him hi for me.

He's here with us. He says hi too.

Okay, guys. We've exchanged e-mails. I think we're getting to know each other better. You know I'm not some nut and that I have an image to protect also. I want to know just what you two are looking for. Do we move forward? Or are you just having fun chatting with people?

No. We really want someone to play with us.

You don't have much experience with this, right?

Not much. We've played around a little. But we want someone we can trust.

You want a steady boyfriend. Is that it?

Yes. Exactly. And you have experience. You told us in your previous e-mails that you have. But what kind of experience?

I've had some brief flings. But I was with one couple for a few years. I met them on a trip. We found we had good chemistry and coincidentally lived in the same town. So we kept things going after the trip.

But what was your role in the relationship?

I didn't have a "role". We'd get in touch and make a date to have sex. At first, in small hotels then later on at their house.

Did you have sex with them both?

No. I'm straight. I don't do gay sex. If that's what you want, count me out!

Relax. No. We're straight too. I was just asking. I only wanted you to describe a little of what the three of you did, to see if we're on the same page.

And to be able to move forward with her research, Simone needed to know more about how people behaved and what they felt.

The husband fantasized about seeing her having sex with other men. Sometimes, he just watched. Sometimes, he joined in. But always us two with her, never us two!

Don't get me wrong, Victor. But I haven't done much of this and neither has Paul. So we're not sure how we'll react afterward. Paul has the same fantasy. But I'm afraid afterward he'll get jealous and that will spoil the good relationship we have. How did the husband feel?

Look. When I wasn't with them I don't know. When I was with them everything was fine. He and I became friends. Sometimes, we'd even go out for a beer and talk about life.

So you think he didn't get jealous?

She told me the few times I was alone with her — because I was always ethical and never tried to make a date with her — that he was very jealous of her. She said she couldn't understand that because of his fantasy and that he was real neurotic. But he wasn't jealous of me. On the contrary. When he and I would go for a beer afterward he'd tell me he'd use the episode as a fantasy when he was alone with her.

Maybe it'll happen to us then…jealousy.

I can't say for sure, Claire.

Simone decided to change tactics because she needed more information. She inserted Paul into the conversation.

Victor, Paul's going to talk to you now. Okay?

Okay. Hi, Paul.

Hi, Victor. I'm a little worried about this jealousy business because that's how I feel. I'm very jealous of Claire usually but I have this crazy fantasy.

Yuh…I think that's just how it goes, Paul. I've had other shorter relationships but it was always that way. Jealousy, desire, but everything controllable. I think you two have to be sure of what you want before you really get started.

Right. I think so too. But we like this approach we're making. Without pressure.

Yes. I understand and I want you to understand that I too am worried about the risks of the unknown. I want safety and security. I've got a family and I don't want to hurt anybody. I just want a few moments of pleasure.

Oh. You're married too?

Yes, I am. I've already told you that. I need absolute secrecy.

Yes. I'd also like to know about you, Victor. How did you feel in those relationships? Did you ever fall in love with the woman? Did you ever want to have her for yourself?

Yes. Of course. That happens. But then you've got to end it. There's a life outside the bedroom. In that life, I have someone I love and I wouldn't risk everything over a passion for a type of woman I wouldn't want for myself.

Whoa. Now it's me, Victor. It's Claire. You wouldn't like to have a woman like me for yourself. For what then?

Claire, don't be offended... I very much value your type of woman for that...for an adventure...for a little excitement in life. But for my everyday life, I couldn't handle it. The games we're talking about are too over the top. I'd always be wondering if my wife wasn't going beyond her fantasies and living them out behind my back.

Understood. I'm not offended. But in your previous experiences have you ever seen this kind of suspicion in the husbands? I'm worried about Paul.

I have, Claire. Yes. In almost all of them. And I've seen other men's jealousy, as I've said. Not just of me but of everybody. I have trouble understanding it because if the man is jealous and at the same time wants to share his wife with somebody else, that has to make him suffer. But I'm not a psychologist. I'm just someone who enjoys the fruits of other people's fantasies.

Simone easily categorized what he was saying. Pain, pleasure, pure masochism. Giving your wife to someone in order to feel pain and taking pleasure from it. And after the pleasure, more pain. The vicious cycle of masochism. She'd jot down notes after the conversation.

Victor, Paul says he'd like to meet you. If he thinks you're what we're looking for, I'll go to the following meeting.

I'll be away this week. I'll be back next week and I'll contact you then. I definitely think we have to meet. If there's no chemistry, there'll be no reason to go any further.

Agreed, Victor. Have a nice weekend and a great week. Paul says likewise.

Same for you. By the way, let's try to schedule our next conversation on a weekday. My wife's usually nearby on Saturdays and Sundays.

Fine. No problem.

The chat ended and Simone wrote down her notes. She felt almost certain that masochism really was one of the driving forces behind this type of fantasy. She had decided to post an ad from someone who wanted to be number three in a ménage-à-trois in order to get the view from the other side. She wasn't in a hurry. She was meticulous. She wanted precision.

She looked out the window and saw that the light rain had stopped and night was falling. The day had ended. Saturday was over. She was starting to feel the need of a little company in her life. Maybe someone to have dinner with? Who? She set aside the idea and decided she'd eat something and then read a bit more.

She went to the kitchen and made some popcorn, then she sat in her favorite spot on the couch, put a soft blanket over her freezing-cold feet and sighed.

Work, work, work, she thought Perhaps that was all there was to life. Perhaps she was only cut out to work, and love was for other people, for those less lucid and with their eyes half closed. Nobody could stand up to her clinical analysis for more than fifteen minutes. Within the first hour of conversation, she'd know the psychological profile of most people and also grasp their intentions. That made it very hard to fall in love. To fall in love required a little dose of blindness and a huge one of faith. She wasn't blind and she had little faith in "true love". The thought didn't make her sad, only more resigned. Resigned to the fact that she might spend the rest of her life alone…that the most she might wish for was to find happiness — or at least satisfaction — in her work and in the few close friendships she had.

With that thought in mind, she picked up Carl's manuscript and opened it. A few minutes later, she lost herself in the text yet again.

Mark's Journal — Exclusivity

After the night she spent in my bed, Lara disappeared again for ten days. I called once or twice but got no answer. I thought it best to leave things as they were. She enjoyed playing games. I wasn't like that. I was simple and direct. If a woman wanted me, fine. If not, there were lots of fish in the sea.

Having made that decision, I felt better. But my desire to see her was overwhelming. I thought about her constantly and couldn't get our lovemaking out of my mind. Then I ran into her when I was going to a delicatessen in SoHo.

She was walking into a restaurant with a man who was all over her. The sight of the two of them together really hurt. Jealousy drove its knife deep into me. The man was kissing her on the neck when she spotted me.

"Maaark, dear. You here! This is my friend Tony. Tony, this is my friend Mark."

It was easy to see that we were all "friends" of Lara's. Fun friends. I don't know what I was thinking. I felt so much hatred. It was okay for us men to be that way. I myself had had various female "friends". But I didn't want to be just another of Lara's "friends". My macho moment of the year appeared.

"Have you traveled again, Lara?"

"No, I've just been around here."

Then her "friend" added some clarification.

"She doesn't always perform her vanishing act. Though she does it a lot!

Aha. So I wasn't the only frustrated one. Good. At least I could console myself with the thought that he was getting the same treatment I was.

"I have to go. Good night to you both."

"Good night, Mark. I'll call you." She kissed me on the cheek.

"Good night, Mark. A pleasure to have met you."

"Same here, Tony." *I hope you get hit by an express train, you piece of shit*, I thought.

And so, out the window went my illusion of having a different kind of relationship with Lara. I realized she was just a good-time girl. She'd never promised me anything. *Au contraire*. She'd warned me about getting "greedy" when I'd talked about having more time together. My mistake. I was a moron and felt like a patsy. I wanted to kick myself in the ass. I didn't recognize myself in the pathetic role I'd been playing.

I stood in front of the restaurant for a few minutes, trying to decide what I should do next... I considered murder but in the end, I decided to call Peter to see if he'd go for a drink. It was almost 8 p.m. and it would be nice to talk to someone. If I went home alone now, I'd be miserable.

"Hi, Peter. Want to go have a couple?"

"Hi, Mark. I'm fine, thank you."

"You'll have to excuse me. I feel a little weird today."

"That's all right."

"How about a drink?"

"Sure, why not?"

Where do you want to go?" I asked him.

"Where are you now?"

"In SoHo."

"Okay. Meet me at the Boqueria. We can get something to eat too. I haven't had dinner yet."

"Boqueria. I think I've been there but I can't remember where it is."

"Spring Street. I don't know what number."

Boqueria is a small restaurant. From the outside it looks like a grocery store but inside it has the cozy atmosphere of an Italian canteen with hams hanging from the ceiling. I asked for a discreet table next to the wall and waited for Peter.

When Peter arrived, he gave me a hug. But he must have sensed my sinking ship mood because he wasn't so effusive with his greetings. I ordered a double shot and Peter a glass of red wine.

"What's so painful, my friend? You look as if you've either lost a big case, a tooth or you've got hemorrhoids."

"Jesus Christ, Peter. Can't you ever be serious?"

"What for? Life's serious enough as it is. I'm not going to add to it by being just one more sad sack. Speak to me."

"Lara."

"Oh no. You've fallen for Lara? I warned you. Look. I adore her. But you can't sail the sea of love in a sieve."

"It's too late now. I can't get the bitch out of my head. And to make matters worse, I bumped into her today. She was going into a restaurant with a guy and they were all lovey-dovey."

"That's Lara."

"What do you mean 'That's Lara'?"

"You didn't hear a word I said the other day. Lara doesn't go steady. I never see her holding hands with anybody for very long, and you thought you'd be different. My friend, I don't know what to tell you. Maybe you'll really get there. You're charming, successful and handsome. What I'm saying is you'd be a fantastic fairy."

"Peter, I'm going to seriously consider the gay scene. I don't understand women!"

"Okay, I'll give you a free tour if you want. But it seems you don't understand that girl and that's why you're down in the dumps. You're in love with the mystery. Snap out of it, my friend. Face reality. Take what she has to offer and decide if it's enough or it's not."

"I want exclusivity. I want all of her for me!" I told him emphatically, pointing at my chest.

"You're obsessed. That's all. Goddamn human beings are so masochistic. They can't take no for an answer. The more they're rejected, the more they love!"

"It's not like that, Peter. Or maybe it is. What do I know? I like her flakiness. I like the way she smells. I like her unpredictability."

"That unpredictability is fucking you up!" Peter pointed his finger to his head and said, "Think rationally. If you want her, demystify her. Use your head or she'll devour you!" As Peter is Peter, he formed claws with his hands and roared at me like a lion. If I had not been in such a blue mood, I would have laughed…

"How?"

"Huh?" Peter sounded surprised at my question. "That part I don't know. In fact, I have no clue. I've got a good line but I'm the most masochistic gay man in New York City. Reject me and I fall in love. Sometimes, I even think I'm in love with you. You reject me so much." And he put a hand over his heart, playing the tragic prima donna.

"Oh fuck you, Peter. You've really got a classic case of cranial-rectal insertion syndrome. And I thought you were the voice of wisdom."

"Sure. The wisdom of someone who always gets hammered. Experience makes us wise…makes us sound wise, at least."

"Any brilliant ideas?"

"I'll ponder it. I'll throw a party at my place and invite you both. Set you both up. And I'll ask her to bring some beautiful gay man so I'll be golden too." His eyes sparkled as if he were already at the party.

I scowled at him and sobered.

"You're very selfish, you know?"

"But let me think," Peter went on. "I like you both. It would be good to bring you together. Water and oil, I'd say. But opposites always attract. Of course, afterward they repel. But by then, I don't know if we'll all still be alive. When was the last time you went out with her?"

"Ten days ago. She invited me to a party. It was really weird. We screwed in the car and the driver was watching us. The woman's insane. I think she doesn't like smooth surfaces, just obstacle courses."

"Smooth surfaces mean beds. Beds mean involvement. Involvement means relationships. In other words, my friend, she doesn't want to relate. She wants to bang. Bang the shit out of her, for Christ's sake! You are the man here!"

He pointed his finger at me and I could see nails were painted with a sort of transparent polish... How weird could the guy be?

"Okay. Let me finish. Then we went to somebody's party, some "friend" of hers whose apartment she'd designed. We met a woman there named Sabine who said she was Lara's mother. Lara treated her like toxic waste and dragged me out the door."

"Sabine? Lara's mother? Oh man, what a bucket of worms." He looked really surprised.

"Why?"

"I don't know the story. Nobody talks about it in that family. But the mother abandoned them for a senator or something like that. I know the parents had been separated for a while before I got to know Lara and the others. The mother was always a taboo subject." Peter spoke in a very low tone, as if he was telling me a deep, dark secret.

"Taboo?"

"Well, I mean nobody would talk about her. The kids were raised by Lara's father and her grandmother Emma. Emma was even crazier than Lara."

"Crazier than Lara? What did she do…screw stallions in a side show?"

"Well, I can't say she never did that. She was irreverent. She had zero respect for conventions. She drove a motorcycle and we had a lot of fun with her. It was as if we had a teenage friend with experience. The advice she gave us was fantastic but real. We adored her." Peter smiled as he talked about Emma; apparently he held great respect for the lady.

"She died?"

"Yes. Around four years ago. It was tough for all of us. I truly suffered and it devastated Lara. It was one of the few times I saw her feelings rise to the surface. Absolute desperation over the loss of her grandmother."

"Wow, Peter. Thanks for telling me that. You know, after we ran into her mother, Lara wouldn't talk about her at all. I took her home with me and put her to bed. She asked me not to leave her alone. I thought maybe we were starting to understand each other. But she slipped away early in the morning and hasn't answered the phone since."

"I'll sound her out for you. I'll be subtle about it and try to see what's happening. I won't let on that I know anything about you two. You guys just met at my party, okay?"

"But that's a really bad strategy, Peter. It won't work."

"Do you have a better idea?" Again that manicured finger pointed at me…

"I'm going to talk to her. Thank you anyway, my friend. Just listening to me has helped a lot."

"That's what friends are for." He sang it in a loud voice and stretched out the last word.

Everybody around us turned their heads. Peter was being Peter.

I went away tipsy and feeling courageous. I took out my cell phone, rehearsed ten times or so what I was going to say and then went home to bed.

Mark's Journal — Who's the Boss?

The day after my chat with Peter I was busy at the office, sitting in the meeting room, surrounded by books and papers, studying a complicated lawsuit, when the phone rang. I thought to ignore it when I saw it was Lara calling me.

"Hi, little goat." Her voice had the husky tone of someone who'd just gotten out of bed.

Whose bed, I asked myself.

"Hi, Lara." I promised myself I'd cut out the game of "I don't know who you are and I don't know what I want."

"Let's go out to dinner," she said.

"Sure."

Life should always be that simple. She calls. I answer. She says what she wants. I accept. But whenever I called, she never answered the fucking phone!

"Anywhere special you'd like to go, little goat?"

"You choose."

"There's a great Indian place called Amma. Ever been there?"

"No. Where is it?"

"East 51st. Shall we meet there?"

"No. I'll pick you up. Okay?"

She said nothing for a few moments, as if thinking about her reply. "All right. What time?"

"How does eight o'clock sound?"

"Fine. I'll make reservations. The place is usually pretty crowded and a bit small."

"Good idea. See you tonight, Lara." I was not in a mood to extend the dialogue

"See you then, Mark."

Progress! I remembered I was the lawyer there. I gave the orders. I was the master of words. To hell with little goat this, little goat that. If I looked even remotely like a little goat… I would have been one of those big, strong motherfuckers that roamed the mountains. Leader of the pack. I felt *muy* macho! But the feeling only lasted five seconds…until I saw the pile of papers I had to analyze before I'd be free to have dinner. I set aside my machismo and got back down to work.

* * * * *

At eight o'clock, I parked in front of Lara's building and she was already waiting for me. To my surprise, she wasn't dressed to kill. She was wearing skin-tight jeans — on second thought, maybe she was just a bit dressed to kill — high-heeled boots, a high-neck blouse and a touch of makeup. Her hair hung loose and she smelled great. She greeted me with a peck on the lips.

I opened the car door for her, helped her in, took the wheel and headed for the restaurant.

Leave it to Lara to discover a place like Amma. It was tucked away and tiny with no more than ten tables. The cozy and simple décor featured salmon walls and inexpensive but attractive furnishings. I immediately understood Lara's casual attire. My suit felt a bit out of place. But I was a lawyer and it was part of me. Nevertheless, I took off my tie and loosened my collar.

I'd always liked Indian food. As we perused the menu, I suggested my favorite dishes: Cochin crab cakes, naan, rice with mint, and butter chicken. I was in charge. The Gewurztraminer wine I selected proved the perfect accompaniment for a spicy meal.

After ordering, we got down to conversation.

"You're not too big on answering the phone."

"When I don't know what to say I prefer not to answer it."

"What did you think I wanted to say to you that made you prefer not to answer? Or, generally speaking, don't you ever know what to say to me?"

"I didn't want to talk about that night at the party and I also don't know what to say to you."

That surprised me because she talked all the time. Maybe Peter was right. Feelings upset her. Was she feeling something? Definitely. That something could be repugnance. Loathing is a feeling.

"Does that mean you'd like me to stop bothering you?"

"No. It means I don't have answers to the questions I know you have."

Aha. So she knew I had questions, I thought ironically. "And what questions do I have?"

"Why won't she do it in bed? Why won't she answer the phone? Why does she disappear? Why can't we spend more time together? Why did she sneak out of my bed? Why was she mean to her mother?"

How nice. The lady possessed awareness of her own behavior.

"And what…possibly…might the answers be?"

"I don't have any. I just live, Mark. I don't plan. You, on the contrary, seem to do nothing but plan. But maybe I'm wrong. We hardly know each other."

"And you don't want to know more."

"But I do… No, I don't… I don't have an answer for that either. I get all mixed up around you. There's a sweetness about you that disconcerts me. I'm used to rough stuff…to people jumping all over each other. You're kind. You're nice. You're polite. I don't know what to do with you."

"But you know what to do with the guy you were with yesterday." I thought she'd claim he was just a friend, or rather, they were only good friends.

"Yes. With him, I know. We want the same thing. To have fun and that's that. You want more. I feel that in you."

"Then give me more!"

There it went. There went my pride down the drain. I did want more. I didn't want any more fucking games!

"I can't do that. It's not in me. But I like being with you. I always come back for more. I just can't handle getting close."

"Then learn. You're a very intelligent woman."

"I am." She laughed sadly "But I'm too rational. Don't get me wrong. I'm not cold. It's just way too much for me. When I get emotional things get out of control."

"And you like to have control."

"I need it for my sanity. Mark, I'm thirty-five years old. They haven't been thirty-five years of roses."

"I'll never hurt you," I said, because her words showed she'd been deeply hurt in the past. I tried to assure her I wouldn't continue her suffering.

"Never is a long time and nobody hurts anybody on purpose, unless he…or she…is a sicko. You are nothing like that."

"Let me get closer to you."

"I believe I can do that…if you respect my space, my escapes that are really my encounters with myself. Do you believe that is possible?"

"I'll try. At least answer the phone and say, 'Not today' or 'Today's okay' and I promise I'll abide by your wishes."

"Okay. It's a deal!"

"And another thing. Please don't call me little goat anymore. It's irritating!"

The dinner turned out perfect. The spices were strong and sensual and left our tongues throbbing. Every dish, from start to finish, was well prepared and mouthwatering. After our initial humorless *tête-à-tête*, the evening grew light and filled with laughter. Lara was extremely funny and broke me up with a potpourri of amusing and scathing observations.

I took care of the tab and invited her back to my apartment. She accepted. She knew I was the boss. I almost beat my chest like Tarzan.

I was the boss 'til we reached my place. Lara went into the bathroom. She came back out naked, wearing only her high-heeled boots. Luscious. Drooly. Okay, she was the boss. I was on my knees again, or rather, she was. She began to suck my cock. Her mouth was a fiery furnace fueled by Indian fellatio food. The burning sensation consumed me, overwhelmed me. I squeezed her shoulders while she devoured me, dominated me.

When I finally caught my breath I picked her up and put her on the dining room table.

Now it was my turn. I began by sucking her full breasts. For the first time, I noticed a faint trace of an incision beneath them. Silicone. No problem. They were beautiful.

My tongue licked and tickled its way downward 'til it reached her honeypot. Her pussy was hot, wet and perfumed by desire. I lovingly lapped it. I gradually moved in on her clitoris and began to suck. She moaned. She groaned ecstatically, scandalously, helplessly. I was proud of my prowess. I was making that gorgeous, glorious goddess give in to me.

As soon as she came, I drove deep into her right there on the tabletop. With her boots still on, she wrapped her legs around me and we humped 'til we erupted in a volcanic climax.

"It was really good," she said and smiled a sweet, serene smile.

"Yes, it was."

"But for someone who wanted to go to bed, that cold table seemed a bit odd."

"You don't give me time. You strut nude into the middle of the room and expect me to think about a bed? The only thing I can think about is fucking you as soon as I can. But…let's go to bed?"

I was afraid she'd say no, put on her clothes and vanish from my life for another ten days.

"Yes. Let's."

We screwed until we were exhausted and I think at the end, we were doing it to feel satiated from each other and not because we were still horny. We simply did it 'til we passed out.

* * * * *

The following morning, Lara was lying beside me with her hair spread across the white pillow and her face buried in the covers. I smiled. I felt in command once again. I was the boss.

Chapter Nine

Present Day – Simone

Simone's eyes were burning when she heard the bell. She opened the door to find Edward holding a bottle of wine with one hand and trying to control a bag and an umbrella with the other.

"You wouldn't answer the phone so I decided to come over. I was positive you were slaving away on Saturday. Enough's enough, woman. We'll drink some wine and I'm going to cook for you."

"You're heaven-sent, Edward. I put the phone on mute because some lunatic kept calling and hanging up. But yes, I was working on that New York client's text… It's wonderful you're here!"

For most people, it's a case of bad manners to show up at somebody's house without notice. But not for Simone and Edward. They enjoyed a type of rarely used intimacy that allowed one of them to appear on the other's doorstep if they needed emotional support. Neither would show up at the other's place if one or the other was involved in a romantic relationship of some kind. At the moment, that wasn't an issue for either of them.

"Let's go into the kitchen, Ed. What's on the menu today?"

Edward liked to cook. He prepared simple but always delicious meals. He didn't cook to impress people. He did it to please his friends.

"How about pasta with Alfredo sauce?"

He showed her the ingredients he'd brought and started taking utensils out of cabinets. He was familiar with the house, having visited it many times. Simone opened the wine, poured some into two large goblets and handed one to Edward. She grabbed one of the bar stools and sat at the white marble-top island to savor her wine while she watched Edward cook.

"Okay, my friend, now that you're getting your hands dirty, tell me. What's up?"

"Noah." Edward sighed with dismay. He began to prepare their meal, moving quickly, putting water in a pan and the pan on the cook top, then grabbing a cutting board and knife to slice up ingredients.

"What's wrong now? Beth being obnoxious again?"

"No. I caught him smoking marijuana. It was my turn to have him yesterday. I went to play tennis at the club. I took longer than I'd planned to because I drank a few beers afterward. Noah stayed home. He always brings a friend with him, and this time he invited a kid I'd never met before. When I finally walked in the door, my apartment was a damn smoke house." He stopped chopping, went to the fridge and got some butter.

"My God. Isn't he a bit young for that? He's only twelve!"

"I don't know. Kids aren't my strong suit." Edward got a casserole dish, put some butter inside and started to melt it. After a while, he tossed the mushrooms inside, turned it a little bit, added some white wine he had brought and then some cream.

"What did you do?"

"I kicked out his friend then I grabbed Noah by the collar and took him home to Beth. And then, my dear, you can imagine the scene. Screaming, hollering, recriminations." He finished the sauce, put it aside and then checked the pasta to see if it was ready.

"She wouldn't be Beth if she didn't throw a shit fit."

There were times Simone simply couldn't understand how Edward could handle being in the same room with his ex-wife. She was a twenty-four carat cuckoo clock of a raving maniac. But he was levelheaded and always tried to maintain his equilibrium. Today, however, he didn't seem at all well.

"Simmie, can you set the table, please?"

"Sure. What are you going to do?" She got two placemats, two plates, forks and knifes and her white linen napkins and arranged them quickly. She was not very good at domestic tasks but she could set a table at least.

"I don't know. I'm looking for a psychiatrist." He chuckled.

"I think you should have him examined to see if he's developing a problem with drugs."

"He swore it was the first time. He said he was just seeing what it was like. But I don't know…he's not the same boy who used to trust me and tell me everything."

"Welcome to adolescence, Ed. I've always thought kids should hibernate between the ages of twelve and twenty-one. The world would be a lot more peaceful. The next few years will be hell if he's already started messing around at twelve."

"What if I take custody of him, Simone? What's your opinion? Does he need a male influence on a more regular basis?"

Edward was truly worried. They talked about Noah awhile longer. Simone advised Edward to schedule a meeting with a colleague of theirs, specialist in teenage behavior. Edward accepted the idea — in fact, he seemed extremely relieved and pleased to have something productive to do, and after a bit, he finally started to relax. The meal was wonderful, everything you could ask for on a rainy Saturday night.

Simone began to talk about her research. They read some of the e-mails and laughed a lot.

"You know, Simmie, I think our idea's crazy. But at least it's a lot of fun."

"It's really crazy. Today you spoke to a guy and almost set up a meeting. You'll have to do it soon because I want to analyze this character. I've already obtained a lot of material just from one simple dialogue. It corroborates everything my patients tell me. There's always a degree of masochism involved in that type of fantasy."

"I spoke to him?" He guffawed. "Simmie, you're nuts. Let's be careful with that research."

They were both laughing at nothing now, no doubt due to the wine they'd consumed. They were on the second bottle now. *What a wonderful feeling the complicity of friendship is*, Simone thought. *It's infinitely better than a complicated romance.*

"You've got sauce on your mouth, Ed," she said.

She ran her finger across his lower lip to clean off the little bit there. He took her hand

and affectionately kissed the back of it. The delight she felt at the touch of his lips on her skin startled her. Her whole body shivered. She blamed it on the wine, on her loneliness and the marvelous presence of her friend. She touched Edward's cheek and said, "Thank you for rescuing me from a dreary Saturday."

She looked at him and saw that he, too, had been affected by the sudden tenderness. *Oh, that wine. Better watch out because it wouldn't be good to give free rein to feelings other than those of friendship.*

"I'd better get going, Simone. I'm already tired and the wine's making me lightheaded."

"Wait a minute. I'm not letting you drive home in that condition. You're going to stay here."

"You sure?"

"Definitely. You know where the guestroom is. It's always ready. You'll find an extra toothbrush in the medicine cabinet."

"I love you, Simmie."

There was great feeling in his words, more than usual.

"I love you too, my dear friend. Now let's turn in because we're both almost sleepwalking."

Simone went to her room and Edward to his. She was exhausted but happy to have someone precious close by.

* * * * *

Simone woke up late the next morning. Edward had gone by then but had left breakfast for her on a tray. Though the coffee was cold, she found a note thanking her for a wonderful evening. She put on her gym suit and went for a jog. The rain had stopped and the weather was cool.

She showered when she came back, dressed comfortably and went to her kitchen to make some tea. She carried her mug to the sofa, set the tea on a nearby coffee table and settled in to resume reading. Today, she'd finish Carl's text, or at least attempt to do so.

Mark's Journal — Routine

After our conversation, my relationship with Lara evolved into a kind of routine. She came and went. I respected her space and she didn't disappear anymore. She simply told me whether she wanted to go out or not.

It wasn't easy for me to understand. I hoped in time she'd trust me and maybe things would change. The truth is that I was desperately in love. I'd never been close to feeling that way before. Perhaps, as Peter constantly told me, I was obsessed. Passion turns us into idiots. I felt lobotomized and incapable of dealing with my emotions.

Despite my hopes that Lara would change, I was trying to get on with my life as if she didn't exist. Sometimes she seemed like nothing more than a mirage.

I tried going back to an old girlfriend I used to have fun with. Samara was an attractive, interesting woman. Needing to rid myself of my obsession with Lara, I took Samara to bed, but that only made things worse. Comparisons were inevitable and Lara won by miles and miles. I even ended up frightening Samara because I let out all the stops the way Lara liked me to do. Samara didn't appreciate that. She liked to make love. Lara fucked.

Lara was an enigma. Fear and distrust pervaded her behavior. Clearly, she was terrified of relationships. I was nowhere close to deciphering her but I kept trying.

Sex with her was always surreal and explosive. We continued screwing in the god-damnedest places and sometimes in my bed. She'd nestle in my arms 'til morning and then I often wouldn't see her for a week. I tried to take Peter's advice and just live. Or do what Lara told me and not plan. But I was not myself, definitely.

I called her one night and asked if she'd like to go to Behind the Door. I wanted to get supercharged again. She immediately said yes.

Lara wore a raincoat on the way there. When we arrived she took it off, revealing a bitch-goddess of a dress underneath. Motherfucker! The gown was low-cut to the navel and full of slits down the back and at the waist. I didn't know how it made her feel but I was completely turned on just looking at her.

We went through the same procedure as the first time, body searches for cell phones and cameras. We walked in, danced a bit and drank a few shots of whisky. My head began to spin. I took Lara by the hand and we slipped through the portal to the inner sanctum.

That night, it hosted a sparser gathering and I had a better sense of the surroundings. Glimmering globes and vermilion velvets framed a garden of Eros with an ambient melody of sighs, moans and lamentations of lust and coital climax.

We strolled hand in hand through a dim labyrinth. A drop-dead hot redhead approached me and ran her fingertips across my chest. Lara immediately slipped her hand inside the fox's blouse and felt her up. *Tonight's my night!* I thought. My fantasy served on a silver tray. Lara pulled the woman to her and stuck her tongue down her throat. They swapped spit right before my eyes. I felt like a teenager and almost came, just watching them. Then Lara did the unexpected. She shoved the woman away.

"Buzz off, bitch," Lara snapped. "This one's mine!"

Ciao ciao, bambina. Ciao ciao, dolce illusione. I didn't even have time to savor the pleasure of seeing Lara jealous. I felt so damn frustrated. I'd already been imagining those two luscious, lascivious ladies naked, and the three of us doing it all together.

Lara turned to the wall with her back to me and implored, "Drive it in hard and fast! Now!"

She didn't have to ask twice. I took out a condom, put it on and jammed my joystick in up to the hilt. I could feel her ass pressing against me. I thrust with such force that I thought I was hurting her. But I didn't care. Adrenalin coursed through me. My cock throbbed violently. I placed my arm around her neck to support me and she moaned.

"Squeeze!" she begged.

I squeezed and she cried out.

"Harder!"

As I applied more pressure to her neck, I began to feel the satisfaction of totally dominating a woman. I had her under my yoke, impaled and helplessly restrained. I had complete control and it made me feel twice the pleasure. It was the thrill of sex and of power at the same time. We came 'til our legs buckled. After catching my breath and getting rid of the condom, I remembered I squeezed Lara's neck hard and that worried me.

"Did I hurt you?"

"No, Mark. Not one bit. That was our best fuck ever. Feeling my neck squeezed is ecstasy."

I looked around and saw people watching us. I felt ashamed and at the same time powerful for having made this woman come cataclysmically for the crowd. I reveled in my power and quickly forgot my shame.

"You got really horny when I kissed that woman," Lara remarked.

"I did. That scene was pure fire. I want to see it again."

"All right. C'mon."

After we straightened our clothing, Lara led me by the hand over to where a man was running his hands all over the redhead, who was clearly trying to push him away. Lara pulled her close to us, took my hand, placed it on her breast and began French-kissing the redhead. Then she asked me to sit down on a bench and put on a condom. She mounted and began to ride me, positioning the redhead so they could continue kissing while the redhead fondled Lara's breasts.

"Kiss him," Lara told the redhead.

The woman complied immediately, nearly swallowing my tongue. Molten lava engulfed me. My cock was in one woman's vagina and another was sucking my mouth dry. I couldn't take it. When I felt Lara coming I let myself go and we blasted off together.

"That's great for you two. What about me?" the redhead protested.

"You've already gotten what you deserved today, girl," Lara said. "Now go find your own man. This one's all mine."

"Cunt!" the redhead snarled, baring her teeth.

"You keep singing and I'll keep turning the pages, bitch!" Lara retorted and pinched one of the redhead's nipples.

Wow! A cat fight over me! I was the cock of the walk.

"Okay, Mark. You're hot. And I have to admit I'm not the only one who thinks so." Lara didn't look very happy about admitting it.

I had to laugh. I felt like God's gift to women. Lara had admitted she loved to fuck with me and had even become jealous over me. Not to mention the mind-blowing sex we'd just had. This was good. Maybe this would be enough for me; maybe I really didn't need a relationship.

We screwed once more, this time in a private nook, and then we left. Lara said she wanted to spend the night at her place and asked if I wanted to go there. Progress was being made. I'd be sleeping in her bed for the first time!

When we got to Lara's building, it was almost one in the morning and her mother was slouching half asleep on the couch in the fancy entrance hall.

"What the hell are you doing here at this time of night?" Lara asked.

"Lara, we need to have a serious talk." Her mother stood.

"Sabine, fuck off! I haven't acknowledged your existence for twenty years and I'm not about to lower myself now."

"A serious talk"—she looked at me—"alone."

"Now hear this! I have zilch to say to you. Nada. I'm not going to waste five minutes of my life listening to your bullshit and if you don't get your cheap ass out of here right now, I'll call security."

"Lara, listen to me," the woman begged.

Lara turned to the doorman and asked him to request security to escort "that woman" out of the building. She also made it clear said woman was absolutely never to be permitted onto the premises again.

"But, Miss Lara, she said she was your mother." The doorman looked as confused as I was about Lara's reaction

"I don't have a mother. That woman is *persona non grata* and a certified bucket of afterbirth! Sabine, out! Now!" Lara pointed toward the street, shaking with rage.

"Lara, take it easy, please. Let's go up." I led her to the elevators. "What's your floor?"

"Fifth," she snapped.

At that moment, I glanced over my shoulder. Sabine had gone.

"What's happening, Lara? This is the second time you've run into your mother and completely lost it. Excuse me. I know this is none of my business. But I don't like to see you in this state."

She didn't answer. She just trembled. She stepped into the lift and we went up. She took the key out of her purse but couldn't manage to insert it in the lock because she was still shaking so badly. I took the key from her and opened the door.

A bright and cheerful atmosphere greeted us. Paintings hung on the walls. Colorful cushions lay everywhere. I might have been in a harem. The apartment shouted "Lara" from every nook and cranny. Her décor was whimsical and full of fun. She left me alone for a few moments and I just stood there looking around. What a delightful surprise to find myself in such a cozy place. I'd expected a den of steamy sensuality and exotic eroticism. But it felt so much more like a home!

Mark's Journal – Mommy Issues

"I don't know what to say to you, Lara. I've never imagined anything like what happened down there. What brought that on? You tarred and feathered your own mother. I've never had a mother."

"You're lucky."

It was painful to see Lara so rude, so furious, so downright cruel. She lost control only when she was having sex. Otherwise she was friendly and kept her emotions in check. My insistence on wanting to find out why she'd treated her mother with such brutality seemed to unnerve her.

"I'd like to know. Maybe if you tell me, I'll understand. I swear, the way you behaved with your mother was awful... It's too much for me!"

I'd lost my mother when I was two. I'd spent my life wishing I had one. I couldn't fathom how someone who did have a mother could treat her so horribly. Was it because of the divorce Peter had mentioned?

"Okay. You asked for it. You want the whole nine yards. You insist on seeing the dark side of the moon. I hope you've got the stomach for it!"

What could be so unspeakable? I couldn't conceive of anything involving the lovely and elegant woman I'd met that would engender such hatred.

"When I was very young, my father owned a large construction company. He was tight with a powerful senator in Washington, where I was born. His name's beside the point. Most of the work that built my father's fortune came from the senator's connections. I was used to him and his family coming to our house and to us going to theirs. We were all friends and the senator was like an uncle to me."

Lara paused and went to the fridge. She got some ice cubes, poured herself a whisky and took a swallow. She forgot to offer me one. Her hand was shaking.

"The senator had a son twenty years older than I am. I'd known him forever but he went to school abroad, in England. I never saw him much and when I did we hardly spoke. I was just a kid and he was a grown man. When I was twelve he came back to the U.S. for good. He was elegant, well dressed and worldly and he began to show an interest in me. When he came to our house he'd bring me presents — the kind all little girls adore. Lipstick, a barrette, a CD, a comic book — just trifles. He was the first man who ever gave me any attention."

I felt queasy right from the start of the story. Something bad was coming. Should I ask her to stop?

"He'd also take me out for rides. He'd buy me ice cream on hot days. He drove a convertible and would drop the top and play my favorite music. He was pretty cool for an old man, I'd thought. He was thirty-two. He told me about the world, about places where he'd lived. He was very sophisticated. I felt grown-up when I was with him. His attention lasted throughout that summer. I was barely twelve and felt like a woman. I didn't want to be a child anymore. His interest in me proved I was an adult."

"Did you fall in love with him?" I felt insanely jealous of that man.

"In love? I don't know. Maybe during those rides. I think I was in love with the attention he showed me, with the fascination in his eyes that I didn't know how to explain but knew was for me."

"A little girl Narcissus drowning in her own reflection," I said.

"That's it. A little girl's vanity. Besides, I was a needy child. One day, we went out for ice cream. I was wearing a cute and colorful summer dress. He drove to a quiet spot, a half-deserted park. We were parked there just talking about music when he moved closer to me and kissed me. My first kiss. I felt a rush I'd never felt before, a desire I couldn't understand. He stuck his tongue in my mouth and I shivered with fright. I didn't know a kiss would be like that. Then he put his hand on my thigh and began slowly moving it upward. I felt a mix of desire, curiosity and fear. Something inside me was telling me it was wrong and that I should stop him. But he had great authority over me."

"What a sick son of a bitch! You were just a kid!" My stomach clenched as if I might be sick.

"I was. And all those conflicting feelings overwhelmed and confused me. He slipped his hand onto my pussy and for some strange reason, I got wet. That had never happened before. I told him I was sorry. I said I didn't know why it had happened and he answered it was because I wanted him. I was very ashamed. I tried to get his hand off me but I couldn't. He stuck a finger inside me. It hurt a little but then he put another finger on my clitoris and began to rub gently. I got really turned on and I think I came because it suddenly felt wonderful."

"Did he rape you?"

"No. That day, he just fondled me. When he stopped he told me I was a beautiful woman and he loved me. But the grown-ups wouldn't understand so it was better not to say anything. He kissed me and drove me home in silence. We spoke only to say good-bye."

Lara swallowed some whisky and continued.

"When I got in the house I felt dirty. I felt as if I'd done something awful. I ran to take a shower and then I went to see my mother. I said I had to talk to her. She told me she was about to go out to dinner and asked if it was important. She was in a hurry. I said it was. I said the senator's son had put his hand on my leg and stuck his finger inside me. She slapped my face and told me not to make up stories about someone like him. She said he was the son of the man who'd done the most to help my father and our family. She called me a horrid little liar and then she left."

"Your own mother said that to you? That refined woman I spoke to? I don't believe it!"

"I didn't either. But there's more to the story. If you want to hear it."

"If you want to tell me."

My stomach turned over, thinking about the defenseless little girl Lara had been and that monstrous abuse. It explained a lot about her, the nameless suffering in the depths of her eyes.

"I began to avoid him. Whenever I knew he was coming over I'd invent an excuse not to be around. I was going to play at a friend's house or do homework, I'd say, or I'd just hide. I didn't want to see him anymore. But one day, he caught up with me. He arrived unannounced. It was a Sunday. The servants were off. My parents had gone to his parents' house and had taken my brother and sister along. I hadn't felt like going. My mother seemed to understand my reasons. I was alone that afternoon but I was happy because I wouldn't have to see him. My mother was finally starting to believe me, I thought."

Her expression turned bitter and sad and then she continued.

"He arrived. He had a key. For sure, my dearest mommy had given it to him. He opened the door. I didn't have time to react. I was watching TV and he took me by surprise. He told me I was a bad girl, that I was running away from him and I shouldn't do that. He hugged me. He said he'd missed me and I was his little doll. He started kissing me. Again I felt desire, fear and shame all at the same time. He tore off my clothes. I still remember I was wearing cotton panties with teddy bear prints. He took me to a bedroom and took off his clothes. He began to run his hands all over my body and then he started sucking my pussy, something I'd never even imagined was possible. I was terrified and yet turned on. Then he forced his penis into me. It hurt a lot but he put his hand over my mouth to keep me from screaming and kept pumping until he came. I began to cry. I was hurt and filled with fear. I hurt all over and there was blood on the bedspread."

"Lara, can you give me a whisky? I need it." I had to interrupt. I felt sick.

"Of course. Take mine. I'll pour another one."

She handed me her glass. She seemed to be calming down, amazingly enough.

"He told me not to worry. The first time it hurt but from then on it would be different and I'd like it. He said I shouldn't tell my parents what had happened because they wouldn't understand. He took me into the bathroom and washed me. There was semen on my legs but back then, I didn't know that's what it was. I just knew it was something slimy that I didn't know how to explain. But then, I couldn't explain much of anything else that had happened either."

"Did he use some protection? Was he worried about you?"

"He was worried, all right. About himself!" She laughed sardonically. "Imagine. I wasn't even menstruating yet. He still made me take a pill. Looking back, I think it was a morning-after pill or something like that. He was about to announce his candidacy for some office or another. The last thing he needed was to be accused of knocking up a little girl! And get this... That same day, he decided I'd have to enjoy myself too. He spread my legs again and this time I really liked it. But I was still ashamed. A shame made worse because of the pleasure I felt."

"What about your parents?"

"Conveniently, they didn't get back until late. By then, we'd screwed three or four times. I was in a lot of pain. But now I knew what an orgasm was. I must have taken five showers by the time they came home. I felt filthy. I needed to feel clean."

"Didn't they notice the stained bedspread or anything?"

"Nothing. He found another and made the bed before he left. He took the bloody one and my torn clothes with him. When my parents arrived my face was swollen from so much crying. My shame overwhelmed me. He'd said that what had happened was my fault because

I'd provoked him. I was wondering how I could have done that. He called me a naughty little slut and other ugly things several times while he was inside me. I didn't even know what that meant. When I finally found out I felt so dirty and ashamed.

"My mother asked me what was wrong. I asked her to come to my room and I told her everything that had happened. My state of shock grew worse because she said he was like a son to her and my father and if he wanted to screw me, I should be grateful. She said if I had pretty clothes, expensive toys and a beautiful house, and if I went to the best school in town, it was thanks to his father. The least I could do in exchange for all that was to make his son happy. She said if I behaved myself, she was sure someday he'd marry me."

"Holy shit! Your mother should be shot!"

"Take it easy; there's more. I screamed. I said she was crazy. I might have been just a kid but I knew that was wrong. I said I'd tell my father everything. She laughed. It was a sadistic laugh. I can still hear it today if I close my eyes. She said she had a present for me. She was going to tell me a story. She said it wouldn't do any good to tell my father anything because he wasn't even my father! She said her gynecologist had gotten her pregnant and my father had raised me. I was nothing more than a child my real father didn't want. So, she asked me, did I want to upset him with a story like that? Did I want to damage his career? If he found out he wasn't my father, would he still love me?"

"You weren't your father's daughter? Or was it just something she made up?"

"Do you think I had the courage to ask my father at a time like that? Years passed before I learned the truth. I turned into a depressed little girl. I always felt dirty, guilty. I was afraid my classmates would find out I was a little whore. I began to isolate myself. I felt my mother had abandoned me. It was the worst time of my life."

"And that guy kept on abusing you?"

"For three more years with my mother's help. She fabricated 'school trips' so he could take me wherever he wanted. After he lost the election, he decided to go to France for six months. I'd been to France with my grandmother when I was eight and had loved it. My dear mommy invented a student exchange program. She said it would be wonderful for a girl like me to learn French and she sent me with him. To cheer him up on the trip! I have no idea what she told my father."

"You lived with him in France for six months?"

"That's right. I was almost fifteen and he was happy to be able to walk around town, dragging me by the hand. I was already pretty tall at that age and could pass for being older."

"And how did you feel?"

"It's hard to explain, Mark. After a while, abnormality turned into normality. I didn't feel guilty anymore. I developed a kind of emotional dependence on him. I went everywhere with him. We slept together. We had fantastic sex, for a little girl like me, at least. I loved it whenever we did it. He taught me things. He showed me the city. I'd already fallen for Paris when I was there with my grandmother. That didn't change. My love for the city deepened. I adored everything in Paris…its art, its restaurants."

"He'd go out with you like that, holding hands with you everywhere?"

"Not here. But in France he did. Hardly anybody knew us and no one suspected how old I was."

"You got used to the situation?"

"Yes. I got used to being his Barbie doll. Put this on today. Say this. Eat that. Suck my cock this way. Do it that way. I was a damn puppet. I had no will of my own. I couldn't. My mother had made sure I'd only do whatever he wanted. I think she believed we'd get married and she finally would become a card-carrying member of high society and not just a wannabe."

"When did it end? It did end, right?"

"Yes. We came back from Paris and I had to return to school. Normal life, studies, hard work to make up for my lost six months. The other girls were dying of envy because I was more grown up, more sophisticated, full of Parisian airs. I'd talk about things they'd never seen. I told them about theaters, operas, restaurants, *foie gras* and *confit de canard*. I wore sophisticated clothes and makeup. I felt like an ET around them. I was too old for my age and too young to have lived what I'd lived."

Her eyes grew moist. She looked as if she was fighting to hold back the tears.

"I turned into a loner. I was ostracized for being different. But then I met a boy about my own age. He was a nice kid, studious. We grew close and he helped me overcome the difficulties of having been on another planet for six months. We did our homework together. He was kind, polite, affectionate and easy to be with. We fell in love. For the first time, I felt young love. It was light and innocent and everything I wasn't anymore."

"How old was he?" In the middle of a horror story I was jealous of a kid.

"The same age I was. Maybe a month or two older. We were fifteen."

"And how did you get rid of the other one?"

I didn't dare to ask his name. She didn't tell me his name.

"Oh. That wasn't so easy. He had an apartment where we'd meet. He'd call me and I had to go running to service him. But one day, I got ahold of myself and went to talk to him. By then, I had a key to the apartment. He always ordered me to show up there bathed and perfumed and dressed in such and such a way. Whatever. I went in. I waited. When he arrived and saw me he was all smiles and he kissed me. He said he wanted to play our favorite game again."

"What game was that?"

"In Paris, he'd started going to swing and sadomasochism houses like Behind the Door and he'd take me with him. He developed a taste for masochistic games. He'd handcuff me and put a collar on me when we had anal sex."

"Just when I thought the bastard couldn't get any sicker…"

"Oh, yes. That's what I thought too. I got to like it after a while just like everything else. I think I've always had a strong sexual appetite, especially because of the way I'd been initiated. I managed to separate sexual pleasure from my other feelings. When I had sex with him I'd block out any kind of aversion I felt for him. It was as if my body and my feelings lived in different worlds."

Mystery solved, I thought. *She's still like that today. Feelings don't enter into her sexual relationships.*

"And then?" I asked.

"I told him, 'Not today! Not ever! I don't want you anymore! I'm in love with someone else!' I spewed out the words like puke all over him. He slapped me and told me to shut up. He said I was his property and he'd do whatever he wanted to. He told me to stop the being-in-love bullshit. He threw me on the bed and jammed his prick up my ass. Because I fought and struggled, he hurt me badly that day. But that was his great misfortune and my salvation.

"I got home with a horrible black eye. The first person I ran into was my father. He was in the living room and asked me what had happened. I was so devastated, I couldn't lie. I told him everything, right from the beginning. I told him what my mother had said. I told him about Paris. I told him I thought I wasn't his daughter. I told him what had just happened, in detail. I just couldn't stand all the secrecy anymore."

"And what did he do?"

"He totally went to pieces. He cried a lot and asked me to forgive him. He said he'd never suspected a thing. He said he was my father and my mother was a goddamn liar."

"And what happened with your mother?"

"When she got home it was like World War III had erupted inside their bedroom. I don't know what they said—they were used to fighting behind closed doors—but she left carrying her bags. For years afterward, I heard nothing from her. Those were the best years of my life."

"What happened then?" I couldn't avoid being curious about the whole story.

"Everything. My father already had business interests up here. We moved. He cut all his ties with the senator. He pounded the shit out of the senator's son and put him in the hospital. All that got hushed up. My father had a huge fortune by then. My mother didn't dare try to get any of it. First, because their marriage didn't involve community property, they had a wonderful pre-nup my grandmother forced Sabine to sign, and second, because my father threatened to blow the whistle to the media and ruin the senator. Oh, yeah. And we found out that my mother had been having an affair with him for years."

"And your brother and sister?"

"They were small. Sean was eight and Debbie six. My father got custody of all of us. Sabine didn't try to contest it. Kids weren't her thing. She'd just used us. We put our lives back together. My grandmother Emma, who hated Sabine, came to live with us. She was the best mother anyone could have. We succeeded in overcoming a lot. Considering the circumstances, we almost became a happy and normal family. I'll never forgive Sabine. As far as I'm concerned, she's a snake. A child trafficker. The worst and most selfish human being I've ever known."

"Lara, please forgive me. I had no right to make you remember all that. I don't know what to say to you."

"That's okay. It was good. This was the first time I've talked about it outside a shrink's office and with someone other than my father and grandma. It was liberating. It seems it's all in the past now. Thanks for listening."

She began to sob. I hugged her tight and she cried until she seemed to run out of tears and dozed off in my lap. I carried her to her bedroom. I undressed her and tucked her in under the covers. Then I snuggled up beside her. I understood the woman. At last. I just didn't know if that was a good thing.

Chapter Ten

Present Day – Simone

Simone was used to emotional disturbances. It was her job to treat them. But tales of child abuse always rocked her. She felt physical pain whenever she heard stories like Lara's.

She couldn't understand why an adult would torture a child, as the senator's son had done. It wasn't hard to read Lara's personality now. She was a typical victim of abuse. She had suffered a kind of Stockholm syndrome, bonding with her oppressor because she saw no way out. She had developed an extremely distorted view of sex and relationships. She was deathly afraid of becoming someone's puppet again. Lara was no goddess. She was a twisted rag doll, struggling to keep her head on straight.

What an atrocity! Utter madness! Simone felt nauseated. She thought about her daughter and couldn't see how any mother could serve her own flesh and blood on a silver platter to a pervert. She was in shock. She needed air. The walls seemed to close in on her. She went outside and tried to clear her head. But she couldn't shake the images of a defenseless little girl betrayed by the person she most needed at her side.

Simone never treated pedophiles. She couldn't — she always sent them to other professionals. Child abuse was a very sensitive subject with her. She always suffered with her patients who had been victims of this perversion. Simone decided to call Carl to state her initial opinions. She got her cell phone and dialed his number.

"Hello, Simone, how've you been?"

"Great, and you?"

"Very well and anxious for news…" he replied. "Have you arrived at a conclusion?"

"Not a conclusion yet but a very strong first impression."

"Ah…" He sounded disappointed. "And what is your first opinion?"

"Clearly, Lara had acquired a taste for masochism as a result of preadolescent horrors. Chains, collars, handcuffs and anal sex might be enjoyable and erotic for adults who had freedom of choice. But a child? It would disturb the rest of her life, and it did."

"So you've reached that point in the story…hard to know, hmm?"

"Yes, very."

"And about her death?"

"I haven't gotten that far, but at this point, I can tell you it's reasonable to assume Lara's death was an accident. I still need to finish reading and then talk to some people — Mark, for instance — but…well, I've told you what I think right now."

Carl sounded relieved after that. He truly believed in Mark's innocence. Simone was heading there too. Most likely, Mark had only been fulfilling Lara's fantasy when things got out of control. There had been no intent to kill. Her death had been an accident.

"It's going to be necessary to finish reading the text before drawing a definite conclusion but this last chapter had been a revelation to me."

"Could you write a report for me, Simone?" Carl asked her.

She promised to write one for him the following day, with references to pertinent case histories, and assured him the job would be finished in another week or two. Simone had been at it for three weeks. The contract specified forty-five days. But she understood why Carl was in a hurry.

"Goodbye, Simone, thank you very much for the help."

"You're welcome, Carl."

Even after Simone hung up the phone she couldn't get the story out of her mind. She felt sorry for Lara. She felt sorry for Mark as well because he probably had had no clue what he'd gotten himself into. She'd help Carl get the poor man acquitted.

Chapter Eleven

Present Day - Simone

Simone hit a brick wall after reading Lara's story. She sent the report to Carl but hadn't been able to pick up the manuscript again. She was in deep distress. She called him and told him about it. He said he understood and that if she needed more time to finish the job, she could have it. She accepted the offer.

"Carl, I sincerely thank you for your understanding. This task is taking much more time than I expected."

"No problem, Simone. What happened to Lara was a living hell. I reacted the same way you did."

"The manuscript is so heavy. Have you read all of it?"

"Several times!"

"How's our deadline, Carl?"

He hesitated before answering. He seemed to be thinking. "The trial hasn't been scheduled yet. I'm in a rush because my defense will rest on what you come up with. But I can wait a little longer."

"I promise I'll do my best to finish soon.

"Let's do it this way, Simone, if this works for you. I'll come see you on Saturday. I have questions about your report. We'll have lunch and discuss the case. How does that sound?"

"That would be perfect for me!" And, she thought, she'd still have a week to read further and prepare something more concrete for Carl.

But Simone's good intentions were for naught. The week got off to a hectic start.

Edward did volunteer work for the local police, helping them to clarify criminal behavior. He was a certified volunteer and had received the one hundred hours of training required to be one, and when they called him for help on a case, Simone picked up some of his clients. Deciphering criminal minds was Edward's passion. He'd published two books on the subject and used his pro bono work to develop his theories. His activities had earned him considerable respect and a fat appointment book. Unlike Simone, Edward had no interest in teaching. But he was a great researcher. On Sunday, he'd gotten an urgent call, which meant Simone would be seeing twice as many patients for the foreseeable future. She'd interview the ones who needed prescriptions and the rest could be rescheduled.

Two women had been murdered in the city during the past twenty days, and the police suspected the crimes were possibly the work of a serial killer. The detectives were getting nowhere. A third victim had been found on Sunday. All the victims appeared to have been tortured over a period of time. The telltale signs on the bodies had clearly been inflicted prior to death. The killer had masturbated on the bodies. At least, that was what the police thought, because there was no sign of rape...just semen.

The semen didn't match that of any known killer, which left the police without a lead. The only way forward was to construct a new criminal profile. The problem was that the murders had just two elements in common. The victims were always female and the same man had left behind his semen on each victim's body. Their families had never reported the women missing because they were thought to be traveling. As far as the police could discern, the women hadn't known one another, either. They were just everyday people of no particular note in the community.

The killer never left traces. No fingerprints, hairs, blood, skin under the victims' nails or anything else to help identify him. The bodies were always dumped in parks on rainy days when the water would taint any potential evidence. It was a wet time of year. The season favored him.

Simone watched as Edward drove himself crazy struggling to solve the puzzle of these cases. He always seemed to hit a dead end. A shrink had to create a pathological profile to be able to help the police. The situation Edward was grappling with made this extremely difficult.

A pattern of torture existed. All the earliest marks on the victims' bodies looked to be from five to seven days old. The victims' disappearances always coincided with upcoming short absences they'd informed their families about. For a week or so, the families didn't think their loved ones were missing. They were just traveling and out of harm's way. This meant the murderer had a few days or a week to torture them before the kill. All without exception had sent text messages saying they were fine. One of the victims had even called to say she was having a good time.

The police were trying to ascertain whether the victims' trips had something to do with the killer. Had he induced them to travel? But nothing added up. One had gone on a pre-planned vacation, the second on a business trip. The third had gone for a job interview. There was no link.

Serial killers follow patterns that unmask them in the end. This one's pattern included torture, victims' absences, violent deaths and no rape, just semen. Semen was his trademark, his morbid signature, and always found on the victims' breasts and bellies. He'd left the women facedown to protect the semen so it could be identified.

The first woman had been strangled, the second smothered. The latest, as Edward explained to Simone on the phone, had probably been thrown down a staircase. Forensics was still working on it. Firearms weren't involved in any of the three cases and there was no blood. But there were signs of torture.

Edward returned to the office on Monday just as Simone was leaving. It was eight in the evening and she'd just seen one of his patients. He looked totally burned out, with dark rings under his eyes.

"Eddie, my friend, you're a wreck! Is there anything I can do for you?"

"Besides what you've already done today? Simone, I can't thank you enough for your support. I don't know what I'd do without you." He hugged her tightly, as if seeking comfort.

When he finally released her, she asked, "And so, how was it this time?"

"The usual. But he gave it a new twist. He made the victim swallow melted butter. When it cooled, she suffocated. And the burns! The butter must have been horribly hot. Then he threw her down something, probably a set of stairs, as I told you on the phone. Can you imagine what that poor woman went through in the final moments of her life? And afterward of course, he ejaculated on her." Edward's expression defined loathing and disgust.

"Melted butter? Hey! I've been watching a French crime series on cable called *Caïn*. That's what the killer used in the latest episode."

"Is that the show you told me about with the crippled cop? You said you loved it because it's so politically incorrect."

"That's it. And butter was the murder weapon. No masturbation but the same bizarre crime."

"Did you record that episode, Simone?"

In spite of his wasted condition, Edward's face suddenly lit up.

"I did. I'll put it on a pen drive when I get home. I think I've got twenty episodes or so. I copy them in case I want to watch them again. If you think it can help…"

"I'd like to see it because I'd never seen a death by suffocation with butter before. And now you tell me about this coincidence. Please, let me have it. Are you going home?"

"Indeed, I am. I think you should too. Nothing else to do here, my friend. It's late. You need to rest. I'll bring you the show tomorrow. Relax and take a long, hot, lazy shower."

"Your prescription for everything."

"That's right. It always does the trick. A psychologist would say it has something to do with returning to the warmth of the womb. Go for it."

"I will. But nothing is easy after seeing a dead body."

"By the way, after the shower, have a big glass of wine. I could never do a job like that. Not my cup of tea."

"You are, nevertheless, helping a lawyer to acquit a killer."

She detected an out-of-character undertone of criticism in Edward's voice. She wrote it off as irritation due to fatigue and stress.

"I'm not so sure he did it intentionally. I'm leaning toward a sex-game accident. But I haven't reached a conclusion yet."

* * * * *

Two days later, Edward and the police were celebrating. Simone had given Eddie the thumb drive, which held almost the entire season of *Caïn*, and at last, he and the detectives had discovered a pattern in the killer's behavior. The man would imitate a given crime in a given episode. Thank God his schedule didn't line up with the series or there'd be two murders per week.

At the end of the day, Simone went to see Edward as he was leaving the office. She wanted to hear more details because he'd called to thank her for the lead her idea had given him.

"Anything concrete, Eddie?"

"Not yet. But we've narrowed the field. Only subscribers to cable TV can watch *Caïn*. We're trying to get the channels that carry it to give us their lists of *Caïn* fans. There shouldn't be that many because the show is in French. If we can identify the program's viewers, our killer might be among them."

"I'll be a suspect. I always watch it."

"Take it easy, Simmie. Since when do women leave semen on murder victims? Besides, the body was dumped on Saturday and I was at your house, remember?" He laughed.

"I just don't want the cops asking me why I watch a particular TV show. I don't have time for that."

"It won't happen. Everyone at the department knows you were the one who connected the crime to the series. No killer would do that. Nobody's going to bother you.

But tell me…why do you like that show so much? In my opinion, it is pure crap!"

"I used to watch *Dr. House*. When it ended I felt like a widow. I signed up for *Caïn* to give it a try. It's a sort of a French *Dr. House* but even more politically incorrect."

"And you love political incorrectness, right?"

"You know what I think of nondiscriminatory speech." She made quotation marks in the air to highlight her point of view." It's the death of creativity. And *Caïn* is really sexy. I want a man just like him."

"Crippled?" he blurted.

"No, dummy. Sexy!"

"And there's no one like that on the horizon?"

"Well…that lawyer I met in the city. Maybe…after I finish the job. I never mix business with pleasure. It always results in half-baked work, a half-baked affair or both."

"You're right. But what's the attraction? Is he politically incorrect?"

"I don't know. I haven't made up my mind yet. I do find him handsome and interesting."

"A lot of guys fit that description. What makes him different?"

"I actually haven't stopped to think about it. Maybe, my friend, I find him so attractive because I really need to get laid. Soon!"

She grabbed her coat and kissed Edward on the cheek and left.

Chapter Twelve

Present Day - Simone

The four o'clock patient had arrived, a thirty-three-year-old man with very short hair and soft-brown eyes. His eyelashes were as long as a girl's, which made him more pretty than handsome. Simone had been treating his chronic masochism for six months. He was always pleasant and polite. And despite the gravity of his condition, she got a kick out of working with him.

Philip suffered from overpowering sexual compulsion. If he couldn't have sex at least once a day, he'd end up masturbating five or six times. Sadomasochistic fantasies were hurting his marriage, though he swore he loved his wife. Simone had him on a course of drugs and therapy. She'd adjusted prescriptions and doses several times until the latest had begun to take effect. She was pleased with the results and so was he.

The early treatments had left him sleepy and with erectile dysfunction. For a sex addict, it was a jolt to go from one extreme to another. The current regimen had reduced his compulsion while leaving him able to have a normal sex life with his wife. He was getting better and Simone felt optimistic.

However, Philip had been taking the same small dosage and was now at the point where his medication probably needed to be increased. He didn't want that. He worried about losing his erections. During this session, Simone planned on trying to persuade him otherwise.

"Philip, how nice to see you!"

"Same here, Doctor. Always a pleasure. Hey, I've brought you some double-fudge, chocolate-chip brownies I made this morning." He handed her a bag.

"Thank you so much. I'll have a cup of coffee when we finish and try them then."

"Make it strong black coffee. Brings out the flavor."

"I'll do that. Now, how have things been going?"

"Well, my fantasies are driving me berserk again and I'm not getting enough sleep."

"What do you mean by not enough?"

"Only about four hours a night. I'm bushed!"

"I understand. But as I told you, I believe your body has adjusted to the medication and that's why you're beginning to have trouble again. I really think you need to take a larger dosage."

"And if I can't get it up again?"

The possibility frightened him. His voice held a note of despair and he started to tap his right foot in a clear demonstration that he was a bundle of nerves.

"That won't happen. We've already seen that this medication doesn't affect you that way. Every patient reacts differently to a drug. Trust me. Increase the dose by half a pill, okay?"

"I will, Doctor. I trust you. I need to get my head on straight."

"Good. So what happened with your fantasies this week?"

"The usual. I pestered my wife to have sex with an ex-boyfriend of hers."

This was a recurrent product of Philip's fancy. He was always imagining his wife making love with other men. He suffered when it happened but it turned him on.

"Did she do it?"

"Yes. She didn't want to at first. They split up a long time ago and she had no reason to see him again. But when she finally agreed she found she liked it. We filmed the whole encounter. I must've walloped the ol' bishop at least ten times while I watched the video. But I think I damaged myself. It really hurts. No way can I strum it today."

"Now do you see why I want to increase the dosage, Philip? You were okay. The masturbation and the fantasies were under control. Now you're back to square one."

"Yes, Doctor."

"Please describe the events and how you felt about them."

"Sure. Nothing new. She went to see the guy, an old flame from before my time. I helped her choose her outfit. She could have given a dead man a hard-on. Black bra and panties, garters and stockings. She filmed everything with our key-ring recorder."

"And you watched?"

"Yes. I was in a meeting at the office during their…tryst."

Philip owned an accounting firm and had a number of employees.

"I knew she was with the guy, betraying me. She was getting off with someone else. The mere mental image caused me to leave the meeting twice to stroke it in the bathroom. Everybody must have thought I had the runs."

"Probably." Simone muffled a chuckle.

"When I got home we watched the video together. I noticed she was seducing the guy differently from the way she does with me. He said it was good how they always used to do it. Memories. She chewed a lot on his cock. They sixty-nined. She certainly gave him a much better blowjob than the quickie ones she used to give me. And he Hershey highwayed her. He did that first and she loved it. We don't do that. I got really horny and jealous. We screwed but it wasn't enough. I had to pound my pud mucho as I watched them."

His characteristically quaint language always challenged Simone's determination to keep a straight face.

"And afterward?"

"I hated my wife. I was so pissed off I wanted to tar and feather and draw and quarter her. I went to sleep in the guestroom. I could see her feelings were badly hurt. She always says she doesn't like it when I give her to other men. She feels unloved. The worst part is that I do love her. I'm dying of jealousy. I can't stand it when men check her out on the street!"

"It's pain and pleasure, pleasure and pain. The same old story. Time and again, I tell you it's pure masochism." Simone paused and raised her eyebrows at him. "Okay, I know you're not going to like this idea. But now that we're stabilizing you with medication we'll have to return to your childhood. We need to know what happened back then because something made you the way you are today."

"Mommy damnedest?"

"Not always. Do you have any recollection of being abused?"

"No. None. I don't think that's the problem."

"I'd like you to talk to me about your childhood."

"All right. If I really have to."

"You do. Masochism has a variety of causes. Sometimes it's abuse. Sometimes it's sibling rivalry. We need to get to the root of yours."

"I think it's sibling rivalry. I'm the youngest of three brothers. My mother only had eyes for Christopher, the oldest. He was her pet. She'd always say Chris was going to be very rich and successful because he was the smartest of us three, and he'd always help us because he was kind and generous. What a joke! The retard couldn't even get into college. Today, I'm asshole golden boy's boss! I'm his goddamn employer!"

"Did you feel loved?"

"By my father. My batty mother made me feel like an unnecessary auto accessory. I wasn't even the spare tire… You know that saying, an heir and a spare? My middle brother was the spare."

"And why did she have three sons? Do you know?"

"Indeed. I do. She was dying to have Michelle, her imaginary daughter. She wanted her first child to be a boy. She got her wish and she got a big head. But when she went for her ideal one-boy-and-one-girl family plan, my other brother came along. I was the final failed attempt. And as she made it a point to inform me—in public, in the middle of a family cookout after she'd had a few—when the doctor pulled me out and slapped me on the backside her first words were, "Shit! Another boy!"

"Aren't you exaggerating, Philip?"

"That's an abridged version, Doctor. And to pour salt on the wound, she said she was sparing me years of therapy by telling me."

He then recounted his difficult childhood, detailing how jealous he was of his brothers. His was a classic case of masochism. Philip loved a mother he knew would never love him the way she loved the others. The pain of sharing a mother he knew would never love him back as he deserved eventually turned into adult sexual paranoia. Philip was giving his wife to other men because he feared she'd never really be his.

How beautiful and complex the human essence, Simone reflected. And how difficult the art of raising children. A mother should never conceive of behaving that way, but throughout her years as a psychiatrist, Simone had met quite a few who'd done things that were even worse

By day's end, Simone was exhausted but she still had to go to the university to see the dean. She was going to ask him for a six-month break from classes so she could finish her research and concentrate on her new book. He'd okay her request. Yale supported its researchers. Each book published was more than just a feather in the cap for the author. It was a splendid trophy for the whole school. It proved that research and science were the university's driving force.

She left the office and paused in the front entrance, one hand on the doorknob.

"Going home?"

Simone jumped and spun around, heart racing.

"Dammit, Edward, you startled me!" Why the hell did he always have to skulk around like a damn cat?

"What else is new? I always do that." He laughed.

"It's not funny! Try to walk like a normal human being, would you?"

"How does a 'normal human being' walk?" he teased her.

"Well for one thing, they make noise!" She drew a shaky breath and released it on a sigh. "No, I'm not going home yet. I'm headed over to the university. You?"

"I'm going to take that long hot shower you recommended. Then exercise, dinner and peace and quiet. Not necessarily in that order."

"Will you do me a huge favor? If you have the time?"

"Of course. What is it?"

"We need to make progress on researching those e-mails. Talk to that Victor who wants to set up a meeting. Read the chat record first to situate yourself, okay?"

"I certainly will. Leave it to me."

"I love you, Ed."

"I love you too, Simone. A lot!"

* * * * *

Initially, the dean wasn't very keen about Simone's request to take a leave of absence. However, the prospect of a new tome in the university library brought him around. He granted her three months. Though only half of what she'd asked for, it was enough to do the research. Later on, she'd figure out how to find time to write the book.

She picked up the manuscript once again when she got home. Carl would arrive on Saturday and she wished to read a bit more before speaking to him. Her definitive diagnosis would have to wait until she finished but she had a good idea of what it would be. Nevertheless, a further exchange of ideas and impressions might bear some fruit.

Simone was delighted Carl was coming on a Saturday. It was a good sign. Men with fiancées or girlfriends didn't schedule meetings on Saturdays.

Mark's Journal – Let's Go to Disneyland

Life went on with Lara. It went on without her too, during the periods she'd absent herself. Just when I thought I was breaking down barriers and getting close to her, especially after she'd told me about the pervert and the mother from hell, she'd cloister herself. Then days later, she'd reappear. Her behavior confused and frustrated me. But I loved her. I'd accept the distance between us and wait patiently until it grew shorter and shorter.

One night, Lara, Peter and I went out together – the first time we'd done that, even though Peter was much more to us than just a casual friend. I was happy.

"Hi, kids! Great to see you! Did you know you're a really cute couple? If Mark and I were to hold hands, that would be even cuter but we know he refuses to come out of the closet."

"Peter, bend over and I'll drive you to Cleveland." Sometimes, Peter pissed me off with his bullshit. He acted like a one-man gay pride parade. But despite his nonsense, he truly was family.

"We make a gorgeous threesome," Lara remarked, dismissing the remotest notion of a couple.

"Yes, indeed. Even sexier!" Peter agreed. "Nevertheless, Lara, wanting to be you doesn't mean I want to ravish you. The idea conjures up codfish. Yuk!"

He made his customary over-the-top grimace.

"Thank you ever so much for comparing me to a dead fish! Now I'm all set for the evening! But think about it; if you're really ravenous, you can ignore the scent."

"I'll die of sexual starvation before I do that! I've never had a woman in my whole life and I'll go to my grave without trying one!"

"But how do you know it's so bad if you've never taken the plunge? C'mon, Peter. I know a host of voluptuous volunteers who'd love to help you go straight." Lara laughed heartily.

"Mission impossible!" I chimed in.

"Go ahead. Ridicule this queen of whom ye doth speak. Idiotic ideas aside, Lara, I agree we are a resplendent trio. But you two are queering my pitch. Is there any homosexual worth his salt who'd want someone seen hanging out with you? Get real! A threesome is beyond the pale! I'll die alone and you'll be to blame! You should split; Mark and I together would be more attractive."

"Peter, you are one sick man," Lara declared. "You're lucky you're funny. But I think there's someone eyeing you over there at that table, despite the company you're keeping. Check out that guy." She nodded toward the middle-aged man ogling Peter.

"Suffering sack of shit! That's goddamn Jonathan Harris, back from the dead. We are definitely *Lost in Space*. I'm Mr. Gay America and you're trying to fix me up with a refugee from a cemetery! Some friend you are! You know what you deserve? A good spanking with cleated Louboutins!"

Lara and I roared with laughter at Peter's indignant expression.

"You two think it's funny, don't you?"

"Sorry, Peter," I said. "But it was irresistible to make fun of you for a change, and anyway, who the hell is Jonathan Harris?"

"Who is Jonathan Harris! 'I'm a doctor, not a space explorer!' 'Black was always my color.' Oh, Google him, for Christ's sake!"

"Fair enough. I'll let it go this time... Hey! Did you guys know that the three of us have something truly special in common?"

"Besides being beautiful?" Lara chirped.

"We do, Peter?" I could only imagine what it was.

"We're all former in-laws. Mark used to be married to my sister and I was Lara's brother's boyfriend. That makes us relatives!" He was three sheets to the wind now and began to hug and kiss us.

"That's true. We have that in common," I said.

"What are you two going to do this weekend?" Lara asked out of the blue.

Whatever you want to do, I thought. "No idea," I said.

"Me?" Peter shrugged. "I'll probably do a *Godfather* marathon. I'm single. I'll console myself with Corleone Junior."

"Peter...again? That would have to be the tenth time this year. You've lost your marbles," Lara said.

"Hey! What I eva done to make you treat me so disrespectfully?" Peter blurted, imitating Don Corleone.

Lara suddenly raised a finger. "I have an idea! Let's get on a plane and go to Disney World! We can be there in two hours, and all the rides will be waiting for us!"

She was as excited as a little kid about the idea. I saw a side of her I'd seen only on the day I'd met her. The smile that could bend anyone to her will. The mischievous look. The happy child who still lived within her. I'd have done anything to see that side more often.

"I'm in!" I exclaimed. "How about you, Peter?"

"Michael or Mickey? Mickey, of course! Let's spend the weekend laughing. If it all goes wrong, I'll end up in Goofy's arms."

* * * * *

And so, the three of us went to Disney World. It was one of the best weekends of my life. Lara turned into a lighthearted child. She laughed at everything. She wanted to go on all the rides and I discovered she was crazy about roller coasters. She'd get off one and jump onto another. Fortunately, the lines were shorter that time of year. It was hilarious to watch her screaming hysterically on Splash Mountain. At the end of each ride, she'd be soaked and smiling. She'd happily lost all sense of past and future there.

If I wasn't already in love with Lara, I fell for her forever at that moment. She'd become a little girl before my very eyes. You should have seen her with two big ears on her head being photographed with Minnie Mouse.

Peter was fantastic company too. He clowned around and laughed at everything. And he thoughtfully disappeared at day's end, claiming he had a date with someone he met in line at It's a Small World. He'd gone there by himself because Lara and I chose not to. We were too tired and hungry.

Sex that weekend was atypically soft and sweet. All the excitement and the walking had worn us out. Still, I felt light and happy. I was in love and felt closer to Lara than ever before. It was a weekend to remember. I forgot about normal life. I forgot I was a respectable lawyer.

* * * * *

When we got back to New York, I hoped Lara would come to my apartment or invite me to hers.

But she kissed me lightly on the mouth and asked, "Will you drop me at my place?"

"Certainly," I said.

I was hurt but didn't let on. A perfect weekend and suddenly nothing more. So close and yet so far away. But I'd come to understand you didn't ask Lara the whys and wherefores of her decisions. You just respected her. And in time, she taught me that I too had the right not to have to explain. I too had the right to live more in line with my own wishes and less in line with the expectations of others.

She taught me to be looser and more carefree, to go with the flow. I began giving myself permission to not attend events that didn't interest me, to live life as I pleased. Lara's lessons always had an upside, the side of being free.

She loved to be free. Freedom was everything to her. She'd do anything not to be caged. By grasping that, I began to grasp her. I learned to leave the door open, so my bird of paradise could come and go as she wished. And she always returned. That was enough for the time being. Maybe the idea of marriage was wrong. Maybe a healthy relationship wasn't an eternal "Good morning... Good night" but rather a "Hello, I missed you. It seemed like a mighty long time".

Mark's Journal — Oh, No! Mommy Again.

Lara phoned and asked if she could come. She was neurotic about not dropping in unannounced on others. She was equally neurotic about others not doing the same to her. She always called first and expected others to do so too.

She was tense and nervous when she arrived. I gave her a big hug but she quickly slipped away and went to the window. She opened it as if she needed air and stood there awhile, looking outside. I usually didn't ask a lot of questions when she acted like this and gave her time. At last, she turned and looked at me. Then I spoke to her.

"What's going on, Lara?"

"Can I have a drink? I need one because I have to tell you about another tragedy. I think I'll appoint you the depository of Lara's tragedies."

"Bad day?"

"Bad life!"

I poured her a whisky, handed her the glass and said, "Speak to me."

"Okay. Debbie called."

"Who's Debbie?"

"My sister."

"Oh. You told me her name once but I didn't remember. Excuse me."

"That's all right. Sabine called her. Debbie's a fragile little thing and she decided to see Sabine after that asshole persuaded her it was important."

"Your mother? What did she want?"

"To try to get Debbie to feel sorry for her...and she succeeded. She said she's dying of cancer!"

"Is it true?"

"You never know with Sabine. But I don't think we could be that lucky."

"You said that to your sister?"

"I did. And she got really annoyed. She said she didn't understand. She said no one had ever spoken to her about our mother. Sabine wants to see her granddaughters and says she's full of regret."

"Your sister doesn't know about what happened to you?"

"Worse than that. We decided not to tell her. Debbie's always been the easygoing type. She doesn't ask questions. We told her the fucking bitch had left us for the senator and Debbie was devastated. But she accepted it. She was little at the time. As for Sabine...well, she never cared about kids. So now, here comes the cunt with this bullshit about dying, with a complete motherfucker story, and I don't know what to do!"

When Lara was irritated, her vocabulary turned vulgar. I could only guess where she had learned those kinds of words...

"Want advice?" I'd learned from having listened to Lara's story that it was better to ask first before opening my mouth.

"Yes! Because I'm worried. That monster wants to get close to Debbie and my little sister has young daughters. I'm afraid she'll dump them on the market the way she did to me. Besides, I don't want that sack of shit in our lives again! Please understand me, Mark. Whenever I'm forced to look at that fucking bitch, *everything* comes back to me!"

I motioned for her to come and sit next to me before she wore a hole in the rug from striding back and forth so much. She sat down, gripping her glass with both hands.

"Go talk to your sister. Tell her the *whole* story. In detail! She has the right to know why you feel the way you do. Your statements and behavior where your mother is concerned won't make sense to Debbie, otherwise. You're a warm and loving person. You'd never turn your back on someone who's terminally ill." The time I'd spent with Lara had shown me her compassion for the needy, for sick animals, for friends in difficulty. There was nothing cold or callous about her. In fact, her suffering was the product of extreme sensitivity.

"Why do you think I should do that?"

"Because if you don't, your sister will never understand. Sabine will be back, big time, and don't doubt for one split second that she'll turn herself into grandmother of the year."

"God! Just when I thought I'd put all that behind me, I have to relive it again. But what you're saying makes sense." She covered her face with her hands. "I don't know if I have the strength."

"Only you can decide that. But if you can, I think it's the best thing to do. You should get your therapist's opinion."

"I've already spoken to him. He said the same thing you did."

"And what about your brother? Does he know the story? I think you should talk to him too."

"He doesn't know either. There was a big age difference between us. Sean was only eight when my parents split up. There was no way to tell him then. I think deep down he suspects something more was going on. It was a very sensitive subject and my father and I didn't want to talk about it."

"I understand that, Lara. But I think with the passing of time, and without knowing the truth, it's only natural for your brother and sister to want to see their mother again. They have no concrete reasons to hate her. Is your father still alive?"

"No."

"There it is. His death has left a vacuum for your repentant mother to fill. Besides that, they think the problem was between your father and mother. The kids didn't get divorced. She didn't mistreat them, did she?"

"Just wasn't around much. She'd see them for a few moments when they were scrubbed and shiny. As she used to say, quality time was better than quantity time. That meant do everything you can do with your kids in fifteen minutes a day."

"Fifteen minutes?"

"Oh yeah! Sometimes, she didn't see us at all. But weekends we were The Brady Bunch— everybody brushed and bushy-tailed for the portrait of the perfect family."

"Okay. So there are no real bonds of affection. But from what you're telling me, you're close to your brother and sister. What were you like around them?"

"I wore the mask of the happy, smart and carefree sister. They always looked up to me. I never let them see my dark side. I learned early on to masquerade, Mark."

"Does it still hurt much to think about what you went through?"

"I think it will always hurt. It's as if there's a rupture inside me. I try to forget but something always comes back to haunt me."

"What's the pain like? Do you want to talk about it?"

"It's a deep sensation of loneliness. Not the kind a person feels when they've lost someone close to them. It's the kind a person feels when they've lost a piece of themselves. It's not easy to explain. It seems I'm always incomplete. I look all around to try to fill that void but I can't. And whenever I try to be happy, the Sabines come out of nowhere, the images. And there's that hunger inside me I can never satisfy."

"Can you identify that hunger?"

"Hunger for the part of me I lost. My best part. My innocence. But I'm gonna hammer that woman!"

The way Lara refused to put up with pain for long impressed me. It was there, clear and palpable and very near the surface, but when it became too much to bear she'd put on her mask and the lost child would vanish, giving way to a strong and determined woman.

"You're right, Mark. I'll call them. I'll set up a meeting with them. It's the best thing to do. Maybe I can exorcize my demons once and for all."

She grabbed the purse she'd tossed onto a chair and headed for the door.

"Can't you stay for dinner? Nobody fries an egg like I do."

"No, not today. Even though the egg's tempting." She winked at me. "I'm going home to clear my head and do some serious thinking. But you're right, Mark. I just need courage."

Lara ended up disappearing for a few days and afterward returned to report she'd spoken to her brother and sister. An urgent appeal to Sean had brought him up from Texas. The three of them had sat down together. The meeting had been excruciating.

"Almost *opéra bouffe*," Lara said.

The sincerity of her account made her brother and sister decide to keep their distance from Sabine. They agreed to repel her advances and her sudden surge of maternal love. Lara had emerged victorious. But she was emotionally drained. She needed to escape to Paris. She called me and I thought, *there she goes for a couple more weeks*. But before the gloom could descend she gave me the good news. She wanted my company!

I did what I would never have done before. I postponed hearings and canceled meetings. I took a short leave from my classes. I packed up and went to Paris. For once in my life, I acted on the spur of the moment!

Chapter Thirteen

Present Day – Simone

Simone didn't feel tired. The text she'd been reading was absorbing. Had it been a novel, it would have been a bestseller, a page-turner. She'd forgotten life, food, rest. It was almost midnight and there she sat, curled up in her favorite chair with a glass of wine and a growling stomach.

Finally, she wondered what there was to eat. She went to her kitchen and opened the fridge to find the unappealing macaroni and olives salad Lola had left. Simone ransacked her cupboards for a quick fix and came up with popcorn. She microwaved it, filled her glass again and went back to reading. *A bit more,* she thought. *Just a few more pages.*

Mark's Journal – Paris

Lara loved Paris. She told me that despite everything she'd been through with the senator's son, she'd loved it ever since she'd first set foot there at the age of eight, with her grandmother.

For Lara, Paris was a magical refuge. Whenever she needed to find her center she headed there to the hideaway she'd inherited from her grandmother.

I'd been to Paris only one other time and I hadn't seen much. I'd gone there to represent a client at an International Chamber of Commerce arbitration hearing. The impression I'd gotten was of an old city full of grumpy people who ate raw duck. I didn't grasp the nature of the place. So my memories were very different from Lara's.

I went to Paris with her only because I knew a week with her would be like spending a week in paradise. I'd have gone to Mars if that was where she wanted to go. I also knew she needed a break after her recent family travails.

From the moment we arrived, Lara's fluency in French astounded me. My vocabulary consisted of *bonjour*, *merci* and *au revoir*. Lara communicated perfectly. Of course, my notion of perfection was speaking rapidly and being understood.

The vision of the Eiffel Tower was surreal. As we moved closer to our destination, it increasingly blurred everything else.

"*La vieille dame!*" Lara murmured reverently.

"What?"

"The old lady." She pointed toward it. "Whenever I see it, I know I've come home."

"Paris is home to you?"

"Paris was a tough row to hoe. But it was also Emma, who was half French. That makes me an eighth!"

"I didn't know that! I thought you were Italian!"

"Why?"

"Your hands are always moving!"

She squeezed my nose.

"Ouch!"

We reached the building where Lara had her hideaway. She informed me proudly that the edifice was two hundred years old. I'd never been big on old things. But as soon as she opened the great iron door on the rue Saint-Dominique by punching a combination into a keypad, the atmosphere of the buildings and the interior courtyard knocked me out.

Almost all the older structures in France were made of sandstone blocks, and for being two hundred years old they were very well preserved. Lara's building was U-shaped with a beautiful interior courtyard. I needed to lug my suitcase across the courtyard because the taxi had left us on the sidewalk. Lara explained that because the whole place was a historic preservation site, vehicles were barred from entering it.

Luckily for me, Lara had brought just one piece of hand luggage. She told me she kept clothes in the hideaway. Fantastic! A woman who didn't take the whole house with her when she traveled.

There were three entrances to the building, one on each side of the U. Lara's was the middle one. She typed another combination that opened another iron door and we stepped inside the building itself.

"Those two-hundred-year-old keypads look pretty modern to me," I joked.

"Smartass." She shoved me gently. "They're no more than ten."

"And I thought French technology was advanced."

"France will make you swoon yet, silly. Get in that elevator."

The thing was bizarre. It looked like a jail cell hanging in a stairwell. My suitcase and I, or Lara, could fit inside if I avoided breathing.

"Fifth floor, Mark. I'll meet you there."

She gave me her piece of hand luggage, shut me in the calaboose and turned to run up a set of stairs. Apparently, she still hadn't realized I was a gentleman.

When I caught up with her, she was panting and rummaging through her handbag for the key to her door. She finally got it open and we went inside. The tiny apartment struck me as a merry pencil box with multi-colored pencils. Enormous windows with transparent curtains let in the sun.

The dollhouse-sized kitchen was green and tucked into a nook. It had a microwave, a cabinet with three doors above the sink and three below, and two hotplates. I also noticed a single machine that functioned as both a washer and a dryer squeezed in there too. Talk about economic space utilization!

The living room was walled with shelves bulging with books. There were two ancient, orange-upholstered chairs with an even older trunk between them, along with a few lamps. A comfy blue sofa sat against one wall, facing a small fireplace.

Though cramped, the hideaway had gorgeous decor that showed excellent taste. Colored carpets lay on the floor. Cushions of various sizes were strewn here and there. The whole scene displayed Lara's talent for turning a small space into a cozy, chic and captivating abode.

There was even a modern bathroom—except for the antique, claw-foot bathtub—and a bedroom.

"Your apartment is splendid!"

"Say it this way, Mark—*a-part-a-mahn*."

"Okay. Peter would love to purse his lips like that."

"Delighted you approve. Come over here and check this out!"

She opened a window onto a wrought iron Romeo and Juliet balcony and proudly introduced me to the view. I could see the Eiffel Tower, or rather, about a third of it.

"I'll be damned! Your very own piece of the Eiffel Tower!"

"I'm so happy here!"

Her smile radiated joy. I could not have been more pleased that she was sharing her little piece of paradise with me. At that moment, I came to love Paris as seen through Lara's eyes, and I loved her even more.

Lara had me sample the dishes the City of Lights had to offer. She warned me that prejudice had no place at its tables.

"You can't dislike what you've never tried," she said. "That's ignorance. So taste and dislike or taste and adore. But taste!" That was her philosophy.

She took me to a traditional restaurant called *La Fontaine de Mars* on the same street as the apartment. After she ordered, she told me I wouldn't be trying anything too risky on our first day. When the entrées arrived I saw a little plate with six little round holes and something dark covered with olive oil and herbs. God alone knew what awaited me there.

"What's this, Lara?"

"Take the plunge. If you don't like it, I'll order something else for you."

"Without knowing what it is?"

"Perish the prejudice."

She picked up a tiny fork, speared something that looked like rubber and popped it in her mouth. At that moment, I began to suspect it was escargot. I'd never had the courage to try it before. But I braced myself and decided to go for it, especially after seeing Lara's reaction.

She closed hers eyes and chewed slowly. Then she opened her eyes and exclaimed, "God exists! He does!" And she'd told me she was agnostic.

I followed her lead and was astonished at the heavenly flavors I found in that morsel. The herbs. The butter. Exotic. Mysterious. I loved it.

"This is great, Lara! I've seen escargot before but passed on it. I never dreamed it could be so good."

Lara had chosen a bottle of Sauterne to accompany the escargot. It was slightly sweet, made from grapes that were collected at just the right time, almost raisins. If time had stopped then and there, the moment would have been perfect. I had the best company in the world and food and wine of the gods.

The second course was *confit de canard*. Lara said it was a duck thigh cooked for hours in its own fat with a thick, dark, sweet sauce. Cubed potatoes cooked to a golden brown accompanied it. Absolutely delectable.

Each subsequent dish was accompanied by an excellent wine that Lara selected.

"Eating like this, how do the French stay so thin?"

"I think people walk more here. That compensates for all the fat and butter in their diet." She broke a piece of bread, soaked up some sauce and put it in her mouth. Then she went on. "They also eat a lot of bread."

During the following days, we took in the sights, including museums and expositions. Lara dragged me all over town, mostly on foot. She believed that was the best way to get the feel of a place. Occasionally, we rode the metro. Lara said it would be impossible to see everything if we used a car, or rather, half a car, because she had a convertible Smart car. I don´t know how we fit in there but at night, we used it.

As you explore Paris, you start to think of it as a gift that has been specially wrapped to delight all your senses. Art is everywhere. The food is divine. I was always savoring something new. Lara found cause for laughter wherever we went. I fell in love with the city.

Lara was loose, happy and carefree. We slept in each other's arms. And when we made love, it was in bed.

On Thursday, three days before flying home, we walked around less. Lara wanted to do some shopping for a client's apartment. She also told me she had something to show me that night.

In the evening, she put on a black dress that instantly gave me a hard-on. Her back was bare to the point of revealing a tiny moon tattoo at the base of her spine, just above her derrière. She wore high-heeled boots, dark, smoky makeup and her usual perfume. I wanted to devour her right there in the living room. But she insisted we go out.

She asked me to dress casually in slacks, a shirt and a blazer. There I was, all set for one more adventure with my sorceress of surprises.

We caught a taxi. The driver could hardly speak French-there are many foreigners driving cabs in France, many of whom can barely speak the language. I felt right at home as Lara guided him to our destination. If daytime in Paris is spectacular, nighttime is like a hallucination. Bright lights and romance rule the city. It's like a gigantic Christmas tree.

We headed for the second arrondissement, a neighborhood not far from the opera, and stopped at a private club called *Le Mask*. Lara said something to the greeters and they let us enter. We paid the cover charge and picked out masks, which concealed half our faces. The atmosphere was sensual to the extreme. Lara's black lace mask lent glamor to her features. Her greenish-blue eyes glittered and her lips were a scandalous scarlet.

Another swing house. No doubt about it. A masked man approached Lara and, as she translated, explained the house rules. You couldn't be naked at the bar. Everything else was fine. As we walked across a dance floor, Lara pointed upward to the transparent glass roof high above us. It was easy to see that the people on the mezzanine were naked. The sight turned me on. Lara looked at me as if seeking approval, and I nodded. I was ready to try anything with her.

We sat down on a soft velvet couch. Lara asked what I wanted to drink. Domestic champagne, of course!

The waiter filled our glasses with *Veuve Clicquot*. Lara took a healthy sip and shared it with me as she kissed me. That was one of the most erotic acts I'd ever experienced. A drop ran down my chin and she licked it, slowly.

The woman was bent on making a maniac out of me. The only thing I could think of was fucking her. She always came up with something new that made me want her even more.

We drank half a bottle. Then Lara took me by the hand and led me to a locker room like the ones they have in schools. I took off my clothes and stashed them. She slipped off her dress but left her boots on. She wasn't wearing panties.

I had a bolt-upright boner, which made me happy. I would have been embarrassed to walk around the place dangling a wet noodle. Not being able to get it up is most men's nightmare. And in that regard, at least, I'm like most men.

We went into a room where absolutely everyone was naked. I'd never seen that before. There were beautiful bodies and not so beautiful bodies, but one and all appeared uninhibited. I was having fun. The scene was so erotic that my penis bobbed and throbbed. Whatever shame I might have felt left me to be replaced by total desire.

As we made our way through all that skin, hands ran all over my body. Now a "veteran" of that game, I reciprocated. A man with the kind of body that would shame Adonis began to feel up Lara. Jealousy seized me.

Lara must have noticed because she softly said, "Mark, relax. It's only pleasure. I'm not going home with him."

Then she drew closer to the man and planted kisses on his neck. He took her buttocks in his hands. I didn't know what to do until Lara included me in the festivities. She backed up to me and I took her breasts in my hands. Though jealousy tortured me, my lust was even greater. I couldn't think straight. This was high-voltage eroticism.

We went to a couch in a corner. Condom dispensers hung on the wall. Lara gave one raincoat to me and one to Adonis. We put them on and Lara began to suck his erection. I was behind her and had no doubt what to do then. I drove it home. It was the first time I'd had anal sex with her. I didn't care if she liked it or not. I felt hatred and my hammering hard-on at the same time.

Lara began to moan, enjoying my penetration or maybe the Frenchman, who was licking her now — or probably both. Then she positioned herself on top of him to welcome his superman´s cock into her pussy. He was saying something in French. He injected his and I jammed mine in deeper. I could feel the three of us breathing almost in sync. I think we all came in less than five minutes. Impossible to say. It was the most hardcore sex I'd ever had.

When we finished fucking, Adonis kissed Lara on the cheek. She wouldn't let him kiss her on the mouth. We untangled ourselves. He went his way, and Lara and I went to the bar. I was silent. I couldn't understand what had happened. I'd just let the woman I love chew and screw another man before my very eyes. I'd taken part and had had the greatest pleasure anyone could possibly feel. I was going stark-raving mad.

We ordered a drink. My head was flying off my shoulders. We were seated at a counter. Lara didn't speak, either. She sipped her drink. Her eyes flamed like those of a beast that had just spotted the perfect prey.

She finally took my hand and said, "Come with me, Mark. Payback time!"

We approached a petite woman wearing a red mask. She must have been five inches shorter than Lara and had brown hair and light eyes. In the penumbra I couldn't tell what color they were. She appeared to be quite young, no more than twenty-five. Her body was perfect with small, firm breasts.

"I have a present for you, Mark."

Lara then whispered something in the woman's ear and nodded toward me. The little lady stood looking at me like someone admiring a pair of shoes in a store window. To my good fortune, she nodded her consent. She moved closer to me and stared into my eyes. Her eyes were blue, she-devil Babaloo blue.

Allo, Marrrk!" she greeted me, with an absolutely French "r".

I had no idea how she knew my name but it didn't matter.

She ran her long fingernails across my chest and when I placed my hands on her breasts, she moaned. She kept looking into my eyes as she slowly got to her knees. She fondled my balls, rubbed my dick and took it into her mouth. Lara approached and slipped her index finger into my mouth. Then she tongue-kissed me. I almost shot my wad down the French girl's throat. *Ménage à trois*! I'd almost gotten there with Lara and that redhead she'd chased away. Now my dream was going to come true.

The two sirens led me to a sort of bed. I lay down on my back, put on a condom and the petite woman mounted me and began to ride. Lara sat on my face. The height of the erotic. One woman fucking me and another's smoldering muff on my mouth, a muff that had just had another man's cock inside it. I don't know how long we did that. The two of them came. I held off longer to enjoy it more.

Lara lay down beside me and asked me to fuck her. She grabbed the French girl by the hair and made her lick her while I screwed her. She was eating Lara and licking me at the same time. When it was all over, my head went spinning down, down, down into a bottomless whirlpool. The French girl kissed Lara on the mouth and then left us. We were alone.

Lara looked at me and asked, "Had enough or do you want more?"

The whole experience had made me slip my moorings. I'd seen Lara doing it with another man. I'd pooned another woman. Naked bodies. Too much champagne. I pinned Lara against the nearest wall, put my hand around her neck and started to squeeze.

"That's it, Mark! Hate me! It makes me so horny! So horny! Squeeze my neck hard! Hard!"

I squeezed it hard and jammed my cock into her. No condom. No nothing. Just brute force. I wanted to hurt her the way she'd hurt me by making me share her with another man. I shoved it in deep, up to the hilt. That goddamn woman! Instead of whimpering like other bitches would, she howled with pleasure. And the harder I squeezed her neck, the more she enjoyed it.

We both calmed down when we finished. We rode home in complete silence. She cuddled up to me and slept on the way. My eyes remained wide open as I tried to make sense of the hatred inside me.

The following day, Lara didn't go anywhere near the subject and neither did I. I didn't feel up to it. I kept telling myself I was the one who'd ended up spending the night in Lara's arms. But my old-fashioned mind tormented me. I felt cheated. I felt ashamed for having allowed it to happen. I tried to console myself with the memory of the hot sex I'd had with the French girl. Lara went back to being herself as she always did after seismic sex. That helped me relax, have fun and experiment, not plan or make judgments based on my traditional view of the world. At least while I was in her company.

Just when I thought all of the Paris surprise packages had been opened she handed me a beaut. Lara told me she had something to do on Saturday morning and asked me if I wanted to go with her. Naturally, I said I did.

When we arrived at *Parc Monceau* around eleven, three elderly gentlemen awaited us on a bench. They greeted Lara joyfully and she introduced them as Grandmother Emma's longtime, dear friends, the three musketeers. Lara had inherited them upon Emma's death.

Hervé, Théophile and Maurice were very *sympathique*. They all more or less spoke English with an extra dose of the Gallic "r" but I understood them fine. We went to a nearby restaurant and the mood over lunch was merry. The old boys were loquacious and full of fun. We enjoyed a traditional ratatouille, a delicious vegetable stew.

"Mark, *vous avec de la chance*! Mark, you're lucky!" Hervé translated. "Lara is an enchanting girl. She takes after her grandmother."

"Emma was even more beautiful." Théophile sighed.

"As beautiful as Lara and just as enchanting," said Maurice.

"From what I see, you were all great friends of Lara's grandmother."

"Ah, yes. Emma was the most fantastic woman I've even known." Théophile sighed again.

"Théo," I said, addressing him by the name he'd insisted I use when we were first introduced, "it sounds as if you were in love with her."

"We all were," Maurice said.

"All of you? And you're still friends? No question about it?"

"Of course not. Emma belonged to no one. She belonged to the world and we were privileged to know her. She taught us much about *joie de vivre*."

"This girl here inherited a lot from Emma, except her height," Hervé said as he caressed Lara's hair. "Emma was this size." He held out his hand to show how short Emma had been. "You must be special, Mark. Lara has never brought anyone to meet us before."

That bit of news made me forget all about *Le Mask*, betrayals and conflicting feelings. I was filled with the sensation of being unique that everyone in love feels when someone tells him the object of his affection does something with him and him alone.

"My friends, Mark is indeed special," Lara said and smiled at me tenderly.

Ask me to jump off the Eiffel Tower and I'll do it right now, I thought.

"Mark, take good care of Lara or you'll soon see the three musketeers in action," Maurice admonished me with a raised finger.

I have a fertile imagination. I envisioned those three creaky senior citizens with capes and swords and I had to smile.

As we took our leave after lunch, Lara promised to see them again soon. We returned to the *Parc Monceau* and sat down on a bench near the *Colonnade* just to watch the world go by. Priceless moments of intimacy.

"Do you visit them every time you come to France?" I asked.

"I do. I always make time for them. They're part of what remains of Emma."

"She was very important to you, wasn't she?"

"She was my safe haven in the middle of a storm. She made sense of everything I went through and showed me how to plant my feet on the ground."

"She helped you after the…episode." I didn't know how else to put it.

"Yes. She always came to my rescue. When we moved to New York she all but moved in with us. She had an apartment there she kept for her *escapades*. But she began to supervise and take care of us."

"Were you close to her before that?"

"She hated my mother and had distanced herself. She said she didn't want my father to feel she was always looking over his shoulder. She respected his choices but she was the one who introduced me to Paris when I was eight. She wanted to teach me about art and beauty. I always loved her."

"She must have been a very wise woman."

"That she was. Wise. Crazy. Sweet. All that in just one person."

"Did she know what happened to you?" I looked at her, seeking approval to pursue the subject.

"My mother had made a point of keeping my *studies* in Paris a secret. I think she believed Emma might go there and unmask her. When my father found out about it, he told Emma. I was unable to talk about it. As you well know, I still find it hard. Back then, it was very recent and I was a tangle of fear, insecurity and guilt."

"Guilt?"

"Guilt. I felt dirty. I was always wondering why I'd gotten myself into that situation. My childish efforts to turn the head of a much older man had made me his plaything for almost four years and had destroyed my family."

"My God, Lara. You were a little girl. How could you be guilty?"

"That sick relationship had given me pleasure, Mark. The sex gave me pleasure. The stay in Paris gave me pleasure. I felt horrible. I felt unclean. My father was left without a wife and with a problem daughter on his hands. My brother and sister were motherless. We lost our childhood home and with it our friends. I felt I was the cause of all of it."

"You weren't guilty of anything, Lara. Your mother betrayed your father. She sold you to that piece of shit. How could you possibly have been guilty?"

"Because…if all that were true and I wasn't guilty, then why did I enjoy having sex with him when I despised him? I *did* enjoy the sex. All of it."

"Because sex is good!"

"Yes, it is. Very good. But then Emma came along. Unlike my mother, who never would stop to have a serious conversation about it, Emma began to talk to me. She explained the facts of life. She made me understand that sex and feelings don't necessarily walk in lockstep. She told me sex is a physical need and doesn't have to be tied to emotions. One time, she said, 'Sex, Lara, is good. Even when it's bad. But the thing is that when you do it with people you don't feel anything for, they should turn to dust and the wind should carry them away after they give you an orgasm.' Emma was right."

"Emma was wonderful. She was very progressive for a grandmother, wasn't she?"

"She was young in spirit, a free spirit. She dated, traveled, had countless interests and talents, danced the tango, loved to dance in general, was an accomplished astrologer, spoke several languages, painted and told stories. She was fantastic. Emma had tons of fans and friends. All our friends who came to our house loved to be around her, to listen to her stories and her advice."

"It seems she was like the mother a lot of people would want to have."

"More than that. She was the heart and soul of the family. My father went to her for comfort. My brother told her about the strange feelings he had for men. She helped him confront and accept his sexual orientation and come out of the closet. My sister wanted to be a little girl, play house, have children and be happy that way. Emma gave her love and support. For me...she made the world make sense."

"Do you miss her a lot?"

"Every day. She's been gone for almost five years now..." Lara said emphatically, eyes full of tears. "Losing her was a disaster for me. I held myself together only by remembering what she had taught me. At the end, she was very ill and she prepared me for her departure. She was cremated. We all came to Paris to toss her ashes off the top of the Eiffel Tower, just as she wished. She wanted the wind to take her in a thousand directions, she said. Since she couldn't be everywhere in life, she wanted to accomplish that feat in death."

"I think you have a lot of her in you. That free spirit."

"I do. But I have my monsters in the closet. Emma didn't. She didn't believe in the past. She believed in today. She always said yesterday's gone and we don't know if tomorrow will come. Only today matters. She had no bones to pick with the past. Everything was settled."

"And you? Any bones to pick?"

"Several. I didn't inherit Emma's peace of mind. I'm very bitter sometimes and I have thorny unresolved issues."

"If I were you, I would feel the same way."

"Really, Mark? You seem so centered. Everything by the book. Orderly life. Successful career. Your parents must be proud of you."

"My father is. My mother died when I was two and I never had an Emma."

"I didn't know that! Did your father remarry?"

"Worse than that. I think he loved my mother with the kind of love they don't make anymore. He never wanted anyone to take her place. He raised me by himself."

"So, my dear friend, mothers are not our strong suit."

She moved her chair close to me and put her head on my shoulder. And we sat there, just passing time in complete harmony.

Chapter Fourteen

Present Day — Simone

Saturday finally arrived. Carl called Simone in the morning and suggested a change of plans. He'd get to town about four. They'd discuss the case and then go out to dinner. She readily agreed and told him they could talk at her office. She told herself that at least part of the time during their meeting she should behave professionally, despite the sexy jeans she planned to wear.

Carl showed up a bit later than expected at Simone's office. He'd driven up. He said he liked to drive. He explained he'd gone to lunch with his friend Peter and hadn't been able to break away sooner. Simone opened the door for him, as she was the only one there today, and he gave his hand to greet her in a very formal way but then moved close and kissed her on the cheek. *A promising start,* she thought.

"Wonderful to see you, Simone. Please excuse my impatience to talk to you before you finish the material. But I really need to understand things better. This case is driving me nuts."

Simone made a mental note about his lack of compliments such as, "You're looking very pretty" and so on. That indicated a certain absence of personal interest. Oh well. Another man attracted only by her intellect. The thought pained her.

"As I told you on the phone, Carl, I still don't have any definite conclusions. I've read up to where Lara and Mark go to Paris and I can tell you what I've got so far. But please bear in mind it might change by the time I've reached the end."

"Great. Perfect. I *need* that." He rubbed his hands together.

That's understandable, Simone reflected. Carl was dealing with an ethical question. He was defending someone who was either innocent or guilty. But even for an experienced lawyer, defending someone innocent would have to feel infinitely better than defending someone who was not.

"I'm practically convinced of Mark's innocence," she stated hesitantly. She hated to offer an opinion before finishing a job.

"Practically?"

"Yes. As I said, my beliefs might change."

"Of course."

"He seems to be a man of principle—I might even say rigidly so. Nevertheless, at a certain point he allows himself to be swept along by Lara's behavior. But that's quite normal. Correct and organized people tend to be attracted to those who are anything but, and vice versa. Flaky people tend to seek the equilibrium they lack in the equilibrium of others. This usually doesn't work. They end up leading the others over the cliff."

"Do you think she actually grew to like Mark or was he just someone to lean on?"

"I can't say for sure. But it's clear she felt something for him. Maybe she only appreciated the sense of security he provided. He was always available to her, as far as I can see. But based on what he wrote—and that could be just his perception—it seems to me Lara had feelings for Mark."

"Why was Lara the way she was?"

"What do you mean, specifically?"

"A loose cannon, a wild thing, extremely promiscuous."

"It's a long story. From what I can tell, Lara had a sadomasochistic personality with self-destructive tendencies. She loved danger. Sex with strangers, roller coasters, risky places. It was as if she was unconsciously seeking to be punished for enjoying the abuse she'd suffered in childhood."

"Sadomasochistic personality? You're saying she liked to inflict pain or took pleasure from feeling pain, right? I'm a lawyer, Simone. I hear that term but its meaning is always more complex than it seems."

"Yes. To oversimplify, that's sadomasochistic. People like Lara get pleasure from pain, their own or another's. It's masochism when it's their pain. It's sadism when it's someone else's. But in reality, they're two sides of the same coin."

"The one who causes pain suffers too?"

"Not on purpose. But yes. He or she suffers. Lara suffered in various passages. I think Mark wrote down what he saw. But we have to get beyond his *impression* to see deeper. There's a clear indication that Lara didn't want to be the way she was. And the way she was made her suffer."

"Was there any way for her not to have been the way she was? Did she have a choice?"

"Probably not, Carl. She had a lot of unhealed wounds. She was treated cruelly at an age when her personality was forming. Adolescence is a time of rebellion. But paradoxically, it's also when you want to be part of a group, to be *one of the gang*. Lara neither rebelled nor belonged. She couldn't rebel because she was dominated and blackmailed. She couldn't be part of a group because she was different from everyone else."

"Poor Lara."

"Poor Lara. Poor Mark. He was attracted to a woman who was a lot more than he could handle. He doesn't seem to be sadomasochistic. But he adapted to Lara. He took part in playing out her fantasies to make her happy."

"But he also played out his own."

"Did he? I think it's more likely his one and only fantasy was to have that woman all to himself without her let-it-all-hang-out behavior."

"I'm not so sure about that. He got off on that wildness of hers."

"Fair enough. But we have to bear in mind that his narrative is written just from his point of view. That's why I need to speak to other people who knew Lara. Even Mark himself. It's one thing to put your feelings down on paper. It's quite another to talk about them with someone else who sees your body language. That would provide a more nuanced understanding."

"Certainly. You can speak to whomever you wish. But I'd like you to finish the text and give me your conclusions before you do. Then you can interview other people. Your thoughts will be less biased that way."

"Do you believe what Mark wrote?"

"Yes. Mark's what you say he is. A strictly by-the-rules type. He's no liar. He's very honest."

"I believe it too. But there's still a lot of work to be done. And I agree with you about completing my reading before I approach other people. By the way, to keep myself from being unduly influenced, I haven't looked up anything on the Internet, just as you requested. I'll do that when I'm finished. And Lara. Do you think he gave a faithful description of her?"

"I think he described everything he was able to remember."

"Speaking of which — what a memory!"

"Lawyers."

Carl fell silent. He walked over to the window with his hands in his pockets and a pensive air. Then he turned and said, "What's your initial verdict, Simone?"

"Without having finished? I don't know. I'm not on solid enough ground to say. But I'll give you my impression up to now. As I told you when we began this discussion, I think if there's an innocent party in this story, it's Mark. The unfolding of events makes me believe Lara was lucky not to have been killed while she was still a teenager. Fate dealt her a dead man's hand during her adolescence. It just took a while to happen."

"You believe in Mark. I can see that." Carl looked clearly relieved.

"Up to now."

"You don't see the slightest possibility that he intentionally killed her?"

He stood next to the window, revolving a crystal ball that sat on a side table, the only gesture that showed his uneasiness.

"I can't say that, Carl. There are psychopaths who appear to have Mark's characteristics. They're solid, successful, even family men. Until the day they start to kill. But he hasn't killed again...or has he?"

"No."

"Good. He's not a psycho. When they start, it's hard for them to stop. They just pause for a while and it´s almost impossible to know what will make them start again."

They exchanged ideas for a bit longer, until about six o'clock. As it was too early for dinner, Simone invited Carl for a drink at her house. He accepted and followed her in his black Mercedes.

He parked his car in front of Simone's house while she parked in the garage and they met at the front door. Simone easily found the key where she always kept it, snapped into place inside her neatly organized purse.

"You have a beautiful house, Simone," he said upon stepping through the door.

"Thank you, Carl. Make yourself at home. Take a seat. What are you drinking?"

"A glass of wine, if you have some."

Carl chose her favorite spot on the sofa but she didn't react... She did a mental note to talk to Dr. Edgar about this new obsession of hers...

"Of course. I'm no connoisseur but I have a friend who makes suggestions. I have red and white. Which do you prefer?"

"White."

"I have a Chardonnay Chateau Monthelena. Is that to your taste?"

"Excellent. Your friend knows his stuff. That vineyard's won quite a few prizes."

"Good."

She got the wine from her small wine cooler in the kitchen, opened the bottle slowly as Edward had taught her to do and poured two glasses while silently thanking Edward for the selection. As she approached Carl, goblets in hand, she glanced out the window and saw a yellow taxi parked out front. Had someone come to see her?

"Just a minute, Carl. It seems I may have unexpected visitors."

"Take your time. Mind if I look at your pictures?"

He took a step toward the piano.

"Go ahead."

When Simone opened the door and looked outside, the taxi pulled away. *Wrong address,* she thought and returned to her guest.

They talked for a long time, mainly about the case, before going to eat. As they went out the door, Simone spotted the same taxi, this time across the street in front of the neighbor's house.

Carl asked her for a recommendation on a good restaurant, and they proceeded to Simone's favorite, Alice in Wonderland, a nice contemporary place.

The atmosphere there was romantic, a few well-placed lights, nice tables, well-dressed and friendly staff who knew exactly when to appear and disappear...

They chose a table near a window where, thanks to the outside lighting, they could see a beautiful garden.

They quickly chose the food and wine, and spent the next hour or so making small talk. Carl was very reserved and other than a few personal, irrelevant observations, his remarks were all about the world and nothing about his personal life.

After dinner, to her frustration, Carl took her directly home. He said he had to get back to New York. She'd had high hopes of a more satisfying outcome that night.

She planted herself in front of the TV and promptly dozed off, either because of the wine or her disappointment. She awoke with a start a little later, thinking she'd heard a noise. *Just something on the tube,* she told herself. She clicked off the television and went to bed.

Chapter Fifteen

Present Day - Simone

Simone woke up early that Sunday morning. She went to the side door to see if the newspaper had been delivered. She'd told the paperboy to leave it there. At one time, he'd tossed it into the front yard and the neighbor's dog had peed all over it.

Simone opened the door — and let loose a scream. A naked woman lay inert on the steps. Simone started to shake uncontrollably and the tachycardia she had made her feel as if her heart was outside her chest, so strongly and fast was it beating.

"Breathe!" she told herself, making a supreme effort to calm down. She closed her eyes and sucked in air, filling her lungs and then slowly exhaling. After repeating this several times, she opened her eyes again and glanced down.

"Now you have to check to see if *she's* breathing," she said. "And then you have to call someone."

Gathering her courage, she leaned down and hesitantly placed two shaking fingers over the woman's carotid artery but the moment she touched the woman's cold skin, Simone realized the person lying on her doorstep had probably been dead for a few hours.

Still shaken, Simone found it difficult to walk. Dazed, she made it to the phone and dialed Edward's number.

"Ed? For the love of God!"

"What is it, Simone?"

"There's a dead body lying at my door!"

"What?" he shouted. "What do you mean a body at your door? How did it get there?"

"A body! A naked woman! Dead on my doorstep! Someone put a dead woman at my side door!"

"Don't touch anything. Stay inside the house. I'll call the police and come right over."

"Make it fast, Ed! Fast! I'm terrified! I touched it! It's clammy cold!"

"Try to keep calm. Take a hot shower. I'm on my way."

Edward got there in record time. The police arrived minutes later. They all went and gathered around the body—a young woman who appeared to be about thirty years old. There were no apparent signs of violence except for marks on her neck, suggesting the probable cause of death was strangulation. But there was semen on the body. It looked as if the serial killer had struck again, even though the usual indications of torture were missing.

One of the policemen turned to Simone and said, "Dr. Bennet, we'll need you to come down to the station to make a statement."

Edward addressed him before Simone could reply.

"Carlo, could we do it tomorrow? Simone's just had a severe shock. I promise I'll take her there first thing in the morning."

Carlo hesitated a moment and then gave his okay, and a few minutes later, an ambulance arrived to take the body to the morgue.

"Officer, is there some way to have the press stay out of this?" Simone asked. "I don't want my name involved with a possible serial killing."

"It will be nearly impossible to keep the press from finding out about this but I think we can manage to at least keep your name and your address out of the news. So far, we've been able to do that with the other peripheral victims in this case," Carlo replied. "We're doing our best to keep things under wraps until we get more leads. We'll be running two risks with too much media coverage—either the killer will be scared off and start killing somewhere else and we'll lose track of him. Or he'll get the attention he may be craving and kill more often."

"I understand. I appreciate anything you can do. Thank you, Officer."

Carlo nodded. "Try to relax, Dr. Bennet. I know it won't be easy." Turning to Edward, he continued. "Are you going to stay with Dr. Bennet? If not, I'll leave one of my men here. I'm worried."

"I'm staying and I'll let you know if anything happens. I brought my gun. I'm worried too. Simone made the connection between the crimes and the TV series she was watching. It looks as if the killer wanted to send her a message."

"If that's so, Ed, it's bad news. It means there might be a killer among us. Only the police, you and Dr. Bennet knew about the tie-in with the series."

"Christ! That hadn't occurred to me, Carlo. We have to find out where the leak is."

The police left and Simone and Edward went inside.

"What do you think, Ed? Could it be someone close to us? A cop?"

"I don't know. Maybe, maybe not. We discuss the case on the phone. Somebody could be listening. I don't even want to think about a cop being involved. Cops have access to all kinds of weapons. Our killer hasn't used any firearms…so far."

"Do you think that body was a message to keep me quiet?"

"Too soon to say. But you did find it a few days after you connected the dots between the killer and the TV series. Hey. Does the body on the steps have anything to do with an episode you've seen?"

"Not that I can remember. But there are two episodes I haven't seen yet."

"It certainly seems to be a message. Anyway, c'mon. I'll make us breakfast. How ya doin'?"

"Feeling first-hand how it is to be traumatized for life. I don't think I'll ever open that door again without expecting to find a body."

Edward put his arm around her shoulders. "Take it easy. This'll pass. We're lucky our training has given us mechanisms to help us cope with things like this. If it gets too much to handle, I'll try hypnosis on you. We'll face this together. I'm here for you."

"Thanks, Ed." She leaned her head on his chest. It comforted her to have such a friend at her side. "For the life of me, I don't know how you can work with the police…having to see all those corpses. I had a hard time dealing with the cadavers in med school. That's why I never wanted to be a surgeon."

"I don't see that many in person; I usually just review the crime scene photos. But whenever I work on a heinous crime I remember that it might go unsolved if I don't help, so it makes me feel better. I think trying to do good comes naturally to human beings and counteracts the dark side of life. You'll get over this, my friend. I used to have nightmares when I first started helping the police. They pass after a while."

"Time heals everything," Simone said. "In mythology, Saturn, the god of time, ate his own children."

"That's the greatest of all truths. Nothing like time. Don't forget that."

"I won't. We can eat after I take a shower, okay?"

"Sure. I'll get things ready."

* * * * *

The day flew by. Edward kept Simone company and refused to leave her by herself. He took her to his apartment, where she spent the night. In the morning, they went to the police station to make their statements.

Simone had never been to her local police department and the atmosphere inside the building was strangely calmer than she expected—maybe because it was still early in the morning, she thought.

Carlo met Simone and Edward and accompanied them to a small interview room. The walls in the little room were painted a stark white, and there were no pictures or other frivolous décor…just a small, plain brown desk with a computer and some very uncomfortable chairs around it. Carlo pointed to the chairs, indicating they should take a seat, and he went around and sat behind the desk. After fiddling with the computer keyboard for a moment, Carlo told them the woman had been killed at around eight o'clock Saturday night. The Glaister equation, which calculates how fast a body's temperature drops after death, had helped them to reach that conclusion.

"Dr. Bennet, I need to ask you some questions here. Where were you at eight o'clock that night?"

"Having dinner with a client, Detective."

"Can he verify that?"

"Why? Am I a suspect now?" She pointed at herself. "Remember, Officer, I'm a woman. There was semen on the body."

"No, Doctor. It's simply a question." He gave a quick shake of his head. "Do you think your client would verify your whereabouts?"

"I'm sure he can. But I don't wish to involve him. As I said, he's a client. I'm working on something for him and he came up from New York to talk to me. Besides, there were a lot of people in the restaurant who can vouch for me without inconveniencing him."

"I didn't know your client was in town," Edward remarked with surprise in his voice.

"He was here for a few hours," Simone answered quickly.

"Did he spend much time with you, Doctor?" Carlo asked.

"Yes. We spoke for a while at my office, had some wine at my house and then went to dinner."

"What time did you get home that night?"

"About eleven."

"And your client?"

"He drove back to the city."

"Maybe we will have to talk to your client.

"I must insist you only disturb my client as a last resort. He is a lawyer and I'm positive he is not going to like being interrogated by the police!"

"I will do my best, Dr. Bennet. Did you notice anything strange that night, Doctor, or hear any strange noises?"

"No. I didn't see or hear anything out of the ordinary. But the side door isn't visible from the street."

"Think hard, Doctor. What you can remember?"

"Oh, wait a minute. On second thought, there was something. I fell asleep in front of the TV and a noise woke me up about midnight. But I thought it had come from the TV."

Carlo nodded and said, "We're going to run tests on the semen to see if it matches our killer's. Also to see how long it was on the body. We'll probably find that the noise you heard was the killer putting the body in your yard."

"This is so creepy. It makes me very nervous. I've always felt safe at home. Now I don't know anymore."

"Anything else you can think of? Sometimes, when a person suffers an extreme shock, they have a hard time remembering certain details but memories will come in time, and although they may not appear important to you, they can provide a clue for us," Carlo stated.

"Yesterday, while I was at home with my client, I saw a taxi parked in front of my house. I thought somebody was coming to visit me. But when I opened the door it drove away.

Later on, I saw it on the other side of the street in front of the neighbors' house."

Edward gave Simone a look of concern. No doubt, he was wondering why she hadn't mentioned this earlier.

"Who are they?"

"The Peddinghouses...a nice, quiet, elderly couple."

"We'll have to talk to them."

"Some other strange things have happened. But I don't know if they have anything to do with any of this."

"Such as?"

"Several times in the past few weeks, I've come home and gotten the feeling someone had been there. Just a feeling. Picture frames out of place. But nothing stolen. The other day, a window was open and I was sure it was closed when I left for work. I thought perhaps my cleaning lady had changed her schedule without telling me. She's the world champ at cleaning and dusting and not leaving things as she found them."

"Doctor, I'd like you to talk to her about this. I'm afraid for your safety. Maybe someone is getting into your house. Call her now from right here. Depending on what she says, we might have to do a thorough search of the premises. In that case, I'd strongly advise you to stay somewhere else for a while."

"What? Get out of my house? That's all I need," she said sarcastically. "Okay, I'll call her now. I can ask her to pack a few things for me." She pulled her cellphone from her purse to call her maid but the detective stopped her.

"Doctor, would you mind using our phone? I'd like to be able to hear her answers, firsthand."

"No problem, Detective."

Simone gave him the number and he dialed the phone on the desk. As it rang, he pressed a button and engaged the speaker.

"Hello Dr. Simone, can I help you?" Lola had a strong Latin accent.

"Hi, Lola, how've you been?"

"Fine, Doctor, is everything okay with you?"

"Yes, yes. Listen, Lola, I'm calling to ask if you changed your cleaning day at my house last week. Did you happen to come on Saturday?"

"Never, Doctor!" Lola sounded scandalized by Simone's suggestion. "I wouldn't do that without talking to you first."

"I need you to be sure, Lola."

"By all the saints, by the Holy Virgin Mary, I swear I wasn't at your house on Saturday."

"Okay, Lola, no need to swear; I know you're telling the truth but it was important to know you were certain. Thank you."

"You are welcome, Doctor. By the way, I'm in your house today. Is that okay?" She sounded worried.

Simone sighed. Lola came by every Monday, Wednesday and Friday. Since today was Monday, she was scheduled to be there. "Sure it is. No need to cook dinner, though; I'll eat out tonight. Have a nice day."

"Same to you, Doctor."

"Do you believe she is telling the truth?" Carlos asked.

"I'm positive, Detective. She is a truthful woman and a devout Catholic. She would never swear by all the saints if she were lying, for fear she'd burn in hell," Simone assured him.

"Well, if your maid wasn't responsible for opening that window or moving things around, then I'm sorry, but that means we'll have to go over your house with a fine-toothed comb."

"I understand," Simone said, but she was highly displeased.

"C'mon, Simone, you can stay with me. You know you're more than welcome and I can keep an eye on you. I couldn't let you go back to your house alone anyway."

"No, Ed. I'll only be in your way."

"No, you won't! It's me, remember? Besides, you'd do the same for me," he reasoned.

"How long before I can go home, Officer?" Simone asked.

"Not until we get some answers. The killer knows where you live. That's a fact. And this week, you helped us understand part of his M.O. Your house isn't safe."

"You're right. Would you like me to go there with you now?" she asked.

"Well we can set up a time that's convenient for you. Ed tells me you've got a full plate today."

"Thank you. I'll be free at the end of the afternoon, about six."

They scheduled to meet at her house and then she and Edward left for the office.

Chapter Sixteen

Present Day - Simone

Simone braced herself to face the lunacy of her psychiatric practice. Stressed out and in erratic orbit herself, she didn't relish the thought of spending that day with lunatics. As Edward drove to their office, she had time to think and analyze, and she sensed an existential crisis coming on. Had her choice of profession condemned her to a lifetime of repairing the works of twenty-four-carat cuckoo clocks?

Philip, her favorite patient, arrived in the afternoon. At least Simone would get to see a kind patient today—*a little nuts but kind of loveable,* she thought.

"Hi, Doctor. Wow! You look pooped. Aren't you well?" Always considerate, he handed her a gift-wrapped box. "I brought you half a dozen of my homemade chocolate-covered creampuffs. The custard filling's my grandmother's recipe. I used real vanilla bean, not that bottled biodiesel that smells like bat piss."

Simone eyed the psychedelic green bandana he was wearing around his neck. He either had a humongous hickey or he was now an aspiring country-western singer. Only the ten-gallon hat and cowboy boots were missing.

"Thank you, Philip. Your treats are always welcome. I'm fine. Nothing a hot shower won't cure. Is there a problem with your throat?"

"Nope. It was the *kinbaku*."

While Simone puzzled over what kind of sushi had gotten stuck in Philip's gullet, it crossed her mind—no doubt thinking a little slowly this morning due to the recent events—that kinbaku sounded like the name of a Japanese food—he removed the bandana to reveal enormous red splotches. He also proudly rolled up his sleeves and his trouser cuffs to show similar ones on his wrists and ankles.

Simone couldn't prevent an eyebrow from arching. Despite years of effort to control it, the eyebrow insisted on betraying her moments of astonished disbelief.

"*Kinbaku*?" Simone futilely ransacked her brain for the term and how it might relate to sadomasochism.

"Japanese sadomasochistic rope art!" Philip replied, as pleased as if he had told her he'd just created ikebana with wildflowers.

"I think you've gone too far this time. You're covered with wounds."

"No, I'm not. They're just the marks the ropes leave. They only hurt once in a while. But when they do, I remember the pleasure and get a humdinger of a hard-on."

"Could you describe for me just what you've gotten yourself into?"

"Sure. My wife was still pissed off about what happened the other day when she got it on with her old flame. Remember?"

"Perfectly."

"So she asked me to play out a fantasy with her. She suggested we go to a submission house because she wanted to see me pussy whipped. We went to New York to avoid being recognized around here. You know how it is. Small town. When we got there we saw some people practicing *kinbaku*. They're ropes tied to restrict your movements, to control you and give you pleasure." Philip sounded as if he were describing a scientific experiment.

"I loved it when I saw two women doing it. I asked if I could join them and the dominatrix gave the thumbs up. I asked my wife for permission and she said yes. So I stretched out on the floor, belly down, and they tied my hands and feet together behind my back. Then the dominatrix put a rope around my neck and chest and ran it through the ones on my hands and feet. She started pulling on it, tightening it. The more pain I felt, the more pleasure I felt.

She started easing off and the rope began cutting into my wrists and ankles. I got so hot, Doctor, you can't imagine!"

Simone could. That was the worst of it.

"And your wife?"

"She got really horny seeing me under the yoke. She lifted up her dress and the shameless hussy wasn't wearing panties. She masturbated…right in front of me and all the other people who were there. I'd never seen her so turned on. We're gonna join a sadomasochist club."

"Is that a mutual decision?"

"Oh yeah. She liked it a lot. I was happy because it was something we enjoyed together without my asking for it or her doing it to please me. Understand?"

"I do. But you'd better be careful. People die doing that sort of thing."

"That won't happen. The dominatrix has things under tight control."

"And if the dominatrix loses control?"

"Loses control? I think I might faint. I almost did at the point when she pulled all the ropes tight and left me without air."

"And how did she know when to stop? Did you agree on a safe word?"

"We did. But I didn't use it. I wanted to find my limit of pleasure and pain. When you get there it's very hard to cry uncle when you can't breathe…"

"You might find your death. I'm really afraid of that."

Philip's foray into masochistic practices alarmed Simone. Apparently, the medication she'd prescribed had eliminated the sexual compulsion but not the masochistic one. Now he was getting into high-risk activities.

"I started thinking about that. If dying wouldn't be pleasurable."

"And you want that? You want to experience death?"

"I don't know, Doctor. But when the rope tightened around my neck the pleasure grew. And also the sensation that I'd leave my body at any moment in a cloud of pleasure. I felt all my problems would go away. I felt deep peace."

"When you're having sex or see your wife having it, you don't feel the same way?"

"No. That was the first time I ever felt anything like that."

Philip's emotional state looked truly critical now. A Freudian theory dealt with the subconscious death wish after traumatic experiences and Simone couldn't get it out of her head.

"Did you also have sex that day?"

"Not penetration. No. Just domination. I enjoyed it a lot. I really blasted off."

"What was it like?"

"My wife was watching while I was tied up. She went off somewhere and came back with a stranger. They positioned themselves very close to me where I could see them. Even smell them. He ran his hands all over her body. He fondled her breasts and began to suck them. She was moaning and looking at me. He turned her toward the wall and took her from behind. He held her shoulders and drove his cock into her until she came. Then he turned her to face him. She wrapped her legs around his waist and he put it to her again. He took hold of her buttocks and moved her back and forth. The whole time, she was looking into my eyes. I felt as if I was between them. When she reached orgasm, drooling with her eyes closed, he had an earthquake of a climax and I squirted and squirted and squirted, tied up in the ropes as I was. The dominatrix didn't like that at all. She pulled the rope hard. If I'd had anything left to shoot, I'd have come again. Then I felt at peace."

"I'm worried."

"Why, Doctor? For the first time in a long time, I don't feel neurotic. I'm happy. My wife is happy. What's bothering you?"

"I'm working on a case involving practices very similar to what you've described. But they don't involve ropes. They involve strangulation. With hands."

"And?"

"And the woman died."

"I won't die unless I want to."

"No one wants to die. If he's well."

"Anyone who comes close to the experience I've had will long for the feeling of peace that death provides."

"I'm going to change your medication."

"Again? Why this time? What I'm on is good, Doctor!"

"Philip, the medication you are taking doesn't have the same side effects you experienced with the previous one, but there *are* side effects, and one of them is depression. And if you're talking about seeking the peace of death" — she made quotes in the air around the phrase — "then it looks to me as if you might be experiencing a bit of depression. I can't take the risk, trust me."

"I always do, Doctor; you know that."

I'm going to give you a new medication and we are going to see if we can balance things a little better. I like what we're doing now but something's missing. A better medication has come out recently and I'd like to try it. Fewer side effects."

Philip laughed. "This reminds me of a line out of that Garfield movie, Doc. When John tells Garfield he's about to eat a new and improved food, and Garfield says, 'So the one you used to give me was old and worse?'."

They both laughed but Simone quickly sobered. Philip's sudden death wish wasn't uncommon. Some people wanted to die "with their boots on"—while having sex. Others sought the peace death would bring.

"Philip, understand me, you've never shown signs of depression. Sure, sometimes you were sad but never to the point you wanted to die. I really need to alter your medication." She refused to risk having a suicide or homicide on her hands. In the field of medicine, especially psychiatry, there were no certainties, only probabilities and elimination. Philip's death wish stood a good chance of passing with the new medication.

After writing the prescription, she said, "Try to ignore the description and the label. They'll influence you. Just tell me what's happening, okay?"

"Okay, Doctor. As I said before, I totally trust you."

Philip seemed resigned to the new medication and said nothing more.

"Any questions?" Simone asked. Whenever she changed his medication he usually had a few.

"Do I stop taking what I'm on now?"

"Yes. Start on what I've just prescribed tonight before you go to bed."

For the remainder of the session, they discussed some of the effects of the new medication and other details. But this case had Simone's warning signs all flashing red alert.

Chapter Seventeen

Present Day - Simone

That afternoon, Simone returned home with Edward and the police. The mere thought of anyone examining her personal belongings horrified her. The cops were after fingerprints because she had reported certain objects being out of place. Simone's and Lola's prints would be separated from any others. They suggested Simone install a security system with cameras and alarms, which would enable her to reoccupy her house. A private and reserved person, she hated to inconvenience others. Edward was a great friend but to have to stay more than a very short time at his apartment made her ill at ease.

The police told her it was still too soon to reach a definite conclusion. However, the results of the semen test had come in and pointed to the serial killer. The apparent lack of torture probably meant the body was a warning for Simone to stay out of his way and to stop helping Edward and the police.

Investigators had learned that the victim had not been on a trip. She had simply gone to the local supermarket late Saturday afternoon to stock up for the weekend. Her husband was at their son's Little League game. When he returned at around eight, he found a message from her saying she'd be back soon. He couldn't say what time the message had been left. He called the police around ten o'clock, after trying his wife's cell phone several times and getting only her voice mail. Someone must be absent for twenty-four hours to be considered missing so the police took no action immediately. The supermarket's security cameras only showed her entering and then leaving with her purchases.

In the previous cases, the victims' bodies had shown multiple signs of torture. In this case, the killer hadn't taken the time to play cat and mouse. He'd apparently murdered this latest victim just to drop her on Simone's side steps. The police believed he'd acted out of necessity and not for personal pleasure this time.

Simone locked the doors and called an acquaintance who owned a security firm. She asked him to install a system at her house. She said it was urgent but didn't explain why. The man promised he'd send someone over the following day to do an appraisal and then he'd give her an estimate. At last, the day ended and she went with Edward to his apartment.

"Hey, Simmie. I can see you're dying for your magic remedy for days from hell, a glass of wine and a shower."

"First the shower and then the grapes. You read my mind!"

"I'll cook us something. Monday's your low-carb night, right?"

"How did you know that?"

"Because every Monday you leave the office frowning and grumbling, "Low-carb night."

"Edward, you are a prince. Will you marry me?" She gave him a light kiss on the lips.

He pulled her closer and reciprocated. But his embrace bore intentions other than friendship. For a few moments, she let him linger and the sensation electrified her. Heat waves swept through her body. Then she remembered where she was and who she was with. She gently withdrew.

"Excuse me, Simone. I got carried away."

"That's okay, Ed. I did too. We're both stressed out. I'm going to take my shower."

As she stood there beneath the caress of the warm water, she couldn't get the kiss out of her mind. She hadn't realized Edward harbored such passion. But that wasn't the point. They'd been friends for so many years. She couldn't even think of him in a romantic way. To do so might only spoil their friendship. Now was not the time to let a moment of vulnerability confuse things. But how should she behave now? What should she say when she went back to the kitchen? She decided to pretend nothing had happened.

Fortunately, Edward must have had the same idea. When she saw him, he acted as if nothing was different.

He'd set two places on the kitchen island with its cook top, range hood, sink and stools. He reigned supreme there and ceremoniously announced dinner was served. Simone accepted the glass of wine he offered, a vision of paradise at that moment.

They kept things casual, chatting about work and the recent crime. Neither dared mention the kiss. Afterward, Simone went to her room to read more of Mark's journal.

Mark's Journal – Jailhouse Rock

I was sound asleep when the phone rang. It was Peter, stammering and shouting.

"That you? That you, Mark? That you?"

"Hey, Peter. What's happening? Is it your turn to drag me out of bed to discuss affairs of the heart?"

"Don't try to be funny, Mark. Lara's been arrested! I need your help right now! Can you get her out of jail?"

"What do you mean 'Lara's been arrested'? What happened?" I sat up in bed now, completely awake.

"I don't know. Even I don't understand. We were out dancing at a nightclub…me, her and a friend."

What friend? I wondered. But I put that thought out of my mind because Peter sounded so upset.

"Okay. Calm down. Tell me about it."

"Like I said. We were dancing. I went to get a drink and when I was coming back I saw a man go up to Lara. I didn't know him. I thought he just wanted to make a pass at her. She didn't want to have anything to do with him. She tried to leave the dance floor but he went after her. Lara threw a drink in his face. Then she went at him and began to hit and scratch him. I'd never seen her like that."

"And then what?"

"Then her friend thought the other guy had attacked Lara first and jumped the guy and they began to fight. Lara tried to hold Leo back and ended up in the middle of it. Then everything was all chaos. The cops came and Lara and Leo were arrested."

So…Leo was Lara's friend, not Peter's… "You stayed out of it?"

"I don't get into fights. Suppose I break a fingernail! I kept my distance! I detest gratuitous violence. Michael would never dirty his hands in a catfight."

"Michael? Who's Michael?"

"Corleone."

"Pete, sometimes you're on another planet. Do you know where Lara is now?"

"Yes. I'm on my way over to get you to take you there. And I've got money to pay her bail."

In the final analysis, despite my previous comment, did the guy have his head on straight or what?

I didn't know whether to go to the police station and identify myself as a lawyer or to go armed. To kill Lara! She'd gone out with another man and then gotten herself into a jam. And exactly one week after we'd returned from Paris! That woman was bringing out the worst in me.

When we arrived at the station Peter stayed in the car. He said hospitals and police stations gave him the creeps. I found out what had happened, posted bail and went to her cell. Luckily, she was alone—no cellmates. She was curled up in a corner, looking all disheveled, her makeup smudged and smeared. She'd obviously been crying rivers. The situation must have turned ugly because Lara wasn't a woman to solve problems with tears.

I took her out to my car and she said she wanted a taxi. I lost it. I grabbed her by the arm and threw her into the back seat. Peter looked at me bug-eyed from behind the steering wheel.

"Now look, you goddamn Duchess of Disaster! It's four fucking a.m.! You get in a brawl, get me out of bed, drag me down to the calaboose to bail your ass out, and you have the nerve to want to slip off?"

"Mark, take it easy. She's in a state of shock."

"Oh yeah? Well, she'll be in no state at all if she tries to get out of this car!"

I was furious and my fury had a name. It didn't have a last name because I didn't know it yet. Just who the fuck was Leo?

"Mark, I know you're upset but you have to go back inside. Leo's still in there." Peter sounded like an intimidated little boy.

"Leo can sit on this and rotate! I don't know him. I don't even know who he is."

"Of course you know him," Lara said, emerging from the stupor she'd been in. "You met him at Behind the Door. Remember? The first time we went out."

"Leo? The gay guy on the dance floor?"

"Yes."

Only then did I start to get hold of myself. I wanted to crawl under a rock. I'd manhandled a woman who was clearly in shock. I'd been a jerk to my best friend. And why? Because the thought that Lara had gone dancing with another man had driven me wild with jealousy.

"Yes, that's him," she went on. "I wanted to introduce him to Peter. So we all went out together."

"I'll go back in and get Leo," I said meekly. "Wait here. It won't take long."

"We will," Lara and Peter answered together like a couple of chastened children.

I rescued Leo and he walked out, clinging to my arm and swearing everlasting love. I told him to get a taxi. Peter then took Lara and me to my place. Only after we went inside did I ask her to explain what had happened.

"I was all happy and dancing. He came up to me out of the blue. I was terrified. It was as if I was a kid again and he had me under his spell. I tried to get away from him but he came after me. I just wanted to escape from him."

"Him. You mean *him* him?"

"Yes. Him!"

"How did he find you? What did he want?"

"I don't know. I think he was with some people there and he recognized me. It wasn't a swing house or anything like that. Just a nightclub. When he appeared, I didn't know what to do to keep him from talking to me. I threw my drink at him and attacked him! And then Leo thought *he* was attacking *me* and came over to defend me and all hell broke loose."

"So he didn't succeed in talking to you?"

"He just said he needed to talk to me. Just his being there and the sound of his voice made me feel so fragile. I felt as if I'd lost all my strength, Mark. I turned into a silly little girl again. If I hadn't flipped out the way I did, he could have started giving me orders and I'd have done whatever he wanted."

"Okay. We'll talk later, Lara. You need to rest now."

And I needed to get my nerves under control and put my feet on the ground. That woman had me tottering at the edge of the slippery slope to perdition.

Mark's Journal – Soirée in the Seraglio

Lara called me a couple of days after the jailhouse episode. She wanted to express her gratitude for my "extricating" her from that "*contretemps*."

"Mark, please come over tonight. I'd like very much to thank you."

"No need for that, Lara. But it will be a pleasure to see you."

"Get here about eight."

"Dinner?"

"Middle Eastern fare," she said in a sultry whisper.

"Hmmm. Sounds good."

"You're gonna love it."

We chatted for a few more minutes. I'd thought Lara couldn't fry an egg, and there she was, ready to make my dinner. Things change, *n'est-ce pas*?

After I left the office, I went home, took a shower, changed my clothes and headed happily to her place. On the way there it crossed my mind to pick up some flowers. But I decided not to. I couldn't imagine Lara holding a bouquet. Flowers and Lara? Apples and oranges. Maybe a cactus, I thought a bit snidely.

The doorman at Lara's building, by then my good buddy, told me to go right up. Miss Lara had given explicit instructions to that effect. When I reached her apartment the door was ajar. Even so, I rang the bell. I too believed in respecting others' privacy.

"Come on in, Mark. Make yourself comfortable on the couch," Lara shouted from some inner sanctum. "I'll be right there. Don't turn on the lights."

Penumbra pervaded the room. The shiny surfaces of numerous colored cushions reflected flickering candlelight. Could I be in for a romantic, exotic and even erotic evening in the seraglio? The table hadn't been set. Lara was probably in the kitchen. I waited patiently on the couch.

The strains of flutes and the beating of drums suddenly spiced my surroundings. Lara was certainly taking our Middle Eastern repast seriously. A woman in sheer red veils appeared. She swayed to the rhythms with swinging arms and revolving hips. My hostess materialized, perching beside me to take in the show.

The sultry dancer's eyes gleamed. Shorter than Lara and raven-haired, the dancer boasted seductive curves and firm, full breasts, a harem girl floating in gossamer and music. She turned, slipped a veil and tossed it to me. Her tawny, oiled body glistened. Her bejeweled bra sparkled in the half-light.

She undulated in sync with the sensual music, whirling closer and closer to me. My mouth opened. She was impossible to resist. The tingling in my crotch intensified as her castanets tinkled like bells.

The music stopped. The voluptuous odalisque knelt before me. She tossed back her tresses and raised her arms. Lara went to the couch opposite us and took a seat.

I didn't know what to say. I just watched the show in a trance. The woman moved closer and sat down in my lap. I looked at Lara and she nodded her consent.

"Touch her, Mark. Go ahead. Touch her," she said.

I took the siren's breasts in my hands. I removed her bra and began to lick her nipples. She backed off, shed her skirt and undressed me. All under Lara's attentive gaze. She took my penis in her hands and rolled it between her palms. She put it in her mouth and began to suck. Then she took it out and nestled the shaft between her breasts. She squeezed them together and began to move up and down, up and down. Skin against skin. Slipping and sliding in lubricated heat. My dick turned into an ICBM about to blast off. I closed my eyes.

"Open them, Mark. I want you to look at me while you play with Fatima."

Lara stood beside us, watching us. For a split second, I felt rage. She didn't give a shit that I was with another woman! But as this had now become routine, a more powerful feeling — raging lust — overtook me.

I removed my penis from Fatima's cleavage and she gave me a condom. I put it on, laid her down, drove it home and began to do her methodically. She moaned in ecstasy. My long, slow strokes soon made her beg me to give it to her harder. All the while my eyes were on Lara's. It was as if I was having sex with her. By now, Lara had taken off her clothes too and was fingering herself.

After Fatima reached her first orgasm, I rolled her over, set her on all fours and started off slowly once more. I changed positions a number of times, after each of her climaxes. I have no idea how long we had sex. Lara finally came all by herself. That's when I finally shot my wad. I couldn't take it anymore.

I stretched out on the carpet, catching my breath. I noticed that Fatima had gathered up her things. I heard faint murmurs. Lara must have taken her to the door.

"I hope you enjoyed your Middle Eastern appetizer," she chirped as she knelt beside me. "Are you ready for the *pièce de résistance*?" She pointed to her luscious body.

As ever, Lara had the knack of making me laugh. I pulled her down, laid her out and ran my hands all over her. Then I began to lick her. I started with her feet, slowly, and lapped my way up her legs. Just as a teaser, I brushed against her pussy, leaving it to savor later on. I nibbled her belly and took one of her breasts in my mouth. She squirmed and thrust with lust.

"Mark, this is delicious. Keep going. Give it to me!"

"Are you in a hurry?" I asked. "I'm not in the least bit."

I turned her face down and ran my tongue over the curves of her buttocks and up her spine to her nape. I dallied to lap her there. I knew she desperately wanted me inside her. But I preferred to torture her until she begged me.

"Bite me!" she begged. Bite me there!" She grabbed a handful of my hair.

I bit her gently on the neck and she really moaned.

"Now I want you to ram it in and bite me harder while you fuck me. Pull my hair. I want to feel pain!"

I didn't stop to consider her request, found it impossible to think at all. My dick throbbed too much. I obeyed her and drove in deep as I tugged on her hair and contorted myself to bite her neck.

"Mark! No mercy! Bite harder, Mark!

"If I do that, I'll hurt you."

"I don't care! Bite me! Scratch my back! Dig your nails into my back! Hard!"

I humped for all I was worth as I raked her and clamped my teeth onto the skin of her neck. She shook, unloaded, exploded in an orgasm foretold by moans that must have been heard three or four floors below us. I felt as if I came in quarts.

We lay there on the carpet in silence, lifeless for several minutes. Then I began to gently kiss her arm and shoulder. She forced herself to her feet and staggered over to switch on a light. The condition of her back shocked me. I glimpsed ugly wounds there.

"Lara, I've hurt you badly."

She pulled her hair to one side and uncovered all the deep bites and scratches. "Don't worry, Mark. They'll heal fast."

"That's not what worries me. I made you suffer! I lost control!" My lack of control and my ability to hurt someone scared me. Outside of a few teenage scuffles, I'd never harmed anyone, much less a woman. What more was I capable of?

"No you didn't. You made me come hard! That's what you did! I was hallucinating when you bit me and scratched me and yanked my hair! It was awesome! Oh how I love to feel pain when I fuck!"

Strange. Pain and pleasure. Pleasure and pain. First squeezing her neck. Now this. Making me hurt her on purpose. I didn't know if I was more appalled by her behavior or by mine. I'd gone way over the limit. I'd actually sunk my nails and teeth into her as if I'd been some wild beast in heat. And she'd loved it! Our relationship was definitely perverting me, debauching me. I didn't recognize myself anymore!

Lara put her head on my shoulder.

I began to run my fingers through her hair and plucked up the courage to ask, "How long have you been like this?"

"Since he taught me. Whenever he had sex with me he'd come up with a little surprise. Sometimes, he'd grab my hair and almost pull it out. He'd bite me. He'd tie me up and hit me. Sometimes, just with his hand; other times, with a small riding whip. He even did it with flowers. He used to tell me he was *sculpting* me to his pleasure as if I were a piece of marble."

"Christ!"

"It didn't hurt that much because he'd screw me or masturbate me at the same time. The pain became pleasure. It complemented the pleasure."

"That's not normal."

"I don't know. For me, it always was. I learned to link pain with pleasure when I was young, and now when I feel pain my pleasure is even greater."

"Did he ever injure you?"

"Yes. Never seriously enough to leave scars, though. Sometimes it hurt a lot. But when it did it was always the prelude to seismic sex."

"How old were you when he started this sadistic stuff?"

"Fourteen, almost fifteen. When we went to Paris. I think he felt freer there to do whatever he wanted. No one would call him on it. Whenever I was covered with scratches and bruises, we'd stay home."

"Did you learn about group sex from him too?"

"Everything I learned, I learned from him. He was my teacher. I knew nothing before I met him. I'd do whatever he said was good and normal."

"How did it start?"

"A good-looking young man came to the apartment one day. I think he was a male prostitute. My *sculptor* told me to put on sexy lingerie. Then he blindfolded me. I found out what was going to happen when I felt four hands feeling me up. Then I felt a tongue licking one of my breasts and another at the same time licking my pussy. I got too turned on to think about anything else. And there was no one to tell me that wasn't right. If there is such a thing as right."

"And that led to other things."

"Exactly. We started to screw in swing houses. He even got me a fake ID so I could cross the doors with no questions. We had sex with lots of people. One time, we even tried to get it on with a Brazilian transvestite. But it was a flop. He didn't like chicks. Later on, my sculptor began lending me to his friends so we could *play* together, or so he said."

"Lending you? As if you were a goddamn baseball glove or something?"

"Friends of his would come to the apartment to talk and have a drink. He'd make me wear sexy clothes—short shorts or see-through blouses without a bra. The order of the day was to drive them wild. When he saw they were getting interested he'd tell them they could play with me. He enjoyed watching."

"How did you feel about that?"

"It's hard to say. I had fun turning on his friends. Some I liked and some I didn't. Most were about his age and were in good shape. They were rich, good-looking and well groomed. I usually liked having sex with them. And when I wasn't in the mood, he didn't try to force me. But afterward, he'd punish me in some way."

Lara took a deep breath before continuing. I had the sense she wanted to exorcize her demons by talking about the past.

"I got addicted. I always wanted to fuck with two men. He always let me, provided he chose them. The only time I tried to choose… Well, you know what happened. Later on, when I was free of him and had my own boyfriends, it was hard for me not to try to get them to play the games I'd gotten hooked on. It shocked me when I found out what I'd been doing wasn't normal."

"It truly horrifies me whenever you tell me about all this, Lara."

"I know. But I want you to understand that for me it wasn't horrible. I didn't know anything else. Later on, I discussed things in detail with Emma. I mean I held *nothing* back from her. She never blamed me at all and through her I began to understand that sex could be different. But I think by then it was too late."

"You wanted to be different?"

"Oh yes. Very much. I've talked about it a lot with my therapist. I want to be satisfied with just one man. I want not to want to feel pain. And I do feel pain, physically and emotionally. But the pleasure that goes along with it is beyond belief! When I saw you having sex with Fatima a little while ago, it hurt me terribly. But the pleasure it gave me at the same time was indescribable. There's no way I can explain it."

"What does your therapist say?"

"It's sadomasochism and it's difficult to cure. It would be easy to cure if there were no reward. But the pain triples the reward. The pleasure! I think it's like being a chocoholic. You know you're going to get fat. But the pleasure makes the chocolate irresistible."

"Did you miss your life with him, after you broke up with him?"

"I put that life behind me. I didn't want it anymore. In some remote corner of my subconscious, my intuition was telling me that what I was doing with him—just being with a man twenty years older—was wrong. But after you leave a life like that, there's something that tries to pull you back. It seems there's a void that needs to be filled. Know what I mean? Right, wrong, normal or abnormal. It was the life I'd known and I felt a need for it. I'd been that man's slave. But at the same time, I'd been the center of his existence. And afterward, well, I wasn't the center of anyone's existence anymore." Lara paused. "And there you have it. I felt guilty. Not just for wanting what was bad. Oh no. I felt guilty for everything! I was forged, Mark. Sculpted. I wasn't raised."

Her eyes were wet. I could almost feel her pain.

"Lara, what the hell am I going to do with you? You're so different from anyone I've ever met!"

She said nothing. She just looked at me and smiled sadly. But she was calm. She leaned against me and quickly went to sleep. I remained there on the carpet, stroking her hair, too shaken to sleep. For the first time, I thought I should seek professional help, a psychologist or someone like that. I was in way over my head. My mind couldn't handle it. And, for sure, Lara was in orbit around the seventh moon of the fifth planet from the sun in a solar system in a galaxy that had yet to be discovered.

Chapter Eighteen

Present Day — Simone

Simone put down the manuscript. Chills wracked her body. They froze her desire to sleep. How Mark must have agonized as he'd listened to Lara's tale of life in hell. As a scientist, Simone had the harrowing case of masochism and post-traumatic personality disorder she needed for her new book. But as a human being, she recoiled at the heinous, systematic torture of a pubescent girl. It caused her violent visceral pain. She drank some water, got a grip on herself and decided to resume her reading. Sleep would have to wait.

Mark's Journal — Get Out, Man

Whenever Lara opened up and took a step toward me, right afterward, she'd take two steps back. I was getting used to it.

I decided to see a shrink. I needed help to understand what was happening to me, to Lara and to our relationship. I'd gotten in deep.

I had three or four sessions with a therapist. The woman said I was settling for too little and my relationship with Lara was poisonous. She told me I was like a battered woman who tries to justify an abusive relationship with a husband or lover. Her exact words were, "Mark, one of these days you'll come here and say, 'Lara's a wonderful person. She's only bad when she goes off the deep end.' Then you'll add, 'She's off the deep end all day long.'"

Leaving Lara was not in my plans. I was convinced she needed me and, of course, I craved her madly. I left the therapist instead. Peter was a splendid therapist, I thought. I decided to talk to him. I told him as much as I could. I said nothing about the abuse Lara had suffered because it was a secret of hers and not mine to reveal. But I did tell him sex was always over the top and sometimes it really troubled me.

"Get the hell out," Peter said.

"Why?"

"I've already told you but you're a cement-head and nothing sinks in. I'll say it one more time. That woman's not for loving. She's for laying!"

"But I've fallen in love with her!"

There. I finally managed to put into words what I'd been feeling for some time.

"Dog shit and double dog shit! Fall out of love! She's a whacko. You're fine. You're normal. She's a deep-space dildo!" Peter's fury turned his face purple. "I introduced you because I thought a piece of ass like her would get you out of your *Leave It to Beaver* rut. I didn't do it for you to join a carnival in some surreal red-light district. Taking a walk on the wild side is one thing, Mark. Living there's like living in a parallel universe!"

"First of all, you didn't introduce us. And second, where the hell is your compassion...your friendship? I think she suffers..."

"Fuckin' right, she does. She suffers from nymphomania. You are *never* gonna be enough for her! I can just imagine you without your suit and tie and all decked out in black latex with your pink ass sticking out and a whip in your hand. That's ridiculous! That is so not you! And don't question my friendship. That's why I'm telling you to get out!"

Peter had been emphatic. The therapist had been clear. But I wanted Lara. I believed I could save her, bring her back to normality. As long as I did it little by little. Yes. I could save Lara. But then I ended up asking myself who could save me from her.

I was so pissed off when I left my "session" with Peter I decided to break the rules. I headed off to visit Lara without calling her. When I got to her building the doorman greeted me with a smile and let me go right up. I intended to tell Lara I loved her and that even if she felt only remotely the same for me, we'd work things out together. We'd do our best to live a normal life. I'd help her get over her pain and suffering.

When I reached her apartment loud music boomed from inside. I automatically rang the bell despite realizing it wouldn't be heard. *Wow*, I said to myself. I hadn't known Lara was into 1960s rock. But there was the sound of The Doors and Jim Morrison's unmistakable voice singing *Back Door Man*!

I tried the knob. The door opened and I stepped inside. I froze. An undressed man was wandering around the living room. Lara was naked on her hands and knees on the floor. An equally naked big black guy was taking her from behind. Lying on his back under Lara, another man was licking her.

She didn't notice my presence at first, engrossed as she was in the business at hand. Paralysis and pain prevented me from reacting. The black guy yanked on Lara's hair as he fucked her. She wept and wailed as he whipped her buttocks, gripping her blonde mane like the reins of a horse. The guy underneath wiggled his toes in obvious delight.

The crescendo of Lara's carnival-esque carnality at last climaxed in a mushrooming thermonuclear orgasm. The black guy withdrew his huge cock, rid it of its raincoat, pulled Lara's head into a propitious position and ejaculated into her mouth.

At that moment, Lara spotted me. She wiped her chin with the back of her hand and screamed, "Get the fuck outta here!"

And that's what I did. I left with the certainty I never wanted to see that princess of perversion again. My sanity was at stake. I didn't know where to go. When I got outside it was raining. I sat down on the curb with my feet in the gutter in front of the building, lifeless and desperate. I buried my face in my hands.

I don't know how long I sat there in the rain. The black guy who'd been with Lara suddenly appeared and put his hand on my shoulder. I wanted to take a swing at him but I felt as weak as a kitten.

"Hey, man, come with me."

I followed him to his car and got inside. I couldn't refuse, couldn't find the strength to.

"My friend," he began, "I don't know who you are but I saw you up there and how shocked you were."

"I'm not your friend," I snapped.

"And I'm not your enemy. You were watching what was happening. And I can tell you are in love with Lara…big mistake! She's a sex-goddess but she's community property. I'll tell you straight. From the looks of you I can see you deserve the truth. That happens all the time. Me, her, somebody else, her and other people. It's always a gang bang with her."

"Who the hell are you?"

"John Meyers. I once fell into the trap you're caught in now. She ripped my heart out of my chest with her bare hands and ate it right in front of me. Finally, the nickel dropped that she's just a fantastic fuck. Fuck her when you can. But don't expect exclusive rights to her. Avoid her like the plague. If you're with her for sport, that's okay. But I see that's not your case. If it's love, get out! Or she'll chew you up and spit you out!"

I didn't thank him for the same piece of advice I'd heard for the third time in a week. I just got out of the car. My mind was made up to steer clear of Lara for good.

A few weeks went by, the worst of my life. I felt like a complete asshole. I missed her. I missed her body. I missed her smell. Then she called me.

"Mark?"

"Lara. Can we talk?"

"What for? Didn't you tell me to get the fuck out? Well, I'm out!"

"Out of the apartment. Not out of my life. I need you." She was sobbing pitifully.

I was such a stupid piece of shit. Hearing Lara breaking down and saying she needed me was the same as pushing the play button on a remote control. I rushed to her.

Lara was a basket case. Her coiffure by Porcupine Hair Design perfectly complemented her makeup by the Cry Me a River Salon. She had an ugly black-and-blue lump on her face and bruises on her arms. She was wearing a soiled pair of sweatpants, so old they were practically falling apart. Her old T-shirt with the words "Girls have more fun" was in a similar state. The sight of Dulcinea in distress turned me into Don Quixote. She needed me and I was honor-bound to succor her in her affliction. Her presence, as had happened so many times before, dimmed my wits and gave me amnesia. I hugged her to my breast and tucked the memory of John Meyer fucking her under my mental carpet.

"What the hell happened to you, Lara?"

"He came here."

"Who's he? Attila the Hun on horseback?"

"No. Arthur."

"Who's Arthur?"

Lara had the irritating habit of assuming I knew each of her vast circle of "friends".

"The senator's son!"

Oh, I thought. *So now I know his name.* I'd always wanted to ask but could never summon the courage.

"But how did he get in?"

"That fuckin' asshole doorman let him come up. When I went to open the door I thought it was a neighbor or a Federal Express delivery. And there he was."

"And?"

"I tried to slam the door in his face but he pushed me away. He started shouting at me. He called me an ungrateful slut and said I had to go see my mother in the hospital."

"What did you say?"

"I told him in detail what I thought of him. I'd waited years to do that. I said he made me want to puke. I called him a pig fucker and a pedophile and said my mother was a scrofulous piece of shit."

"How did he take that?"

"He belted me so hard I landed on the couch. Then he grabbed my arms and shook me damn near senseless. He swore he'd never again gotten involved with someone so young. He said he had been crazy about me and he loved me. He claimed he'd been waiting for me to grow up so we could get married and that my mother had only helped him because she knew all about it."

"You didn't believe him, of course."

"Of course I didn't. What kind of love was that? Like my mother's? I know jack shit about love but I can tell you what they were up to was the opposite!"

"What are you going to do now?"

"Avoid them like the fucking plague like I've always done. Mark, for Christ's sake! I couldn't think straight when he was there. I just wanted to run, not listen." Lara covered her ears with her hands. "The son of a bitch wouldn't stop talking and I started to feel like I did when I was a little girl. I felt as if I was losing my strength and that if he ordered me to do something, I'd do it. His voice was making me remember…"

"What?"

"The torture, the suffering he put me through. The punishment when I didn't behave."

To imagine Lara in a session of sadomasochism was one thing. But to imagine her being a fragile and defenseless victim was something else. The woman was an Amazon.

"You've never spoken to me about the punishment. What kind of punishment?"

"I'm really ashamed of it."

Lara cringed on the couch. She drew her legs up to her chest and started to sob. What could I do? I wanted to race to my therapist. I was afraid what she might tell me would drive me mad.

"Come here, Lara. Cry all you want. Tell me *everything* there is to tell. I can't take this death by a thousand cuts anymore. You have to pour it all out into the light of day. I have to know what's hidden inside your head or I can't help you."

I pointed at her head for emphasis.

"He'd hit me when I still shied away from group sex. He'd hit me when I said no to his sadomasochistic games that always hurt me. He'd hit me when I refused some friend of his. He'd hit me a lot but not in the face. Today was only the second time…"

I remembered when she'd told me about the first time. She'd gone to her father afterward and told him everything. Lara's apparent lack of limits did have a limit. Being hit in the face was her limit.

"Or he'd leave me locked up in the apartment with no food. I don't know where the fuck he'd go. The bastard would take the key to the kitchen. I'd have to drink water in the bathroom. Sometimes, he'd stay away for a couple of days. Then I'd promise to be good and he'd feed me. I finally found a hiding place where I could keep cookies."

"What a sick son of a bitch!"

"After a while, I believed I was to blame for going hungry or being beaten. He always said, 'It's your fault. If you were a good girl, none of this would happen. It's your fault I don't give you food. It's your fault I hit you. You make me do it. You could have chosen to eat. But you chose to disobey me'."

"Do you understand now that he was completely deranged?"

"I do. It was one of the first things the therapist that Emma and my father took me to explained. Aggressors like him always say it's the victim's fault and eventually, the victim believes it. An adult does. Imagine a kid! And today he said he loved me."

"Lara, that's not love. It's sick. He's a psycho and a pervert. Never let him into your mind to convince you otherwise. Love has nothing to do with that. Lara, we need to get a restraining order against him. Let me do this for you. We'll get one against him and another against your mother. They won't come anywhere near you!"

"Ever?"

Her voice had turned childlike and my heart hurt for her. She was like a little girl, asking her father to promise the monsters would never again appear in her dreams.

"For as long as the order lasts, at least."

"What do I have to do to get it?"

"We'll go to the police right away to show the marks on your body and name the attacker."

"But his father used to be a senator. He knows everybody!"

"Look. This building has security cameras. I'll go down and get the tapes now. And God help that idiot of a doorman if he won't give them to me. We'll keep those bastards away from you. Trust me, Lara."

"I trust you, Mark. A lot! You're on my list of people I know I can count on."

"I love you, Lara. Let me take care of you! I can't promise I'll never hurt you. But I'll never do it intentionally. I promise you that, and I promise I'll take care of you."

Lara didn't answer. She just sat there with her head on my shoulder and squeezed me as if I were a tree trunk in the middle of raging floodwaters all around her.

"I don't want you to tell the whole story. Can we get the order without having to do that?"

"Leave it to me. Don't worry. We'll show your bruises and the tape of when Arthur enters the building. He and your mother will want to avoid a scandal and they'll back off. By the way, I'll need their full names."

"Okay."

At last, I learned the rat's name was Arthur Ranking Eberle. Son of the illustrious former senator Ruggiero Eberle.

We went to a police station and had Lara's injuries verified. Neither friendly persuasion nor nasty threats could get the doorman to give up the tapes. I needed a court order for that. But twenty-four hours later, we had the restraining order. And now that I knew the degenerate's name, I dug up some interesting information on him.

His father had been out of the senate for years and Arthur was now a prominent banker in Washington. He'd recently opened a branch office in New York. Negative publicity would damage him. My experience as a lawyer had taught me that the richer someone was, the greater his need to keep the skeletons hidden in the closet.

I got Arthur's office phone number, faxed him the restraining order and after that called him. I hated that scumbag so much I was shaking uncontrollably. His secretary or whatever told me he was unavailable. I told her to put the fax on his desk immediately and have him call me before noon or Lara would be giving an interview to the media. I also advised her to make sure he got the message. The idea of the interview came to me on the spur of the moment.

And the bluff worked! In a few minutes, Arthur was on the phone, wanting to know what was going on and who I was. I explained to him about the restraining order and its implications. I explained the legal consequences of violating it. I threatened to blacken his name and ruin his life. After all, he'd had no qualms about committing heinous crimes against a defenseless child.

"See here, counselor. You don't know that girl. She's always been unbalanced. She ought to have been institutionalized long ago and put in a straitjacket. She has a warped imagination. She's demented. And she's as cold as ice. I went to see her because her mother is in the hospital with terminal cancer. She wants to see Lara before she dies and God knows Sabine deserves a decent goodbye from her children."

"Now listen to me, Arthur, you sick fucking son of a bitch. I know everything. I know about Paris. I know that Mommy dearest aided and abetted your pedophilia. It's not hard to make a case against a thirty-year-old child molester who takes a girl of thirteen to Paris for six months. So I suggest, for your sake, and for the sake of your loving stepmother, that you comply with the restraining order and stay light years away from Lara. And make sure you relay my message to your pimp of a stepmom. If you don't, her name as well as yours will figure prominently in the media. I hope she dies a painful death. In no way, shape or form is Lara obliged to give a sentimental sendoff to someone who deserves to croak choking on swine swill."

"I understand. Can we make a deal?"

"Yes. Keep away from Lara. That's the deal. No contact with her of any kind. No visits. No phone calls. No telegrams. No e-mails. No text messages. No voice messages. No telepathy. If that word's too erudite for you to comprehend, it means don't even think about her. *Capisci*?"

"Perfectly. Can I count on your canceling the interview?"

"As long as you keep your end of the bargain."

"And what about the accusations you made to get the restraining order?"

"Behave yourself and we'll withdraw them in a few days. Lara doesn't want to see you, even in court."

"And what about her mother? What do I say to her? She's desperate to see Lara before she dies."

"She deserves to suffer a million times what she put her daughter through. My sincerest wish is that she spends eternity in the hottest region of hell. Furthermore, I order you to stress that not only will she not see Lara, she won't see Sean or Debbie either. That dots the Is and crosses the Ts."

"All right."

I hung up, secure in the knowledge he'd gotten the message. To be doubly sure, I made another phone call.

"Lara, pack a suitcase. You're moving to my place today. You'll stay just until this situation blows over."

I went on to tell her what I'd done. I left out certain details such as the state of her mother's health. She didn't need that and besides, I wasn't sure it wasn't another lie.

"Okay, Mark," she meekly replied. No argument, no resistance. We were entering a new era.

Lara stayed with me for a week and then another. A month went by. We picked up clothes and other things from her apartment and occasionally slept there.

We began going out and around holding hands like a normal couple. We talked about everything, or I thought we did. She went to work during the day and I did, too. I gave my evening classes and she painted. We were settling into that way of life. Her nieces even came to visit and I saw how Lara turned into a happy child when in the company of children. A new thought crossed my mind. If Lara wanted to have a baby, I'd embark on that adventure with her.

Our idyll lasted three months, the best months of my life. They were months in which, though she never said she loved me, I felt her close to me. She was happy. Mine. She seemed to have put her demons to flight. We had superlative sex on the living room rug, on the kitchen table, in the bathtub. Even in bed. But always just the two of us. In fact, all third parties were held at arm's length, including Peter. He told us he was getting jealous and feeling left out. But we really wanted to be alone.

Present Day – Simone

Simone put down the manuscript and finally went to sleep. It was after midnight, and the next day promised to be forty miles of bad road.

Chapter Nineteen

Present Day - Simone

The next morning flew by and before Simone knew it, the day was nearly over. She'd had a busy morning and early afternoon, spent handling her clients as well as some of Edward's. He'd been tied up lately, toiling away nonstop on the case of the corpse on her steps. When she stepped out of her office to go grab a cup of coffee toward the end of the day, she was surprised to find Edward there in the reception area.

"Hey, girl, how was your day?" he asked, giving her a peck on the cheek.

"Great, Ed, lots of patients—and some of yours weren't very happy to see me instead of you—but they're all settled. How are things going with you?"

"Working hard with the cops but now the police chief decided I and all the cops on the case should give semen samples. I told them I'd do it but not until next week; I am way too busy right now."

He clenched his jaw and rubbed his hands together, both sure signs that Edward was stressed and irritated.

She laid a comforting hand on his arm. "I'm sorry, Ed, but I guess it's a good thing they're trying to rule people out."

"Just what I needed," he grumbled. "Look at a *Playboy* centerfold and masturbate into a plastic cup. As if I have nothing better to do with my life! And with so much free porn on the 'net I'm surprised those kinds of magazines still exist!" At last he made an attempt at a joke.

"I hear you, my friend, but hey…maybe they give you a tablet instead of a magazine these days." She laughed at the thought.

"Funny…"

Simone's cell rang and she hurried back in to her office to snatch it up off her desk. She pressed the talk button without looking at the display and held it to her ear. "Hello?"

Once again, she heard heavy breathing and the sound of music in the background but not a single word from the caller. After everything that had happened lately, the call took on a new, more ominous meaning.

"Hello?" she said again and when no one responded she scowled. "Listen, if you're not going to speak, don't fucking call this number again!"

She clicked the end button and dropped the phone back onto her desk.

"What was that all about?"

Simone turned to find Ed standing in her office doorway.

"Um, Ed…I think I forgot to tell the police something. Something that might be important."

"What's that?"

"I've been getting weird calls. I answer the phone and there's heavy breathing and music in the background but nobody says anything and the number's blocked."

"How long has this been going on, Simmie?"

"Well, I got two calls before I found the body and this makes three. I shrugged them off but now I'm getting nervous."

"Me too. We'll let the police know right now."

Edward phoned the chief investigator on the case. He gave him Simone's number and received some instructions.

"Simone, the police are going to bug your line. The next time you get a call like that, try to start a conversation. I know it might be a monologue but we need time in order to trace it. The best thing would be to keep talking for at least a minute."

"Damn it! My house has become the setting for a reality show with cameras everywhere…and now a phone tap! Where's my privacy, Ed?"

"I promise you'll have it back when we nail this maniac. He's starting to get sloppy. He was careful up to the last murder. Now he's killing without planning. Soon, very soon, he'll be ours."

"And until then?"

"Until then we have to watch our step. This guy doesn't fool around. And he doesn't just scare people. He kills them."

"I know. But I hate it when my life gets out of control, when nothing feels normal."

"It'll all get back on track. Meanwhile, let me take care of you, my friend. I know you're the most independent woman in the world but I'm here for you. Count on me."

"Ed, that's all I do lately! I'm a burden on you."

"Take it easy. You've always been there to listen to my problems whenever I've needed you. What kind of friend would I be if I only took and gave nothing back? I have to do something for you to make me feel good. And I'm not that altruistic. I need you to be close."

Edward gently touched Simone's cheek and then left.

At that moment, something occurred to Simone. Edward was probably the best person — and most interesting man — she'd ever known. Why had she never seen him that way? Because, to answer her own question, maybe if they'd mixed things, the relationship they had would have ended long ago. Love only causes confusion. Friendship is a much more straightforward feeling.

Philip would be in that day. He had been a nervous wreck when he had called earlier and said he needed her help urgently. She'd managed to juggle some appointments in order to accommodate him.

He looked downcast and downright depressed when he arrived. Simone reflected that he'd no doubt describe himself as feeling like "homemade shit". His clothes were rumpled. He had dark rings under his eyes. He appeared exhausted. And the clearest sign that things were not well — he bore no package of goodies under his arm.

"What happened, Philip? What's wrong?"

"I feel like homemade shit, Doctor. I caught my wife cheating on me."

"What do you mean 'cheating' on you? Aren't you the one who likes her to betray you? I thought you two were doing fine, practicing domination and submission?"

"I did too. I was happy! And then. I found out everything. That club she *suggested*—she's been going there for some time. Alone. And that guy she dragged in front of me when I was all tied up—they've been lovers for a long time."

"She told you?"

"No. Yesterday I went home early, very early. I wasn't feeling well. I thought I was coming down with the flu. I opened the door and I heard moans. My wife doesn't moan much, at least not with me. So I thought she'd decided to surprise me and arranged someone for me to see her with to get me all horny. But right away, I chucked that possibility because I usually arrive three hours later."

"And?"

"I crept into the bedroom. She was on our bed with the guy from the submission house. She was on her hands and knees. I love it when she does that because her ass looks so hot when it's bare. He was deep inside her and they were both moaning. She was saying, 'Come, my love. Come inside me. Feel good, my love. Please.' I didn't care that she was having sex with him. But the 'my love' shit really made me suffer. Her love was me, not him! And she never talked dirty to me…but there she was, talking dirty to him."

Philip began to sob. Simone handed him a box of tissues. He calmed down a bit and continued.

"I stood there beside the bed and they didn't pay any attention to me. They were making love, doing everything she said she didn't like. She always told me she wanted heavy duty, 'send-it-in-daddy' sex. But here was this guy caressing her body and porking her slowly. She turned over and he put his mouth on hers. They were kissing as he was diddling her gently."

"And they didn't see you at any time?"

"Their eyes were closed. When they finally fired their afterburners, they noticed me. I was expecting some creative explanations but he just said to her, 'Darling, I think you two should talk. Will you be all right?'"

"That must have been heartbreaking for you, Philip."

"I thought I was going to die then and there, Doctor."

"How did she attempt to justify her behavior?"

"She said she needed to have something of her own. She said our sexual practices were short on intimacy and she had more of it with her lover. More intimacy than she had with me? We did everything together!"

"What's going to happen now, Philip?"

"She wants to leave me. She says she's going to live with her lover, that she's fed up with my looniness and that she's never felt loved. She says that my giving her to others means I don't care for her. But her lover cares and wants her only for him and him alone."

"Philip, that's one of the risks in this kind of sexual practice. Somebody loses."

"I've lost her, Doctor. And the worst thing is I don't know what I'll do without her. It's exactly the opposite of what she thinks! I love her more than anything. Letting her have sex with other men was a way of always keeping her satisfied. I thought she wouldn't need to cheat on me."

"But let's face it; it was also a way for you to have fun, Philip."

"Yes, it was, Doctor. But also a way for her to get more fun out of life. That way, she wouldn't have to chase other men because I'd always give her all the men she wanted."

"If she asked you to cut out your fantasies…all of them…would you? Would you be true to her?"

"I would, Doctor. She's the most important thing in the world to me! But I think it's too late now."

"Philip, it's never too late. You have to tell her everything you've just told me. You have to make her understand you've let her have other men because you were afraid of losing her. In reality, it's that old childhood fear of being overshadowed by your brothers and sisters, the fear of never being able to shine in the eyes of the woman you love."

"You think if I do that, she'll come back to me, Doctor?"

"I can't say for sure. But I do believe your sincerity will go a long way. If she truly wants an intimate relationship with just one man, tell her you're the one. It's your only chance."

"I'll try," he replied, perking up a bit.

When the session ended Simone felt all in. Poor Philip! Sometimes she felt powerless. She'd hoped the psychotherapy would bear fruit earlier. If Philip's nickel had dropped sooner, he might have saved his marriage.

Her final patient of the day canceled and she decided to use the free time to keep reading the text Carl had given her.

Mark's Journal – How About Having Some Fun?

Lara woke up happy and we lolled around in bed.

"Hey, Mark. Want to go dancing today?" she chirped.

"Sounds great, babe. Where?"

"I don't know. I thought maybe a new place." She glanced at me mischievously.

"Okay." I returned her glance. "Is it swing?"

"Yes, but I hear the music's great and you don't have to do anything."

"Ha. Don't forget, lady. I know you. You're up for some fooling around, right?"

"Yes, to tell you the truth."

She looked at me with puppy-dog eyes. How could I refuse?

"I'm in," I said.

I knew what lay ahead. But I'll be honest. I wanted some action too. Just the thought of it tickled my prostate. I forsook hypocrisy. I could live on caviar and champagne every day if I had to. But variety is the spice of life. If I were able to change the menu once in a while, with the consent of the partner, what would be wrong with that?

The recently opened club was not far from Penn Station in midtown Manhattan and was called Silk Lips. My growing excitement amazed me as I got ready to step out with Lara. My heart raced and my hands grew ice cold.

The place was discreet with private parking—highly unusual, considering its location. We entered a corridor lit only by the computer for registering customers. No formal ID required, just our names for the night.

"I'm Luca and she's Jane," I told the greeter.

Lara smiled and said for my ears only, "Me Tarzan. You Jane."

They gave us a plastic card with a number to pay for our drinks. We walked through a doorway onto a dance floor with a pole in the middle. A few couples were boogying to 1970s disco music. Luca and Jane eagerly joined them. The dance floor filled up as we bounced around. A number of women risked their necks amateurishly on the pole. What a spectacle! By day, they were probably demure damsels or prim housewives. Now they were naughty, nocturnal New Yorkers, displaying their drawers and *derrières* for all the world to see.

A counter running the length of the wall separated the bar from the dance floor. Half-naked, frolicking women hung from rails suspended above the counter. At first, I had no idea whether they were employees or customers. Lara clarified the situation when she asked my help to get up there.

She was wearing a very short violet dress and stilt-like silver high heels. I did as she requested and she began to perform provocatively. A lot of men soon took notice. She was a sultry, swaying sexpot and loose as a goose after three whiskies. I watched her with wonder and jealousy. My girlfriend, if I could call her that, looked gorgeous. And despite my jealousy, it was fantastic to see other men lusting after the woman I was with. I felt powerful.

After a while, she came down and we had another drink. Then we headed for the dark "labyrinth", the place where couples traded partners. Only silhouettes appeared in the dim light given off by red lamps tucked away in corners. There was a corridor with tiny side rooms, each of which had a sofa around five feet long. The doors had windows for passersby to see the goings-on inside.

Two copulating couples had squeezed themselves into one of the compartments. Probably a switcheroo. I began to get horny. Lara and I wandered around, taking in the sights, holding hands. Mine were getting sweaty because I was in heat, surrounded by unfettered fornication, raw sex without preliminaries. One woman we saw pressed her face against the glass to take it in the ass. She looked directly at us, a patent demonstration of exhibitionism because she'd turned up the interior light. She wanted to be seen, admired and desired. I felt a number of hands touching me as we stood there.

Lara pulled me away. We entered a room that had a community bed with a tangle of people on it. Others were just hanging around, watching the show.

We moved closer. Two women were getting it on. One lay on her back with the other on all fours on top. The latter had three fingers in the former's pussy and had the pecker of a fully dressed, gray-haired man, who had slightly lowered his trousers, penetrating her from behind. He climaxed, pulled out, removed his condom and gave way to another guy who'd been there ogling and playing with himself. The woman on all fours was taking on all comers. Have an orgy! Monkey business in the monkey house!

"You want a piece of that?" Lara asked, pointing at the woman. "She's just warming up."

"*Moi*?" I replied. The idea of putting it to a woman who'd already taken on the Chinese army and was about to engage the Russians did not appeal to me. But I was witnessing an extremely erotic tour de force. The scene had boosted my adrenalin level a thousand percent. My heart hammered. My testicles tightened. My cock hardened. I urgently needed to get my rocks off.

We departed that den of debauchery and entered another. Again, an orgy was in progress on two beds, or rather, two mattresses upholstered with a glossy fabric. Everybody was doing it for the benefit of a few spectators like Lara and me. A daisy chain of two couples humped and bumped about while others took part in sundry activities lying down. A lone man went around feeling up all the women he could lay his hands on. Another guy just stood there masturbating.

Amid all this jerking and jostling, one scene struck me as especially memorable. It was reminiscent of an episode of *Wild Planet*—the one about how snakes have sex. A gorgeous goddess who was being penetrated by a handsome guy performed cunnilingus on an equally delectable deity. There were good-looking people on that mattress. The beautiful blonde goddess being licked looked in my direction and nodded at me to come over. I turned to Lara.

"Go for it, Mark," she said.

I didn't hesitate. The woman's statuesque curves must have been sculpted by a personal trainer who was the reincarnation of Michelangelo. She said nothing when I approached. She simply shoved away the woman who'd been sucking her snatch, pulled down my zipper, slipped the condom Lara handed her onto my pulsating penis and put my cock into her mouth. I closed my eyes and let her do the job. Her tongue was agile and slick. It slipped around and around and tickled the tip. A little longer and I'd have come in her mouth. The only thing that stopped me was the reduced sensitivity caused by the condom. She took my member out of her mouth and led me to a mattress. She pushed me down, mounted me and rode me savagely until we both came and came and came. That venue was void of foreplay. Adrenalin reigned supreme.

The woman dismounted and I lay there comatose for a few moments. When I snapped out of it, I looked around for Lara. I spotted her with her skirt raised, sans panties and fingering her sweet spot, no doubt inspired by the scene she'd just witnessed. A man stood behind her with his hands on her breasts, which were now visible because he'd dropped her top. Another man came up and began to suck one of her nipples.

A third man appeared. Lara had her eyes wide open and was aware of everything that was going on. He was about fifty and not at all attractive. But in the half-light he looked lean and dapper. He took his monstrous meat out of his pants and showed it to Lara to get her okay. She readily granted his unspoken request and pushed away the man sucking her breasts. The guy with the big one put on a prophylactic and skewered Lara right there while on his feet. They began to bump and grind. The other two guys fondled her breasts while she moaned. Lara and the stallion climaxed together and then separated. One of the guys who'd been feeling her up whispered something in her ear. She shook her head no. He then came over to me.

"Your lady's a fox. I want to fuck her. Please ask her to let me."

What a loon! The guy was begging me to convince Lara to spread her legs for him. If someone had told me a short time before that such a place existed, I'd have asked him what he'd been smoking. Strangely enough, this time I didn't get jealous. I think my senses were still deadened by that drool-sex with the goddess.

"Mark, want to do a switcheroo?" Lara asked.

"What?"

"There's a nice-looking couple sitting over there." She pointed to an attractive twosome agape at the sights in Sodom. "I'll do him and you do her at the same time."

"Sounds good."

Lara went to them and negotiated. They agreed, and the four of us headed to another corridor that had rooms like jail cells with mattresses on the floors and bars on the windows. We entered an empty one. I closed the bars. Lara and the man went at each other right away. The woman was on the shy side and nervous. I slowly and gently began to caress her neck.

"Take it easy," I whispered. "I'll only do what you want."

"I'm frightened," she replied. "I've never done this before. It was his idea."

She gestured toward her husband who had one of Lara's tits halfway inside his mouth.

"No problem. As I said, we'll just do as you wish. And I won't hurry you."

"Thank you."

I rubbed her shoulders lightly and then began to nibble the back of her neck. She let out a deep sigh. I ran my tongue down her back and then turned her around and began to suck her breasts. I lifted up her skirt, slipped my hand inside her panties and massaged her moist pussy. Not many women can keep cool while enjoying that.

I continued patiently to wear down her resistance. Finally, she moaned. I obeyed her wishes, leaving her in control. I put on a condom and slipped my penis into her vagina. She was tight. She was delicious. And as I watched Lara and the man screwing rhythmically, I sped up my thrusts and made her orgasm one, two, three times. She couldn't stop and pleaded with me to keep going.

"Give me more. Give me more. I've never come like this before!"

Maybe she was just turned on. Maybe I'm a super stud. Who knows? But I was extremely pleased to see that we wrapped things up well after Lara and the man did. They just sat there watching us. Lara looked frustrated. *Grrrreat!*

When we finished, my partner whispered in my ear, "Give me your phone number. I want more. Nobody has ever made me get off like that."

I felt like King Kong but answered, "I can't. I'm with her." I nodded toward Lara. It would be madness to cheat on someone who gave me such freedom.

Lara took my hand and led me to another room, one with windows. She growled between her teeth, "Fuck me, Mark! Make me come! I need to come! That quick draw sack of shit over there couldn't finish the job!"

I felt proud of myself. *That's what Lara gets for her smart ideas! In the end, what's new isn't always what's best.* Lara had to work to get her wish. After all, it was my third time that night. Only when I was a teenager—and now, when I'm in a place like this one—could I perform such feats. We returned home in the wee hours, looking like a couple of scarecrows—disheveled, sweaty and with the smell of sex about us. But we were together and holding hands.

Chapter Twenty

Present Day – Simone

Mark's accounts of his erotic nocturnal adventures intrigued Simone. They contained so many details and such precise descriptions that she felt transported to the very locales. Did he have a photographic memory or just a vivid imagination? Suddenly she had an idea. She'd visit one of those places to learn the truth. She'd separate fancy from reality. A field trip would also be fruitful for her book. What kinds of people go there? And why?

She called Carl and said she'd like to visit one of the swing houses Mark talked about. She didn't disclose her motives. She asked if he could find out if those nightspots really existed in New York. He told her he'd call back later with the information. When he did, he said the places existed and were still operating. One was open from Tuesday to Sunday and the other kicked off the week on Wednesday. Simone asked if he would accompany her to one of them. Carl sounded a bit reluctant. He said he could if it was on a Friday night. If not, he'd find someone else to go with her because he would be busy from Monday to Thursday night this week.

They scheduled the expedition for Friday. Simone would meet Carl in New York early in the evening. He informed her that the swing houses opened after eleven. He suggested they first have dinner at one of the restaurants Mark talked about in the text. He seemed to understand what she was seeking to accomplish. Simone thought it best not to discuss her plans with Edward. Something told her he'd be against the idea. She wondered whether it was correct and professional or just the product of her curiosity. She ended up telling him she'd be going to New York for work.

Edward informed Simone he'd set up a meeting for them on Friday with Victor, the e-mail contact. As Simone had told him she'd be with Carl, Edward said he'd figure something out. He added that maybe it would be better for him to go alone to see the fellow anyway.

Alvin was Simone's final appointment on Wednesday. They'd agreed it would be at his regular time. She didn't like him at all, though she couldn't decide just why. He seemed polite and well mannered. But she had the impression that everything he said was nothing more than a set piece performance, completely phony and designed to shock her. What was his motive?

Why would someone spend good money to shock a shrink? It didn't make sense.

"Good afternoon, Alvin. How are you?"

Simone offered him her hand. He took it with his fingertips, raised it to his lips and kissed it. Simone wanted to go to the girls' room and wash. She had an innate aversion to reptiles.

"Good afternoon, my lovely doctor."

Better not to get carried away, she thought. The guy had hardly gotten seated when he began to talk about his off-the-wall week.

"I did it again, Doctor."

"Did what, Alvin?"

"Sex with strangers. And this time there was a bit of bisexuality."

"Could you explain that, please?"

"There was a very handsome man in the place I went to. An orgy was in progress. Everybody was screwing everybody, and when I spotted him he and I began to get it on."

"Active or passive?"

"Me? I was passive."

"And?"

"I found it interesting for a change. Do you think I could be bisexual?"

"Based on just one experience, I can't say."

"And if I like it and want more?"

"Look, Alvin. Let me explain something. Usually, bisexuality is a euphemism for people who can't come out as homosexuals. Some can live with that their whole lives. But others eventually need to come clean about their true nature. If you did it just once, it was only an experiment. Sure, it may have been pleasurable. But it's mere curiosity. Now, if you start desiring men more often, it's a clear sign of homosexuality."

"Homo or bi? I could be flex, right?"

"Bisexuality is usually the lack of courage to come out or a profound ignorance of real feelings. People like that suffer. Coming out has huge consequences. So to think of oneself as 'flex' is easier than to face reality and the costs that accompany it."

"I'm not a coward, Doctor."

God give me patience, Simone thought.

"I'll give you my professional opinion, Alvin. We need further meetings for me to reach a conclusion. At this point, I can say you're showing listlessness with regard to having sex with women. You have almost no interest in relations with your wife. You need a large amount of adrenalin to get aroused. Recently, you've had a homosexual experience that you wish to repeat. This might indicate a search for something that only now is starting to come to the surface."

"Desire for men?"

"Have you felt that before? Was it your first experience of that kind?"

"Intercourse, yes. I'd sucked men's cocks and been sucked in a few unprotected group sex sessions. But I'd never reached this point. It surprised me because I enjoyed it much more than with a woman."

"A few group sessions...with total strangers?"

"No, the group sex wasn't with strangers. They were people I knew well."

He was grasping at straws. Simone realized the people he "knew well" part of his statement was probably another lie.

"So you have had unprotected sex several times with other people. I misunderstood you during our first meeting. You told me the other day that it had happened just one time…"

"Perhaps I expressed myself poorly. Is that important?"

"It is. Have you been practicing group sex for very long?"

"Yes. For a while."

Simone didn't believe a word of what he was saying. Everything seemed geared toward unsettling her and testing her reactions."

"What is it like?"

"Very intense and very good. There are always various people, men and women. We constantly switch partners. Nobody cares about who they do it with. Only about getting off. All the bodies are there to give pleasure. Conquest is unnecessary. You just go up and get it on with whoever's available. Or you join a party of two, three or sometimes even more people."

"Does that give you the most pleasure? Sex with a lot of people?"

"No. That's the problem. It seems I only feel satisfied when I experience something new. Different."

Simone got the impression that what Alvin was saying had come right out of a book on sexual behavior. It was as if he were regurgitating what he had read somewhere. But that didn't make sense.

"That doesn't surprise me. The incessant search for pleasure usually means a search for your hidden side. Maybe it's emerging."

"Yes. Maybe. I'd like to be able to resist these impulses, Doctor. There's no way I can let myself turn gay. I have a wife. I have a child. I'd never want to let them down," he said, but he spoke without a trace of emotion.

Simone thought she'd once read something similar to the story he was telling. But she couldn't remember where.

"Perhaps it's only a part of your bad habit, Alvin. Do you enjoy sex with women too?"

"Yes, I do. But only with women I don't know. If it's the same woman all the time, not much. But this experience I just had with a man — truth to tell, it was sublime. And it terrifies me!" But he didn't seem terrified.

"We'll need to reduce your sexual compulsion if it makes you feel that way. We could try medication."

"If that helps me to keep away from men."

"It will reduce your libido in general. There's no way to be selective. I just don't know how you'll handle that."

"Chemical castration?"

"Let's not exaggerate. But because of your fears, we have to try to control you until the therapy takes effect."

"I *told* you seeing you just once a week isn't enough, Doctor! Now I'm going to turn gay and it's *your* fault!"

She scrutinized him to try to determine if this angry, threatening outburst was just an act. Almost immediately, she saw real anger there. His tone was hostile and he jabbed his index finger at her.

"I've already explained to you that my agenda is full, Alvin. Unfortunately, I'm dealing with cases even more serious than yours. I can't just drop them."

"Is it about money, Doctor? I'll double what they're paying!"

"No, Alvin. It's about ethics! How would you feel if I dropped a patient to see you? Would you believe I wouldn't do the same to you if a *better opportunity* arose? I've got possible suicides to worry about."

"Fuck your ethics, Doc! And let your patients kill themselves if they want to! My problem is serious. I'm turning gay and you're not doing a *goddamn thing* to help me!"

"I suggest you calm down, Alvin. I'm doing my best but you have to help yourself. You need to have willpower and we'll start you on medication immediately."

"You're a useless cow. You can't treat me, so you want to stuff me with pills. You're a fucking farce. You're just a frigid bitch. All you know about sex is theory. You must spend hours dreaming up theories about what sex is like in practice."

"Alvin, I don't think I'm the best person to provide your treatment. I'm going to refer you to a colleague who has more time. I agree that your case requires more attention. But I simply can't give it."

Simone went to her desk to find the number of another psychiatrist for Alvin. When she turned her back, something whizzed past her ear and smashed against the wall. Alvin had thrown the glass ball that had been by the couch.

Simone yelped in fear. Thinking fast, she reached a shaking hand beneath the lip of her desk and pressed the panic button, which would signal Mona, who was, luckily, still in the office.

"You're a sadistic snot! You're not professional at all! Goddamn you, you owe me more attention!"

"I don't owe you anything."

Simone tried to remain calm and had gone around behind her desk for protection when Mona opened the door and entered the room without asking for permission, planting herself between Alvin and Simone.

"Mona, please show this gentleman to the door. He is no longer my patient."

"You tight-ass cunt! You think you can get rid of me just like that?" He continued to rant.

A lifetime of discipline enabled Simone to appear cool. Inside, she wanted to kick the asshole in the nuts.

"Alvin, control yourself. If I call the police, you'll be in a world of trouble. I'll transfer your records to wherever you wish and we will no longer work together."

Mona took Alvin firmly by the arm and led him outside. She was not a small woman and she had no trouble handling him, despite the fact he continued spewing expletives.

"You are going to pay dearly, you bitch," he shouted back over his shoulder.

Simone's legs were trembling so badly she collapsed into her chair.

"Are you all right, Doctor? He's gone." Mona appeared at Simone's side with a mug of hot tea, her remedy for all the trials and tribulations of the world.

"I will be, Mona. Thank you. My intuition told me that guy would be a huge problem from the second I first saw him. Oh, Mona. I'm getting too old to handle so many lunatics all the time. Lately, I haven't seen anyone remotely normal."

"Well, if makes you feel better, I never seen any normal around here. You need a vacation, Doctor," Mona sympathized as she handed her a saucer for her tea.

"You're right, Mona. And thank you for the tea."

Mona nodded once, patted Simone's shoulder and then left her alone to sip her tea.

Simone called Edward and told him what had happened.

"That's awful, Simone. Lately, I've been thinking seriously about getting a security guard for the office. Things are no longer the way they were when we started out. It seems more and more people out walking around should be straitjacketed."

"We're in the age of 'me first' and 'just for me', Ed."

"And that's why I'm thinking about me, about us. I'll hire someone, Simone. I'll hire us a guard to be on duty during office hours. That Alvin character could have hurt you."

"I don't think so. He's the type who just blusters. Deep down, he's a coward. I'll have to call Dr. Schuster to tell him I can't treat his referral. But I'll do it tomorrow. Right now, I just want to go home and lie back with my feet up. What an infernal week."

"Want some company?"

"No, my friend. But thanks for offering. Today, silence is what I need."

Simone went home to be by herself. They'd installed the security system the day before and she'd returned. But after the body on the steps, the house felt spooky. Every little noise gave her chills and made her jumpy. She'd have to do something to take her mind off the noises and to forget the dead woman.

She decided to read. She was getting to the end of the text. Had it been a novel, she would have read rapidly. But it was in fact a document that demanded thorough analysis of minute details.

Mark's Journal – Mourning

Everything seemed fine. Lara and I were happy. Once in a while, I'd give in to her itch for adventure. But generally we sailed along upon calm, sunny seas. Such waters, however, can be the harbinger of hurricanes.

Peter called me at the office one afternoon. He asked my secretary to interrupt whatever I was doing because it was urgent. I'd turned off my cell phone and was working on a complicated case and had made it clear I wasn't to be interrupted unless there was an emergency.

"Hi, Peter. What's up? Where's the fire?"

"Hi, Mark. I couldn't get you on your cell."

"Is everything all right?" When Peter spoke in a restrained tone, it was always a sign of trouble.

"Lara's mother died. Lara's taking it hard. Debbie called me and said she couldn't reach her. Lara's probably shut herself up in her apartment and doesn't want to talk to anybody. Debbie's worried."

"When did she die? I was with Lara last night."

"I don't know. Lara, Sean and Debbie found out this morning. A lawyer contacted them about reading her will."

"Leave it to me, Peter. I'll go talk to Lara."

Lara really wasn't taking calls. I dropped what I was doing and went to her apartment. The doorman was warier now—though he'd often seen me with Lara—and didn't want to let me go up since Lara wasn't answering the interphone. He also said he believed she wasn't there. I thought it was just an excuse Lara had asked him to make. I explained the gravity of the situation and he at last gave in, no doubt fearful of a court order.

I repeatedly rang the bell with no success. I considered breaking the door down like they do in the movies, but it was heavy and solid and I feared the consequences for my shoulder. I asked the doorman if he kept a spare key. He said no and I called Peter.

"I'll see if Debbie has one, Mark."

She didn't. No one did. I cursed Lara's obsession with privacy. I ended up breaking in, saying a quick prayer she wouldn't do anything crazy like press charges. Night was falling, the apartment was chilly and a window was wide open with curtains billowing in the icy wind. I went over and closed it. I looked in every nook and cranny but no Lara. In the dead quiet, I grew extremely worried. I called Peter again.

"She's not here!"

"She might be in the Hamptons. She has a house out there."

"I remember. You told me about it. You think that's where she is?"

"I'm not sure. But I can't think of anywhere else."

"Paris! It would be just like Lara to get as far away as possible."

"No. Forget that. Debbie said Lara was sobbing and all broken up. I don't think she was in any condition to go to the airport. But wait. You never can tell. You go to the Hamptons and I'll go to the airport. Whoever finds her first…"

"Okay. Give me the address. I don't think the airlines will give you any information about a passenger without a court order but it's worth a try."

I raced out to Long Island. I had a hard time finding the house. It was in a remote spot in Westhampton and night was falling. Luckily,

Lara's car was parked outside. I called Peter and told him.

The house looked beautiful from what I could see in the dark. It was made of wood like almost all the others around there. I couldn't be sure of the color — maybe beige, maybe white. A sand driveway went up to the front steps. The door was unlocked and I went inside.

I found Lara right away, barefoot and sitting on the floor. She was wearing torn jeans and a loose T-shirt, and her eyes stared lost and vacant out of a puffy, tear-soaked face. She was a picture of palpable pain and suffering. I texted Peter to tell him I'd found her.

I approached her slowly. She raised her head and looked at me but said nothing.

"Lara, my love, what's this? What's going on?"

"I killed my mother!" Her wavering voice showed she'd had at least one too many.

"You didn't kill your mother. Why do you say that?"

"Mark, you don't understand. I always wanted her to die. Now she's dead."

"She died because she was sick, Lara. Not you, not anyone, can kill someone just by thinking it."

"I let her die alone. I didn't believe she was sick."

"Lara, your mother did everything possible to die alone. The way she treated you! Everything! If she was alone when she died…and we don't know that…she had a husband and stepson…it was her choice. The choices we make in life determine our future."

"I know. I thought I hated her. But now I feel alone. I don't have my father. I don't have my grandmother. I don't have my mother anymore. I'm alone!"

"Lara, you never had a mother. You had a pimp. But you have your brother and sister and nieces. You have me. You have friends. You're not alone."

"Yes I am. I'm more and more alone. People are going away. They're leaving me. I'm not worthy of being loved."

"Listen, Lara. You're drunk. You don't know what you're saying. People haven't gone away. They've died. They had no choice between staying and leaving. And you deserve all the love in the world."

Now she uttered the immortal words of the indignant lush: "I am *not* drunk. I'm fine."

She struggled to her feet and tried to cross her legs to show she had perfect balance. If I hadn't grabbed her, she'd have gone ass over teakettle. Her glass fell from her hand and shattered on the floor.

"Lara, relax." I put her on the couch.

"Goddamn you. I want another drink."

"Don't even think about it. I'm going to make coffee and then you're going in the bathtub. God knows you need one. You smell like a skid-row wino. How long since you've had something to eat?"

"I don't know… I'm such a scumbag, Mark. I killed my mother. I split up my parents first."

"We know that's not true, and that's that. Stay here. I'll be right back."

I went to the kitchen, a lovely room decorated in all light-beige, with a glass wall that probably faced the sea. It was dark and I could only guess. I found an espresso machine and some capsules. I made a rugged cup of coffee as fast as I could and took it to Lara.

"The room's spinning, Mark. I close my eyes and everything goes arounnnnd…"

"I believe you."

I went into a greenhouse-like bathroom, bright and glassy. I opened a tap and let the tub fill up. I returned to Lara and started stripping her.

"I don't want to fuck just now, Mark. World is spinning too fast."

"I don't either. You stink like an old port´s tavern. You're going to take a bath. It'll do you good."

I lugged Lara to the bathroom with her head resting on my shoulder. I checked the water temperature and cooled it a little. I lowered her into the tub, took a sponge and a bar of soap and went to work. I found some shampoo, washed her hair and rinsed it with a hose and nozzle I took from the wall. Lara behaved like a docile child, quiet and obedient. *I should always keep her pickled,* I thought.

I found towels and a robe in a cabinet. I lifted her out of the tub, dried her off and slipped the robe on her. Then I carried her toward a bedroom.

"Not that one," she mumbled. "That's Emma's. Nobody uses it. Mine's at the end of the corridor. The pink one."

So I headed there. The room was dark and I flipped on the light switch. To my surprise, it was a kid's room. It was all pink, including the curtains, with stuffed animals on a shelf. A guitar lay forgotten in a corner. None of this fit with what I'd known about the woman until then. Lara was showing an ever more fragile side of herself. She hadn't had a proper childhood and seemed to want to remain forever at the point before it had been torn away from her. *May her mother rot in hell.*

I pulled back the covers, removed the robe, propped up the pillows and laid her on the bed.

"Stay here, Lara. Rest. I'll get you something to eat."

"There's nothing in the house. You'll find phone numbers for pizza and stuff on the fridge." The booze seemed to be wearing off. "My head hurts," she moaned. And the hangover was setting in.

I found numbers galore. That woman couldn't fry an egg. I called a few take-out places and a local supermarket. They promised to send my orders right over. I had aspirin coming too. It was almost ten o'clock. Out there, "right over" meant eleven.

When I finally had food and a glass of juice on a tray, I took it to Lara. She was sleeping peacefully. Great. I settled into an easy chair and chowed down. Then I fell asleep right there, exhausted.

The following morning, before Lara woke up, I fixed breakfast in the kitchen. I called Peter right afterward, asked for Debbie's number, phoned her and introduced myself. Though I'd babysat her daughters with Lara, I'd never actually spoken to Debbie before. I described the situation. She told me she and Lara were supposed to meet with a lawyer about Sabine's will. She asked me if I would accompany them. I said I would but suggested we wait a couple of days because Lara needed time to pull herself together.

I canceled my immediate appointments, handed off others and took care of Lara for the next three days. Immersed in a personal hell, she spoke very little and ate even less. I spotted storm clouds on the horizon.

We scheduled the reading of the will for Friday and Lara agreed to go. She, the lawyer, Debbie and I were present. Sean refused to travel to attend what he called "Sabine's final performance".

And he had hit the nail on the head. Wonderful he wasn't there. None of us should have been there. Sabine had left a letter to her children. She blamed Lara for her life's misfortunes. She said her daughter hadn't realized that all she ever cared about was her "wellbeing". The whole screed was a potpourri of falsehoods and execrable excuses, certainly concocted so she could die in peace. She left properties and valuables to be divided among the three survivors. If the bitch hadn't died already, I'd have hunted her down and killed her for what she'd written.

Dear Children,

I am about to depart this life and will do so alone because you, Lara, have misunderstood everything that took place in your childhood. All my actions were conceived to ensure you a safe and secure future. But they have resulted in the irreparable estrangement of us all. You were so young, Lara. We were all too young to grasp the true nature of things. I have never wished our lives to turn out this way. More than anything, I have yearned for us to be a family. Now it is too late. Our mistakes have been made. Our wounds have been opened and I know they will never heal. I forgive you, my daughter, and ask your forgiveness and that of your brother and sister for not having been a better mother.

I recently found out that Sean has turned gay. Listen, my son. It is just a phase you're going through. You will grow up to know better. You have always had a curious mind and liked to try new things. I am certain this will pass.

Deborah, you are the perfect child all parents would love to have. You are stable, normal, a born mother! I was so surprised to hear my little baby now has her own babies. I have not had the pleasure of meeting the girls but I am positive they are as beautiful and sweet as you are.

Now I am going away and I hope that I am leaving you with at least one small remembrance of happy moments we have shared together. I bequeath to you everything that I have built in my life as proof that all I have ever done I have done for you. And especially for you, Lara, my eldest and dearest child.

Love,

Sabine

"I don't want one fucking thing from that bucket of toxic waste! Donate everything that's coming to me to charity! I don't need anything from her."

"Lara, I'd like to keep the jewels. They remind me of my childhood. I thought Mama looked so pretty when she wore them."

"They're yours, Debbie. But always remember she sold me to get half of them."

Lara looked awful. She'd lost weight in the past few days and had stopped wearing makeup and doing her hair. She almost never spoke. I desperately wanted to know what was happening inside her tormented body and soul. But she'd shut me out of her world.

Chapter Twenty-One

Present Day – Simone

Simone's days had been busy. Thursday began like a blow to the solar plexus. She stepped out of her house in a hurry, her phone in one hand, her purse in the other. After dialing Mona's number, Simone propped the phone on her shoulder as she closed the door and engaged the house alarm.

"Hi, Mona," Simone said when the other woman answered. "I'm leaving home now; do you know if I have any open space on my schedule today?"

"Good morning, Doctor. Nope—you're all booked up, except for one hour to have lunch."

"Nice, and I didn't have breakfast. Oh well, thanks, Mona." She climbed into her car and drove directly to the office.

When Simone arrived at the office, Mona greeted her with magic words. "Doctor, your first patient called to say he is going to be at least ten minutes late, so I took the liberty of preparing you some breakfast. It's waiting for you in the kitchen." Mona smiled sweetly.

"Thanks, many thanks. Mona, you made my day…as always!"

After her quick breakfast she started to receive her patients and couldn't stop to breathe until noon. She hoped to break for an hour to have lunch and to rest before getting back in the ring for round two. Mona came to her just after twelve to discuss Alvin, the madman who'd whizzed the glass ball past Simone's head.

"Doctor, I'm sorry to disturb you during your moment of peace but that man, Alvin, is calling every fifteen minutes, insisting I make an appointment for him. I'm having a difficult time making him understand you aren't interested in seeing him."

"Mona, I have to talk to Dr. Schuster about that man. Please call the doctor's office and if you get him on the line, transfer him to me. Tell him it's urgent. Oh, and please order me a salad and grilled chicken breast." *There goes lunchtime leisure,* she thought to herself.

In no time at all Mona was buzzing Simone to say Dr. Schuster was on the line. Simone had Mona put the call straight through.

"Hello, Simone. Gustav here."

"Gustav, thank you so much for taking my call so quickly. I need to discuss a former patient of yours, one you referred to me. Alvin Ormand."

"Was that recently? I don't remember an Alvin Ormand, Simone."

"He came in about two or three weeks ago, saying you'd sent him."

"No. No referral that recent. And whenever I refer someone to you I always call to fill you in beforehand."

"You do. I hadn't taken that into account."

"So what he said isn't true. You'll have to find out where the man came from, Simone."

She said goodbye to Gustav and buzzed Mona.

"Mona, please call that lunatic."

"Which one, Doctor?"

Simone couldn't help laughing.

"Good one, Mona…our current problem."

Alvin didn't answer. Simone then asked Mona to transfer him to her the next time he called. She added that, if she was with a patient, to have him call her on her next break or to get a number where he could be reached. Simone was worried but soon her afternoon patients took her mind off Alvin.

Just before closing, Mona buzzed to say Alvin was on the line.

"Transfer him to me, please, Mona." Simone's heart started to accelerate.

"Okay, Doctor…and, um…and if I may give you a little piece of advice? Tell the man to go straight to hell if he tries to mistreat you."

"Ha! I certainly will, Mona, thank you!"

The intercom fell silent and a moment later, the phone on Simone's desk rang. She picked up the handset.

"Good afternoon, Alvin."

"Good afternoon, my dear doctor. I see you've given in and decided to talk to me."

"Only to tell you to stop bothering my secretary. I've spoken to Dr. Schuster. He doesn't know you. What are you trying to pull, Alvin?"

"Dr. Schuster is a smelly, senile old fart. He treated me for months and used to doze off during our sessions."

"We both know that's another lie. Dr. Schuster's father may be an old man but he's not my colleague and he is retired. Gustav Schuster is only fifty, far from being old and senile. What do you really want with me?"

"To be treated by you, Doctor. I know you can cure me."

"Suppose I told you I think nothing that comes out of your mouth in my office is true?"

"I'd say you were mistaken. By the way, please forgive my behavior the other day. I've been very much on edge lately."

"Certainly, Alvin. Let me give you the number of a colleague, Dr. Klein."

"I've already told you I don't want any of your fucking colleagues!"

"I'm no longer available to treat you, Alvin. Please jot down the number."

"Listen to me, you mangy bitch! Do you think you can go around ruining people's lives any old way you want?"

"Alvin, I think you're overexcited and if you continue to speak that way, you'll force me to hang up."

"Nobody's forcing you to do anything, sweetness. You do whatever you want. You're not a good person, Doctor. You're just a bitter, nasty, useless little cunt, and I'll turn your life into an infernal cesspit if you won't treat me!"

Simone slammed down the phone and made a mental note to talk to Edward the next day. That lunatic was definitely crazier than the others.

* * * * *

Simone headed for New York on Friday afternoon. She called Carl upon her arrival, and he told her he'd pick her up at her hotel at seven. They'd go for a drink, then dinner and then get down to business.

Carl showed up at the appointed hour. They had cocktails at the hotel because they didn't want to face the hellacious traffic. Around nine, they took a cab to Amma, the Indian restaurant Lara had taken Mark to on one of their first dates.

As soon as they entered, Simone took note of the décor and the smells, the tiniest details. They took their seats. A waiter who spoke minimal English brought them menus. He suggested various dishes and they ordered. From start to finish, Mark's description of the waiters, the wall colors and everything else was right on the money. His accuracy impressed Simone.

Carl was wonderful company, ever eager to hear Simone's thoughts on what she'd read so far. Now she was almost finished and he was pleased with her progress. Though they mainly exchanged ideas and impressions regarding the text, they also made small talk, as if they were just another couple out on a date.

Simone told him about the body she'd found on the steps the morning after he'd been to her house. He seemed sincerely startled. He had seen something on TV but hadn't connected the news to her, and he asked questions about the serial killings and how the investigation was going.

"Slowly," she stressed. "The police keep coming up empty in their search for a suspect. Nobody has a clue about the killer's movements. He's a clever and careful psychopath." She went on to tell him about the connection she'd made with the French TV series.

They finally began to talk about which swing house they'd visit. Carl suggested Silk Lips. He explained that, according the information he'd gotten during his earlier research, Behind the Door was very bad news lately.

As they stepped onto the sidewalk outside the restaurant, Carl spotted a taxi across the street. He hailed it but it drove away. It took a while to find another.

A bit after eleven, they arrived at Silk Lips, a low-key establishment without signs. They registered, gave a phone number, paid the cover and received numbered cards to keep track of their consumption. A girl in a short skirt and high boots body-searched Simone. A burly bouncer searched Carl. They left their belongings in a locker. Simone went over Mark's description in her mind and found it exact.

They stepped through a door into a "ballroom" with a stripper pole in the middle. People jostled one another at a packed bar in one of the corners. A long counter separated the bar from the dance floor. Rails hung above the counter. No one was dancing up there yet.

Everyone was scantily clad, dressed to provoke and seduce. By comparison, Simone looked like a nun, with her jeans and bare shoulders, which she'd thought would be sexy. Carl looked even more out of place, attired in a suit and tie, which made Simone feel better.

"How about a drink, Simone?"

"No thanks, Carl. I want to keep lucid."

"Shall we see the rest?"

"Absolutely."

At the back of the dance floor, they entered a corridor faintly lit by red lamps. The tiny rooms lining the hallway contained red couches and had windows on the doors so the activities inside could be observed.

The corridor led to a room with a community bed. Three couples, side by side, were screwing on it. The scene was a turn-on. Simone hadn't been tuned up in quite a while and felt embarrassed with Carl at her side. She kept quiet. God bless the loud music.

They continued onward out of the room into an adjacent one where two beds were covered with red satin. One was unoccupied. A couple of women were engaged in heavy petting on the other.

The rooms Mark had described as being similar to jail cells lay ahead in another corridor. He'd related them in exact detail. Carl and Simone strolled along until they returned to the corridor with the windowed rooms. Perhaps due to the early hour, just one was occupied. A young woman was "servicing" two men, one most likely her husband. He seemed a serious sort, with salt-and-pepper hair. The other looked much younger than his two companions. The woman climbed aboard the younger man and rode him until he came. Then she mounted the one with the salt-and-pepper hair and they humped until they both blasted off. The younger man then beckoned her over and she did him again.

Simone was getting excited and by the expression on Carl's face, he was feeling the same way. They looked at each other. Carl placed his hand on the back of her neck, drew her to him and began to kiss her. She didn't resist. It was out of the question. She was too turned on to even try. Carl drove his tongue deep into her mouth. His kiss was demanding and hot and delivered with skill. Then he pulled back but only for a moment before he leaned in again and went to work on her neck. His hands slipped up to her shoulder straps. He lowered them, exposing her hard nipples, which he started to suck. Then he leaned her against the wall and began to run his hands all over her body.

The three occupants of the room had concluded their business and wished to leave. As Carl and Simone were pressing against the door, the others began to beat on it. The sudden noise caused Simone and Carl to pull back from each other.

"Simone, forgive me. I don't know what got into me."

"Me too, Carl. The atmosphere here is torrid. We got carried away. Forget it."

Simone's head was back on her shoulders again. *Unfortunately,* she thought. But she was here to work and Carl was still a client. Intimacy wouldn't do. Yet her entire being shouted, "Fuck me!"

They explored Silk Lips for a bit longer and then left. Carl took Simone to her hotel. On the way, she started a conversation to break the uncomfortably silent environment inside the car.

"Carl, I hope to have a full report on Mark's manuscript for you next weekend. If that's the case, how would you like to proceed?"

Eyes still on the road, Carl said, "Can you bring the report to me so we can discuss it? I'm going to be really busy and I can't travel, but I can spare time to talk about it. Would you do me this immense favor?"

Will you finish what we started at Silk Lips? she thought in frustration.

"I have to check my schedule," she said, "but I believe that will possible"

"Thank you very much, and thanks for all you have done, Simone. Your work has been extremely important to my case."

Does your thanks include kissing me, caressing me and allowing me to melt in your arms?

Lost in thoughts of their aborted steamy encounter at the swing house, Simone fell silent once again. What the hell had come over her lately? She'd kissed two men recently due to exceptional circumstances. Edward, because they were involved in a hideous situation. Carl, because they'd been surrounded by sensuality. She longed to kiss someone for the pure pleasure of it, without having to consider the consequences.

As they pulled up in front of her hotel, Carl turned to face her—the first time he'd looked her in the eye since they'd left Silk Lips.

"Good night, Simone, I wish you a safe journey back home."

She heard no emotion in his voice, no regrets, no joy.

"Thanks, Carl, have a good night."

He leaned toward her and she braced herself, eyes wide, but then her cheeks heated as he gave her a light peck on the cheek before straightening.

Simone snatched up her purse and climbed quickly from the car, feeling inexplicably embarrassed. As she strode into the hotel lobby, she shook her head derisively. *Well*, she thought, *at least he didn't try to shake my hand.*

She returned to Connecticut the following day.

Chapter Twenty-Two

Present Day - Simone

Simone had been home only a short time when she received a call from Edward, who asked to hear about her trip. He also wanted to tell her about his meeting with Victor, "Claire's" research correspondent.

"I think we'll dump this guy, Simmie. He acted weird yesterday."

"Why do you say that?"

"He got annoyed because you didn't show up. He called us a couple of assholes and said we think we're dealing with some punk."

"He said that?"

"In detail. I reminded him he'd agreed to meet me first but that didn't calm him. I have no doubt he has a serious personality disorder. The other day, he was calm, cool and seemed collected. But our meeting got all my red lights flashing. Let's scratch him off the list and look at someone else."

"Okay, my friend. I have complete faith in your good judgment."

"And how did New York go?"

"I made serious headway. I visited two places mentioned in the text and confirmed that Mark's descriptions are wholly accurate."

"That's wonderful! It's good to hear that. I should have offered my help before. If you think you need it, you can count on me. Even though sexual issues are at the heart of the matter and that's not my field, maybe I can help with personality analysis."

"Thank you, Ed. You're too good to be true. You're up to your ears in work and you still make time for my problems. Will I ever be able to repay everything you do for me?"

"You do that every day. Just being at your side is enough."

They chatted a little longer and discussed the therapist Edward had hired to treat his son Noah. Then Simone hung up and took it easy the rest of the day. She had a lot on her mind and needed to relax.

On Sunday, she slept late and then, as she usually did on Sundays, she put on a pair of sweatpants, put on her sneakers and went for a run. The fresh air and exercise had a wonderful effect on her. She loved the streets in her neighborhood, which were lined with big trees, and today the weather was cloudy but warm. Back home, she ate breakfast sitting in the kitchen while she read the news, after which she decided to take a long, hot bubble bath. She then washed her hair and prepared herself to face Monday, so it was late in the day when she finally got back to Mark's journal.

Mark's Journal — My Way or the Highway

Lara was an emotional wreck. Her comings and goings resumed. She'd disappear for days, return, and disappear again. At first I didn't press her about it. Her pain and suffering were plain to see. Her mother's death had dredged up sunken traumas. Lara seemed to have dived into the deep, and apparently she couldn't get back to the surface.

Then she simply went off the radar for two whole weeks, her magic number. She didn't even answer the phone. I got worried. I went to her apartment and the porter told me he hadn't seen her for quite some time. Déjà vu all over again.

I called Peter. He and Lara were tight. Maybe he knew her whereabouts.

"Peter, Lara's vanished. Have you heard from her?"

"She didn't say anything to you? She didn't leave a note or anything? I thought you two were about to enter into wedded bliss. I even considered volunteering to be a bridesmaid."

"So funny, Peter."

"No sense of humor on your body! I don't know anything about Lara. You're telling me she's not at home?"

"She's not at her apartment. You think she went to Paris?"

"Your best bet's the Hamptons. She's been there a lot lately."

"How do you know?"

"We're friends and I'm worried about her too, Mark. She's not well."

"She doesn't answer her home phone or her cell or her phone out there."

"So go to the Hamptons. That's where I'd try. But I don't know. What kind of fantasyland are you cooking up? Listen, Mark. She parked her ass in your life for a while. She does that once in a while. I've seen it before. That doesn't mean she's going to change and go out and buy a wedding gown, you know?"

"I *don't* know, Peter. She was happy. At least she seemed to be. Her mother's death fucked her all up."

"No, it didn't; she was *already* fucked up!"

I headed for the Hamptons, secure in the knowledge that I was a knight errant off to rescue a damsel in distress. No doubt all of Lara's demons had returned to afflict her upon Sabine's demise. Her guilt must have forced her to flee. Perhaps she believed she was unworthy of being loved. My head swam with suppositions. I drove recklessly and got to her house in less than two hours. To my surprise, at least a dozen cars were parked outside.

The house was wide open and brightly lit with some sort of festivities underway. When I stepped inside I was confronted by a mass of naked people engaged in a variety of sexual activities. Three sixty-nines were in progress. Two women were eating at the Y on the floor in a corridor. Two men were doing the same on the living room rug. A man and a woman were munching away on a plush divan. Everywhere I looked I saw intimate body parts engaged with other equally intimate body parts. Lara was complicit in this bacchanal. She was not slouched on a couch all disheveled and lamenting her mother, as I had imagined she would be.

It took me a while to locate her, what with the loud music, people moaning and groaning and nobody properly attired. It's hard to single out an individual in a sea of squirming skin. I stepped over the two sixty-niners, slipped past a *ménage a trois* and zigzagged through numerous asses and elbows. Nothing in this scene made me horny. I was too angry.

At last, I spotted Lara. She was standing in a corner, in her birthday suit, of course. She was wearing a collar with steel studs around her neck. The chain connected to it was held by a man I didn't know. He was on his feet behind Lara. Her voluptuous curves gleamed with sweat. John Meyers, the big black guy, was flagellating her with a cat-o'-nine-tails. Her body was covered with red welts, her eyes were closed and the expressions on her face were either of pain or ecstasy. I couldn't tell. Before every lash, John declaimed an epithet.

"Slut! Harlot! Strumpet! Nasty bitch! You deserve it! Messalina!" And so on. A rich vocabulary. And the guy knew some history.

He paused to catch his breath. Then he instructed the fellow to pull the chain so that Lara would have to lean back. When he complied, I couldn't see Lara's head anymore. She was too arched over. But I could see her torso and her pussy. Now John brutally spread Lara's legs and thrust his titanic tool into her. She moaned. I don't know if she was suffering or enjoying it. But I heard what she said to the guy holding the chain.

"Pull hard!"

John kept pile-driving his dick into Lara. No mercy. I had never been so brutal with her, not even in the moments when I'd lost all sense of time and space. The man behind her kept the chain taut. Lara shuddered. I could only stand there and watch. The scene was overwhelming. Lara and John were magnificent physical specimens. The act was sheer savagery. When it ended, they both collapsed. Lara was black and blue all over. Goddamn! John Meyers had told me the truth about her. This was standard operating procedure for Lara. I felt like a cretin with mental retardation. Christ! Trying to transform a degenerate into a princess!

I don't think Lara saw me right away but I heard her calling to me as I was leaving. I swore to myself I'd take all the advice I'd been given and quit her for good. I was at the end of my rope. I couldn't endure her anymore. Hatred of my jealousy mixed with the pity I felt for her. She was an addict with no hope for a cure.

"Mark!"

She came running after me. Stark naked. She tried to hug me, but I stiff-armed her.

"Lara, go back to your party. It's a success, by the way. Everybody's having fun! You don't need me. You've got tons of meat here."

"Mark, my mother's dead. I feel awful."

"I just saw you in mourning."

"It's the only way I can ease my guilt." Her eyes filled with tears.

"I know. I believe you." And I really did. That's the way she was. But it was light years from enough. "I just can't handle it."

I didn't know what else to say. I turned and walked away. There was no remedy for her. As for me…well, I wouldn't see her anymore. My entire being screamed, "Get out! Don't look back! It's her way or the highway. Take that highway!"

* * * * *

One warm summer night a month later, I found Lara parked in front of my apartment building. I had just returned from teaching a class at the law school. At least my doorman was on the ball and hadn't allowed her to charm her way in. I opened the garage with my remote control and when I pulled into my spot there she was. She'd walked down the ramp. I'd have to get rid of her.

"Mark."

"Good evening, Lara. Is there a problem?"

My heart pounded just seeing her. She was thinner and had dark circles under her eyes but she was as gorgeous as ever. I'd resist her. Lara's beauty was like that of a carnivorous plant waiting for a fly. I had more self-esteem than an insect did.

"I need to talk to you."

"You think we have something to say to each other?"

"I do. At least I have something to say and I'd like you to hear me out. Afterward, I'll leave."

"That's what you always do, right?"

"Mark, please."

"Okay, Lara. Let's go up. A garage isn't the best place for this."

The doorman arrived and asked me if everything was all right.

"It's cool, Oliver. Nothing to be concerned about. Thank you."

I was already a bundle of nerves by the time we entered my apartment. Lara's presence always had a way of keeping me off balance. If she'd been my adversary in a courtroom, I'd have lost to her every time.

"Okay, Lara. Out with it. You have fifteen minutes."

"Can I have a drink?"

"The ice machine's broken, the bar's closed and the clock's ticking!" I hadn't the least intention of being her bartender and needed to get rid of her.

"Understood."

"What do you want, Lara?"

"My mother's dead."

"Old news." I spoke without showing the least bit of concern. After all, if she didn't give a shit about me, why should I give a rat's ass about her?

"That destroyed me! I always hoped my mother would die and die in agony. And it happened just that way, even though in my mind I wanted her death to be even crueler. Then came the freak-out."

"I know. I saw it. It was huge and black."

"No, Mark. Please understand. Make an effort. John is a friend who knows how to be dominating. I go to him when I need to hurt myself because I know he won't go too far."

"And the rest of the party? Is that your way of being sad?"

"No. It was just a group of swingers I get together with once in a while."

"Listen to me, Lara. Your world and mine…our paths never should have crossed. I've tried. But I'm not like that. I'm not so detached that I can share a woman with other men whenever she wants me to. I'm not so liberal that I can accept a woman I love lending me to other women. It's too much for me. I'm a dinosaur, okay? I liked the man-woman swing thing. Of course. It was great to live out a fantasy. But I don't want it to be part of my daily existence. I'm an ordinary guy. I can't stomach orgy after orgy after orgy."

"I know. And that's why I'm here. I need you. I need you to help me to change. I don't want to be this way either. But sometimes the emotional pain I feel is so severe and overwhelming that I think I'm going to get lost in it and never find my way back. So I need thrills and physical pain to relieve my emotional suffering. And I've discovered that not having you in my life hurts a lot too. No one has ever made me feel the way you make me feel. No one. I love you, Mark."

That was everything I'd always wanted to hear her say. But it was the wrong time and the wrong place.

"Sure. I make you feel like disappearing. I make you feel like vanishing into thin air without a word for weeks. I make you feel like having other men. Thanks! But no thanks. I can do without your feelings."

"What if I change?"

"How do you propose to do that? Go live in Paris?"

"I don't know. I've changed therapists. I'm starting to see a psychiatrist. He's going to put me on medication."

"Medication won't do a goddamn thing if you don't want to change, Lara. I think you like to disappear."

Lara suddenly took off her blouse. Her back was a mass of bruises and ugly welts. She looked much worse than when I'd found her at the party. That meant the party had continued long after I'd gone. The sight left me speechless.

"This is what I did to myself over the past few days. To punish myself. This time, I did it to kill the pain of my mother's death. But I do it a lot. That's why I disappear. Because when the emotional pain is unbearable I need physical pain. What you see are the consequences of those actions. The disappearances last as long as it takes to heal the wounds. I don't disappear because I want to. I do it because I don't want anyone to see me like this!"

"Lara! You can't go on like this! It's sheer madness!" That was all I managed to say. She was a mess in every sense of the word. For a moment, I set my anger aside. I stopped feeling sorry for myself and became a compassionate human being who wanted to help her, the woman I loved.

"Mark, I need you! I need your normalcy, your affection. I need you in my life. Those months we were together were the best days of my life. I was happy for the first time in a long time. And then the wicked witch died and I thought I'd go crazy. I felt as guilty as I did when I was a child."

"I don't know what to tell you, Lara. I don't know what I'd do if you suddenly ran off again or if I had to deal with your needs for other men. I'm not built like that. I'm the guy whose idea of an adventure is to have a drink with a friend after work."

"And what if I can change?"

"I don't know. I don't know if I think you can do it."

"Maybe I'll never stop wanting to mix pain with sex. But I have hopes for the medication. And we could try to keep the rough stuff just between us."

"You want me to do that to you?" I pointed to her beaten body. "No way, Lara. The most I can do is squeeze your neck a little. The rest is too much for me."

"You don't even want to try?"

"What would the ground rules be? How would we proceed?"

My head screamed for me to run but my heart was stone deaf. I thought I must be having a midlife crisis. I'd never ever been in a situation like that before. My reason had always won out, but then…

"Let's try to be a couple. Just boyfriend and girlfriend. We'll live separately. At least for now. I don't feel up to anything more yet."

"And if you freak out?"

"I'll talk to you and you'll help me?"

Her eyes were wet, begging, impossible to refuse. Common sense urged me to flee her treacherous tears. But I threw common sense to the wind and decided to risk it. *You only live once.*

"Okay, Lara. Let's try."

Mark's Journal – Normal Life

We were a "normal" couple for a while. Lara made an effort to share her pain and suffering with me. She had heaps of it. At times, I thought I'd be dragged into a bottomless pit when her crises struck. But somehow, we'd manage to pull through. Her scars weren't scars but deep, open wounds. She had nightmares. She had deep fears. She was much more fragile than I'd ever realized. Sometimes, she was the goddess of savage sex; other times, she was the terrified child in need of shelter. I used to see just the goddess but now…

Through it all, I loved her and she made me happy. And I tried to make her happy too. But just when I thought I was getting somewhere, there would be disappearances and tearful pleas for forgiveness. But at least she swore — and I had to believe — she never went back to swing or sex with other people. She usually ended up in the Hamptons to enjoy a few days of silence.

After a while, I gave up trying to understand and just lived from day to day. I believed we were a couple able to have a life together, despite our abnormality. We actually did take a few steps forward. I gave her my apartment key and she gave me hers.

Sometimes I'd go there and cook us dinner. She couldn't handle more than microwave popcorn. Sometimes, she'd surprise me with a feast. She'd buy it at a delicatessen but that didn't matter. What counted were her efforts to set a table and create a romantic atmosphere.

One day, I went to her place with a bottle of champagne. She'd called to tell me she'd been chosen as the architect of a huge new luxury hotel. She sounded elated, absolutely thrilled, on the phone. *Wonderful,* I thought. *The dark days are history.* But there was nothing like something tangible to jolt you out of your dream world. I found it in her apartment—a plane ticket to Paris for the following afternoon. She'd said nothing to me.

I didn't even try to understand why. I felt brutally betrayed. I'd been sharing my life with her, been honest and open with her. She'd been treating me like a goddamn mushroom, keeping me in the dark. I left the bottle of champagne and a note next to the plane ticket. *You'll never change,* it said. I walked out the door and didn't look back.

Chapter Twenty-Three

Present Day – Simone

When Simone arrived at work on Monday morning she found Mona in a heated argument with Alvin. The security guard Edward had hired, Gregory, held Alvin's arms behind his back.

"What's going on here?"

"Good morning, Doctor. These two idiots won't let me talk to you!"

"Alvin, please leave without making a scene. If you don't, I'll have Gregory forcibly remove you and I'll call the police."

Simone went into her office and closed the door on Alvin's foul language. *What a great start to the week*, she thought.

For some reason, Mona did not come back after lunch, nor did she show up the following day. The office was in chaos. Edward and Simone had to make do as best they could. Fortunately, Gregory the security guard pitched in but it wasn't the same.

"Simone, have you reached Mona? It's pandemonium around here. A full slate of appointments, patients wandering in and out and meeting each other and the woman simply vanishes!"

Psychiatric patients hated to meet each other. They always felt embarrassed, and Mona always scheduled the appointments far enough apart to avoid such encounters.

"I called her house but no one answered, and her cell phone's out of the area. I don't have another number. I'm really worried. It's not like Mona to do this."

"As soon as I get five minutes free, I'll take a look through her desk to see what I can find."

"Okay, Ed. Let me know."

Later that day, Edward found Mona's mother's number. When he called, the elderly woman said she had no idea where Mona could be. They hadn't spoken in days.

"Ed, let's call the police."

"Think so? I'm worried too but—"

"Ed, let's call now. I don't like to trust my sixth sense—there's no scientific proof that something like that even exists—but I have a feeling there's something very bad about this disappearance."

Edward called his friends down at the station. What he told them got their attention in a hurry. The most recent body they'd found had been a warning to Simone. Her secretary's disappearance now left them in an uproar.

They promised to start investigating right away.

"Any more patients today, Simone?"

"Just one. I'm free after that. And you?"

"I'm finished. I've promised to take Noah for pizza. I'll get him and then come back here and follow you home, okay? I'm worried."

"Thank you. Offer accepted."

* * * * *

At day's end, Edward arrived, and he and Gregory walked Simone out to her car, ready to follow her home.

"Dr. Bennet, isn't that Mona inside your car?" Gregory asked.

"Yes, I believe it is but how the hell did she get in there? I'm almost positive I locked my car doors."

As they neared the car, Edward put a hand on Simone's arm, and they all stopped.

"Wait, Simone. She's not moving." Edward opened the passenger-side door, where Mona was seated. She appeared to be staring off into space, her eyes wide open.

"Oh, Lord...is she...?" Simone couldn't bring herself to finish the question.

Edward cast her a grim look and then leaned in, placing two fingers against the side of Mona's neck. After a moment, he straightened and shook his head. "Nothing."

Simone began to cry. She moved to go around Edward, to see to her friend, but Edward blocked her path.

"Don't come any closer, Simone. She's dead. Gregory, call 9-1-1; I'm going to settle Simone in my car and call my contact at the police department."

"Sure, Dr. Reynolds."

As Edward turned, Simone got her first good look at Mona. Her face was pale and a tiny trail of blood had trickled down from one corner of her mouth. Simone reached out, hand shaking.

"Oh my god!" She staggered backward, would have fallen if Edward hadn't put his arm around her.

Simone allowed herself to take in the full horror before her. Mona was naked from the waist up. A sticky substance that appeared to be semen had run down her breasts and belly and had stained the front of her skirt. And the killer had apparently added a novel touch. A hair clip secured a note to the skirt. *It's your fault, bitch,* it read. The note had been typed. The killer was careful.

"Oh no, Edward!"

Simone could say nothing else. The weight of the past few days, of the recent discoveries, had left her empty and exhausted. Nothing made sense anymore. And now she felt responsible for another death. What had she done? How had she caused this? How could she be responsible for such atrocities? She felt almost a physical pain for losing her friend in this brutal way.

"I'm going to call the police, Simmie. That whacko Alvin must have done this. Mona threw him out, right? She told me he was shouting that you'd pay for the way you've been treating him and right afterward, she disappeared."

"I refused to treat him. He's a lunatic. But I don't think he's a killer, Edward. I'd have noticed the signs."

Simone refused to accept that a murderer could have been right under her nose without her knowing it. If she was wrong, she'd retire, go home, give classes. But she wouldn't practice any longer if her instincts were failing her. That was inadmissible in her profession.

"Come here, Simmie. I'll take care of everything. Come over to my car. Noah's there. I'll take you to my place. You'll be safe there. It's a building, much safer than a house. Don't even think about going home today."

Simone let herself be led away. She was badly shaken. She lacked the will to protest. Edward put her in the back seat of his car.

"Sit here, darling," he told her as he helped her with the seatbelt.

She seemed to be having a difficult time controlling her shaking fingers.

"Noah, stay here with Simone, please, and keep her company. I'm going to call the police station…let them know we suspect Alvin and why."

He took out his cellphone and walked away a few paces while Simone sat silently, staring off into space and wondering how on earth she'd gotten herself involved in such horror.

* * * * *

The police picked up Alvin a couple of hours later. Preliminary investigations revealed he was unmarried, childless and had had a twin brother. The brother had died in an accident, along with his wife and child. Alvin was a loner, a computer geek.

At his house, the police found a laptop he used to track all of Simone's e-mails. He also corresponded with a certain woman named "Claire" under the pseudonym Victor, his dead brother's name. There were a number of calls from his cell phone to Simone's and the dates matched those of the anonymous calls she'd received.

Edward and Simone told the police who Claire was. The police were sure Alvin had a serious problem with Simone and were almost certain he was the serial killer. They confirmed right away that Alvin had corresponded with Simone/Claire. Almost all the proposals "Claire" had received had come from Alvin's machine, which contained several false e-mails with corresponding pseudonyms.

Alvin was questioned the following day. He categorically denied any connection with the unsolved crimes but he didn´t deny or explain the emails. Immediately afterward, he took a semen test, the results of which would be back in less than twenty-four hours. There were no fingerprints on the note found on Mona's skirt to be compared with his.

To everyone's surprise, the next day, the semen test showed no compatibility with the killer. Nevertheless, Alvin's behavior remained suspect. The police began to wonder if more than one killer was involved, or if Alvin had an accomplice who carried out the murders he masterminded. They learned his software company was quite lucrative. He would have no problem hiring someone to do his dirty work. They had a number of theories but no concrete proof of anything, and now Alvin had made bail.

Alvin's lawyer informed the police that Alvin wanted to talk to Simone to clarify the situation. He claimed the conversation would clear his client. The police asked Simone if she felt up to the task. They understood Mona's death had shaken her but they also thought such a meeting could yield valuable information. Simone agreed to do it.

Alvin and his lawyer sat down with Simone in a room at the police station where everything would be filmed and recorded.

"So, my lovely doctor. You had me arrested," Alvin began.

"Victor...Alvin. Who are you, anyway? And what do you want with me?"

"Alvin, Doctor. That is my real name. I just wanted to meet the woman who killed my brother!"

"Your brother? I never met your brother! I just found out you had a twin!"

"You knew his wife very well. Madeleine Kevingston."

"That's true. She was my patient. But she discontinued her therapy a long time ago. I haven't seen her since."

"You convinced her to leave my brother! He went crazy. He began to stalk her. Then one day, he got drunk and persuaded her to get into his car with their young son, whom Victor hadn't seen for a couple of weeks. He drove with them head-on into a trailer truck."

"How do you know it wasn't an accident?"

"My brother was a race car driver. He wouldn't get into an accident."

"What do you know about your brother's and Madeleine's relationship?"

"He was crazy about her and their son! He'd have done anything for them."

"Your brother was a violent man, Alvin. He beat Madeleine regularly. She ended up in the hospital several times. The last time, he gave her a severe concussion. She almost died. I obviously advised her to leave him because her life was at stake."

"That's not true. My brother was gentle. He wouldn't have hurt anyone!"

Alvin was visibly irritated at the idea that his beloved brother might have had faults. Simone's diagnosis had hit the mark. He'd made up everything he'd said in her office—she'd known he had because he'd shown no emotion when he'd spoken. Now that his words were genuine, emotion punctuated them.

"There's proof, Alvin. There are hospital records. As a relative, you can have access to them. I have copies. I'll let you see them. Madeleine lived in constant fear. I know it's hard for you to hear this. He was your brother. But it's the truth. She told me her heart pounded in terror whenever she heard the door open. She never knew how he'd be. Would he be a raving maniac or gentle and kind? He often arrived infuriated and beat her for no reason at all. On one of those occasions, she lost a baby!"

"Is that true, Doctor?" He finally seemed to be coming around.

"Yes, it is. She also filed a complaint with the police that she later dropped. I don't know what your brother told you. Madeleine did love him. She just couldn't endure living with him any longer."

Alvin looked disconsolate, his face showing signs of disbelief and pain.

"He was much more than just a brother, Doctor. He was my other half. He told me you advised Madeleine to leave him and he didn't know why. He had plenty of money and provided a life with all the comforts for Madeleine and their son. There was no reason for her to leave him. They had a beautiful house and cars. He gave her a lot of expensive jewelry…"

"When he beat her he gave her jewelry. Jewels were his way of begging forgiveness when he was sober. Madeleine told me she didn't even wear them because each one reminded her of a horrible episode."

"That's not the brother I knew, Doctor!"

"I understand but you have to realize there was another side to him. He was jealous, possessive and violent. Especially because he had a drinking problem. He drank a lot and used cocaine."

"Booze? Are you telling me my brother was an alcoholic and a fucking junkie? He had a few beers once in a while but he was no lush, much less a druggie!"

"You never noticed? Unfortunately, he was a hard-core addict. Madeleine tried to help him. For a while, he went to Alcoholics Anonymous meetings at a church near where they lived. I don't know which one. But he kept having relapses and finally stopped going. He refused to see a therapist. She put up with it as long as she could. The woman loved your brother. She did everything possible for him. But he grew increasingly violent and she feared for their son's safety."

"Did he ever hit the boy?"

Simone almost told Alvin the truth. Madeleine left her husband when he hit the boy for the first time. But Alvin's agonized expression made her think better of it. By the content of his questions, she saw that he had finally started to believe her.

"I don't know. But he often physically abused Madeleine. He nearly killed her. She had to leave him. I was sure he'd kill her. And now you tell me you think that's what he did. I see my suspicions were right."

"I don't know what to think anymore."

"What were your intentions in coming to me?"

"I wanted to expose you. I wanted to show the world your research methods. I wanted to ruin your reputation so you'd lose the thing you love the most, your profession. But now nothing makes sense. I've believed lies and for the past few months, I've been trying to create a web around you to catch you like a fly." He ran his hands through his hair. "I'm going to check on everything you've said, Doctor. But I think you're telling the truth. I have to see…"

"How come Edward didn´t recognize you when you pretended to be Victor meeting him?"

"I hired another guy to meet him."

"Did you kill Mona, Alvin?"

"For Christ's sake, I'm not a killer!" His face showed true indignation. "I never wanted to hurt anyone. I only wanted to scare you a little by pretending to be a crazy patient. Just a few anonymous phone calls…but I think I went too far. I was going to do it only until I exposed you. I heard about what happened to your secretary. She was a good girl. She always stuck up for you. She was loyal. But I had nothing to do with her death."

"I believe you, Alvin. I truly do."

"Please forgive me for everything, Doctor."

Simone saw true sincerity in his eyes.

"Can I ask you another question?"

"Yes, Doctor. I owe you some answers."

"Was anything at all of what you told me in my office true?"

"None of it. I read your book on sexual behavior and pretended to be a nutcase with some of the characteristics you wrote about."

"That makes me feel better because it's what I thought from the beginning. My instincts didn't deceive me. I knew nothing you told me was true." Simone got up to leave. She was tired. But she was also happy because her professional technique had detected the lie right at the start. It reinforced her conviction that Alvin was not the killer.

He called out to her when she got to the door.

"Doctor, when I get out of here, will you accept me as a patient again?"

"I don't think so, Alvin. The bond of trust between doctor and patient has been broken. It wouldn't be ethical."

"That was one of the things that surprised me about you. Your ethics. An evil person wouldn't have any. It made me unsure."

"Can I refer you to a colleague?"

This time, Alvin didn't protest. "Yes, Doctor."

"You have my best wishes," she told him.

"You too, and I'm truly sorry about Mona. Nice girl."

Outside the room, Simone found Edward, a policeman and one of the investigators on the case. They'd been listening to everything.

"Doctor, what do you think?" the investigator asked.

"He didn't kill anybody."

"I second that," Edward added. "But maybe he hired someone to do the job."

"He will remain our primary suspect," said the investigator.

"Let's go home, Simmie."

"Where's that?"

"Wherever you want. From now on, you're under round-the-clock protection. There'll be a police car parked in front of your house and the clinic. We're taking no chances with that maniac running free. He seems to know everything about you while we know nothing about him."

"By the way, Ed. About the taxi that was parked outside. Have they found out anything?"

"The Peddinghouses are traveling. They're on a cruise. We finally managed to contact them. They said they didn't call any taxi because they were already away. They'll be back soon. They said their house has a security camera they'll let police look at to see what's on it. But they don't know if it even works and it's never been checked out. It's very old. Their son insisted they purchase the system years ago when they moved in.

"So the taxi might have something to do with the crime?" Simone asked.

"That's what we think is most likely. The FBI is involved now, Simmie. Everything will move more quickly from here on out. They have a whole team investigating"

"FBI?"

"That's right. They have jurisdiction in serial killing cases. The body on your steps triggered the request for their involvement. Now with Mona's death, they're actively working on the case. Our local police will help with the evidence they've gathered but this is in the FBI team's hands now."

As Simone and Edward were about to exit the police station, they were warned about a crowd of reporters waiting out front. There had been a leak somewhere and all the local media were on the case. The cops slipped Simone and Edward out the back.

* * * * *

The next day, the TV news and papers were full of stories about the crimes. They reported Simone as someone being stalked by the killer and Alvin as a principal suspect, who'd been arrested then freed on bail. The last thing the cops and the FBI wanted was all that coverage. They believed it would make the killer go elsewhere and the case would remain unsolved for years.

Edward wasn't so sure that was how things would turn out. Alvin would still be investigated. He hadn't committed the crime. That was almost certain. But he might have been linked in some way to the killer. He was out on bail but forbidden to travel. But just like Simone, Edward didn't believe Alvin had a part in the murders. Edward thought that because the media's attention was focused on Alvin, it might flush out the real perpetrator. Serial killers generally don't like sharing credit for their atrocities. A possibility therefore existed that the killer might try in some way to make it clear Alvin was not involved.

That night, Carl phoned Simone. Media coverage of the murders was ongoing and widespread. He inevitably had heard about them.

"How are you, Simone? I'm worried about you."

"I think if I'd had less rigorous training in how to analyze and handle problems and emotions, I'd be a basket case now. But as I'm able to put things on a more scientific plane, I'm only sad and very troubled."

"Your secretary was the latest victim?"

"Yes, she was. Mona had been with me for ten years. She was like a daughter."

"I'm so sorry, Simone. Can I help you in any way? Do you need anything?"

"Normalcy. But I don't think anybody can give me that. Thank you for asking, Carl."

"If it gets too much, run away down here to New York!"

"Okay. I'll bear that in mind. Once again, thank you for your concern. I'll try to stay on schedule and finish the text by the weekend."

"That wasn't why I called. I'll understand if you want more time. I don't know how you can read in the middle of that chaos."

"It's the one thing that takes my mind off it, Carl."

They chatted a bit longer. Carl was sympathetic and clearly concerned but the events swirling around Simone had numbed her. No friendly conversation could perk her up. She'd been very fond of Mona and her loss had deeply saddened Simone.

She and Edward had hired Mona when she was just eighteen, right out of high school. She was a girl with few ambitions but always cheerful and eager to help. She quickly became Simone's right hand. She managed Simone's agenda, her very life. She scheduled doctors whenever Simone needed a checkup and Mona knew by heart when and how often. She was always there with a timely cup of tea or some "baked apples", which was what Mona called the ones she warmed up, knowing Simone detested cold fruit. Much more than a secretary, she was a faithful friend, one of the few people who took care of Simone and not the other way around.

I need to cry, Simone thought. She just wasn't able to do so. She felt only exhaustion and profound grief. Maybe the tears would come in a few days. Like a torrent. But now, she felt only pain and more pain at the loss of an irreplaceable friend. She'd read a bit now, as she'd told Carl she would. It was the break in the storm that was raging in a mind frantically searching for answers.

Lara called me almost immediately to talk about the plane ticket. Progress was being made, even though she was trying to justify another unannounced disappearance.

"Mark, I was going to tell you today about the trip."

"Sure you were. Well in advance. I mean, you're leaving tomorrow, right?"

"I didn't know how to explain it to you."

"And now you know."

"Look. I want to tie up some old loose ends I left in Paris. I want to put everything in order for you and me."

"And just what might those 'old loose ends' be? Or do you want to get tangled up in some new ones?" I was referring to the getaways she liked to make to practice sadomasochism.

"No. Nothing like that. It's a personal problem. I don't want to discuss it now. But you have to trust me, Mark. I *am* changing. You know that. I need your vote of confidence. I'm taking my medicine as prescribed. I'm getting better. This situation goes way back. I need to settle it to be able to move on with my life."

"And you want that vote of confidence with no questions asked?"

"I'll tell you everything when I get back, okay?"

"And how long will it take to tie up those loose ends?"

"Well, I also have to buy some things for my new project."

"So that means quite a while."

"Not really. And I sincerely promise I won't go out with anyone in Paris. Except for the three musketeers, that is. I swear to you I won't get involved with other men. You know I want to be with you. It was I who came after you this last time, remember?"

"If you're not going to be with anyone, if you're going for work, then why all the secrecy, Lara? Why are you afraid to let me in on it? How long have you known you were going to travel?"

"I knew I'd have to go when I presented my ideas to the hotel. I just didn't know when. Everything fell into place about three days ago. You and I were doing so well. I didn't want anything to interfere with that."

"It interfered! I'm not your enemy! You don't have to do things on the sly! Just when I'm beginning to trust you, you spring this on me. Lara, there's too much up and down and hot and cold. Can't we just level things off and keep them at a comfortable temperature?"

"Can I come over?"

"It's better you don't. I need solitude once in a while too. I don't feel like being with anyone right now. Have a good trip."

"Please let me come over."

"Oh, Lara. Yes!"

She arrived bearing food, which was highly unusual. She went into my kitchen, set the table, heated what she'd brought and popped open a bottle of wine. She felt guilty, very guilty. It wasn't her style to even go into the kitchen. Sometimes I thought she didn't even know what it was for but that's what she did when she wanted to please.

"Mark, shall we dine?"

"Yes. I'm hungry."

I sat down to eat, still in a rotten mood. I kept quiet and she did too.

Then she broke the silence. "Mark, I'm married."

"What?"

That was all I needed. At any moment, a husband was going to walk in the door and shoot me. I choked on the wine. Those words hit me like a Mike Tyson uppercut. All the outrageous thoughts in the world stampeded into my head.

"Take it easy," she said, slapping my back to keep me from choking on the wine. "It's just on paper. I've been separated for years. I've decided to explain why I'm going to Paris. It's not right to leave you in the dark. Things are going so well for us."

"Right. I want to hear this one! Are you going there to celebrate a wedding anniversary you forgot?"

"Mark, you can be a real asshole sometimes. I'm going there to try for the zillionth time to get a divorce!"

"What do you mean?"

"In detail?"

"All of it. From the beginning."

I had no doubt that what would pop out of the top hat of her past would be a gargoyle and not a cute little bunny rabbit.

"After college, I went to France to do graduate work in architecture. Two years in Paris. Things seemed to be reasonably on track. My life had normal standards, more or less. I was twenty-three."

"And?"

"And Paris. Well, you know how it is for someone twenty-three-years-old and full of professional dreams. Any street in Paris is a class in architecture. I was happy. I'd promised myself I'd act like a normal person. I'd go out with normal guys. I'd have sex in bed. I was trying to adjust to the idea."

"But?"

"I met Nicholas during my second semester. He was forty-five and a professor of lighting. He was a very handsome and charming man. He always wore brightly colored scarves and exquisitely tailored suits. He was the antithesis of garden-variety architecture academics. Most of them dress like street people."

"And you fell in love? Another older man?"

"Yes. Older. Divorced. Had three kids!"

"Motherfucker! Don't tell me you married him?"

"Him and all his problems. Six months after we met."

"Wow. Nobody could ever accuse you of prudence."

"He was so sweet and his voice was so soft. He spoke about philosophy and history. He was mature and very successful."

"Twenty-three years older."

"Twenty-two. Right. The sophistication and experience of older men attracted me. Not consciously. But don't forget. The first man in my life, for better or worse, was experienced. The others seemed like children in comparison."

"And you needed the experience."

"Mark, however much I loved Paris, I was all by myself and far from my family. I was vulnerable to risky relationships to ease my loneliness. I needed to feel taken care of. You take care of children. Men make you believe you're being taken care of."

"Believe? Only that?"

"In Nicholas's case. The marriage lasted a year. He was totally unstable."

Coming from the "queen of flakes," what did that mean? I asked myself. "Unstable?"

"Okay. When I went to Paris I made up my mind I was going to be happy. I stopped seeing my psychiatrist. I wanted to live a normal life. No more tragedies. But I didn't grasp that I was still in the same rut."

"The old search for the oppressor you told me about?"

"That's it. Our emotional sicknesses soon complemented each other. He had serious sexual problems and he knew I had mine. My lack of inhibition that way made it very clear what I liked. I never had the courage to tell him about my past suffering."

"A real marriage based on trust."

"Spare me the sarcasm, Mark. It doesn't look good on you. A real marriage based on my desire to be normal. I don't want to be a victim or deserving of pity.'"

"Okay. Excuse me. It's just that…Lara, I'll be sincere. The very thought that you got married makes me jealous!"

"Look, Mark. It's my past. I can't change it. If I could…"

"I know. I know. I'm being stupid. Go on."

"I have ADHD."

"What the hell is that?"

"Attention Deficit Hyperactivity Disorder. I can't sit still."

"Goddamn. The name alone freaks me out. Please explain."

I'd always known she wasn't normal. But to have a condition like that… It was a good thing neither of us wanted to have kids. I'd worry about how they'd turn out.

"It's the lack of an enzyme in the brain that makes a region of it dysfunctional. High doses of adrenalin activate that region, which is why I'm hooked on adrenalin and powerful emotions. I need them! And I can't stay focused on things. I need external stimuli to make me pay attention. I get bored easily with repetitive activities."

"So your desire for adventures has a cause. Does it come from the trauma in your adolescence?"

"No. It's hereditary. It seems it comes from my grandmother's side of the family."

"Aha. Emma the adventuress."

"That's right."

"And it's always there? It's constant?"

"Yes. If I'm not on medication. But I'm taking my pills. Don't worry. I'm in control. But back then I'd stopped taking them… Ritalin, antidepressants…and my adrenalin addiction had come back full blast."

"And you gave it full rein with your new husband."

"We started swinging and doing *ménages à trois*. What can I say? I was back to my old ways. Then to complicate things a bit, I found out he was bisexual…"

"Lara, are you sure you're not an actress in a Mexican soap opera? I ask that, my love, because only a Mexican soap opera is more melodramatic than your life. *Luz Clarita, Luz Clarita te amo.*"

"Mark, this isn't a joke! It's my life! My goddamn life!" Her eyes filled with tears.

I felt like an insensitive prick. "Excuse me again. I think I'm having a bad day."

"You certainly are. Do you want me to continue?"

"Yes!"

"During one of our sessions he had sex with a young man, much younger than I was. It shocked me at first. But he calmed me down by saying that our marriage was unconventional and that if you get pleasure from doing something, it's not wrong."

"And what did you think about that?"

"My head was so fucked up I accepted it and still do. I don't necessarily think pleasure and normalcy go hand in hand."

"So that wasn't why you split up."

"That's right. He began to play the role of a new Arthur in my life. He tried to control where I went, the clothes I wore, who my friends were, my every move. I realized I didn't have a husband but someone once again thinking he owned me."

"And how did you react?"

"Relax. There's more. Remember I told you he had three children?"

"Yes."

"Twenty, seventeen and fourteen. All boys. They did whatever they wanted. He had no idea how to handle them. He lied to them and he lied to me because he could never keep a promise. It was total chaos. The youngest had to go into drug rehab. The middle one was the most normal. He's an architect today. I think I had an influence on him. The oldest is some kind of post-modern hippie."

"Holy shit! It sounds like something out of *Hieronymus Bosch*. Was your former husband aggressive?"

"Not like Arthur. He wasn't sexually sadistic. But he was verbally abusive. He'd come home yelling and throwing fits. He'd lose his temper for no reason at all."

"How did all this affect you?"

"All my demons came back to torment me, Mark. I lived in constant terror of his rages. At the same time, he'd say things like, 'You'll be nothing without me' or 'You'll never find another man who'll accept you as you are'."

"As if you were a cretin?"

"Something like that. My condition makes me feel that way sometimes. And he noticed it right away. Fortunately, Emma sensed something was wrong. She and my father had gone to the wedding. Just the four of us attended, by the way. They were clearly opposed to it but they didn't interfere with the choice I'd made. Emma began to worry about my silence. She hopped on a plane and landed at our apartment."

"I love that woman retroactively!"

"When I opened the door and saw her there I threw myself into her arms, crying and begging her to help me. Emma never failed to get me to spill the beans. She sat me down on the couch and brought me a glass of water. She gathered my books and things and clothes as best she could. She called a taxi and took me to her place."

"And him?"

"He tried to talk to me a few times at school. Luckily I only had a month to go. Whenever he did, I'd threaten to cause a scandal. He'd get scared. You know…professor, student. Even if they're married. The teacher always comes out the worse. Emma stayed with me until the end and then took me home."

"Why didn't you divorce him before?"

"Because he simply refused and I never wanted to fight about it. But now I've decided I will. The three musketeers already have a lawyer for me. I'm going to make one last attempt to reason with him. If not, we'll take it to court."

"And why were you running away without talking to me?"

"Because I'd turned into a hussy from a cheap novel, as you've just pointed out, and I was afraid you'd lose all respect for me. There are so damn many pathetic scenes in my life."

"Lara, is this it? Is this the last skeleton?"

I felt as if I was working on one of those five-thousand-piece puzzles where there's always a piece missing.

"I think so."

"Do you want me to go with you? It couldn't be now. We'd have to wait a bit."

"No. I got myself into this mess. I'll get out of it."

"Do you feel strong enough?"

"Trust me. I've already told you. I'm much better. I'm centered now."

After dinner and another chapter of Lara's potboiler life, we cuddled up on the couch for a while, listening to music.

"I'm going to miss you," Lara said. Her scent would never leave my nostrils.

"Hey. Me too."

"I want you, Mark."

She began to unbutton my shirt with one hand, massaging my chest with the other. Then she climbed into my lap and wrapped her legs around my waist. She covered my face with sensual little kisses. She nibbled on my lower lip and licked it slowly. She had my penis trying to pop out of my pants.

She ran her tongue down my neck, down my chest and then she slid down on her knees. She undid my belt, pulled down my zipper, took my hard-on into her mouth and went up and down on it, up and down, as if it were penetrating her. When she'd reach the tip, she'd squeeze it with her lips and then go down again. She was driving me wild. She did it over and over and over again, steadily increasing the rhythm. When I was panting and sweating and about to come in her mouth she stopped.

She stood up. She began to remove her clothes. It was an erotic spectacle. Off went her jeans. Off went her black blouse. She was wearing a black bra and black string panties. She left them on but slipped the panties to one side. She mounted me and wrapped her legs around my hips. Lara's heat and the rubbing of her panties against my skin had me ecstatic. Her bra was the frame of an indescribably beautiful picture. She rode me hard until we exploded together. Then she hugged me just as she was, with her legs around me. We stayed that way for a long time as the rain went *rat-a-tat-tat* on the windows.

We slept in each other's arms. She left early the next day. I offered to drive her to the airport. She said she hated *au revoirs* at the runway. I didn't argue. My heart weighed a ton.

Mark's Journal – Choices

The next day, I scheduled an appointment with a new psychiatrist. Less radical than the previous one, he seemed to understand my need for Lara. I'd explained to him all the problems involved. He knew the whole story and was helping me to come to grips with everything. I told him everything Lara had said before she left.

"That syndrome she has is serious, Mark. Many people suffer from it. And it's traumatic because while they're inattentive and bored by commonplace things, they're absolutely brilliant when it comes to what interests them."

"I understand. She seems to be brilliant and batty at the same time."

"Yes. They're really special. But they know it and it makes them sad. I think it's good she told you about it because it helps you to understand her better."

"It does. But the whole thing…the syndrome, that crazy marriage. It was another bomb going off inside my head."

"So she nuked you and took off for Paris."

"She's taking off today. I don't know what time. I saw just the date."

"And you?"

"Although I feel better because I know what she wants to do there, I still feel betrayed by the way I found out she intended to go. It makes me hate her and yet I love her. I feel like a fucking retard the way I want the plane to blow up in mid-air and her to turn into a shower of flame-broiled fragments of flesh."

The shrink laughed.

"I think I'm just like a gay friend of mine now. I've become a tragic figure."

"You'd be just like him if you wanted a shower of sequins. Your hatred is natural. You and Lara are unable to live a normal life for very long and that makes you lose your sense of balance."

"Sometimes I'm afraid of what I might do to her when she pulls one of her stunts. It makes me want to kill her! Especially when she takes off on me."

"That's a natural impulse. But you have your feet on the ground. You wouldn't do it. The desire to get rid of what causes pain is normal. It happens to us all. In life. In a traffic jam. When someone insults us. Sometimes, when someone just tells us no. And Lara's flakiness makes you suffer."

"Do you think she's going to meet some boyfriend of hers in Paris?"

"I have no idea. I don't know her. I want you to answer that, Mark."

"I don't think so. She'd tell me. That's the worst thing about Lara. She does something and she tells you about it!"

"So you don't think she's going to do that?"

"Or that's what I want to believe. I don't know. But when she comes back I'll know. She'll tell me."

"What are you going to do in the meantime?"

"I'll practice detachment. I'll take advantage of her absence."

"I don't understand. Could you explain what you mean by that?"

"I'm going to live my life as if Lara didn't exist. I'll go out with my friends, see other people."

"Other women?"

"You know, Dr. Allan, I'm not so sure this latest story of Lara's is the last Chinese box. I wanted a normal life. I wanted to meet a normal woman for a change. There are a lot of them in this town. I wonder if there's one for me, wandering around out there."

"Do you and Lara have some kind of fidelity pact or agreement?"

"Lara and I? We've never sat down and drawn up a contract to that effect. Life with her is what I've told you. We're like a couple of recovering alkies. We live one day at a time, or one outrage at a time."

"I think you should try to do what's best for you. If something gives you a guilty conscience, don't do it. But if something doesn't, make up your mind. Choices always have consequences, Mark."

"I just don't know. Choosing Lara makes me feel I'm choosing to swim against the rapids for the rest of my life."

"And so it is. She'll make the choices she wants, not the ones you want. It's no good, Mark. Lara has real problems. The syndrome she has…generally, the patients stop taking their medication. Normality bores the hell out of them."

"So you don't think she'll change?"

"Nobody changes for anybody and Lara has deep-seated emotional disturbances. She has traumas. There will be relapses. You'll have to learn to live with that or get out."

"I know. We're talking about apples and oranges."

"You're right on!"

I hated the way shrinks gave their patients a pat on the head to boost their self-esteem. I felt patronized.

"You can choose not to like Lara's apples anymore and not to want them if she makes you suffer more than she pleases you," Dr. Allan went on. "But you can't change an apple into an orange."

"And if I can't live without her?"

"There's your answer. Accept her as she is! You'll suffer less."

I left Dr. Allan feeling as if I'd just left a meeting of diplomats at the UN. The guy gave me no direction at all. He just sat on the fence, waiting for me to jump one way or the other. Choices, choices. *Headshrinker bullshit*, I thought.

I got together with Peter to lunch at a small restaurant near my office, a place called Green Choices, which Peter had chosen, saying something about needing to lose weight. He was very put out that Lara and I were a couple. Sometimes, friends can be more jealous than a girlfriend! I arrived early and got us a table, admiring the simple décor and studying the framed photographs of movie stars that covered the white walls.

"So the princess of darkness beat feet again?"

I glanced up at the sound of Peter's voice. He hadn't even greeted me before he started to criticize me. This definitely was not my day…

"Hello to you too, and no, she didn't disappear; she went to Paris."

Peter didn't bother to say hello back. "Ah. Just as I thought. She's vanished once more and left you playing pocket pool." He seemed really upset about something, making faces as he spoke.

"Peter." I made certain my voice held a note of warning. I really wasn't up for this today.

"Fair enough. But from now on, don't say I never warned you!"

"Far be it from me to contradict you. Look, I've missed you. Stop being such a bitch. Lara and I are your friends. You should be rooting for us."

"Sure. I'm rooting...for her to move to Paris and for you to return to your old rut of a life. But without you going to pieces in the process. She's my ideal of a woman. You, however, are dear to my heart."

"Thanks, Peter. But she *is* changing."

"Has she dyed her hair? Undergone plastic surgery? Those are the only possible changes for her."

"Okay. Enough of that. Let's get serious. How have you been and what have you been up to? You disappeared for longer than the princess of darkness."

"I've been here and there. I even went to China."

"Literally?"

"Yes. I need to see my suppliers up close from time to time. And have fun too."

"In China?"

"Aaah. I sense a certain prejudice about China. Or do you think there aren't good-looking men there?"

"No. I was just curious. Haven't you ever had a serious relationship, Peter? Around here?"

"Good question. I've tried but nobody within a radius of three thousand miles wants to have anything to do with me." He pouted childishly.

"I know. What are you doing that drives men away?"

"I'm too hot for the market. Wanna try?"

"If you weren't my friend, I'd whack you."

"Oh no! Don't do that. I'll go absolutely mad! But if you must, don't hit me in the face."

We kidded around for another half hour or so. Peter had a quality I truly appreciated. When he wasn't being cynical he was a lot of fun, and now it seemed his anti-Lara mood had passed.

A brunette, who was stunning but a bit too scented, came up to us and kissed Peter on the cheek. She gave me a look that said, "I want you. Let's fuck."

"Keyra, dearest, how nice to see you. Let me introduce you to my wonderful friend and lawyer, Mark. Mark, this is Keyra, my marvelous friend. She owns the Planet Teens fast fashion boutiques."

"A pleasure, Keyra."

I extended my hand, and she stepped closer and kissed me on the cheek. It had already occurred to me that women were getting more and more aggressive. This one's perfume smelled like midnight in a Tijuana whorehouse.

"The pleasure is mine, Mark. Peter tells me you're a tax-law genius. I'm really delighted to meet you."

"Peter is a great friend and a challenging client, to boot. I get him out of all kinds of trouble. That's why he thinks I'm a genius."

"I import for Keyra's stores, Mark."

"I thought so. Would you like to join us, Keyra?" I invited her just to be polite.

"Thank you. You're very kind. My girlfriends haven't arrived yet."

Hah, I thought. Girlfriends. *Who knows? Maybe if one's not too hard to look at and smells a bit less like lavender douche…*

It soon became clear her friends would never arrive. After forty minutes of chitchat, the woman was still there. Peter had set me up. I'd have preferred him to have set up my favorite hot dog stand outside my apartment. Well, here was a knockout brunette who was single, as she'd emphatically made clear, doing everything but spreading her legs on the table. Peter's doing. Apparently, the "separate Mark from Lara" campaign was underway.

And just when I thought Peter at least wouldn't play dumb anymore, he came out with, "So, my dears. I see you two are getting along verrrrry well. Unfortunately, I have to go now. I have an appointment."

"Really? With your bed or with Michael?"

"Who's Michael? Do I know him?" The brunette wasn't such a dear friend, after all. She didn't know Michael.

"I think you do," Peter said. "But it's not with him." Then he shot me a murderous glare, as if to say, "If you tell my client I'm hooked on *The Godfather*, I'll cut your balls off with a chainsaw."

"Okay, Peter. You're outta here. But don't think for a minute I don't know…"

"What?" he asked, poker-faced and fluttering his eyelashes.

"Bye, Peter."

"Bye, Keyra and Mark. Kisses, kisses, love you. Don't do anything I wouldn't do." And he strutted away like a peacock.

"So, Keyra, how did you meet Peter?"

"We met at a trade fair. He offered me the possibility of producing my wares in China. At first, I wasn't interested, even though I was working on a new line. But he's very charming and persuaded me I could save forty percent by off-shoring there. And he was right." She related the information without once taking a breath.

"And the quality?"

"Well, I see fast fashion's not your area of expertise. Quality's not a factor. It's all about the number of models and rapid replacement. Teeny boppers always want to be seen in something new. They don't want to leave something for their descendants."

And the young woman, no more than twenty-eight or so, rattled on about the teen fashion market. I couldn't have cared less. First, because I hate to be treated like a fool. Second, because I detest being meat for a matchmaker. And third, or maybe first, I had someone in my life. The days of slam, bam, thank you, ma'am were long gone.

But I was a gentleman. I wasn't going to get up unless the lady did so first. And so another hour went by of her endless monologue. I had to hold myself down in my chair. My foot was jackhammering under the table. It's a defect of mine. Something I do when I'm impatient. She finally stopped babbling and went for the kill.

"Mark, let's go to your place or mine for a drink. We'll be more comfortable."

"Keyra, I'll be frank with you. You're a beautiful woman. At any other time in my life, I'd take you wherever you wanted for a drink and *I* would invite you. I know Peter set this up."

She blushed at this.

"Please don't misunderstand me. I'm in a relationship Peter doesn't approve of. But I love the woman. So I'd feel uneasy going out with someone else, however lovely and interesting she might be." The flattery was a bit forced but I didn't want to offend her. I only wanted to get away from her.

"I feel like crawling under a rock. Peter said you were single."

"I am. In fact, I'm divorced. But I have someone."

"And it's serious. Obviously."

"It is for me. I'm from the old school, Keyra. While it's good, I'm in. When it turns bad, I'm out. I can't have it both ways. I wouldn't get into something to deceive someone."

"You're amazing. Are you from New York or are you from there?" She pointed toward outer space.

"I'm from right here. But I was brought up by a man who loved one woman for his whole life. Unfortunately, that hasn't been my case but he taught me a lot."

"Mark, thank you for your sincerity. Please forgive my theatrics. Good men are hard to find in this town and I can see that Peter was right. You're one of those rare ones who fall to Earth." She stood up, kissed me on the cheek and before leaving added, "If it doesn't work out with that lady, I hope you'll call me."

That's the mistake women make, I thought. *They're too obvious. They leave no mysteries.* But then something else occurred to me. No one had been more obvious than Lara. So what made her different from other women? Why had I chosen her? Perhaps it was the mystery of never knowing if she would really be mine.

Choices. At the end of the day, the shrink was right. If they're the right ones, the feeling is always good. I was feeling good about myself. Sex with Lara satisfied me. If I had had sex with another woman, then it would have been like eating an Oreo cookie after having devoured, a few hours before, a double-chocolate brownie with ice cream, hot fudge, whipped cream and a cherry on top. At least, that was how I felt that day. We'd see in a few more days. Lara had just left for Paris.

Chapter Twenty-Four

Present Day — Simone

Mona's funeral proved to be one of the saddest events in Simone's life. At least the sun shone bright in a cloudless sky. Perhaps that was nature's way of paying tribute to a woman who had always been cheerful and smiling.

The media turned out in force. Family, friends and most of Simone's and Edward's patients appeared, all of them shocked by the brutality of Mona's death. She had always been attentive and courteous with everyone she dealt with. Her passing had visibly shaken Philip. He had enjoyed long chats with her in the waiting room.

"She was special," he explained when offering his condolences.

Disguised FBI agents drifted throughout the crowd. They didn't fool Simone and probably no one else, for that matter. They were hoping the killer would show up to pay his final respects to the victim, as psychopaths sometimes do.

Edward gave one of the eulogies. Simone lacked the strength to speak. She still hadn't wept. But a vast emptiness and deep pain afflicted her.

Edward stepped to the rostrum on the lawn and said, "We all know why we mourn the passing of a young woman who has left us too soon. For some, she was a true friend. For her mother and father, she was a dedicated daughter. At work, my partner and I depended on her to make everything run smoothly. She never let us down. She always received us with a smile. She always had a word of comfort when we were tired after a long day. There was always a cup of tea for Simone and a strong cup of coffee for me.

"Mona could always sense what others wanted and she did her best to provide it. She did not do this merely out of professional responsibility. She did it because she truly wanted everyone around her to be happy and well. Mona was much more than an efficient secretary. She was encouragement and comfort. She was a friend. She was the hand on a shoulder on a sad day. And she had dreams. She was going to school. She wanted to become a landscape designer so she could create glorious gardens to beautify the world. That was the essence of the woman. To make the world a better place for others. There was not a drop of selfishness in her. Not one drop of rancor. Mona was kindness personified. We shall feel her loss each and every day."

As Edward left the podium, the events of recent days at last caught up with Simone. Two deaths, the loss of a friend, patients out of control, aggression, the insecurity of her home. The weight of all this crushed her and she began to cry. Tears flooded the emptiness she felt. They could not be contained. They burst from her eyes and flowed in rivulets down her cheeks. For the first time ever, she did not try to conceal her emotions in the presence of her patients. She did not worry about her image. She simply let it all go.

When Edward saw her in this state, he went to her and hugged her. Then the rivulets turned to rivers, rivers born from springs deep inside her. She felt a grief that could not be soothed. Only those who have lost someone dear can know what it is to face a future without that someone. Only they can grasp that life will never be the same. Only they can understand that a door will never again open to a smiling and cheerful, "Good morning".

Edward led Simone to his car. He gently placed her in the passenger seat. He took the wheel, put his hand on her knee and asked where she wanted to go.

"Ed, can I go home with you?" She could not be alone. She needed her friend's support.

"That's where we'll go."

As Ed pulled away, Simone spotted a taxi heading along the road parallel to them. It seemed to be observing the funeral, and it looked familiar.

"Stop, Ed! I think that taxi's the one that was outside my house on the day of the first murder." She pointed but the taxi was now moving away.

"Are you sure?"

"No. But it seems to be the same kind of car and I remember it had a huge dent on the driver's door, like that one."

"I'll call one of the FBI men."

Edward phoned one of the agents he knew had attended the funeral. The agent told him to continue on his way and they'd look into it. The man called back after a while and Edward put the phone on speaker mode so Simone could listen.

"Hey, Doctor, I've notified my colleagues in the area, but a yellow taxi with no specific identifying characteristics was not much to go on. There are a lot of them that are in pretty bad shape with scratches and dents. You didn't get the plate, right?"

"No, the car was beside us. I couldn't get into a position to see the back end."

"Sorry, Doctor, we'll continue to search and stop all taxis with a dent on the driver's door. I'll keep you posted."

"Thanks, Agent McCormick."

"You are most welcome and thanks for the help, Dr. Reynolds."

After Edward ended the call, he glanced at Simone. "It's not going to be easy to find this guy; he's smart."

"As are all psychopaths, unfortunately," Simone commented.

They continued to Edward's apartment and as soon as they stepped inside, Simone turned to Edward.

"I'm exhausted," she told him. "If you don't mind, I'm going to crash."

"My friend, make yourself at home. You know where your room is. Do you want to eat something?"

"Thanks, Ed. I'm just too tired to think about food. I'm going to my room, if you don't mind."

"Of course not, babe. Just relax, take it easy."

Simone went into the guestroom and stretched out, still clothed, on the bed. In the throes of emotional exhaustion, she quickly fell asleep. Night had already fallen when Edward woke her. Another day had passed in her recently tumultuous life.

She had a light snack and a short chat with Edward. Then she decided to read more of Carl's manuscript. She knew it would be difficult to get to sleep right away after her long nap.

Mark's Journal – To Remember is to Live

Peter called me one day when Lara was in Paris. He said his sister was in town and wanted to have lunch with me. That goddamn fairy. He was still indignant that I wouldn't take his advice. It seemed he'd do anything to drive Lara and me apart. On the other hand, it would be nice to chat with Deena again. Our marriage had ended amicably. We weren't close friends but we did like and respect each other. I called her and we made a date.

We got to the restaurant at the same time. I'd always liked that about Deena. She was punctual. We chose a table, ordered wine and began to catch up on things.

"I've missed you, Mark. How's life been treating you?"

"Fine, Deena. How about you?"

"Fine." That was just about the most bored "fine" I'd ever heard.

"Fine? Really?"

"Really. Or do you want to know the truth?"

I laughed. When we were married, one of us would ask the other "Are you okay?" And the other would answer "Yes. Or do you want to know the truth?" Little joke that only a couple would understand. Old habits die hard.

"The truth."

"I'm under consideration for a federal judgeship."

"Congratulations! I'm rooting for you. It's what you've always dreamed about. That's wonderful. So everything *is* fine."

"Well. It should be. And yes. It was my dream."

"Was?"

"I think I'm going to turn it down."

"But why, Dee? You worked for it your whole life. You always knew that was what you wanted."

"I wonder if it really was what I wanted. I don't know anymore. I think I'm having a midlife crisis."

I started to laugh. But I saw that Deena was serious. She was an attractive, well-kept, intelligent woman of forty. She looked ten years younger and far from matronly, which is what comes to mind when a woman says she's in midlife.

"What happened, Dee? And yes, I want the truth."

"You and I are both middle-aged, Mark. Whether you like it or not. If we're lucky, we'll have forty or so more years. But we're halfway there. That's for sure."

"Ouch! That hurt. I hadn't looked at it that way. That's not how I feel."

"Lucky you. But soon, soon you will. I'm feeling it. It seems I've wasted so much time and energy. The best years of my life. I don't know if I want the second half of my life to be like the first half."

"Why?"

"I did everything expected of me. I was a good student, good daughter. Not that my parents were so good, you understand. But I always followed the script. Good grades, good career. But today, I wonder if I even like what I do."

"You're a great public prosecutor, Dee!" I wasn't just trying to please her. She was a truly excellent professional. She wrote very well. She was passionate about her work.

"But I could have been something else that was wonderful, something that made me happier."

"I can't imagine you being anything but a jurist. So what do you intend to do?"

"I don't know. I'm seeing a shrink. I'm coming up with options."

"How's your marriage going?"

Deena had remarried after the divorce. Her husband was a prominent physician in Hartford.

"It's going exactly the way ours was."

"Hmmm. That's not exactly praising our marriage, Dee."

"If it had been a marriage worthy of praise, we'd still be together. It was an exemplary marriage. Only that. It wasn't what a marriage should be."

"And what do you think a marriage should be that ours wasn't and yours apparently isn't either?" I thought, *Hold on and fasten your seatbelt because the answer's not going to be pretty.*

"Emotion. Passion. Our marriage was perfect, Mark, a perfect pain in the ass! We weren't in the least bit happy. Maybe we were in the beginning. But later on, it turned into the very definition of monotony."

I remembered coming home and feeling utterly listless. It was solitude for two. That killed our marriage. We were simply there without the courage to call off the "perfect marriage" and without any desire to be companions.

"You're right, Dee. At the end, we really were unhappy. I truly want you to be happy now."

"And are you happy, Mark?"

Peter planted that question, I thought. "I think so. As far as possible. At least a little each day."

"That is, your life still has no direction? You live from your career and for it?"

"Christ, Dee! Is that the way you see me?"

"My dear old friend. We were always alike. To tell you the truth, I think I see a reflection of my life here before me."

She took my hand affectionately. I felt nothing at her touch. Everything there was dead and gone. She let go. Affection wasn't Deena's specialty.

"Jesus Christ, Dee." I inhaled slowly.

"You want to know the truth, Mark? We're not in the emotion business. We're in the intellect business. Feelings don't fit into our lives. And as we're so alike…"

"We were always so alike, right? Why didn't things work out?"

"For that very reason. We needed something different in our lives but we fell in love with our mirror images. We ended up not getting that *something extra*, the spice we needed."

"We had so much in common," I thought out loud.

There had been a time when I had believed that to be happy I needed someone with the same intellectual interests. As I watched her sitting there, I knew deep down she'd hit the nail on the head. We were both in the legal world when we first met in a courtroom. We thought, ate and wanted the same things. At home, our favorite subject was "How was your day in court?" We discussed our cases, exchanged ideas about matters in the district attorney's office and about our clients. One day, we reached the conclusion that our home had become a damn law office and we needed a life away from it. So we split up. The same reasoning we'd used to bring us together we used to separate us. No shouting. No recriminations. No pain and suffering.

"Mark, we bored each other. We weren't in love."

"But you married again and you're still not in love," I said.

"Bingo. I repeated the pattern. I'm right where I was when you and I broke up. I'm spinning my wheels and asking myself what I need to change my life."

"And the answer?"

"Courage, my dear, courage. You've got to have courage to make a move and change direction. I want to do that now. Every day I'm putting a little grain of courage in a little bag." She used two fingers to put something imaginary in an imaginary bag. "When it's full I'm going to shit-can everything and maybe study art or something. I don't know. Maybe I'll go to India and meditate."

"You? An artist, Dee?" I'd always thought of her in impeccable professional attire, discussing legal principles. I couldn't picture her paint-spattered or entranced in a lotus position. "Good luck. I mean it. I don't think I'd have the guts. Maybe my midlife crisis still hasn't kicked me in the nuts."

"Sometimes it's unconscious. Peter tells me you are, in his words, 'involved with a woman who belongs in a rubber room' and you need to be rescued from her."

This time, I guffawed. Peter was nothing if not predictable.

"And I am. It's complicated. Peter thinks he introduced us and now he believes he must be the one to *divorce* us, for my own good, of course. He's sandbagging us."

"Peter and his ideas about what's right for other people. As if his life were exemplary. What's she like?"

"Off the wall. Full of highs and lows. I never know what she'll be like from one day to the next. At times, even from one hour to the next."

"Does that cuckoo clock always take you by surprise? Does she keep you off balance?"

"Every five minutes, the ground moves under my feet. I'm in *terra incognita*."

"So, my friend. Perhaps it's time to go for the Russian roulette of a life she's offering you. I think it's just what you need! May Peter forgive me but you have to shed that suit and starched shirt and take a walk on the wild side."

"Hah! Peter wants you to rescue me, not ease my way along the road to perdition!"

"I'm not about to rescue you. I care about you. That woman's good for you, Mark. I saw how your face lit up when you talked about her. Go for it! If you still love practicing law, keep doing it. But that woman really turns you on and, just between us, I'm the one who needs help, not you!"

It was such a pleasure to be talking to an intelligent woman. Lara was a smart cookie but at times, I felt we weren't in sync. We'd speak different languages, talk of different worlds. But right away, I realized that my connection with Deena was just what she had described. It was a relationship with a mirror image that quickly palled. If I was in a midlife crisis as Deena had said I was, I'd do everything differently and jump with both feet into that Alice in Wonderland love.

We chatted for a while longer. Deena said she was worried about Peter. She found him morose and reclusive of late. Maybe he was facing his own midlife crisis. I promised to keep an eye on him. We hugged each other. I smelled her familiar perfume and thought how strange it was that the scent that used to drive me crazy did nothing for me now. When she left, I had the good feeling that someone indeed understood that chapter in my life story.

Lara called me that afternoon. There was a five-hour time-zone difference. I was at the office. She was tucked away in her Parisian garret.

"Oh how I miss my favorite lawyer."

"And I miss my favorite nutcase." The mere sound of her voice thrilled me. If that wasn't love, it was at least mental retardation.

"What are you doing now? I hope you're not with a gorgeous brunette sitting on your face."

"Been talking to Peter, have you?"

"Yes. He called and informed me you had lunch with his sister, your ex."

"Jealous, babe?"

"Of course."

"Don't be. Deena's history. I don't live there anymore. Someone I know said that. Can do nothing about my past. If Deena were important, I'd be there. But she's good people."

"I know. I know there's nothing between you. But I felt a pang."

The thing about Lara was she didn't play games. She took what she wanted, showed who she was and said what was on her mind.

"And so you decided to check on your holdings over here?"

"No. I decided to hear your voice."

"How are things over there?"

"Not at all easy."

"Your ex-husband won't give you a divorce?"

"That's it. He's a spiteful son-of-a-bitch. The years haven't mellowed him one single bit. He's still royally pissed off because I 'abandoned' him, as he sees it."

"Have you spoken to him?"

"I couldn't avoid it. He refused to talk to the lawyer I hired."

"You spoke to him face-to-face?"

"That's right. I had to ambush him at the university. I didn't want to be alone with him in a less public place. If there's one thing I've learned in life, it's that I don't want to be attacked in any way. I also don't have to put myself in situations where that's a possibility. Being alone with him in private would have been much worse than it was."

I understood then and there how Lara felt about my meeting with Deena. It wasn't jealousy. It was the unpleasant realization that I had been in the company of someone with whom I'd tried to build a life. Someone who'd been part of my dreams. Someone with whom I'd tried to make the perfect photo album. Someone I'd slept with.

"Was it really bad?"

"There was a time when he would have gotten to me, wounded me. But now he was just a nasty old man, taking cheap shots, saying things like, 'You're a little nobody with serious mental problems'. I did have mental problems when I got involved with him. That's the truth!"

"Do you regret that?"

"I don't regret anything in life, Mark. Oh, I kick myself in the ass sometimes but I don't suffer. Life's too short to chew pills when they won't do any good."

"I understand. You know, I really want to give you a big kiss. Come back soon!"

"And I want to sit on you and ride you until your balls fall off!"

Lara was so romantic. But just the thought of her bouncing on me gave me a rock-hard boner. The power that woman had over my joystick!

"I can go for that!" I said. "And what else do you want to do?"

"Well...I want to lick you from your neck all the way down to your crotch. I want to put your cock in my mouth and hum on it. I want to run my tongue slowly all around it and then take it all the way down to my throat."

I was so horny I couldn't stand it. I asked her to give me a moment and went over to the door and locked it. Then I returned to my chair, pulled down my zipper, took hold of my whopper and began to stroke it to the sound of her voice.

"Lara, I want you to fondle yourself. Fondle your breasts and imagine I have one of your nipples between my teeth, nibbling it slowly."

"Oh, Mark. I want you to feel you've slipped into me and I'm sitting in your lap. I feel every inch of your hot prick inside me. I'm beginning to ride it, up and down, up and down."

I could feel what she was saying. My balls were getting tighter and tighter when someone knocked on the door.

"I'm on the phone. Wait!"

"Mark, now imagine I'm going faster and faster and swallowing you whole."

"Lara, I'm digging my nails into your back and biting your luscious neck."

"That's it, Mark. Bite harder! I feel it. I'm all wet here."

"How are you dressed?"

"I'm naked. One finger inside me and another rubbing me. And you?"

"My pants are open and I'm playing with my penis. I want to put it in you."

"Now imagine I get off your lap and kneel on the couch with my back to you."

"If you do that I'll shove my cock into you all the way up to your throat! I'll fuck you as hard as I can, you prick-teasing little slut! I'll have you moaning and groaning and begging for mercy!"

"Oh that feels wonderful! What else will you do, Mark?"

"I'm gonna bite your neck and whip your ass until it wiggles like Jell-O in an earthquake! Then I'm gonna fill you up with my come!"

"Oh! Oh! I'm coming, Mark. I'm coming!"

I didn't even think. I began to blast off all over the tabletop and my clients' documents. I'd worry about that afterward. I even forgot the telephone. When my wad was shot I looked at the receiver. She'd hung up. Just like Lara to do that. I tried calling her back a few times but her phone was out of the area. Great! She'd been jealous of Deena and decided to cool me off. Nice to know Lara cared. *Well, time to clean up the mess.*

Chapter Twenty-Five

Present Day — Simone

Edward's knocking on the door woke Simone. She'd slept late and hadn't even heard the alarm clock. She wanted to stay in bed and not go out to face the world. But the world was there awaiting her with a full appointment book. The words of Mark's former wife echoed inside Simone's head. Middle age, changes, death by daily drudgery and all the others danced and pranced together. They caused Simone to greet the new day depressed. And when she remembered that Mona would not be there with her customary cup of tea, Simone pulled the covers over her head.

When she finally got to the kitchen, Edward was on the phone. He motioned for her to take a seat at the already set table. He soon hung up and joined her.

"Good morning, Simmie."

"Good morning, Ed."

She kissed him on the cheek and he sat down.

"News from the police. Late yesterday, they got the list of people who watch *Caïn* and they'll begin visiting them today. Fortunately, there are only a hundred and fifty in the whole town who subscribe to it."

"Huh. Maybe I have bad taste," Simone remarked.

"No, you don't. You and they must be the only ones around who speak French. The series doesn't come with subtitles. You didn't sleep well, did you? You've got dark circles under your eyes."

"I know. I read until late. Just dejected, I guess."

Edward placed his hand on Simone's arm. "It'll pass, Simone. This is a difficult time for us."

"Have you ever thought about what you're going to do with the second half of your life?" Simone asked, looking Edward right in the eye.

"Second half?"

"We're forty, my friend. Will we live until eighty?"

"Whoa! Simmie, let me speak to you like a therapist. We've already got a heap of problems. Maybe we should leave the midlife crisis for later, okay? Today's forty was thirty a generation or two ago. Don't worry about that. Right now, it's too much to handle. Try to solve just one problem a day." Edward raised a hand and shook his index finger. "One at a time."

"That probably makes sense. But thirty-year-old women years ago were useless. All they did was tell others what they should be doing."

"Hey. Enough of that. You're feeling down because of Mona and all those deaths. Me too. But let's not bury ourselves yet. You're a beautiful and intelligent woman. Any man would want to have you. And I swear," he said, clasping his hands together as if in prayer, "you're good for a lot more than just giving advice!"

"Sure. Show me one man who wants me. And please! Not for my brains!"

"You just don't see, Simone."

"Oh. So now I'm blind. I'm alone, Ed. I feel old and sad."

"You're just a bit down. That's all. The rest is in your head." He gently touched Simone's forehead with his index finger. "You're alone because you want to be. You dream about a New York client you hardly know. You don't look around you. You spend twelve hours a day working and researching, instead of going out for a drink once in a while. You've made choices!"

"Look who's talking. Don't you do the same? And as far as I can see, your love life's just like mine."

"But I know what I want in life."

"And what's that?" *Christ,* Simone thought. *What a start to the day. Arguing with Ed bright and early. What'll the rest of it be like?*

"Let's not get into this, Simmie. We're late. Let's have a coffee and go to the office. Please excuse my irritation. I don't feel a hundred percent either."

"I know, Ed. Excuse me too. You're the only thing I have to lean on now."

On the way, Simone asked how the investigation was going. Edward breathed deeply, took a hand off the wheel and ran it through his hair.

"Not well. I think that's why I'm in such a bad mood. Beyond the list of people who watch the series, we've hit a wall. And I've got to give a goddamn sperm sample again! My jizz was the only one the lab screwed up! I found out a little while ago."

"How can you screw up a sperm sample?"

"God knows! Looks as if that psycho's put a curse on me. Maybe they mixed it up with something that was already in the collection jar. I don't know. I've gotta whack it again."

"Ed, I truly understand why you're not yourself this morning. Are you doing it today?"

"With my schedule the way it is? No...I can't. But since I'm not suspect number one I'll do it on Saturday. My only day off and I'm going to practice 'sexual self-abuse', as the nuns would say."

"And the other tests?"

"All negative. No cop is involved. At least no cop squirted the spunk."

"And did you get the Peddinghouses' videos?"

"Yes. They gave them to us. Their security system's obsolete for all practical purposes. But an FBI team's analyzing the films. They have the best technology for doing it but even they are having problems."

"Meanwhile, that loony's on the loose. I've never felt constant fear before, Ed. Now I'm always jumpy. The least little noise terrifies me!"

"At home?"

"Especially."

"Have you considered moving, Simone? Whether you like it or not, a stiff on your steps is not something that's easy to forget. It'll take a while. You should think about getting a new place."

"I have. But I raised Tammy there. It's my home. I built every bit of that house with my own sweat, with my own hard-earned money. I simply can't do it." The very idea practically traumatized Simone. She couldn't face moving right now.

"You don't have to sell it, Simmie. Rent it. Even close it up. You don't need the money. Leave it locked for a few months until all this blows over. Take an apartment. Come to my place."

"My good friend. You are the best person in the world. I couldn't impose. But I will think about moving for a short time. Tammy will be back from her exchange program in France in six months or so. Maybe while she's away, I'll take a furnished apartment or something like that. Let me think about it."

"As far as I'm concerned, having you wouldn't be an imposition. It would be a pleasure. Chew it over. It doesn't have to be right now."

That day, Simone would see an off-again on-again female patient who had never made up her mind about whether she really wanted to be treated. Hers was a complex case. The young woman, only twenty-eight, had become completely unhinged. She used various drugs, recreationally, or so she said, and had no qualms about taking part in orgies or having sex with strangers.

"Hello, Doctor."

"Hello, Helen. How are you?"

"I've missed you!" she replied with a smile. She wasn't pretty but had an interesting face and a vivacity that made her very attractive.

"Helen, today we're going to resume your treatment for the…third time," Simone said as she consulted the woman's clinical record.

"Yes."

"Okay. But this is your final opportunity, all right? Either we continue the treatment or there won't be a fourth try. We need this to be in earnest."

"I expected you to say that. But I feel I'm ready now. I seriously want to get pregnant so I have to get better."

"That's wonderful! So your marriage is going well?"

"Very well. My husband's a great guy." Helen had met him during one of her severe crises. Their union had given her stability. But she'd ceased treatment and Simone had lost track of her. So this was good news.

"And is there a specific reason you've come to me for help just now?"

"To get rid of my lust for her, once and for all."

"Still? For your teacher?"

"Yes. I can't help it, Doctor. She interrupts and disrupts my life. I think about her ten times a day. I want her so much it hurts."

"Her? Or any person?"

"Her. I imagine her body. I imagine I'm kissing her, touching her, tonguing her. I imagine her smell and I go crazy."

"What do you do to satisfy your lust?"

"Wild sex with my husband. He ends up benefiting."

"But does it satiate your desire?"

"No. But it helps a little. What I feel for her is horniness, plain and simple. And I want so much to have a normal life. I want to be a mother. I really want to have a child."

"Whenever you've come here, you've told me you want to have a normal life. And every time you try to take on a role, you don't succeed. It's drugs or risky relations or this obsession for that teacher."

"It's not an obsession. I love her. But I love my husband too."

"You should put off having a child, Helen. The decision is yours but every time you tell me you want a life by the book, I see you taking a way around it. Perhaps you really don't want to be a mother or a wife."

"Why's that?"

"Because you have to resolve these questions before you can be a mother. Does that woman know you love her? The last time you told me you were going to talk to her. But that was four months ago and I don't know what happened."

"I did. But she said she couldn't even imagine it and that she was hetero, even in her fantasies. She's afraid. That's for sure."

"Maybe she really is hetero, Helen."

"Nobody's this or that, Doctor. 'Just try it.' That's what I've said to her."

"You talk to her?"

"Yes. I e-mail her every day. I tell her how I feel, what I fantasize about her. Sometimes I say I'll never write her again and that I'll leave her alone. But that lasts a day or so. Today I sent her a nude photo."

"A naked photo of you, I presume?"

"Yes."

"And she responded?"

"She's a tease. She answers my messages. That's why I don't get it. She must feel something, right?"

"Maybe she does. Or maybe she's being maternal. According to what you've told me, she's someone who's always been there to give you support. Isn't that true?"

"Yes. All I had to do was need. I found that out, so I needed a lot. I needed only so I could have her near."

"Helen, you're harassing that woman and she's keeping you at a distance and taking care of you again. Do you understand?"

"Is that what you think? Sometimes, I think she may be giving herself the time to find out what she feels. She says no. But she may yet say yes."

"Helen, if she says no, it's no. How old is she now, forty-five, fifty?"

"Around there."

"She knows what she wants, Helen. It doesn't seem to me that sex with you is on her list."

"But I need to fulfill my fantasies, Doctor! My whole body begs me to have her. At least for a day."

"And what would you do with that day?"

"Everything. I'd caress her all over. She'd see that a woman's love is different from a man's. It's soft and gentle. I'd touch her everywhere, every place where I know a woman likes to be touched. I'd lead her to discover herself. I'd teach her."

"So now you want to be the teacher? To dominate her? You think if you dominated her, she'd overcome her fears?"

"That's what I think. I would really like to dominate her."

"Let's return to your past, Helen. The abuse. You suffered abuse at the hands of a woman much older than you were. To dominate your teacher now would make you feel you were dominating your abuser. Your teacher must have something in common with her."

Helen was the daughter of a single mother. A woman who lived nearby had taken care of young Helen while her mother was at work. The woman began molesting Helen at an early age. At first, she'd fondle Helen. Later on, she had Helen fondle her. When Helen was old enough to understand what was going on, she told her mother. Her mother didn't believe her and the molestation continued for years. Abuse has consequences. Helen lost her sexual bearings. She ended up feeling she could have sex with both men and women.

"Are you saying that I see that woman in Gloria?" Helen asked.

"The teacher's name is Gloria?"

"Yes."

"I think so, Helen. I think you wish to dominate someone who had power over you. Teachers have power over students. You unconsciously want to dominate that woman and mitigate your hatred for that time in your life. That's not love."

"I'll think about what you've said," she responded after a moment.

"Please do. And try not to chase after that poor teacher. She probably believes she can help you to find yourself again. That's why she pays attention to your messages. If you're not careful, this could turn out badly. She might sue you, Helen."

"Gloria? She wouldn't do that!"

"I'm going to give you something by Lacan to read. It's about obsession."

"But I'm not obsessive!"

"Just read it, okay? It will help you understand a few things. The article talks about hysteria and obsession. They're complementary pathologies. I'd like you to try to decide whether or not the teacher has anything to do with hysteria. Will you do that for me?"

"I will, Doctor."

* * * * *

Philip arrived at the office that afternoon in a buoyant mood. He was absolutely euphoric for someone who, a few days before, had been bemoaning the treachery of his wife. And he was bearing his customary box of goodies.

"Great to see you, Doctor!" he exclaimed, vigorously shaking Simone's hand.

"How are you, Philip? Am I mistaken to think you're happy?"

"I'm happy, all right. Happier than a pig in puppy shit!"

"That's wonderful! Tell me why." Simone clenched her jaw to keep from laughing. Philip's expressions were often coarse but amusing.

"I've got a new girlfriend!"

"You do? Already?"

"Loneliness does nobody any good. And I'm thrilled because this woman seems to understand me."

"Really? That's good. Who is she?"

"The rope dominatrix I told you about."

My God! Simone thought. Just when she believed there might yet be hope for him, Philip regaled her with another display of derangement. "But how did that happen?" she deadpanned.

"I was feeling lower than whale shit. You know, because of my wife and all. So I went to the submission house to have another go at the ropes. It was mind-blowing! Leonora's an expert. She tied me up and I began to have all those sensational feelings I described to you the other day. The more she tightened the ropes, the more I begged her to keep squeezing. Then, just when I thought I was going to pass out from all the pleasure, I said to her, 'Kill me. I want to die!' I was thinking that, in addition to the pleasure, I'd free myself from the pain of having lost my wife. That's when Leonora suddenly stopped!"

"And that was good?"

"No. I didn't know what was wrong. She barked at me to sit down and asked what kind of crap was that, wanting to die wrapped up in her ropes."

"And what did you do?"

"I started to wail like a baby and I told her my story. She untied me and invited me to go for a drink. We've been seeing each other ever since and she understands all my fantasies because that's her business. She's a professional dominatrix!"

Lovely line of work, Simone thought. "And do you think you can feel for her what you felt for your wife?"

"I don't know, Doc. Everybody's different. You can't feel the same thing for different people. But my ex-wife didn't understand me. She went along with my fantasies as if she were doing me a big favor. And I lived in mortal fear of losing her. Although we just got together, with Leonora, I feel I can be myself. As she says, my fantasies are 'child's play' to her."

"I see you have something on your neck again. Is it to hide telltale signs of your activities?"

"Oh no. This is a collar." He was as proud as a peacock to be wearing what appeared to be a rhinestone-covered leather collar for a large dog.

"A dog collar?"

"It is, more or less. Leonora has accepted me as her very own. The collar is one of the manifestations of our relationship. Sometimes she walks me on a leash. It's a sign of property. I love to belong."

"Philip, you're an accountant. Don't you think that would give people the wrong impression?"

"Oh. But we don't go around in the middle of the road. It's just at home and in the nightclub. That's all."

"But you're neither at home nor in the club here and you're wearing it!"

"I know. I wanted you to see it, Doctor. So how do you like it?"

"I don't know. I don't know much about collars. And I don't have a dog."

"No… Not the collar. What do you think of my new relationship?"

"I'd like you to be careful, Philip. You've abruptly jumped into it. Last week, you were crying your eyes out. Now you're on cloud nine."

"But I'm happy, Doctor!"

"I know. I simply would like you to exercise a bit of caution. It's normal for people to go from one extreme to the other when a relationship ends. You've gone from a woman who was reluctant to understand your sexual preferences to one who accepts all your fantasies."

"Isn't that good?"

"Maybe it is. But you should give some thought to what you're getting into. Try to get a clear idea of how far you can go with Leonora. Your ex-wife provided your life with a bit of normalcy and restraint. By setting some limits to your fantasies, she gave you a certain stability. I'm afraid Leonora will let you go wild."

"Okay, Doctor. I'll think about what you're saying. If I'd listened to you before, I wouldn't be separated, right?"

"We can't be sure about that. But think seriously about what you want out of life. Sometimes, we take people too quickly into our lives to fill the void the pain of a separation leaves. But the void is there. And maybe the problems will only get worse."

"I understand."

"I hope you'll think about it. Everyone needs time to heal after the end of a romance. If you don't let yourself feel the pain caused by a loss and just sweep it under the carpet, someday it will slip back out to attack you when you're least prepared for it."

"But I hate to feel emotional pain."

"I know. But pain is part of maturing, Philip. Now I could be wrong and your new relationship might turn into a beautiful love story. I'm just asking you to go slowly."

"How about the collar? Do I have to take it off?" More than anything else, Philip's principal concern seemed to be the collar. It was the clear symbol of someone who wished very much to belong, the symbol of someone who didn't want to be *a dog without an owner*.

"Keep the collar if it does you good. I don't see any great harm in that."

* * * * *

The week had turned into a whirlwind. Simone decided to cancel her Wednesday afternoon appointments. She sat on the couch in her office, missing Mona more than ever. In an effort to distract herself from such melancholy thoughts, Simone decided to finish Mark's journal. She'd complete her analyzation of the text and wrap up the job. Maybe then she'd have a little normalcy in her life again.

Lara called me again. She was happy because things were falling into place. It was magical how a call from her could put a smile on my day and make colors look brighter. Enthusiasm filled her voice as she talked a blue streak. She said she missed me and she'd soon be a free woman.

"Did you get the divorce?"

"Yes! No more chains in a few short months. Now it's just legal red tape. You know all about that."

"Contested?"

"No. Amicable!"

"How's that? The last time we spoke, nothing was budging."

"Maurice had an idea after I told him that Nicholas had dug in his heels. He asked me if I had anything we could use to shake him up. I said I didn't but I knew some things I couldn't prove. I told him about one of the *house parties* we'd had where I saw Nicholas having sex with a man."

"Wow! Maurice didn't have a stroke right there?" I imagined the old codger's purple face when he heard that.

"Maurice? He was one of Emma's gang. I don't know all the details of what the four of them used to do but celibacy had no role in their shenanigans. Those four were a Bangkok sex show! Emma told me I was a nun in comparison."

"I can just imagine those old-timers in a swing house." My imagination is fertile. I pictured Maurice in a daisy chain and I didn't like what I saw.

"They weren't always old-timers. But let me tell you what Maurice did. He called Nicholas and said he was one of my lawyers. He told him he had an envelope with a video made years ago in which a renowned professor was sodomizing a young student. He went on that the envelope was addressed to the university president. But if a certain document were signed, the film would be toast. Once the divorce was final, it would be sent to its featured artist."

"Was that true?"

"Of course not. I have nothing of the kind! But Nicholas is probably still banging boys. Old habits die hard!"

"Never believe someone who says he's a former homosexual. So he swallowed it?"

"He certainly did because I had described his technique to Maurice. Right away, he scribbled his John Hancock. Yeeeesss!"

Her shout almost deafened me. I had to remove the phone from my ear. But I understood her glee.

"And when the divorce is official what are you going to send him?"

"Pocahontas. Whatever. Now I'm free!"

I had to laugh at the idea of a cultured Frenchman discovering he'd been blackmailed with a children's cartoon. *Oh,* I thought, *how we all fear scandal.* More than anything else in life, the threat of our good name being dragged through the mud is the moral equivalent of a nuclear weapon. Clearly, Maurice knew that too. A devil's a devil. Not because he's evil but because he's old! "When are you coming home, gorgeous?"

"Why don't you come get me? We'll fly back together."

"I'd love to but I can't. I'm up to my neck in work. One lawyer's sick and another's on vacation. No way, babe."

"Too bad. We could use the bathroom on the plane for a fantasy I have."

"Speak to me." I had no doubt another torrid tale was on the way to turn me on. She was definitely worried about her absence. Women can be such possessive creatures. Even when they don't want you, they're armed and ready for the least threat they sense.

"First I go into the bathroom and close the door. Then you arrive."

"How do we both fit in there?"

"Easy. It's the sardine-can principle. I leave the toilet seat down. You enter and unzip your zipper. You drop your trousers and sit on the seat. I turn my back to you and slip down on your cock like you're a chair. You hold me in your arms. I go up and down, up and down. Slow and easy-like."

"Hmmm." I began to masturbate.

"I keep going up and down. I squeeze you inside me then release you. When I go down, I release you and when I go up I squeeze you. Then I start to go faster with the help of your hands on my ass. I'm moaning softly, controlling myself so the whole plane doesn't hear."

"And?"

"And when I think you're about to come, I stop. I turn to face you and slip down on you again. I start to ride you, slowly again, and I kiss you and nibble on your lip. I put my tongue in your mouth and, still kissing you, I grab you by the hair and ride you to heaven."

"Crazy lady."

"I come, moaning for you alone to hear. You're biting my neck. It's wonderful. But you don't come just yet. I dismount and take your cock in my mouth. I suck you and suck you until you fill my mouth with your hot come. Then I swallow it all. Not one single drop falls on the floor."

"Lara, I'm going to unload right now, you wicked wench." I was a teenager again. I must have squirted buckets. Happily, I didn't need to wait for her. The moans at the other end of the line told me she too had done herself justice with her own hands.

"Oooowww!" That moan meant pain.

"What happened, Lara?"

"I hit my elbow."

"Where?"

"On the sink in the plane's bathroom."

"Hah! Very funny! I miss you, Lara!"

"Me too. But I'll be back soon."

"When's soon?"

"The truth?"

"Yes! The truth."

"Tomorrow. But I'm going straight to the Hamptons. I'll be a mess and I want to get over the jet lag."

Great. Fifteen days away and upon her return she goes somewhere else, I thought. *Fine. What the hell. It's Lara. What did you expect?* "Okay, beautiful. Have a good trip!"

I was too thrilled that Lara was on her way back to bitch and moan over just one day. I was also feeling the effects of my conversation with Deena. Since our lunch together, I'd reflected a lot about what she'd said and concluded she was right. We were about to embark on the second half of our lives. I shouldn't waste time looking for the ideal partner. It was time to take what life dished up. I had a woman who broke all the rules. She'd never be a conventional wife. But she'd make me very happy. My rational self tried to persuade me otherwise. Sure, she'd make me happy. But maybe that happiness wouldn't be proportionate to the suffering she'd bring. Fuck it. I put reason aside. Deena had nailed it. To live was more important. And in the final analysis, better some nasty moments than an unlived life.

I went to Tiffany's and bought a ring for Lara. A humongous solitary diamond. I know women put a lot of stock in a stone's size, as if they measure love in carats. The center stone was square with smaller diamonds around the edge. I believed she'd like it. I was going to propose to her. A new beginning. If just half a life remained to me, I'd seize it and make every minute count. I didn't feel I was in crisis but Deena had certainly shown me I had to make better use of the time I had left.

I'd been miserable while Lara was away. I'd spent almost fifteen days during which I'd missed everything about her. Her hair spread on the pillow. The tubes of paint she'd leave scattered about. Her general disarray. Even her crises. She'd spent months with me and her departure for Paris had made my life a void.

Then she called me that afternoon, two days after we'd spoken on the phone. I was listening to her hypnotic voice again. She'd returned from Paris. She wanted to see me. At the beach house. Could it be today? She was joyful. She said nothing more would stand in our way. My faith in Lara's words was the same as my faith in the existence of life on Mars. But I was dying to see her.

I tried to leave work early but it was impossible. Two hours on the road lay ahead of me when I left the city at twilight. Meeting Lara was always a hallucination. She made wings flutter inside my stomach. She was always a surprise, always an infinite fountain of fantasy. She scorned normality, the routine. The surprise with her was the routine. I swore to myself that this time I wouldn't seek to change her. It was my last chance to get our romance right. I saw just two options: have Lara forever or lose her by trying to make her over.

She'd be mine. That was that.

I took the sandy lane onto the grounds. I parked beside the house. The murmur of the still sea, with light from a lovers' moon languid upon it, enhanced the silence. I took the side steps up to the front porch. The doors were open and a faint glow flowed from within. Curtains were billowing in the sea breeze when I saw her. She waited for me naked, her blonde hair disheveled. She wore impossibly high-heeled shoes and something like a thick chain around her neck. She strutted toward me, glorying in the lust she always ignited in me and all men.

She didn't say much, something like, "Hi…nice to see you."

She began to kiss me, caress me. I wanted to talk first. To say that I loved her. To ask her to marry me. But right then, all I could think about was feeling her skin against mine and smelling her perfume. We'd talk afterward. She began to unbutton my shirt. She slid her hands down my chest toward my trousers. I tore them off. She gave me a leather glove for one of my hands.

"You don't know how much I want you to bury your cock inside me. Wear the glove."

The bomb that always ticked when we were close exploded. No time for sweet nothings.

Two sweaty, nude bodies glistened in the moonlight. Hands and legs and tongues entwined with sighs and moans and incoherent phrases.

"I want you to squeeze my neck slowly. I want to feel I'm being dominated. I go wild when you do that."

"I know." It was her vice. I wasn't going to try to understand anymore. I'd just do what she asked.

"Use the glove. I want to feel like I'm being attacked by a stranger, that I'm defenseless."

"Like this?" I asked, closing my hand on her neck.

"Harder…as if you want to strangle me. It drives me crazy. Don't be gentle with me. I want savagery."

"I want to feel you come."

"Harder, Mark, squeeze harder. It makes me feel powerless."

"I'm afraid to hurt you," I said.

But the adrenalin was now coursing through my veins. I lost control. All I wanted was to come inside that woman who was driving me mad.

"Harder! Squeeze me hard and give it to me harder! I'm almost coming!"

"You're making me insane, you crazy bitch. I'm gonna squeeze until you beg for mercy!"

I grabbed the chain around Lara's neck and started to pull it. Lara went berserk.

"That's it… Yes… That's it. Squeeze more. More!" She had her back to me. She rolled her hips wildly. She was desperate to reach orgasm. She knew no limits when she wanted to get off.

"I can't hold it anymore! I'm gonna fill you up with come!" I began to feel the fierce pleasure of the approaching eruption.

As we started to come together, I yanked the chain. Immediately, she slumped. She went limp.

"Lara, what's wrong? Lara? You okay? Stop fooling around."

But her stillness told me she wasn't fooling. Something was really wrong. She wasn't breathing.

"Lara, breathe, please. What have I done? Lara, I love you. Lara, breathe. Holy shit! Don't do this to me!"

But she was as lifeless as a pretty little doll.

I tried mouth-to-mouth resuscitation and heart massage, my limited knowledge of first aid. To no avail. I called my father, who gave me the number of a nearby doctor who owed him a favor. He arrived quickly but too late. I had killed the woman I loved. I had killed a part of me. Maybe the best part.

The doctor had to sedate me to protect me from my despair. I was like that until Lara's funeral, two days after her death. I couldn't eat or sleep. The powerful drug just made me dizzy. I felt like a spinning top.

That funeral was the saddest day of my life. I was permitted to attend, the beginning of the rest of my miserable days. I wanted to be able to feel. So I stopped taking the sedative. My head was clear and the pain I felt was physical. It seemed I had a hole in my chest that never would be closed. I was certain my life would never be complete again. On that day, I learned true love comes just once in a lifetime. Shovelfuls of dirt were burying mine.

Lara was interred with the ring on her finger. I had put it there. No one protested. Such was my overwhelming, palpable grief.

My life is now unceasing gloom. Living without her is torture. I've begun to drift, yearning for death. If I were brave, I'd kill myself. But God is punishing me by withholding the courage I need to die. And also the courage I need to live.

Chapter Twenty-Six

Present Day — Simone

Simone put down the text with a heavy heart. She hadn't known Lara but she felt deeply for that disturbed and complex young woman. Just when she seemed to be about to find happiness, her life ended abruptly. Though not without warning. Simone felt for Mark as well. That poor, unfortunate man. He had stood on the brink of having the world in his hands. With those very same hands, he had taken the life of the woman he loved.

Mark's innocence was evident to Simone. There were no culprits here. Only victims. The abstract work was over. Now came the fieldwork. She'd interview people who personally knew Lara and thus finish the job. Simone called Carl to inform him she'd wrapped up her reading. They decided to meet in New York the following day.

* * * * *

Simone got to Carl's office around six in the afternoon. The heavy traffic had held her up. Carl was alone when she arrived. His office oozed elegance with its dark wood décor. Very masculine. Simone praised his good taste.

"Lara decorated this and we've left it alone," he told her.

That confirmed Simone's suspicions. There had been intimate bonds of friendship between the people in Carl's text.

Carl escorted Simone into a meeting room, equally well designed. It boasted a wooden table for fourteen people, black chairs, beautiful paintings on the walls and leafy plants. They took their seats.

"I'm very anxious to hear what you have to say, Simone. You've finished the reading..."

"Yes, I have, as I told you on the phone. So far, I can confirm everything we discussed when you visited my office. I've prepared a formal but not conclusive opinion."

She handed the document to Carl. He took it and fixed his gaze on her.

"So your diagnosis is sadomasochism?"

"That's right. Sadomasochism with strong self-destructive tendencies and profound mood swings caused by the attention deficit disorder Lara said she had."

"It seems that was genetic. She'd inherited it from her father or grandmother..."

"Yes, it's possible. It's really genetic. That condition causes sudden changes in mood…instability. And in some cases…I believe in Lara´s…addiction to adrenaline. But it was certainly aggravated by the abuse she suffered."

"Now that you've finished the text, in your opinion is Mark innocent or guilty?"

"My opinion is that Mark was guilty only of getting involved with Lara. Of course, this is based solely on the text. Her death was an accident and, as I've already told you, it could have happened during any of her sadomasochistic sessions. It's not so uncommon. But I'd very much like to talk to Mark. I need to look at him and ask him some questions, Carl. In my profession, seeing the body language and other signs is crucial to making a diagnosis.

"I understand."

"Could you arrange that? It's very important in order to conclude my work."

"You can ask whatever you wish."

"When?"

"Starting now, Simone. That's why I asked you to come here and not just send me the report. I'm Mark!"

Simone sat stock-still for a few moments. At no time during her reading had she deduced that Mark was in fact Carl. Had her attraction to him clouded her judgment? The impression she'd formed of Carl had kept her from imagining such an earnest and focused man having savage sex in swing houses and falling so head-over-heels in love that he'd risked losing control. She'd fooled herself.

"You're Mark?" Her mouth dropped open. All the self-control in the world couldn't have prevented it.

"That's right. I used my third name in the story so you'd be objective."

"And when are you going to trial?"

"I'm not. This all happened a long time ago. I went to court last year and was acquitted. The jury agreed with you. It was really an accident. But I've been my own judge, jury and executioner every single day since I killed her."

"How did the jury reach their verdict?"

"There were witnesses. John Meyer, the black guy who was Lara's dominator and now my good friend, was one of the principal ones. Other men who'd had sex with Lara also testified, thanks to information John gave. They all said hypoxyphilia took place often in their relations with Lara. My father defended me. He's the best criminal lawyer I know. His team dug up a lot of dirt. Lara was no saint." Carl spoke these last words sadly.

"For me, the worst part was putting together the puzzle of Lara's behavior. For months before the trial and after it, besides feeling guilty for killing her, I felt terrible for seeing her life paraded before the public."

"You didn't kill her, Carl. It was an accident."

"Call it whatever you like, Simone. But I killed her."

"But why all the theatrics? You hire me. You tell me you're working on a case. I could have found out everything on the Internet."

"But you didn't do that. At one of our early meetings, we talked a lot about impartial opinions. I was sure that at first you'd read nothing beyond the text. I trusted your word and I was right. But even if you hadn't given your word, my name was different. Or rather, it was my name too. I'm Carl Anthony Marcus. Either my parents had a dynastic complex or they couldn't agree on the name. As for Lara…well, I wouldn't be able to change her name even to protect myself. Even now, just the sound of it is music to me."

"Peter is Peter?"

"Yes. But it's a common name. Only my name was changed and I trusted your word."

"Why did you hire me, Carl?"

"Because I needed answers no one else could give me. I needed a detached, professional opinion to help me understand what had happened. I underwent therapy after Lara's death. None of it justified or absolved me. Then I saw you interviewed on TV and said to myself, 'That woman can help me'."

"I'm very surprised."

"I know. Please forgive me. But I saw no other way. I decided to write the text. I tried my best to remember everything that had happened in my brief time with Lara. Between the comings and goings, we were together for less than a year.

"When did you start to write?"

"I started not long after she died. Lara kept a diary her whole life. She said it helped her get in touch with her feelings and organize her emotions. So I decided to give it a try when I was in the blackest of my despair. I'd always been a good writer and with every word, I relived our days together. I didn´t pay any attention to vocabulary or style…just let the emotions flow… It did help me. It cut like a scalpel. But it wasn't enough. I needed more help. Your help!"

Deep emotions etched his face. Simone now had a glimpse of the Mark in the text.

"You have an excellent memory. There's a wealth of detail. The events are vivid."

"I've gone over every one of them in my mind a thousand times. I see them all clearly and they give me no peace. They dance around before me. Some nights, I can't sleep. I relive every second of those months. I keep wondering what I could have done differently. I keep imagining new endings to our story. They all end with us together. Forever."

"Is the story true?"

"Everything I can remember is. I didn't make up anything, Simone. I owe this to her. A tribute. To be faithful to her memory." Carl looked Simone in the eye.

She closely analyzed his expression and detected no trace of deception. He was being honest. She saw deep suffering in him.

"You aren't guilty of anything, Carl. You couldn't have done anything differently, anything at all to change what happened. Put your conscience at ease. If she hadn't died at your hands, she'd have died at someone else's. Hypoxyphilia is a dangerous practice."

"For a long time, I wondered if deep down I wanted to kill Lara, if on that day I squeezed harder because I wanted to put an end to the whole sordid business. She was driving me crazy with her fantasies, her comings and goings, her disappearances. I wasn't myself anymore. I'd become a man who took too many risks, who threw caution to the wind."

"No, Carl. You were in love. You'd decided to marry her. You wanted to believe in Lara.

You wanted her for yourself, so you tried to take care of her. But at the same time, your desire to satisfy her was very strong. One of a man's greatest pleasures is to give a woman a fantastic orgasm. Like it or not, squeezing Lara's neck was the way to do it. She was irresistible and she kept begging, and you didn't know how to regulate the means to the end."

"I really tried. I feared hurting her. But she knew no limits. Whenever I thought I was going too far, she begged for more and more."

"They never have limits. I have a patient who uses ropes in his masochism and he tells me that dying during a climax would be wonderful. The human mind is complex and, as far as sex goes, however much you study it, there aren't many keys. There's a lot of speculation. We keep going on what we've learned from other cases. It's hard to understand the nature of desires."

"Simone, talking to you makes me feel better. I don't think I'll ever be able to forget all that and live a normal life. The guilt haunts me. Her loss drives me out of my mind. The pain never goes away. But at least if I could forgive myself, maybe I'd have some peace." He slammed his fist down on his knee in frustration.

"Carl, I'd like to treat you."

Now she'd done it! With just a few words, she had eliminated any possibility of a romance with Carl. She wanted to treat him. Where did that come from? From her compassionate side that couldn't bear to see someone suffering and do nothing about it. Carl was obviously suffering. She had to help him. She'd been trained to cure, not to remain unscathed by the suffering of others.

"I need you, Simone. I need your help."

Carl reached out toward her. She took his hand and he began to sob as if he'd never done this before. The sobs were desperate. It seemed to Simone that they'd never stop, that a dam had burst and the torrent would race forever.

She went to him and embraced him. She put his head on her shoulder. He sobbed for a long time. She kept silent. She understood the poignancy of the moment. Maybe it was the beginning of the recovery of the man's tortured soul.

After several minutes, Carl finally got a grip on himself. He and Simone talked and talked. She didn't know if his life would ever be normal. But she'd do everything in her power to help him. She'd use all the fruits of her knowledge and experience to that end. They left the office and went to dinner. Carl told her stories about Lara. He was less constrained now because he could directly include himself in them. His secret was out. His gestures and movements were more relaxed. Simone could see Mark in him. They were leaving the restaurant when Peter came in.

"Well! If it's not my dear friend and the lovely doctor."

"How nice. You remember me?"

"Of course I do. Beautiful women are unforgettable."

Simone didn't feel flattered. She knew from the text that Peter was over the top.

"By yourself today, Peter?" Carl asked.

"No. I'm awaiting company. And you guys? Having fun?"

He sounded sarcastic, as if he didn't approve of her presence. *Or maybe my nerves are just a wreck lately and I'm imagining things,* she thought.

"You bet. Unwinding after a heavy week," Carl said.

"I've heard the news, Doctor. About all those killings where you live."

"It's horrible. And sadly, there's no end in sight."

"The police don't have any clues?"

"They do. But they don't fit together. Nothing concrete."

"But this is a big deal! Have I heard correctly that the FBI is involved?"

"It seems to be standard practice for them to get involved in serial murders. But it looks as if, so far, they've come up empty as well."

"I guess they're better on TV than in real life," Peter said.

"Who knows? You could be right."

"Peter, we're on our way. Call me and we'll go for a beer tomorrow."

"Okay. Pinkie promise!"

Peter waved his baby finger until Carl faked a punch to Peter's chest and then hugged him.

"Bye-bye, beautiful!" Peter blew kisses at Simone and left.

"You two are close friends, aren't you?" Simone said as they walked away.

"Very close. He was always there for me after Lara's death. He gave testimony at the trial. I could count on him for support. He helped my father with the evidence. Wherever I turned, there was Peter, lending a hand. I'll never be able to pay him back."

"That's what friends are for."

"He's the very definition of a true friend."

Carl invited Simone to spend the night at his apartment because of the late hour. As further proof of the text's accuracy, the apartment was just as described. And the dog greeted them. Now she understood why he'd put her in a hotel before. The apartment would have given away who he really was.

When Simone got in her car to go back home, she felt the urge to remain in the city. She decided not to go home until Sunday evening. She found a hotel on Broadway and called Edward so he wouldn't worry in case he tried to contact her and couldn't. Then she set off to enjoy the delights of Manhattan. She took in a musical, went to a ballet and did some shopping. Her house didn't appeal to her at the moment and she felt safe as just one more face in the crowd.

Chapter Twenty-Seven

Present Day — Simone

On Monday a string of patients awaited Simone, as usual. Late in the morning, she found Edward in the office's kitchen. He was making coffee and she was after a sandwich.

"How was New York?" he asked.

"I finished my work there."

"How did things turn out?"

"Much better than I'd expected." She then told him everything that had happened. And maybe she sounded a bit too enthusiastic about treating Carl.

"Did he ask you to treat him?" Edward sounded angry.

"Hiring me to study the text was already a kind of request. He needed someone to analyze what had happened without initially involving himself."

"You! I don't believe how blind you are!"

Edward seized her arm. His harshness unnerved her.

"Me?"

"Simone, if you're not blind, you're crazy. Can't you see this man is interested in you? And he's a killer!"

"No. He's not interested in me and he's definitely not a killer. What's gotten into you, Ed?"

"You. You're the love of my life."

"What?"

"I've loved you ever since I saw you come into that biology class loaded down with books and notebooks, all clumsy and dropping everything. And I love your mind. You're the smartest woman I know. I love your beauty. I love your smile. I even love the funny way you raise your eyebrow because you've trained yourself not to wrinkle your forehead. But you don't see it. And now you're going to get involved with that maniac. God alone knows the truth behind that so-called novel he wrote! He might be behind all those killings!"

Simone felt as if she'd been kicked in the head. Of all the answers she could have expected from Edward, this was the only one she had never foreseen.

"I'm not getting involved with anyone, Ed. I want to treat him! If I wanted to get involved, I wouldn't become his therapist! As for your feelings, I never suspected a thing! I'm a specialist in human behavior. Nothing of what you're saying has ever seemed possible to me."

And that was the truth. She'd never considered the possibility.

"Because I've never wanted to show my feelings. You were already going out with Jack when I fell in love with you. He was my best friend in those days. Then came Tammy and then you married. Later on, I met Beth, and Noah came along. You and I were partners when we both got divorced. You didn't even notice that when you got divorced I got divorced right afterward. But then Beth started to make my life a living hell and you rushed to give me your support. There was no way I wanted to put you in the middle of all that. And when the nightmare finally eased up, you were in another relationship and seemed to be happy. And so it went. When I was with someone, you were alone and vice versa. I always put our friendship first. But now I can't take it anymore, Simmie! I want you for myself! Enough's enough! I'm just not going to stand on the sidelines anymore! I've been waiting for twenty years for you to notice me!"

Edward's words were the last straw, the *coup de grace* that destroyed Simone's perfect world once and for all. Her best friend! Her rock! Now what? She didn't know what she felt. She didn't know if she could feel something for Ed other than friendship.

"Ed, all this. I can't even think. Give me time to digest. Please. And don't get me wrong. I simply can't fit all of it inside my head right now!"

"I know, Simone. Everything seems to be coming out of the blue at a time when both our lives are in turmoil. But today's the day when I reached the limit. I saw you heading into a new relationship and I got desperate."

"New relationship, Ed? Where? I've just told you I'm going to treat the guy!"

"You came back all bright-eyed and bushy-tailed from New York and I've been aware of the dinners and the comings and goings."

"My friend, you've got it all wrong. All those dinners and comings and goings were on a strictly professional level. I wouldn't get involved with a client. You know that! And I spent the weekend all alone in Manhattan!"

"I've told myself that a million times, Simone. But the fear of losing you one more time…" Edward covered his head with his hands. "Simmie, forget what I said. Let's just go on the way we were as if nothing had happened. Worse than to lose the woman I love is to lose my friend. If that's all we can be, I'll take it and be thankful."

"It's just that now everything's changed, Ed. We can't go back!"

"What are you going to do?"

"I don't know. I just don't know. Until now, you've been my Gibraltar, my friend, my shoulder to lean on. Now all of a sudden, in the middle of the mess and the fog in my life, you've become part of what isn't clear."

"Simmie, let's leave this as it is…"

He was visibly terrified that what he'd just revealed had irreparably damaged his friendship with her. And she was plainly lost in the tangle of twists and turns and emotions of recent days. Dead people. Cops. Patients freaking out. Nothing was clear. All was chaos.

"I'm going out. I'm going for a walk, Ed. Will you please ask the new girl to cancel the rest of my appointments? I can't handle them today."

"The new secretary's name is Joan," he said in exasperation at Simone's failure to remember the woman's name. "Wait a minute. I'll call the police to keep you in sight."

"I'm not going far. I'm just going to sit on the bench in that park on the corner. There's no problem at this time of day. I need to be alone, Ed. Please don't call anyone."

"Okay. It's early. I guess it'll be all right."

Just as she was leaving, Simone encountered Alvin in the hallway. *Lovely*, she thought. All the crazy people could get together and she'd change the sign on her office door to "Auntie Simone's Loony Bin".

"Doctor, could I have a word with you? Everything's okay," he said making the peace sign with his hand. "It's just that I've been trying to put the puzzle together about my brother and his wife and I'd like some information."

"Excuse me, Alvin, but it will have to wait for another day. Yes, I'll help you. Please see the secretary and schedule an appointment."

"Couldn't it be today? It's pretty urgent. I'll wait." He pointed to one of the chairs.

"You'll have to pardon me, Alvin. Today, I just can't do it."

"Doctor. Really. I have to talk to you!"

He grabbed Simone's arm but she yanked it away.

"Make an appointment, Alvin!" She hurried off before another crazy supplicant appeared. She'd have a shit fit if one more crossed her path today.

She walked to the park on the corner, a few houses away from her office. In reality, it was almost a vacant lot. It had two benches with a gray cement fountain between them. There were a few trees. Ideal for a quick lunch in the shade. It had been built by the people who lived in the mainly residential neighborhood.

She couldn't even think about eating. Edward's words kept echoing in her mind. Edward was in love with her. Edward?

She took a seat and stared into the foaming fountain in an effort to calm down. A jumble of thoughts tumbled around in her mind. Her head was spinning. Her heart pounded. She didn't hear anyone approach but she felt someone place a cloth over her mouth and then felt nothing more.

Chapter Twenty-Eight

Present Day – Simone

Simone awoke suddenly. She was naked, wet and inside what seemed to be a cage less than three feet in height that hung from a chain. Squeezed as she was into a crouch, her legs ached from being folded up to her chest. She didn't know how long she'd been there. But the pain she felt told her it must have been at least a few hours. She couldn't alter her position in any way.

Where in hell was she? What had happened to her? She remembered only sitting in the park and nothing else. She was terrified. She was certain the killer had her and that the torture had begun.

A drop of water fell on her head at regular intervals. It explained the wetness she felt and also the cold. The dripping maddened her. She ordered herself to stay calm. No doubt the killer would appear soon. She had to keep lucid to try to understand the situation. It was her only chance to get out of there alive.

She remembered some meditation techniques and began to practice them. She did her best to empty her mind to ease her extreme discomfort. But all the meditation on Earth would not make the water, the pain and the cold go away. Before long, she felt she'd panic. God! What had she done to end up in the clutches of a monster? Was he one of her patients? Was he someone she knew or had she been chosen at random? Victims weren't usually chosen because they'd done something to a psycho but because they had a quality that set off his madness or bore a resemblance to someone who did.

As the hours passed, she went over psychiatric theories in her mind. She recalled books and cases to try to keep herself together and to try to alleviate her physical pain. She also thought about all her patients. None seemed capable of torture or murder.

Her nose started to run. She was shivering and catching cold. Time kept slipping away. Day turned into night and no one arrived. Overcome by horrible pain, cramps and numbing cold, she slept or passed out for a few hours; she couldn´t tell. When she came to, she felt utterly disoriented. Now her throat hurt along with the rest of her body. To make things worse, she was famished, which made her feel even colder. She hadn't managed to touch her food on the day she'd been snatched, which meant at least twenty-four hours without solid food.

"Are you hungry?" a metallic voice asked. Some electronic device disguised the true voice.

"Yes, I am. Who are you? What do you want of me?"

"I am death, Doctor. We are having an encounter."

"Why me?"

"Oh how tiresome you all are. 'Why me? Why me?' Because you have decided to cross my path."

"What have I done?"

"Doctor, you know what you have done."

"Get me out of here. Please. We'll be able to talk. Whatever you think I've done, let's be rational about this."

"Okay. Perhaps it is time to get you out of there, Doctor. Perhaps not. How do you prefer to die?"

"In my bed at the age of ninety."

She attempted a bit of humor. Maybe it would cause her tormentor to form a bond with her. That had happened in some similar cases she'd read about.

"Bzzzzz!" He made a sound like something used during TV game shows. "Denied! Please choose another manner. I could strangle you. I could throw you down a staircase. I could suffocate you with a pillow. I could hang you."

"And why never knives or guns?"

"Because they cause bleeding. I detest blood. It leaves stains. Evidence. It spoils everything."

Oh, great news, she thought. At least he wasn't going to cut her. But now she felt he'd moved closer to the cage. She saw a flame. Probably from a lighter. She smelled cigarette smoke and then felt a burning on one of her feet. The pain was unbearable. Then came another and another and another... He kept going back and forth from one foot to the other. She howled in pain. Tears flowed down her cheeks. Finally, after a number of times more, he stopped and moved away. Her suffering was so great she forgot the cage, the dripping, the cold and her hunger. Her feet were on fire.

A steel door crunched shut and footsteps trudged away. The cage slowly lowered and touched down. A dim light came on. She saw the cage's door and easily opened it. She dragged herself as best she could out of the cage and lay down on the icy floor. It was either cement or granite, some freezing-cold material like an autopsy table, she thought. She hurt so badly she couldn't move another inch.

She looked around her. The room contained a long table, a wooden, straight-back, 1960s chair and a faucet. The windows were blocked with metal plates welded to the frames. The door was no doubt locked but she lacked the strength to go check it out.

Her feet hurt horribly. So did her bones, back, legs and throat, violently inflamed now. She increasingly suffered from cold, hunger and exhaustion. She dragged herself over to the faucet, turned it on and put her feet under the tap. The cool water, the best first aid for burns, soothed them.

Suddenly, hellish music began to play, hard rock so loud it threatened to explode her eardrums. A number of lights then turned dusk into daylight. She quickly realized that the fiend was now bent on sleep deprivation, one of the most diabolical forms of torture. It would eventually result in a victim's utter insanity.

Mind control, she thought. She needed to control her mind. But for how long? There was a limit. Mind control would weaken as the victim's resistance broke down. He usually spent a week with his victims, she thought. She estimated that she'd been in his hands for a day or so. Who was he?

The music changed little by little. Riffs became strident and cacophonous. Her strength was seeping away. She lacked the calories to keep her body warm. She developed a fever in addition to her other miseries. And the son-of-a-bitch had only just begun.

Despite all this pain and pandemonium, she lost consciousness. But something that felt like handcuffs being placed on her wrists jolted her awake. Her arms were pulled above her head and she felt skin scraping off as she was dragged across the floor. A hand on her neck forced her face under the faucet she'd used previously to soothe her burns. A brutal jet of water hit her flush. The hand mercilessly held her there. She found it almost impossible to breathe. She fought frantically against drowning in the torrent that pounded her nose and mouth.

Then it stopped. She coughed convulsively. Her head ached from the water that had ripped its way up her nostrils.

"Wake up, bitch!" The flat of a hand rapped her face.

"I'm out of it. I'm burning up with fever. I won't last much longer." She gagged on her own words.

"You will soon beseech all the powers of heaven and hell not to last any longer! They all implore me to free them from their agony. And then I do so. Life slips from their bodies and they find peace. As you yourself will see."

Simone truly believed him. The victims must have begged for death. "Why me? Who are you?" She looked at him for the first time. She tried to recognize him but couldn't. Something like a gas mask concealed his face. Definitely a man. His torso seemed familiar but in her condition she was unable to remember where she'd seen it. A long, blond wig covered his head.

"You are such an asshole, Doctor. So trusting. And so romantic. Does anyone know how romantic you are, Doctor Bennet?"

"Why do you say that? Do you know me?"

"I've been your shadow, you quack! I have often been inside your house. I have seated myself upon your couch. I have looked at the photos of your daughter. She certainly is cute. Perhaps after conversing with you, I shall do the same with her."

"Leave my daughter in peace!" It was normal for psychopaths to enjoy making their victims beg. But she refused to do that. Maybe she could find a way to control him by doing the unexpected.

"I have to leave her alone for now, Doctor, while she sojourns in Paris. But I may seek her out shortly. If you fail to behave yourself."

"You were the one who broke into my house." She realized the whacko had been ransacking her very existence of late. But why? "What did you want there?"

"To analyze your way of life. To understand you. I have even paid tribute to you!"

"Tribute?"

"Oh, you ungrateful slut! Yes! I suffocated one of the victims the way it happened in that television series you like and I killed the others just as they were killed in the other episodes. Yes, indeed! I liked it too! I watched a few episodes ensconced on your couch, sipping your wine. Surrounded by your ridiculous flowered cushions. I have been in every nook and cranny of your house."

"But no fingerprints were found."

"Do you think I am some sort of idiotic amateur? Do you give me no credit for my prudence? I wore gloves and overalls whenever I visited your residence."

"You went there more than once?"

"Yes! On a number of occasions. But then you installed security cameras and deprived me of my fun. But you did take your time. No one could accuse you of haste. And know what? I must tell you that your taste in clothes is very poor. You are not an unattractive woman, Doctor. But those schoolteacher outfits do nothing for you."

"My clothes. Why criticize my clothes now?"

"Because I went through your closets. Sad. Very sad."

She got the urge to vomit just thinking about him parading through her house. She'd never be able to go back there. She'd feel his presence in every corner. *Who are you kidding?* she asked herself. *Your next residence until the end of time will probably be the cemetery.* But she wished she could go home even for just a day. Alive.

"Enough of this chitchat, Doctor. Shall we play a little game of elastic band?"

"I prefer to sleep."

"I prefer to play. Here the toys are mine, and we shall play whenever I wish to and stop whenever I say."

He picked her up in his arms and carried her to the table. She didn't resist. She'd only waste what little strength she had left and she needed it to keep her head clear. He laid her down and tied her wrists to the sides of one end of the table and her feet to the sides of the other. Spread-eagle. Then he left and she thought he'd just leave her there in the cold. She felt a bit relieved. But then she heard a humming sound and noticed that the table had a kind of electric device that was elongating it. Her body was being pulled and stretched. She screamed in pain. She felt what seemed to be a rib cracking and passed out.

Chapter Twenty-Nine

Present Day — Simone

Excruciating pain racked her body when she came to. She knew the killer was there, looking at her, from the sounds he made. She felt as weak as a rachitic kitten. She still lay on the table but it no longer moved. She made a superhuman effort to talk to him. She needed to force the words out of her mouth. She needed to understand.

"Where do you want to go with all this? Who are you?" She would have screamed this at the top of her voice had she been able to.

He stood leaning against the wall with a foot raised against it and his arms crossed, just watching her. At last he said, "You have the effrontery to cross my path but you don't know who I am?"

"I'm not sure. If I could see your face. Have we ever met?"

"We certainly have, Doctor. And I have observed you up close and personal, as well. You lead such a shithouse life. Work, home, work, home, books and more books. Why you do not commit suicide is beyond me. Such tedium. I believe I shall be doing you a big favor by putting you out of your misery. You should be grateful."

"Alvin?" No sooner had she asked than she remembered Alvin was much shorter. And her tormentor's physique was more athletic. She'd seen that torso before. She was sure.

"My goodness! Alvin? Now who might he be? The fucking chipmunk?"

"I'm dead tired."

"You really should have considered the consequences before you spread your legs for him."

"For who?" She couldn't help laughing. Or trying to. She hadn't had sex in months and now she was being tortured for having had it.

"What do you find so amusing? Idiot!"

"I hate to disillusion you, my friend. But I haven't been laid in ages."

"Liar!" he shouted.

"Though I wish I had."

"And Carl?" That was the giveaway.

"Peter?"

"Oh. Your memory is coming back."

He removed the mask. Simone never would have suspected him. She'd thought he was a fun guy. From what she had read, he possessed a mordant wit and detested violence of any kind. And from what Carl had said, Peter was a bosom friend, someone Carl could count on.

"Peter, I only helped Carl to understand what happened to Lara. I never had sex with him and I never crossed your path on purpose."

"You must think I am a cognitively disabled person. All those hours locked away with him here and there. Always needing to 'discuss' a dead and buried case! I've seen those romantic dinners, the swing house, that night in his apartment. Are you telling me you two were playing video games?"

"We were working."

"You have changed your profession now? Dead donkey-dick-sucking whores actually work?"

"I swear it's the truth."

"You can swear 'til pigs recite the goddamn Gettysburg Address. But now you are mine!"

"Why does Carl matter so much to you?" She had to get him talking in order to find the key to persuading him to let her go. He was a psychopath. There were ways to influence a psychopath. Suddenly she felt she had the energy to try to control the situation. Survival was the name of that energy.

"*I ask the questions here!* Why does Carl matter so much to *you*?"

"He's a client, like any other."

"He is not just anyone. Carl is everything!"

"To you? To me, he's just a client. I want to help him. That's all. He's that important to you, Peter?"

"Yeeeessss. I fell in love with him the first time I saw him. But there was always someone who got in my way. The first was my shithead sister, who introduced us."

"You were jealous of your sister?"

"I absolutely hated the guts of that little sweetie-pie, deadheaded dildo! But one cannot kill family. At least, not while Mother is alive."

"Corleone? Corleone? You sounded exactly like him." She remembered Carl had told her Peter was hooked on the *Godfather* Trilogy.

"Yes. My hero!" His voice turned childlike and he looked proud of himself.

"I really like those films too. Especially the first one." She was managing to make contact with him.

"Then that raunchy retard Lara came along."

"But you were Lara's friend."

"Lara was family too. Long before Carl. And Lara was me and I was Lara. So I forgave her. Because every time she was with him, I was too. Understand? But she was not supposed to remain with him. I thought he would quickly drop her. She was deranged."

"Yes. I do see what you mean. You would like to have been Lara?"

"I *was* Lara."

Now was the moment to be careful. He was starting to fantasize about being another person.

"Do you see my ring?" He held out his hand and showed her the diamond ring. It looked similar to the description of the one Mark planned to give Lara in Carl's text.

"When she died, it was the only thing of hers I could have. Before they buried her, I slipped it off her finger. Isn't it beautiful? Whenever I wear it I feel powerful. She enters me and we are one. And we love Carl. He is ours!"

"Did you kill Lara?"

"Not me! Carl killed Lara! She was crazy! But I killed her mother. That bitch would never die and I knew her death would fuck up Lara. I had to do it because Carl was getting in deep with her and soon he would not need me."

"How did you kill her?"

"She was in the hospital, alone. I went to visit her. With a gun. I made her write a love letter to her children. Three assholes she had raised. I turned off her oxygen. After she suffocated, I turned it on again. We were avenged."

"Who?"

"Lara and me."

What madness! He wanted to be Lara. He wanted to destroy Lara. Complete insanity! Years dealing with the human mind and she had never been face-to-face with anyone so disturbed.

"But I truly wanted to get Lara away from Carl. They were not allowing me to participate, to be with them."

"Do you love Carl?"

"Carl is everything to me!"

"Peter, you have to tell him that. You have to tell him how you feel. That you love him!"

"But he cannot understand that this body here is the wrong body. That I am a woman inside a man. He is unable to forsake his prejudice and look inside me. To find Lara."

"I'm going to help you. We'll be able—"

"We shall not be able to do anything, you slutty scumbag! You are simply attempting to deceive me with your shrinky sweet talk. Come here!"

He dragged Simone by the arms to the middle of the room, where the cage had been. He unhooked the chain from the cage and hooked it to her handcuffs. He went to a control panel, pushed a button and up she went with a jerk until she dangled in the air. She shrieked.

Her wrists had snapped. He then lowered her and left her. Naked. Bound. On her knees. For the first time, she began to cry. And crying turned into deep sobs. She sobbed and sobbed in utter despair. She saw no way out. He was totally twisted, removed from reality. It was impossible to maintain contact with the flicker of lucidness within him. He was going to kill her.

She finally got hold of herself despite her extreme suffering. Her only chance to survive was to overcome it. She was aware she had briefly succeeded in getting through to him. Maybe she could do it again and persuade him to let her go. How much more could she take?

He left her alone for hours, without food or clothes or water, but in peace. Suddenly, he appeared again. Her heart raced, fueled by fear-induced adrenalin. He unhooked the chain, grabbed her by the hair, dragged her away, picked her up, sat her in the chair, removed her handcuffs and tied her arms and legs to the chair with leather straps. She felt almost dead. She couldn't tell where the pain was the worst. Her entire body ached.

"I wish to converse, Doctor."

"I'm too weak."

"Want an apple? Did you know that an apple a day keeps the physician away?"

And how many would it take to keep him away? she wondered. "I do, Peter. But I won't be able to eat it unless you untie my wrists. Please."

He did so and handed her the apple. The simple act of holding it caused excruciating pain. She nevertheless ate ravenously.

"Want another?"

"Yes."

He gave her another and waited patiently for her to finish. She had never imagined an apple could be so delicious. She ate slowly because she hadn´t the strength to do otherwise. And because she wanted to gain time. What was coming next? She was in no hurry to find out.

"Ready to chat, Doctor?"

"About what, Peter? Could I have some water?"

He went over to a sink and returned with a glass.

"Thank you, Peter!"

"My name is Lara!"

"Of course, Lara. What is it you want of me?"

"Tell me everything. How many times you fucked Carl and where."

"Never. We never did anything like that! I'm ethical. I would never do that with a client."

He'd arrived in the room with a watering can. He picked up the can, grabbed her by the hair, yanked her head back and began pouring water into her mouth. She was sure she was going to drown then and there. Then he stopped and waited for her coughing to subside.

"Don't lie to me!"

"No, Lara. I'm not lying to you. Carl has always been yours. The whole time. He came to me only because of the pain he felt when you went away. He would have gone mad if he couldn't understand what had happened. I just helped him. That's all."

"He loves me?"

"More than he loves himself." She thought she'd calmed him down a bit by joining him in his fantasy.

"Then why can't he see that I'm right here?" He pointed to his body.

"It takes time for some people to get used to new forms and shapes. I think Carl is very traditional."

"I do too. But I hope someday he will look at me and see me here."

"You have to tell him. I know this seems like a psychiatrist's baloney but you must be sincere with him. His prejudice isn't allowing him to see you, Lara. But he doesn't know you're there either." She pointed at his chest.

"What if I tell him and he rejects me? If he does not believe me? Mother did not believe…"

"What didn't your mother believe?"

"That the babysitter forced me to do disgusting things."

"What things?"

"She made me suck her rotten, smelly cunt every day when Mother was traveling."

"Your mother didn't believe you?"

"No. She did not believe me. And the babysitter would not stop. Every day. Every day I had to suck and suck. I would even vomit. But she kept forcing me."

He sat down on the floor with his legs drawn up and began to cry like a baby. Simone felt true sorrow for the child he once was.

"And your sister?"

"She was far away at boarding school. I could not speak to her. I had to endure that for a year before they sent me to the boarding school to learn how to stop telling lies. But I went happily because I would be far away from that woman."

"I believe you, Peter." She was certain he now was Peter.

"You believe me?"

"Yes, I believe you. Is that why you hate women? Is that why you started to kill women?"

"Yes. But I wanted to kill her."

"The babysitter?"

"Yes. I hated her so much! One day I went to Disney World and she was in line with a child my age. I killed her. She was going to do evil things to little Peter again."

"How old were you when it all started to happen?"

"Five."

"Peter, let me help you. I can take care of you. You'll get well."

"You are a liar! All women are liars! She told me I would learn to like what she was forcing me to do. But I hated it more and more."

He sobbed and sobbed in anguish, covering his head with his hands. Then he got up and left. She heard the door being locked. He'd probably kill her when he came back.

In her mind, Simone reviewed her life. From her childhood to the present. She went over her relationship with Edward. Whenever she was in need he was there. He was her guardian angel. Her friend. Her adviser. Oh. If she only had time she'd give him a chance to see where they could go together. She'd do it right now. But it was no longer possible. He was surely the best person she'd ever known in her whole life. She wouldn't be able to tell him that. She was as good as dead.

She remembered her pregnancy. Unwanted, at first. But it brought her Tamara, a beautiful baby girl who gave new meaning to her life. She remembered Tamara as a little girl with golden curls and angelic blue eyes, always playing with dolls.

Simone was feverish. Delirium and lucidity came and went. She didn't know how much time had passed. She'd lost all track of it. She just felt the pain and the cold and no longer the hunger. She had a vague notion that natural light came and went. Perhaps a day or two had come and gone. She didn't know. She didn't care. She just wanted the pain to stop. He'd been gone for a long while.

Suddenly the door opened and she tried to prepare herself to die. The high fever had brought on intense hallucinations.

"Simmie, my love. What have they done to you?"

She thought she had died. She heard Edward's voice and felt something warm on her body. Someone untied her hands and feet and placed her on a table. He was going to stretch her again.

"I'm dead. I can´t stand it anymore. Kill me, please. Quickly."

"No, my love. It´s me, Edward. You'll get better. Everything will be all right. I promise. No one will ever hurt you again. I promise. I'll always protect you."

It really was Edward's voice. He was holding her hand. She opened her eyes a little and saw policemen searching the room. She was carried away. She was exhausted and closed her eyes. She woke up in a hospital. Edward sat next to her asleep in a chair.

Chapter Thirty

Present Day – Simone

"Ed?"

He leaped out of his chair and went over to her.

"Simone, how are you feeling?"

"Like I've been through a meat grinder. Everything hurts! What happened? Why am I in a hospital?"

"Pneumonia, two cracked ribs, broken wrists, dehydration, burns. That's all."

"Have I been here very long? I don't remember…"

"Three days. They've kept you sedated… You're still on powerful analgesics."

"What happened? How did I end up here?"

"Rest, Simmie. You're safe now. We'll talk later."

She went back to sleep. She dreamed that a man wearing a gas mask was chasing her. She awoke screaming with her daughter, Tammy, at her side.

"Mom! It's okay! You're safe! I'm here." Tamara hugged Simone and started to cry. "I thought I was going to lose you!"

"Tammy, why aren't you in Paris? What are you doing here?"

"Don't you remember what happened, Mom?"

"Unfortunately, yes. But you should be in Paris. There's a maniac loose, killing women, and I don't want you here. Or have they caught him?"

"No. He's still out there. But nobody's going to hurt you."

"How did you get here?"

"When you disappeared, Uncle Ed went nuts. He went absolutely berserk. He made the FBI guys work overtime to enhance a video to try to see a taxi's license plate number. They finally did and it was from a little town outside New York."

"It was?"

"It was. The taxi belonged to a man from India. They took a whole day to find him and they thought he had you. But he'd only rented it to some 'nice guy', he said, because he needed the money to pay for his taxi license. He told them the guy had fantasies about making love in a taxi or being a taxi driver. He'd show up once in a while and rent it for a few days.

He'd pay big money for it. The man never suspected there was anything wrong."

"Did he know who he was?"

"No. That was the worst part. He just said the guy was white and dressed well and was obviously loaded and always paid in cash. Not much to go on, right? Uncle Ed tried to beat the crap out of him!"

"Out of who?"

"The taxi driver. The cops had to tear Uncle Ed off him! After that, Uncle Ed sent me a ticket and told me to come home."

A nurse came in and set a tray beside the bed. "Good morning, Dr. Bennet. Would you like some soup? You can eat normally now."

"Good morning, nurse. Are you saying I couldn't feed myself?"

"No. We were feeding you intravenously. The doctors preferred to keep you sedated because of your pain. Are you feeling better?"

"I still hurt all over. But I'm sure the analgesics are keeping it from being much worse."

"You can receive visitors now if you wish, Doctor. There's a man named Carl waiting to see you. He says he's your client. The police are questioning him as we speak. Do you know him?"

"Carl is welcome."

"I'll ask them to let him come in. But eat first."

Tamara helped Simone with the soup, which she got down with difficulty. Then a smiling Carl walked in.

"What are you doing here, Carl?"

"You're famous. I want your autograph. Bad joke, Simone. Forgive me."

"No. It's okay. This is my daughter, Tammy. Tammy, this is Carl, a business associate."

They shook hands and then Tammy went out for a cup of coffee.

"So you know what happened, Carl?"

"Yes. I followed part of it in person and part on TV. Your boyfriend went ballistic when you disappeared."

"My boyfriend?"

"Dr. Edward. He was moving mountains to find you. I've heard he even broke the taxi driver's nose.

"But how did they find me?"

"It was in all the papers. They said you were missing, showed your picture, a picture of the taxi and its license plate number. An anonymous call led the cops to you. They still don't know who rented the apartment where you were. Whoever did, provided a false identity. Apparently, it was where the maniac tortured all the women he killed. He'd soundproofed the rooms. A goddamn twenty-first century dungeon! He left the taxi there and someone saw it. Nobody saw the killer, unfortunately."

"It was Peter, Carl." Simone was surprised. She thought they'd already known that.

"Peter? My friend Peter? What does he have to do with all this?"

"Peter snatched me! And tortured me! He killed Lara's mother to make her freak out. It was him the whole time!"

"Impossible, Simone. Peter's in China. And besides, he's one of the best guys I've ever known!"

"No, he's not. It's him. I'm absolutely sure. And he's in love with you!"

"He's my friend, for Christ's sake! Almost a brother! Why would he do that? Telling me this is like taking a part of my life away, Simone. No. I don't believe it!"

"It's true. He told me. He said he killed a woman at Disney World. A woman who'd been his babysitter. She'd sexually abused him when he was a child. You have to believe me! I thought by now everybody knew the truth. At times, he was out of it and thought he was Lara. He said he loved you and wanted you. At times, he was Peter again. Look, I wasn't in the best of shape. But I can tell you for certain it was Peter!" Simone was highly agitated now.

"Relax, Simone. Take it easy. I'm going to tell the police." Carl appeared devastated by the news, his face a mask of misery and shock.

FBI agents came to talk to Simone and she described in detail what she'd suffered at Peter's hands. An arrest warrant for him was issued that same day. Investigations showed that Peter had fled to China as soon as the media carried the initial reports of Simone's rescue. He hadn't returned. They'd learned that the taxi in question had often been parked at a bus station, where passengers arrived from the city where Simone lived. Security cameras showed victims getting into the taxi. The driver always wore dark glasses and a cap. But it wasn't hard to discern Peter's features. That explained the common thread that the victims were always traveling. But it would be impossible to wrap up the case without apprehending Peter and getting a sperm sample from him to compare with the ones found on the dead women.

The disappearance of a woman in Florida was confirmed to have happened at the time Peter, Lara and Carl had all gone to Disney World together. She wasn't Peter's babysitter but after seeing photos of her, Peter's sister said she bore a strong resemblance to the lady who had abused Peter when he was a child. The woman in Florida had been in the company of her four-year-old son and was considered a missing person. The authorities were now looking for locations where her body might have been left, as Peter had said nothing about it to Simone. It wasn't possible to determine whether Peter had actually been responsible for the death of Lara's mother. Too much time had elapsed for a second autopsy to conclude whether the cause of death was oxygen deprivation.

Simone remained in the hospital for another day. Edward spent every night of her stay at her side and left early each morning. On the day of her release, Edward was waiting to take her home. She hugged him tight and thanked him for everything he had done. She had no doubt that only his prompt and energetic efforts had saved her life. That was Edward. He would always be there to rescue her.

"How you feeling, lady?" Edward asked as he caressed her hair.

"The truth? Lost. Hurting all over. Trying to put the pieces of my body and soul back together. I still don't understand. That is, I understand. But…"

"Want to go home, Simmie?"

"Yes, Ed. Finally. It won't be easy to get past those days in hell. But I think every shrink should have an internship there," she said playfully.

"I'll pass!"

"I don't blame you. And I don't know how I didn't go irretrievably stark raving mad."

"I don't either, Simmie. But every human being has a greater or lesser will to survive. Your will is tougher than tungsten steel. Let's talk. I think you should resume your weekly sessions with your psychiatrist. It will help."

"Maybe. But afterward."

"After what? You have plans?"

"Yes."

"What are they?"

"I want to take Tammy back to Paris. She has to finish her program there. Besides, that lunatic is still on the loose. I don't know if he'll come back. I'm going to move her to a different apartment. Just to be on the safe side. Then I'll take a year's sabbatical. I'm going to travel. After that, I'll see. I've lived a millennium in the past year. I need to assemble my mental and emotional jigsaw puzzle. Nothing will ever be the same, Ed. Nada!"

"And your patients?"

"Those who are willing, I can treat online. I'll lose some, of course."

"True. I'll stay here and hold down the fort. For when you return."

"I know. That's the only thing I'm certain of—our business will have a competent manager while I'm gone."

Edward held out his hand and Simone melted into his arms. That was home, a wonderful place to be. But she couldn't stay there just then. Too much had changed in her life and she needed to heal first. Afterward, with her head on straight, she'd decide about the future. Perhaps Ed was the future. She felt if he were with her, she'd be home. She was just sorry she'd taken so long to see that. But now wasn't the time. Who knew when it would be?

The End

About the Author

A. Gavazzoni is the Brazilian author of the newly released novel *Behind The Door*, a sensual romance now available through Amazon.com. She is a lawyer by day and former professor of law; she writes (novels and legal books), but she is also a voracious reader and a writer by night and currently has a law book about international contracts published in Brazil.

She speaks four languages: English, French, Portuguese, and Spanish. She also studies

Chinese and hopes someday she will master it (but it's been a challenge!). Her favorite countries, no surprise, are Italy, France, and the USA. When she is not practicing law, she enjoys many interests and is a very active person. She loves to dance (Tango) and workout. She also enjoys travelling, loves good wine, and has been studying astrology for fifteen years. She paints and loves to cook.

She has two poodles — Juno and Charlotte — and loves all animals. She is an aunt to four nieces who enjoy painting and cooking alongside their aunt. She lives in Brazil and has just finished writing Lara's Journal, the sequel to Behind the Door. She invites readers to visit **her website** for updates on upcoming books and events, and join her on her blog, where she loves to interact with readers and other authors. Readers can also follow her on Twitter @a_gavazzoni.

REVIEWER NEED! Did you know reviews are very important to authors? If enjoy this book please post an **honest** review of *Behind the Door* on Amazon. Thank you very much.

HIDDEN MOTIVES BOOK #2
Lara's Journal
Hidden Motives Series, Book Two

Sneak Peek:

Prologue

The nightclub was dark, a few red lights barely illuminating the smoky, crowded dance floor. Music blared from the sound system, loud and shrill. People bounced wildly, unconcerned with keeping rhythm to the frenzied rhythm, only there to have fun.

At 3:00 a.m., there were very few sober people. She should be one of them, but not today; today she was enjoying life.

Life was unpredictable, she thought. Why not live intensely?

She was not really drunk. She'd had a few drinks—maybe five or six glasses of white wine. Or more...? In any event, she'd drunk enough to relax and loosen up a little, but not so much that she slurred her speech or saw doubles.

A very interesting-looking man sat at a corner table, and he'd been staring at her for at least the last five minutes. Although she couldn't see his features well in the dimly lit club, she knew he definitely had dark-brown hair. He seemed young—much younger than she was—but so what? She wondered what color eyes he had, and decided, if given the opportunity, she'd find out.

He raised his glass in a silent toast, and she smiled back. Deciding to accept his obvious invitation, she nodded, and he was by her side in an instant, bringing two champagne glasses with him.

"Hello," he said. "Would you like to dance?"

"*Hello,*" she answered, accepting the glass he offered her.

They didn't talk; the music was too loud for conversation. Instead, she stepped close to him and wrapped her arms around his neck, still holding her glass. They started to move slowly, following the music, trying to balance their drinks. He put his free hand on her waist, moving sensuously, then slid his hand up to caress her back.

She smiled as one phrase echoed in her mind. *Life is short, too short.*

He took her glass from her hand, put his and hers on a nearby table, took her to a corner, supported her against the wall and lifted her arms. Holding them high, he leaned into her, effectively imprisoning her. Oh, she could easily break free if she wanted to, but at the moment, she wouldn't want to be anywhere else.

He lowered his head and captured her lips with his. His kiss was hot, hard and aggressive and demanded an equal response. His tongue dipped inside her mouth, and he kissed her as if he wanted to dredge her soul. His mouth tasted of champagne. Too much time had passed since she'd last received such passionate kisses.

He ran his hands over her body, trying to feel her through her dress. For a moment, she thought to stop him—someone might see them—but then she figured what the hell? Who cared what people thought? No one there knew her, and there were several other couples doing the same thing in other shadowy areas of the club.

She kissed him back, her arms still draped around his neck, her body burning at his touch, her blood warming as her heart beat fast. He put his hand inside her dress and touched her breast, and a shiver traveled through her.

He might be younger than she was, but he certainly was not inexperienced. While kissing and nibbling his way down her neck, he pulled down one of her dress straps to expose a breast. Maybe in another time or place, she would have been ashamed, but not now. She felt only pleasure at being touched, at being alive.

He started to suckle her nipples, and she grew immediately wet. She closed her eyes to focus on his touch, a spinning sensation in her head brought on by her lust and the alcohol. She was moaning but nobody could hear, the music drowning out the sound.

"Come with me," he said.

At least that's what she thought he said because he took her hand and led her to the men's bathroom.

There were a few guys hanging around the entrance and just inside, but nobody seemed to mind her presence. Her new friend took her into the largest of the five stalls—the one equipped for handicapped entrance—and closed the door. A sink and a toilet were lined up against one wall.

He lifted her dress, set her on the marble sink, and started to caress her again, sliding his hands up her legs. She whimpered and clutched at his shoulders.

Desperate to get her hands on his body, she opened the first few buttons of his shirt. She ran her palms over his smooth, warm chest then scraped his pecs with her nails. Her new lover moaned approvingly. She wiggled her ass on the countertop, signaling her desire for him to touch her, take her.

He grinned before dipping his head to bite at her neck. He rained small kisses all the way down to her shoulder as he pulled aside her panties and put a finger inside her. Excited, wet, and ready for him, she moaned. He worked her for a while, moving his finger in and out, then he gathered the moisture from her pussy and rhythmically swirled it around her clit.

Breathing hard, she opened his zipper, took out his cock, and caressed its length, first with her nails and then with her fingertips.

"*Loca,*" he said, his dick hard, moisture leaking from the tip.

"Fuck me," she commanded.

He reached into his pocket and withdrew a condom. After ripping open the little packet, he tossed aside the wrapper and sheathed his hard dick.

She spread her legs wide, and he stepped between them. He entered her in one long, smooth glide, and she gasped, digging her nails into his shoulders as her orgasm shattered through her.

Holy shit, holy shit, holy shit. She'd never come so easily or so quickly.

She wrapped her legs around his waist to allow him to go deeper inside her, and they started to move. He thrust into her brutally, his face a mask of desperate concentration as he sought his own release.

His charcoal-black eyes were wide open, and he held her gaze, one hand between them, massaging her clit, the other hand clamped on her waist in a bruising grip.

"Yes!" he whispered harshly, slamming into her.

They came together, him releasing a strangled cry and her biting her bottom lip to keep from shouting. Afterward, they stood there in silence, breathing heavily, the smell of sex permeating the air.

She glanced away. A moment ago, they'd been as close as two people could get, but now she felt uncomfortable...exposed. She uncrossed her legs, releasing him, and fixed her clothes while he got rid of the condom. He helped her to stand up.

She wanted to disappear as quickly as possible.

He asked her something but thanks to the noise she only understood the last word. Something about a "telephone"—had he asked for her number?

She refused him with a quick shake of her head, opened the door, and beat a hasty retreat. Without looking back, she lost herself on the dance floor.

Chapter One

Simone – Present Day

Simone sped down the dark hall. Behind her, the masked man drew closer.

Any minute now he'd reach her; she could practically feel his heavy breath on her nape. A staircase appeared before her, and she raced down, jumping the steps two at a time. At the bottom, she came to a closed red iron door. She grabbed the handle, turned and yanked, but the damn thing was locked.

Simone turned, leaning back against the door, breathing heavily and straining to listen for the man's footsteps in the darkness.

Heart racing, she searched her mind for a way out but came up blank. Above her, heavy footfalls sounded at the top of the steps. Simone opened her mouth to scream but found she had no voice.

Simone flew to a sitting position, eyes wide open, a sweat-soaked sheet wrapped around her waist.

"For chrissake," she said, pressing a shaking hand to her chest. "That damn nightmare is going to give me a damn heart attack."

A month had passed since Peter Hay had kidnapped and tortured her, and she'd dreamed of the insane serial killer nearly every night since.

"How much longer will he haunt my dreams?" she said. Although her partner—a psychiatrist who used to assist the police by putting together criminal profiles—had rescued her, and her physical injuries had long since healed, her emotional wounds still remained. The nightmares had started just before she'd left the hospital.

She looked around. What had she heard that had caused her to wake up? On the bedside table, her cellphone vibrated, signaling a call. Simone sighed and leaned over, reaching for the phone. The backlit display showed Edward's name and number.

Why would her partner be calling her this early? She would need to call him back later. Right now, she had to go to the bathroom.

She went into the white marble and glass bathroom, took care of business, then got her Pill case from her cosmetic purse. She popped out one of the little yellow tablets, popped it into her mouth, and swallowed it down with a glass of water from the sink.

After grabbing a towel from the shelf, she opened the shower door, regulated the water temperature, and climbed in beneath the spray to take a good, long, warm shower and allow the water to erase all memory of the nightmare.

By the time she stepped out of the shower, she was feeling much better. However, a quick glance in the mirror revealed dark circles under her eyes, proof her nightmares were taking a toll on her physically.

She applied some light makeup then returned to her bedroom, where she dug out a pair of shorts and a t-shirt from her suitcase and got dressed. Only then did she feel well enough and awake enough to return Edward's call.

"Hello, Ed," she greeted him when he answered. "I'm sorry I missed your call. I was in the shower. How are you?"

"Well…to be honest, I'm worried about you. Your daughter told me you left Paris and were headed back to the US, but that was a week ago, and I hadn't heard from you, so…"

"Don't worry, my friend, I'm okay… I'm in Miami Beach. How could I be better?" Simone laughed.

"Miami? How come?"

"Do you remember that friend of ours from college—Arami?"

"Sure, I do. She was a Brazilian nut if I recall correctly…"

"She's still nuts, but she's from Paraguay, not Brazil. We ran into each other in France, and she invited me to come with her to Miami, and I couldn't say no."

Simone was at a point in her life where she didn't want to deny herself a little bit of adventure, and she'd accepted an invitation from Arami to come stay for a while. Simone was suffering from post-traumatic stress syndrome, but as a psychiatrist, she thought she could work her way through it…could at least handle her emotions.

"Just like that? You go from Paris to Miami…? That's so not you! Where are you staying? Just in case… The police are still investigating your case, and they may need to talk to you again."

"You're upset, Ed. Just give me a chance to get my head together a little bit. I'll be back soon; I promise."

"Okay, but I want you to be honest with me. How do you really feel…?"

"From a layman's point of view, I'd say I'm getting better, but I'm still a little bit messed up. I can't sleep well if I don't take the pills. I have nightmares, but I feel safe here. From a medical doctor's point of view, I need to stop the pills…"

"Treat yourself like a human being, not as a doctor. You need the drugs right now. Take them until you feel ready to stop...and, Simmie...I miss you."

"Miss you, too."

She did miss Edward, her dear friend, her best friend and partner, but his declaration of love — delivered just before she'd been kidnapped — had changed things between them. She didn't know what to do or how to deal with his feelings for her. She couldn't imagine her life without Edward, but she couldn't imagine a life with him as her lover...at least not now.

Simone had never been the emotional kind of woman; she always had a hard time dealing with feelings like love and passion, but she really understood friendship, and Edward's friendship was very important to her. She couldn't loose that, but at the same time, she couldn't even consider anything like a love affair at the moment. She needed to focus on getting well.

They finished the call, and Simone realized her head was killing her — too much alcohol last night — and then she remembered where'd she'd gone and what she'd done. She and Arami had visited a Latin nightclub, and Simone had drunk a lot...and yes...for the first time in her life, she had sex with a stranger. She preferred to forget that part but knew she couldn't. Still, she didn't feel guilty...

Arami was one of those girls from high-class South American society. She belonged to a rich family. Before her father had been murdered, he'd been a general for the dictatorship. Arami had gone to the US to study and had decided to stay. She was a plastic surgeon, a really good one, and she could speak English with almost no accent. Although her voice had an underlying unique quality, she didn't sound like a foreigner.

Simone and Arami had run into each other by chance in a café in Paris. Simone had taken her daughter Tamara to finish an interchange program, and Arami was participating in a Plastic Surgery Congress. They had started chatting over their coffee, and the friendship they'd formed in college came back as if they had only just seen each other the day before. Crazy, considering they hadn't talked since graduation. They had exchanged cards every Christmas and on each other's birthdays, but only that. Some friendships were like that, thought Simone; they would last forever even if you didn't see each other or talk all the time.

When Simone told Arami all about the serial killer, she'd invited Simone to stay in Arami's Miami apartment for a while, and Simone had decided to accept. Although spontaneity typically wasn't part of Simone's psyche, things were so confusing, she had decided to live life without analyzing every move and every act, and she was having a nice time with her old friend; Arami was an easy-going person, and she always seemed to be happy.

Arami's apartment was on Collins Avenue in Miami Beach. The oceanfront property was an example of what good money could buy. Big, luxurious, well decorated, and modern, the suite of rooms had glass walls everywhere that allowed one to see the ocean in all its splendor.

Arami refused to allow Simone to go to a hotel, explaining that Latin American hospitality would never allow a friend to stay in a cold hotel. "You can stay as long as you like," Arami had added. "Forever, if it suits you."

Of course, Simone wouldn't impose for much longer. She was actually thinking about leaving the following week. Not only did she not want to wear out her welcome, she also missed her house and her methodic life.

Someone knocked on her bedroom door, and when Simone opened it, Arami came in like a hurricane, crazy as ever, talking fast, and gesturing with her hands.

Arami was a short, pretty brunette, full-figured and curvy, and she had beautiful, dark eyes that tilted up a bit at the corners, typical features of her countrymen. She really didn't fit the joke that used to go around college—the one about God saying a woman couldn't be a doctor and be pretty—because Arami had both brains and sex appeal.

"Let's go, let's go, girl." She moved her hands like a fan. "We have a lunch date today! Did you sleep well? What a party last night, huh?"

She kissed and hugged Simone enthusiastically.

Before Simone could answer either question, Arami went on.

"What a fantastic night we had! Never saw you drunk before, but I guess people change. That's nice!"

Did she see me with him? Simone wondered. While she'd been dancing alone, Arami had been in the corner, kissing some hot guy she'd picked up at the nightclub. Had she still been occupied when Simone had found her own Latin lover? She sure hoped so, and she wasn't about to say anything unless Arami indicated she'd noticed Simone disappear into the bathroom.

"Where are we going?" Simone asked. "My head is killing me…"

"To my uncle's house in Key Biscayne. They are vacationing here, but you can't go wearing those shorts — nice legs, by the way — but my auntie is going to kill you!"

"Who is this uncle of yours?"

"Cezar Benites. He is a retired general." She made a smart salute. "He is a dinosaur from the time of the Paraguayan dictatorship…old school…my father's youngest brother…you will see…"

"Really? Is he one of those tough, bossy men? I don't know if I can deal with someone like that right now. I've been feeling a little…fragile lately."

"Oh, he is bossy but tough? With you? Are you kidding me? He'll act like a prince, and you'll have him drooling down your neck before you finish saying hello. Don't worry; he is very polite, but he is also a womanizer. Don't wear anything low cut, or he'll dive in…and then my auntie will poison your food." Arami's musical laughter filled the air.

* * * * *

An armored car sat waiting for them out front. Arami explained those were the general's security rules. He was always afraid of being murdered. The driver was also a private security guard.

"Is he really in danger?"

"I really don't know; I believe as a politician in Paraguay, he could be a target...as was my father...but in Paraguay, not here... I'm certain he is a little bit paranoid since my father was killed."

Arami's father had participated in the liberation of Paraguay. He had helped another general, Oviedo, to depose the dictator. Oviedo died in an accident, and her father had decided to run for the presidency after that, but before the elections he was killed in an ambush, and nobody had ever found out who had murdered him. Arami's uncle took his place, but he had lost the election.

They went to Key Biscayne, arriving at a property surrounded by high walls and a tall, iron gate. The sign on the gate read *Paraíso*— Paradise—and "No Trespassing. Private Property".

The gate was opened for them, and Simone had the impression she was entering another country. They drove down a paved road lined with square, sculpted bushes. Beyond the bushes grew palm trees and a very lush green garden filled with colorful flowers—a real paradise. At the end of the drive, they came to a Spanish-style mansion. White with brown balconies, it was huge and beautiful.

Two armed guards stood at the front door. As their car came to a stop, Simone and Arami climbed out. The front door to the house opened, and they entered into a gigantic foyer surrounded by arches. A natural garden stood in the middle of the room. They walked across the golden-brown ceramic tiles and through an archway, whereupon they exited into the pool area. Several women sat on deck chairs, drinks in hand, while two little girls played near another armed security guard. As Simone watched, he arranged his rifle on his shoulder and took one of the girls by her hands and spun her around. The children giggled, obviously having a blast.

I've fallen into a Gabriel Garcia Marque's novel. The Nobel Prize-winning novel, *One Hundred Years of Solitude*, was remarkably similar, she thought. *What kind of trauma will those young girls experience when they grow up, as a result of all this?* Simone's psychiatrist's brain asked. But then she pushed the thought aside. *Not my problem! I have my hands plenty full with my issues and those of my patients.*

The sound of dogs barking echoed in the distance, a parrot sat on top of a huge iron cage, singing a Latin song, and the smell of a barbecue filled the air, but Simone didn't see a grill anywhere.

When she and Arami approached the women, all eyes turned toward them, especially toward Simone. She silently thanked Arami for advising her to choose a more conservative dress, because all the women seemed to be taking her measure, eyeing her from head to toe.

"Good morning, girls." Arami greeted everybody and waved.

"*Buenos dias*, Arami," the women all said at the same time, speaking in singsong voices.

They all looked the same to Simone—dark hair, dark skin, all of them wearing similar, multicolored, expensive-looking dresses.

Where were the men? Simone wondered, feeling as if she'd stepped into a kind of girls' club.

"English, people, we have a guest here, and she doesn't speak Spanish." Arami pointed to Simone. "By the way, this is Doctor Simone Bennet."

A very classy, elegant lady, sporting a short, chic haircut, approached them. Her dress looked as if it was made of pure yellow silk, and she wore a beautiful pearl necklace. And she either had one of the best suntans Simone had ever seen, or she was naturally bronze, like Arami was. The woman kissed Arami and Simone on their cheeks.

"Nice to meet you, Doctor Bennet. I'm Magda, Arami's auntie. She told me she was bringing you for lunch. Welcome to our humble home."

She pointed to the house, no hint of sarcasm in her manner or tone, but Simone figured she had to be joking. Humble...? Hardly!

"Nice to meet you, madam. Please call me Simone."

"And you, young lady, call me auntie."

Impossible, Simone thought, but didn't say a word.

"Auntie" Magda took Simone by the arm and introduced her to everybody else, one by one. So many names and family positions...Simone would never remember them all. She compared them in her mind to the parade of names inside Gabriel Garcia Marques's novel. The more time Simone spent with these people, the more she felt she as if she'd stepped into the pages of the novel.

All the women spoke very good English, some with an accent, some without, but all of them perfectly understandable. After thirty minutes or so of pleasant conversation, a young boy came and said something in Spanish to Magda, and their hostess got to her feet.

"C'mon, ladies, the men wait for us with a nice *asado*."

Simone looked to Arami, eyebrow raised.

"Barbecue," Arami translated in a whisper.

The followed a crushed-shell pathway around to the other side of another large building, which appeared to be some kind of gymnasium — where they found the men. Ten or more men stood or sat near an enormous brick barbecue grill that contained what seemed to be a ton of meat.

Arami kissed the oldest man there. He was very short, no more than five feet tall. She then introduced him to Simone.

"Uncle, this is Simone Bennet, the American doctor I told you about. Simone, meet my uncle, General Cesar Benitez."

"Doctor Simone." He grabbed Simone's hands and kissed them. "A pleasure to have an authority on the human mind in my home, especially when she is also a beautiful woman."

"A pleasure to meet you, General. You have a lovely house, and I would like to thank you for inviting me."

"No, on the contrary, the pleasure is all mine. Anything you need, you just ask."

He gave her a look that a wolf might give to a sheep...*a very hungry wolf,* Simone reflected.

"I would like to have a professional meeting with you next week, Doctor," the general said.

"Uncle, Simone is vacationing here..."

"It won't take long, Arami." He touched his niece's arm in a way that very clearly said "stay out of this" then turned back to Simone. "Once more, Doctor, welcome to my humble home."

Christ sake, what was this "humble home" shit? Simone was intrigued.

"Arami, tell me, this house must be at least four thousand square feet. Why do your aunt and uncle refer to it as their 'humble home'?" she whispered.

"It's a Paraguayan saying, no matter the size of the house. There is no irony in their choice of words, I promise you; it's just a way to tell you that you are welcome."

"My darlings, our lunch is served. Let's got to the table, please," Magda called for them to join the others.

The "table" had at least thirty place settings. Everyone began loading up their plates with an abundance of food — all kinds of meats and side dishes, most of which Simone didn't recognize. She tried a little bit of almost everything, from the meats to *Chipa Guazú* — a wonderful pie made of corn and cheese — but she didn't have the courage to try a black sausage made of pig's blood called *morcilla*. She considered herself adventurous, but that would be pushing it.

"Not going to try our *morcilla*, Doctor?" the general asked, his eyes twinkling.

"No room, I'm afraid. I'm too full from all those other delicious dishes." She mentally patted herself on the back for coming up with a graceful way to refuse.

"You should try it; it's an aphrodisiac, you know." He grinned.

Great! Simone thought. *Just what I need.* I've already had sex with a stranger in the middle of a nightclub…a morsel of the *morcilla* and I'll go to work in a brothel.

"Thanks, General, but we psychiatrists don't believe in aphrodisiac food…just aphrodisiac minds."

"So you are going to like men in Paraguay, Doctor. Latin lovers are the best"

Simone didn´t know how to answer to that remark.

Magda intervened and said something in Spanish to the general, speaking in a tone that sounded as if she was reprimanding him.

"She asked him if he's crazy or just senile, to say such things to a real doctor." Arami leaned close and whispered the translation into Simone's ear. "When they fight, they do so in Spanish, so they have more vocabulary to choose from…"

"I'm sorry, Doctor, my dear wife reminds me that it's not polite to brag about the prowess of our men in public."

"No offense taken, General. Don't worry, few thing are able to shock me."

Magda looked relieved, her shoulders relaxing.

But Simone could tell the general wasn't a bit embarrassed or regretful of his comments; rather, he was amused. *So,* Simone analyzed, *a man who likes to shock others…*

"And there he is! The latest man, ever," the general thundered from the head of the table as he pointed toward the door.

Everyone turned to look.

The newcomer wore blue jeans and a green shirt, and as he strode toward the table he took off his sunglasses and smiled. Simone gasped and grew lightheaded as she stared at the sun-tanned face of the stranger she'd had sex with the night before.

* * * * *

As the general, Magda, and the stranger began speaking to each other in Spanish, Arami translated everything for Simone.

"Father, I was taking care of business. Someone has to!"

"Today is Sunday. I've told you a thousand times…Sundays are holy days," Magda cut in.

The man approached Magda and kissed her loudly on the cheek.

"Sorry, Mamá! I promise it won't happen again."

"Sit and speak English, my son; we have a guest."

Magda pointed at Simone, who was praying—even though she was an agnostic— that the man either wouldn't recognize her or at least wouldn't reveal they already knew each other.

"Doctor Bennet," said the general, "this is my son Armando, also known as Always-late-for-lunch. Son, this is Dr. Simone Bennet; she is a friend of Arami and now a friend of ours. She is an authority on the human mind and also a published author."

My whole curriculum, thought Simone, hoping Armando wouldn't add something like, "And she's also a pervert who likes to bang strange guys in bars".

Armando looked at Simone. His eyes really were black, just as she'd thought last night, and shaped like Arami's were. He too had dark skin and black hair, but unlike his father, he was tall and very sensual looking. She remembered last night very well, and butterflies flittered in her stomach at just the sight of the guy, but what if he recognized her? She'd be totally mortified…

Tell me about bad luck and it being a small world, she thought. But maybe her luck wasn't so horrible. So far, Armando hadn't indicated he recognized her. Maybe he didn't. The club had been dark, and she'd been wearing a ton of makeup, and thanks to Arami's advice she'd also worn false eyelashes... A thousand thoughts flew through Simone's mind.

"Nice to meet you, Doctor, welcome to our home! I hope you are enjoying sampling our customary fare."

He took the empty chair near his mother — the one Simone had noticed and wondered about earlier — which had obviously been reserved for him.

Simone nodded. "Yes, thank you, everything is delicious. And you speak perfect English."

Simone had to say something, and a compliment seemed like a good way to start a conversation. She also hoped he wouldn't recognize her voice, but they hadn't exactly done a lot of talking last night, she reflected.

"He must speak your language well, Doctor; we invested a lot of money in his education, and he loves your country...he spends more time here than he should..."

The father and son rivalry sounded clear to Simone's trained ears.

"Yes, because we have businesses here, and I'm in charge of them. We have a cattle farm in Paraguay, but there's no point in farming cattle if you can't export the meat, and that's what I do in the U.S.…."

Armando sounded at ease, not a bit worried or upset about his father's comments.

Ah, Simone thought, *nothing better than being raised by a dictator.* He seemed to be a man of strong opinions. A general would raise his children with rules and discipline, two factors that, in Simone's experience, produced strong people…the only chance he was a weak or spoiled man was if his mother had protected him from that discipline…but it didn't look as if that was the case here.

"Doctor, the life of a child who was raised by a general would make a nice subject for your couch. I could be your patient. Perhaps I could use a bit of therapy. You wouldn't happen to have an opening in your schedule, would you?"

"Cousin, Simone is here on vacation, not to work. What happened to this family? Suddenly, it seems as if everybody needs the services of a shrink!" Arami said.

Simone didn't disagree. She wasn't in the mood to deal with patients. Some of her more complicated cases she still handled through Skype. The others who weren't dependent upon prescription medication, she'd given some time off. For now, she needed to focus on and take care of herself. Just the thought of working on new cases increased her stress level. Memories of what had happened to her constantly filled her head.

"I really do need to relax while I'm here, but thanks for trusting me. I promise I will think about all your requests." *Maybe in my next life,* she added mentally.

Magda seemed to realize the subject was making Simone a little uncomfortable and changed it.

"Where are you from, Doctor?" she asked.

"I was born in New Haven, Connecticut, where I still work, but now I live in Woodbridge."

"Have you ever been to Paraguay?" the general asked.

"No. I've never been to South America, unfortunately."

"You would love it there. My country and my people are very welcoming."

Simone noticed how often the general used the word "my". My son, my country, my people… The habit was typical of powerful men. On the way to lunch that afternoon, Arami had explained that the general used to command both his business and his family with an iron fist.

The conversation now took a more diplomatic rhythm, appropriate for a lunch.

Afterward, Simone asked Arami for directions to the restroom.

"There's one right inside there," Arami said, nodding toward the big building they'd passed on their way to the table.

Simone excused herself, got up from the table and walked back to the entrance of the building. To her surprise, she found she'd guessed correctly. The building contained I a complete gym, and there were two restrooms and a sauna.

She finished up in the bathroom, washed her hands in the sink, and then opened the door. She jumped back in surprise. "Oh! It's you." Her face grew hot.

Before her stood Armando. She had the distinct and immediate impression he'd planned to meet her alone—he must have followed her. She hadn't fooled him a bit—apparently, he'd recognized her from the start.

"What game are you playing here, Doctor?" he asked.

"Game?"

"You do remember me, don't you?"

"Unfortunately, yes."

He grabbed her arm. "Unfortunately? Why do you say that?"

"Because…" She paused and sighed. "For the first time in my life, I decide to cut loose and do something crazy, and what happens? The very next day, I run into the man I did something crazy with! What are the chances? Next time, I'm going to try playing the lottery."

"I looked for you. Why did you leave in such a hurry? I would like to get to know you a little better. You seemed so...carefree and inhibited. Today, you're completely different— straight-laced and formal. Who are you, really?"

"It's a long story. But I suppose the real me is closer to the person you're looking at right now. Last night...well, I've been under a lot of stress, and I'm afraid I drank a great deal of alcohol..."

Her actions of the night before were so different from how she normally behaved; she found it difficult to explain.

He released her arm. "Can we talk again?"

"I don't know...your cousin is my friend, I'm a guest in her house. At this point in my life, I don't need any more drama." She felt tired and distressed and she couldn't think about relationships right now.

"Are you married?"

"No...no it's not that."

"Then I would like to see you again."

He was definitely his father's son. Simone could hear the similarities in the commanding tone. Although phrased as a request, he was not asking her.

"Let's have dinner tomorrow," he said.

"Okay, call me at Arami's apartment. But I'm warning you; don't expect to meet the woman you were with last night. She doesn't exist!"

"Yes, she does…inside here somewhere…" He pointed at her chest.

The powerful sexual energy between them was impossible to deny. Reminding herself she was there on vacation, Simone decided to abandon reason for a while.

"Okay, let's have dinner."

"I'll pick you up at eight o'clock. Be ready. Wear a dress." He used his father's commanding tone again.

Welcome to the world of macho men, she thought.

They spent the rest of that Sunday at the general's house and returned to Arami's apartment late that evening. Thankfully, the rest of Simone's visit with Arami's family had passed without incident.

* * * * *

The following Monday morning, Simone organized Arami's office, a very modern room in the apartment but a messy one. The décor was probably quite sober under all the disorder, guessed Simone. Grey shelves lined the walls. They were full of haphazardly stacked books, old magazines, picture frames, and all kinds of souvenirs Arami must have gotten while traveling.

There was a glass desk with a modern white computer sitting on it, sharing space with thousands of envelops, pens, post-its, and a dry, half-eaten apple that looked as old as Simone was. A comfortable black office chair sat behind the desk, while two armchairs faced the front of it. Arami had told Simone she could use the space as long as she wanted to.

She spent more than an hour trying to arrange a space for herself on the table without disturbing Arami's order...or lack thereof. Simone loved organization—some might call it an obsession—and to work in an environment such as this one was a challenge to her nerves. And these days, it didn't take much to make her feel nervous.

Even while on vacation, she had reserved a portion of each day to listen to some of her patients over the internet. It was important to them to know she was available to them, but in a week she'd be back in her office in Connecticut.

Today, she had scheduled a meeting with Carl—the first time they would speak since she'd been attacked. Thanks to the work she'd done for him, her life had turned upside down. He had hired her to analyze a journal, to give him her expert opinion so he could defend a client—at least, that's what he'd told her at first—but the truth had been something altogether different, and in the end, his friend and ex-brother-in-law Peter Hay had kidnapped and tortured her.

Friday, he had contacted her, asking for an appointment. She'd felt apprehensive with his request, her heart racing at the idea of getting involved in his problems again, but she couldn't say no to him.

She consulted her clock. In addition to being organized, she was also a stickler for punctuality. Time to talk to Carl… She opened Skype on her laptop, connected to the program, and waited for him to come online. To her delight, Carl was on time.

"Good morning, Simone." He greeted her in his normal, charming way. His chestnut hair looked shorter, which made him appear younger and very handsome in his blue suit, white shirt, and blue-and-yellow tie. Despite the fact his brown eyes had gained some small wrinkles at their corners since she'd met him, he was all charm and magnetism, as always.

"Hello, Carl, how´ve you been?"

"Fine, and you? I'm still feeling guilty about everything that happened to you…"

"You know it wasn't your fault. Relax."

"You almost died…"

"But I didn´t."

She didn´t want to continue talking about it, and she certainly didn't need his pity. She had a hard enough time keeping thoughts of the kidnapping out of her head; talking about the subject was too much for her.

"Tell me what's going on with you. You told me it was urgent that you talk to me."

"Yes, sorry, I know you're on vacation, but I really couldn´t wait."

He began to talk, his words spilling out in a torrent that showed his anxiety. Normally, he was very discreet and restrained in his emotions.

"I´m not okay. I didn´t want to involve you again in the drama that has become my life, but you're the only one capable of really helping me. Selfish, I know, and I'm very sorry to do this to you."

"Don't worry about me, Carl; I'm a professional, and I'm used to dealing with other people's issues. Please, go on…tell me what´s disturbing you so much."

"Lara´s past is back to haunt me…"

Lara had been the love of Carl´s life until she had died during a sexual game they'd been playing one evening. Carl had never really fully recovered from her loss.

"What happened? Is it the usual…you missing her…or something new?"

"Sean, Lara´s brother, called me and told me he wanted to talk. During the trial, he had a few harsh words for me—called me a murderer, killer, vermin, and so on. He always blamed me, and we hadn't spoken since my acquittal. Needless to say, I was very apprehensive about any conversation we might have, but I couldn´t say no…he said it was important…"

"And how did it go?"

"Hard…first of all, he looks a lot like Lara. Same greenish eyes…it was as if she was looking at me through him, and I could barely stand to look at him. The pain was like broken glass piercing my heart… I'd never noticed the similarities between them before because he used to have a beard, but he'd shaved, and this time, it was as if someone had taken a magnifying glass and held it up in front of him. The likeness was uncanny. They even have the same long hands. If he was a girl, I would have fallen in love with him at first sight."

"You'll never forget Lara…" she told him, thinking what a pity it was that the woman would most likely haunt him forever, and a man such as him would never be available to love again. If she wasn't the professional she was, she would have fallen for him and she had to admit he disturbed her; she was not immune to him.

"You're right. How can I? She was the love of my life. I think I'm just like my father; I can love only once."

His words just confirmed her thoughts. Simone redirected the conversation.

"And after the initial shock of seeing him, were able to talk?"

"For at least two hours. It was bad, and it was good…he asked me to explain what happened. He told me he'd hated me for a long time because he was certain I had killed his sister, and not accidentally, but now he believes in my innocence."

"What made him change his mind, and what caused him to seek you out and tell you that?"

"He told me he'd always had a romantic image of his older sister as he was never informed of her situation with the senator's son and all she had been through up until only a few months before her death. He had no idea she'd led such a depraved life full of sexual encounters and other craziness. To see her lifestyle exposed in front of a jury right after losing her was too much for him. He couldn't believe what people were saying, and he thought my defense attorneys had embellished the truth to make me look better and get me off the murder charge.

"Sean and his sister Deborah decided to sell Lara´s New York apartment, and they had to go through her things before they put it on the market. They found a locked box filled with diaries. Do you remember I told you I started to write because I was inspired by her habit of always keeping a journal at hand?"

"Yes…I remember."

"They decided they needed to read them. Sean told me he thought he might find some kind of proof of my guilt in one of them, but what he discovered was something altogether different. Apparently, what was revealed about her debauched lifestyle in court was just the tip of the iceberg. She'd written about her entire life…her childhood, her life in Paris, everything…"

"Those poor people! I truly pity them! But at the same time, I´m grateful they found a way to see the truth. It wasn't healthy for them to go on hating you. The truth can be liberating, even if it hurts. Hate is a horrible feeling, worse for the hater than the one who is hated most of the time. It can eat you up inside."

"He wanted to give me access to the whole story of her life…he gave me a copy of everything. That´s why I need your help."

"Have you read it?"

"I started to, but it was too much for me to stomach. When I came to the part about what that scumbag did to her…I was so angry, plagued by homicidal thoughts; I couldn´t sleep for two entire nights… I realized I need your help, or I was going to find him and kill the piece of shit. The idea of doing so rarely leaves my mind."

"Don't you even think about doing something like that, Carl; it won't bring Lara back, and you would end your life in prison."

"I know! But you have no idea how tempted I am. I would like to hire you to help me through this, Simone. I'll understand if you say no, but I really trust you, and I need your support."

Oh, God, she thought. Could she do this all over again? To read the journals, to analyze them was not the problem; her mixed feelings for Carl were what worried her. From the first moment she'd met him she'd been attracted to him, but they weren't on the same page. He was a lost cause—she'd bet he would never love again… At least, not the kind of passionate love he had felt for Lara—but how could she deny his cry for help? Before her kidnapping, she had promised to help him, but she hadn't had the time to start the job.

"Okay, Carl, what do you suggest?"

"I would like for us to read it at the same time…kind of like a book club mixed with therapy sessions. We'll read a few chapters, and then we can discuss them. Of course, I will pay for your services as I did before, and I will respect your time. We'll work around your schedule, okay?"

"Yes, I´m going to help you. This story haunts my days, too. It will be good to know what happened to her in the beginning…why things turned out the way they did."

"When do you want to start?"

"Let´s do it this way; scan the file, if you can, and send it to me as an email attachment."

"Sure! No problem… Actually…I already did that. You can find the files in your e-mail… I don´t know how to thank you!"

So he'd counted on her help and didn't bother to deny it… *Too sure of himself,* she thought.

They talked for another half an hour, ironing out the details regarding her fee and other practical matters.

When they hung up, Simone sat back in her chair and sighed. She then opened her email box and located Carl's e-mail. Attached to it were scanned files of Lara's diaries. *Progress,* she thought. They hadn't signed a contract yet and hadn't even discussed a confidentiality clause this time. People change, she supposed. The last time Simone had worked for Carl, he'd had her sign a contract filled with confidentiality clauses.

Here I go again, she thought, *losing myself in the mysterious Lara's distorted life.* Simone felt a pang of apprehension, breathed deeply to take courage, and opened the first file.

Lara's Journal

They say everyone has a story to tell, and I suppose that's probably true, but some people's stories are more bizarre than others. I would like to tell you mine. If I had to choose a genre for my life story, I'd have to pick erotica...maybe a little romance...with a healthy dose of horror thrown in for good measure... It's definitely not a fairy tale, although I did have a fairy godmother, of sorts...but more on that later.

Part of the reason I'm writing this is to attempt to organize my mind and my feelings. Homework from my shrink, with love. He advised me that this might be a good way to come to terms with my past... I don't know if that's possible...but I hope so.

What I'm about to tell you is based, in part, on my diaries—I've been keeping a journal since I was a kid. But I'll also have to rely on my memory, as I apparently ripped out some of the pages in a few of my journals—no doubt while in a fit of rage...or out of shame—and some years' journals are missing.

And so, here we go...

About me... My name is Lara Parker... I'm blonde, my eyes are an indefinite color between blue and green, depending on my mood, and I'm very tall—five foot, nine inches. Yes, a gladiator. I'm an architect, and I'm also an interior designer. I love to build homes, and I'm quite good at my work.

I was born in Washington D.C on June 6, 1978. We lived at 4709 Foxhall Crescent Northwest, in a beautiful, two-story brick house with a big, lovely yard. I don't know if the house is still there; once I left Washington, I never went back, not even for a vacation.

From my early childhood in D.C., I have some good memories. I'm the oldest of three siblings. My brother Sean is five years younger than I am, and my sister Deborah is nine years younger.

My parents were working toward acquiring their piece of the American Dream. My father had a prosperous construction firm—he used to build for the government—and my mother was...well...a butterfly, forever trying to make it to the top of elite society through her social contacts. We were very well off, financially.

Although we wouldn't be considered rich, we lived very comfortably, and every year Father seemed to become a greater success in his industry.

For most of my early years, I was raised by a nanny, and as soon as I was old enough for pre-school, my mother made certain I was enrolled. I don't believe my mother wanted me around very much. I always seemed to be getting yelled at for being in her way. She was never a model of maternal devotion. Quite the contrary—and I don't remember getting along with her...ever. She thought I was a strange kid, and I thought she was a complicated person. We didn't find it easy to live together under the same roof.

My father, Laurence Parker, was a nice and very kind man, but he was also a hard worker, and I barely saw him around. He used to leave the house early, and sometimes he got back when I was already sleeping. He wanted to give us the best, and the best had a large price tag. But I always knew, deep in my heart, he loved us.

My mother, Sabine, did nothing but party and go shopping. Um, to be fair, she went to the hairdresser quite a bit, too.

By the way, I refer to my mother by her given name... A little later on, I'll explain why.

My parents didn't get along very well; they used to fight a lot, which, when I was a little kid, used to scare the shit out of me.

Thankfully, I had someone else in my life, someone who truly cared for me...someone who didn't believe children should be seen and not heard and who would take time to answer my dozens of curious question. Emma Parker, my father's mother and my paternal grandmother, was half French and half American. She was also the most fantastic person I've met in my whole life, the best influence a kid could have, and a really wonderful woman. She and Sabine didn't get along—probably because they were such complete opposites—and sometimes, Sabine would refuse to allow me to see my grandmother. But my grandmother was the only real mother I had. I didn't know anything about my grandfather—my father's father—until I was an adult.

Grandmother Emma preferred I called her Emms. She didn't want to be called Grandma, not because she thought it made her sound old—Emms was not like that—but because she wanted me to call her the same thing her friends called her. I guess she wanted our relationship to be based more on friendship than anything else.

Sabine's mother — my grandmother Shirley — was an alcoholic and didn't get along with her daughter or her grandchildren. The few times I saw her, she was weird, mean and bitter, and no one wanted to be near her...not even Sabine, who was a weirdo herself. My grandfather — Sabine's father — had abandoned her when she was a kid. To be honest, I can't say I blame him...

I received my very first diary as a birthday present from Emms one year. I remember thinking what a strange gift, especially compared to all the other fabulous presents she used to give me... She must have noticed my disappointed expression because she took me aside and explained. I remember the conversation as if it happened just yesterday.

"My darling girl, some of the best things we have in life are our memories. Everything else can disappear — people can steal from you, you can lose all, but what you have here" — Emms had pointed to her head — "you will never lose. I want you to take notes of the most important things that happen in your life, and when you grow older, you will read your journals, and you will understand how important it was to create a biography."

"What's a biography, Emms?" I had no clue what she meant.

"It's the story of someone's life, the importance that person had in this world. But open your diary and see… I have another gift for you…" Emma told me.

Quickly, I had opened the diary with its red, faux-leather cover and tiny golden padlock, wondering what would be small enough to fit inside. I flipped through the pages until I reached the middle, and my eyes grew wide. Heart racing, I removed the airline tickets.

"Paris!" I shouted then looked at Emms. "Is this for real? Are you really taking me with you this time?"

Emms had been born in France, and she had used to go back there every year. She'd told me dozens of stories about Paris and the Louvre and all the other sites. I'd pestered her for years to take me with her. France sounded like magic to my ears.

"Yes," Emms had said. "You and I are really, truly going to Paris this summer."

That birthday was one of those days a person never forgets. I wrapped my arms around my grandmother and hugged and kissed her.

"Emms, I love you more than anything!" I'd told her.

"I love you more, my little sunshine."

That's another one of my fonder memories. She used to have all these beautiful nicknames for me—such as sunshine, my heart, and so on.

I really loved the diary because it had a real padlock and a key, and I could protect my ideas from Sabine, who always loved to snoop around in my things.

Even though Emms had explained the importance of me making certain I journaled on a regular schedule, I still had a rough time getting into the swing of things…until I gave my dairy a name. I had decided it wouldn't feel quite so much like talking to myself if I pretended each entry into my journal was another letter to my new friend Martin. Looking back on this now, I have to smile. Who names their diary Martin? But at that time, my favorite movie was *Back to the Future*, and Michael J. Fox played the lead character, Martin. I had so few friends at that time, and I was desperate to have one. Marty—my little red diary—became my best friend, and I used to write to him as if I were sending him letters.

I don't have many friends, Marty. Sometimes, I believe it's because I'm a little bit weird, different from other girls my age, and I spend a lot of time reading. I don't like to play very much, and I think kids are dumb. I also love to listen to music. I got a stereo on my birthday from Uncle Ruggiero and Auntie Valentine…now I need some CDs. I just have one—and here I'd drawn a little sad face. This birthday was super cool! There weren't many children, but a lot of nice people came—friends of my father, mostly—and the gifts were just great!

I used to hide my diary in a hole I'd found behind a drawer and had enlarged, by digging out the drywall with a knife because I was so afraid Sabine would find it and read it. I had explained this to the diary, apologizing as if it had feelings:

Sorry to hide you, Marty, but even if you do have a lock, my mom will find a way to open you... She's like that...nuts...but I believe most grownups are crazy, don't you think? All except Emms; she is the best grandma in the world, and sometimes, I don't believe she's a grownup, she's so cool. I can talk to her, and she treats me like a friend and not like a silly little kid the way other adults treat me. Most grownups think kids don't know nothing. I hate them. But I believe I hate children more because they do act so silly and stupid. I wish I could snap my fingers and become an adult. I want to have a car and go wherever I want.

Back then, to me, having a car represented independence. I thought adults went where they pleased, when they pleased because they could drive.

In the days leading up to the Paris trip, I barely got any sleep.

Martyyyyyyyyyyyyyyyyyyyyyyyyyyyyyyyyyyyyy, I wrote in my journal, tomorrow I'm going to Paris! Just me and Emms. I'm so happy; I can't sleep. Today, Emms and I talked about the trip.

"*Ems,*" I said, "*I'm so happy we are going to Paris. I'm not going to bother you while we're there; I promise!*"

"*But who told you that you bother me, my sunshine?*"

"*Mother told me I'm a bother, and she thinks you are going to complain about me after the trip.*"

"*She told you that?*"

"*Yes…but please don't tell her I've told you. She will ground me. She loves to do that.*"

"*Don't worry, Lara,*" Emms said. "*I will never tell anybody what you tell me; trust me.*"

She'd opened her arms and hugged me, and I was there, in her arms, listening to her heartbeat while we talked about Paris. To this day, I can still remember how she smelled, a perfume mix of flowers and vanilla, and how warm I felt in her embrace, and those memories bring tears to my eyes—me, a woman who rarely cries.

"*Can we go to the Eiffel Tower and Triumph Arc?*" I asked her.

"*Of course. We can go anywhere you like. We are going to see many things in Paris — museums, statues, paintings. There is wonderful art over there. Art is an expression of love. The artist leaves a little bit of his heart in every canvas, every piece of* marble, so we can have a little bit of his soul, of his feelings, and then when you have recorded that piece of art in your brain, a little bit of the artist's love will stay with you forever, too. Those memories will give you happiness because you'll know there are beautiful things in the world."

Emma always had a poetic way to explain things.

My First Trip to Paris

Paris is a party! It's not just a phrase; it is a reality. I fell in love with the city from the moment I first stepped foot there. I adore everything about it — the smells, the food, the people, the crowds.

Visiting there with Emms was like opening a gigantic gift box. She took me every place a kid could go. Museums, galleries, parks, stores, libraries.

My first visit to *Champs Elysees* with its *caffés* made me think I would like to live there as an adult... I didn't know how right I was — or that it would happen long before I became an adult — at least, age-wise.

Emma took me to the Triumph Arc as she had promised. The elevator was broken — nothing unusual these days, I know.

"Madam," a policeman told Emma, "the elevator is broken. You have to use the stairs if you want to go to the top."

Of course, he spoke French, so Emms had to translate for me.

"Thanks," Emms told the officer, and then she turned back to me. "I believe we have to climb three hundred steps, young lady, what do you think?"

"I really would like to go to the top, Emms, can we?"

"Well then, what are we waiting for? Let's go."

Emms laughed and we started to climb. By the time we reached the top, we weren't laughing anymore, though…and we still had to go down…

But first I had to look at the view. I ran to the edge, which was surrounded by a fence to keep people from falling off, but I grabbed the bars and stuck my face in the middle to look down. It was beautiful! All those avenues that meet in the Arc and all so beautiful. The day was clear, the sky a pale blue with a few clouds, and a gentle breeze caressed my face and lifted my hair, making it fly in the air. My heart was full of joy.

"How about it, Lara?" Emms asked me. "Worth the climb?"

"Oh yes! I'm so happy I could shout with joy!"

"Well, go ahead. What's stopping you?"

I looked around us at the other people who'd braved the stairs to experience that amazing view.

"What about them?" I asked, turning back to Emms. "What are they going to think?"

"Do you know them? Are they very important to you?" She gave me a serious look.

"I don't know them at all." I shook my head.

"So shout. Go ahead and scream, kid! Never let other people prevent you from doing something that makes you happy. Their opinions don't matter."

I studied Emms's expression. Was she serious?

She grinned at me and nodded, so I took a huge breath.

"Ya-hooooooooooooooooo!   I'm   in Parisssssssssssssssssssssssssssss!" I shouted at the top of my lungs.

People looked at me, some started to laugh, others turned their face, but Ems was laughing hard, and so I started to laugh, too. I was very happy. I didn't ever want to go home. I wanted to stay there forever with Emms.

Ah…life was so simple then…

In the evening, we went to a nice restaurant Emms knew. It was near the apartment she had there, Fontaine de Mars. Once we were seated at the table, Emms asked me what I was going to order.

"Steak!" I answered quickly. "My favorite!"

Emms frowned. "Don't you want to try something new? I think you're old enough to experience something a little different."

"Well, okay. But what if I order something I've never had, and I don't like it?"

I thought about a big, juicy steak, and my tummy rumbled. I was very hungry.

"Then you'll know you don't like it. But you'll never know until you try. And then you can order a steak and say, 'This is much better than anything else.'"

I nodded. I had never thought of it that way. "Okay…what we are going to try?"

"Hmm…let me choose? Trust me?"

Again, I nodded. I trusted Emms more than anyone else I knew.

Emms ordered, and a short while later, our waiter came over carrying a little round bowl covered in holes. Inside the holes was something brown and juicy looking. I watched Emms use a little fork to pick one up. It looked weird, like a little piece of brown rubber.

"Try this, Lara," she said.

"What is it?"

"Try it first, and then I'll tell you…" She held out the fork.

I leaned forward, closed my eyes, and sucked the little bit of food into my mouth. My eyes flew open at the delicious, buttery taste. It was a little soft but very salty. Some people have a sweet tooth, but I must have a salt tooth because I loved it!

"Well? Do you like it?" Emms asked.

"Oh, yes! Quite a lot. May I have more?"

"Sure. It's called escargot."

"Escargot is good, much better than steak," I told her around a mouth full of another one of the delicious morsels and some bread.

"It's a snail," she told me and waited for the information to sink in.

I stopped chewing. "A what?"

"A snail." Emms smiled.

"Like the ones in our garden? People really eat that?" I asked.

"Yes, you just finished yours and mine, so I'm guessing you really like it."

I glanced down at the empty plate, and my cheeks grew hot.

"I'm sorry," I said. "They were really good. But I can't believe I ate snails!"

"Don't think about what you are eating; just savor the flavor."

I thought about this for a moment and decided Emms was right. After all, I never thought about where steak came from, so why should I think about the snail?

That was how I fell in love with escargots, and to this day, whenever I can, I introduced that food to people I care about. And as usual, Emms had turned the whole experience into a lesson. One I still remember.

"Lara...over the course of your lifetime, you will face many new things. Just because you aren't familiar with something doesn't mean you won't like *it. You cannot form an opinion unless you give it a try. Never judge before knowing — we can only make a judgment based on knowledge, okay?"*

"Okay, Ems," I told her.

To this day, her words have had an impact on my entire life. I have never judged anything before first trying it, and thanks to Emms, I have always loved Paris and trying different things.

On Being "Normal".

Early on, I discovered I couldn't concentrate very well in classes I didn't like. I was a genius when I enjoyed what we were learning and a total disaster when I didn't. One day, when I was on my way to biology — one of those classes I hated — I decided to skip school with a new friend. He was alone and sad, and I invited him to go fishing with me. We didn't go far; there was a little lake behind the school, and we went there.

Later that day, Sabine had a fit. The principal had found out I'd missed class and had called her, and she'd had to come to the school to get me. She told me I was stupid for cutting classes instead of studying. I had tried to tell her I had a hard time concentrating — that my mind refused to focus on my work. Instead, I'd find myself daydreaming…imagining I was an adult and lived in Paris, or I would think about the concerts I'd been to with Emms. I really had a hell of an imagination.

When we arrived home, my parents began shouting at each other. I'd been sent up to my room, but of course, I'd snuck back down and was behind the door, listening.

"Lara is totally irresponsible. I don't know what to do with her!" Sabine said to my father.

"C'mon, Sabine, she's just a kid. Kids do things like that. If you spent more time with her, you could talk to her about responsibility, but then again, responsibility isn't one of your strong suits, is it, so how can you teach her?"

I couldn't stifle my laughter at this, and they caught me eavesdropping. They both shouted at me, Sabine ending by yelling one of her most favorite sayings.

"You're grounded!"

Grounded. Again. Whenever that happened — and it happened a lot — I could read in peace, and I didn't mind being locked in my room.

Made in the USA
Middletown, DE
20 August 2021